HERO DE FACTO

888-555-HERO #1

SUZAN HARDEN

To Ro and Ricardo, two of the smartest attorneys
and most fabulous parents I know

This is a work of fiction. All characters, organizations and events in this novel are products of the author's imagination and are not to be construed as real. Any resemblance to persons, living or dead, is entirely coincidental.

HERO DE FACTO (888-555-HERO #1)
ISBN-13 - 978-1-938745-43-0

Published by Angry Sheep Publishing
Findlay, Ohio

Interior Design by QA Productions
Cover Design by For the Muse Designs

More books by Suzan Harden
(Each series is in suggested reading order)

Bloodlines
Blood Magick
Zombie Love
Zombie Confidential
Zombie Wedding
Amish, Vamps & Thieves
Blood Sacrifice
Love, War & a Bulldog
Zombie Goddess
Ravaged
Sacrificed
Reality Bites (Coming Soon)
Ghouls in the Grocery (Coming Soon)
Resurrected (Coming Soon)

Seasons of Magick
Spring
Summer
Autumn
Winter

Justice
Sword and Sorceress 28 ("Justice")
Sword and Sorceress 30 ("Diplomacy in the Dark")
Justice: The Beginning
A Question of Balance
A Modicum of Truth
A Matter of Death (Coming Soon)
A Touch of Mother (Coming Soon)

888-555-HERO
Hero De Facto
Hero Ad Hoc
Hero De Novo

Miscellaneous
Sword and Sorceress 31 ("Pig-Headed")
Sword and Sorceress 32 ("Unexpected")

For more information or to join her mailing list, visit Suzan's website at www.suzanharden.com

Legal definition from the Merriam-Webster Dictionary:

de facto – in reality, actually

CHAPTER 1

Harri Winters skimmed over the letter in her hand. "Give me a break. Professor Venom? Seriously?" She sighed and tossed the letter into her inbox. "Dammit, I thought he'd gone straight." And a half-assed attempt at a threat was the last thing she needed today.

"He's not dangerous?" Patty Ames, Harri's assistant, plopped into the chair in front of Harri's desk. "Is he a wannabe?"

"He's a wannabe wannabe." Harri shook her head. "He's not dangerous. He's just annoying."

"What's he want?" Patty settled back into her chair with a groan. "Sorry. My feet are killing me."

"If you need to go on maternity leave early—"

Patty shook her head. "Nah. It's just been a busy day." She rubbed her belly and smiled. "Not long now."

Harri smiled back. Patty was a good kid and a great assistant, but Harri dreaded six weeks with a temp. Too many cases, too little time, and by the point she got the temp trained, Patty would be back.

"So, what's the deal with this Professor Venom?" Patty said. Her blond curls bobbed in the direction of the inbox. "He says he's going to melt City Hall, and everybody will die—"

"Unless we give him a couple million dollars. Yeah, yeah. Don't start running yet." Harri spun her desk chair and dug into the file cabinet behind her. "Hang on a sec. I have a picture. You gotta see this guy. He's a total loser." She pulled out the "Professor Venom" folder and spun around to face Patty again.

"You usually show at least some grudging respect for supervillains." Patty leaned forward with a frown. "Is it because he addressed the letter to Harriet Winters?"

"Uh-uh," Harri said. "He doesn't have the ability to carry out his threats. And I don't respect the villains. I respect their assets. The forfeiture on Doctor Malevolent's evil lair gave us enough money to rebuild the Commerce Avenue light rail station and replace twenty smashed police cars. Try getting that kind of bank from a superhero. Cheap bastards." She opened the folder and handed it to Patty. "Professor Venom."

Patty looked at the mug shot and giggled. "Arthur . . . Doohickey? No wonder he calls himself Professor Venom. He's so skinny. And that nose is . . . unfortunate."

"Drallhickey." Harri rolled her eyes. "Lots of desire for elaborate mayhem, but more of a minor annoyance. Biggest thing he's managed to do is melt the paint off a couple of benches in Founder's Green. Which were scheduled for repainting anyway. He saved Dale's guys in public works from an afternoon of sanding and scraping. Dale wants the city to give him a vendor contract so he can buy Venom's acid formula."

Patty flipped through the pages. "I don't see his superhero nemesis in the file."

"He doesn't have one. That's how lame he is."

Patty laughed and handed back the folder. "Oh, that's sad."

"It's all kinds of sad." Harri spun on her chair and put the file back in its place. "Nobody takes him seriously. Poor shmuck. He doesn't have the skills to be a regular criminal, let alone the personality to be a supervillain. I'd hate to see this stupid stunt to screw up his probation." She mentally counted the months. "Or has he finished it?"

"You want me to call Judge Inunza's court and find out?"

"No, I've got his P.O.'s number." She stretched her arms over her head and yawned. "But first, I need some coffee, or I'll be useless this afternoon. I'm buying. You want some hot chocolate?"

"Ooh, yes. Thank you. With extra whipped cream." Patty pulled herself to her feet. "God, my O.B. says I've got another month to go, but I already feel like I'm carrying a toddler around in here."

"Hey, you wanted to experience motherhood," Harri said, and immediately regretted it. She wasn't sure Patty had wanted to experience motherhood. At least not yet. She was twenty-three and all alone. She had no family Harri knew of. When Harri had tried to convince Patty the sperm donor needed to step up—at least financially, Patty shook her head, her eyes shiny with tears, and said that he was gone, he wasn't coming back, and she didn't want to talk about it.

Harri yawned again and realized she needed more than coffee to stay awake.

She decided to take a walk around the park first. She didn't have anything on her calendar for the afternoon. She'd planned to be in a deposition all day with Seismic Shift, beloved local hero and—in Harri's mind at least—menace to society. But his attorney called at the last minute, claiming Shift had an emergency and they'd have to reschedule.

Seismic Shift had the ability to create pinpoint earthquakes, but not pinpoint enough to keep from making a mess, Harri often grumbled to anyone willing to listen. The last one had taken out the Lake County Retirement Home in his effort to stop a couple of kids who'd ripped off a corner convenience store.

The guns they had turned out to be plastic replicas. And worse, one of the residents of the home had died. Shift was damn lucky the dead guy didn't have any relatives to file a civil suit.

Harri kicked off her pumps and fished her sneakers out from under her desk.

But her job was to give the displaced residents a new home. Sure, Shift stopped the bad guys, but he also made a ton of money off endorsements and licensing deals and those ridiculous comic books. If he was so damn civic-minded, why did she have to fight him all the time to get him to pick up some of the tab for everything he broke?

She'd spent a solid week reviewing the thousands of pages of financial and tax documents Shift's attorney had dumped on her in response to her discovery request. With the deposition now put off for another week, she wondered if she should go back through the pile to see if she'd missed something.

She slipped her feet in her sneakers and yanked on the laces. Going through the boxes of documents again would be a waste of time. Federal law gave registered supers broad latitude to protect their secret identities. Without knowing who he really was, she couldn't get near most of his assets. He had to be making more money than he claimed, but she had no way to prove it. She liked the supervillains more because it was a lot easier to pry money out of them. The feds didn't care about maintaining villains' secret identities.

Harri couldn't figure out why people thought Seismic Shift was so damn wonderful. It's not like he was the Ghost Owl. Canyon Pointe's street criminals might not fear the police or the other superheroes, but they were terrified of the Ghost Owl.

Over the last twenty years, he bordered on urban legend. Lots of sightings, lots of stories, but like Bigfoot, only a few blurry photos. In fact, the first thing she'd done when her job granted her access to the federal registry was check if he was in the database. But if he really existed, he was pure vigilante.

Shift was registered, but he was not only a complete phony, he was a media whore. Yeah, he technically had a super power, but the rest was all marketing. From his financial records, she learned the shock of thick blond hair that stuck out above his cowl was fake. Not to mention, he was starting to get a gut. Not quite the sleek, chiseled demigod his publicist made him out to be. He looked about fifteen years younger and twenty pounds lighter in his publicity photos.

Harri pulled her dark shoulder-length hair into a ponytail, checked her teeth for lettuce in the small mirror she kept in her handbag, and frowned at the gray hairs along her hairline—there was a new one every day it seemed.

Both her best friends Aisha and Jeremy had tried to set Harri up with the colorist Aisha used at Jeremy's salon. But she couldn't afford that kind of money, not on a city salary, and she wasn't about to take charity from either of them.

There were a few times when she envied Aisha's position at one of the top firms in the state, but Grandma Harri had drummed public service and standing up for the little guy into her head from the moment she could walk. Besides, she would have ended up like Aisha with all her money going to her ex in the divorce settlement.

With a sigh, Harri dropped the mirror into her bag and slung the strap across her body. The city's superhero infestation hadn't done a thing to deter the city's purse snatcher community. Hell, one of the assholes had nearly strangled her when he grabbed her bag in the grocery store parking lot last month.

"I'm going to do a lap or two around the Green before I go to Java Joe's," she called to Patty as she walked out of her office.

"Forward your phone," Patty called over her shoulder.

"Forwarding my phone." Harri pivoted, marched back into her office, and punched in Patty's extension on her desk set.

Once outside of City Hall, the bright spring sunshine lifted her mood a bit. The park contained its usual assortment of transients, drug addicts, and the mentally ill, but they generally left her alone. Harri was petite, but managed to convey a sense of height. Eddie used to describe her as five feet of rage topped by two inches of woman.

It wasn't rage. It was . . . Harri didn't know what it was. Righteous anger, maybe? She hated bullies. She hated injustice. And in her experience, superheroes were bullies with commercial endorsements. People needed something to believe in. Instead, they got merchandise to buy.

She passed the playground. Two women held their babies while their older children played in the sandbox. It was exactly the domestic scene Eddie had described during their last fight. The one before he moved out and served her with the divorce papers.

Harri snorted and walked faster, annoyed at the thought of her ex. Stupid Eddie, with his new perky young wife and squalling baby and another kid on the way. He'd wanted a domestic family scene Harri had ultimately been unwilling to give him. She had nothing against babies in general, but did they have to be so stinky? And so loud?

Harri told herself that she simply wasn't cut out for motherhood. An essential mommy-ness had been left out of her character and she was being sensible by acknowledging it. But with Patty's baby on the way, part of her wondered if she'd missed out.

"Stupid hormones," she grumbled out loud.

Crazy Jim approached with a hopeful smile. "Miz Winters, how are you this fine day?"

Harri sighed. Crazy Jim was as sad as they came. When he stayed on his meds, he could function. Barely. That he had to do so living on a park bench, while schmucks like Seismic Shift lived like kings, broke her heart. Breathing through her mouth to reduce the smell, Harri said, "I'm fine, Jim. How are you?" She dug in her purse for some money. "When did you eat last?"

"Yesterday, Miz Winters. Yesterday."

"You could eat every day if you went to the shelter." At least until they closed it. The stated plan was to relocate it, but Harri knew better. The mayor had plans for the shelter site in East Downtown, and somehow, a new shelter would never appear.

Everybody would be so bamboozled by the super show, they'd never notice the bait and switch. The mechanics of local government were dull enough without having to compete with a grandiose parade of idiots in their tight, colorful Lycra costumes, creating crisis after crisis. But no help for folks like Jim because he wasn't super enough.

"Can't," he muttered. "Too many crazy people there."

She couldn't argue that point and handed him a couple of bills. Enough for a fast food burger and a cup of coffee. From experience she knew if she gave any of the homeless more they'd forego the food and buy a six-pack instead. She wished she could do more, but what Jim really needed, she couldn't give him.

He thanked her and went on his way.

She stomped across the street into Java Joe's and bought drinks for Patty and herself. She stuck with plain black coffee because she couldn't walk past Crazy Jim and his lost companions with a concoction that cost her as much as the meal she'd bought him.

Back at City Hall, she gave Patty the hot chocolate with the extra whip cream her assistant requested and headed into her own office. Harri took a sip of her coffee and set the cup on her desk.

Before she had time to sit down or even take her bag off her shoulder, somebody out in the hallway screamed. She took two steps toward the door before an enormous wall of hot air pushed her backwards against her desk. Stunned, she saw a masked figure in black step into the doorway.

"I warned you," the person said in a gruff male voice. "Now, I'll take my revenge for you ignoring me." Something green dripped from a tube connected to his outfit. The substance hit the restored wood of the doorsill and sizzled.

"Excuse me?"

"You cannot escape the wrath of Professor Venom!" the figure said.

That's not Arthur Drallhickey. The man was much wider and several inches taller than the real Professor Venom. Not to mention, Arthur could barely meet the eye of his public defender, much less Judge Inunza, after he'd been picked up on the vandalism charge for the park benches.

She should be afraid. This was a wannabe who meant business.

More people screamed in the hallway and Harri became aware of an acrid smell. Smoke, but with a metallic, chemical undertone.

The man in black lifted his arm.

Harri threw herself over the top of her desk and crawled into the leg well. The kick plate and drawers weren't going to provide much protection, but the reconstituted fiberboard was better than nothing. Liquid splashed with a sizzle against her filing cabinet and the wall.

"You're done, bitch." More splashing. Noxious fumes and smoke rose.

Whoever that was, he meant business. But why the hell would any self-respecting supervillain want to claim he was the nerdy, harmless Professor Venom?

More hissing and the kickplate grew hot against her back.

Harri peered around the edge of her desk. Her attacker was gone, but from her vantage point near the floor, Harri could see the carpet in front of her bubbling before it burst into flames. A lake of chemical fire, too wide to jump, simmered between her and the office door. She heard something liquid drop onto the carpet with a hiss and turned to look. The wall beside her was foaming and steaming. Whatever her attacker had sprayed, it appeared to be eating the plaster.

The steaming foam spread to the ceiling and a moment later something dripped onto her shoulder. It crackled on the fabric of her blouse. Pain seared her skin, forcing back under her miniscule cover. The glass top, protecting the wood surface of the desk, would buy her a little time, but she had to get out of her office, and she wasn't getting out through the door.

That left the windows.

The Canyon Pointe City Hall had been carefully restored, in meticulous historic detail five years earlier, after the friction from Blue Racer's super speed had started a fire that gutted the interior of the building. Harri developed a national reputation among municipal attorneys as an expert in winning superhero compensation lawsuits thanks to that case.

As part of the restoration, the building's seventies-era sealed windows were replaced with historically-accurate oak double-hung sashes. Harri's office was on the fifth floor. High enough to be terrifying, but low enough she might survive a fall with horrible life-ruining injuries. She could crawl out on the narrow ledge. From there, maybe she could find an open window. She felt her stomach knot at the thought.

A drop of the stuff falling from the ceiling splashed against the edge of the desk and hit her hand with a sizzle. She yelped in pain and made her decision. Better a fall than being burnt to death. She scrambled out from under the desk, sprinted to the nearest window, and threw open the sash. Taking a deep breath, she pulled herself through the window as more drops of acid splashed on her legs and melted her pantyhose.

Of all the days to wear the damn things. At least, she still had her athletic shoes on.

A wave of vertigo hit, and Harri glanced back. More acid dripped on her desk, setting her paperwork on fire. Including the Professor Venom extortion letter in her inbox. She couldn't go back.

She clung to the frame a moment, fighting off the dizziness. "Don't look down, Harri," she said out loud. "Don't you dare look down."

Instead Harri looked up. A helicopter hovered overhead, a cameraman hanging out the door. He saw her and waved.

She let go of the window frame long enough to flash her middle finger at him, then resumed her grip. "Gotta move, girl," she told herself as a gust of hot air blew outward from her burning, dissolving office. "Can't stay here."

Harri took a few more deep breaths, forced herself to let go of the window frame, and eased along the narrow ledge toward the next window, which opened into Patty's cubicle. Before she reached it, glass shattered, and hungry flames billowed through the opening at the extra oxygen.

Nauseated with fumes and fear, Harri scuttled backward. She was trying to turn around when the ledge broke away from the building. Harri didn't have time to scream before she was falling through the air.

Eyes shut, she felt something hard hit her.

This is it. Funny, I thought it would hurt more.

Except she was still moving, but now she was going sideways. She felt arms around her, and she opened her eyes.

A man was holding her. A man who was flying.

A super.

God, I hope I haven't sued him.

A bright neon yellow and green spandex mask covered most of his face under a dark gray sweatshirt hood. She had time to register a rock hard chest and arms before he landed and set her gently on her feet on the grass of Founder's Green.

"Who else is in there?" he asked.

"My assistant," Harri said. "Blond, really pregnant."

He nodded and took off again. He flew, sleek as an arrow, into her open office window. A moment later, he soared out a window on the opposite side of the building with Patty in his arms. He dropped her off on the roof of police headquarters, across the street, and headed back into City Hall. Harri watched him rescue five more people.

"There you are, bitch," she heard a familiar voice behind her. "Not getting away this time."

A cord dropped around her throat, but she got her fingers underneath it before her attacker could tighten the garrote. But she didn't have the strength to push him off her.

Garish lemon and lime flew toward her in a blur. The garrote loosened, and she heard a cry behind her. She turned and saw—

No, it couldn't be. Crazy Jim sprawled on his back on top of the crushed roof and smashed windshield of a parked car. Blood was gushing from his nose, and he moaned. In the distance, sirens whined.

"We need to go," she heard the masked man say. Before she could answer, he'd scooped her up with one muscular arm and soared upwards. When they flew over police headquarters, she heard the people on the roof clapping and cheering.

I never got to drink my coffee. It was her last thought before she passed out.

CHAPTER 2

Shouts mixed with sirens, but the sounds echoed weirdly. Someone tugged at Harri's clothing. Her skin and throat burned.

Harri tried to force her eyes open, but something covered her face. Panic flared. Someone was trying to choke her. She slapped at the offending material. Plastic and cloth. The guy pretending to be Professor Venom? Crazy Jim?

"Calm down, honey. You're safe." A woman's voice.

Harri fought harder. Someone was trying to kill her, and dammit, she was not going down quietly.

"Hold her." The female voice again, but no one she recognized.

Hands grabbed her wrists, and she bucked against the restraint. Some two-bit supervillain wannabe was not going to—

"It's all right. I have you. You're safe." The male voice crooned the words over and over.

Her panic melted when his mellow tone penetrated her foggy brain. The super who'd rescued her.

"Patty? Is Patty okay?" Her own voice was rough, gravelly, and echoed slightly against plastic.

"She's your assistant, right?" the super asked.

Harri nodded.

"Another paramedic is checking her and the baby."

She sagged against his hold. *God, please let Patty and the baby be okay.*

"If you can behave yourself, I'll take the gauze off your eyes. Give me any crap and it goes right back on," the female voice warned.

Harri nodded again. When the weight lifted, she blinked. Her lids felt like sandpaper across her corneas.

She was in an ambulance. An oxygen mask covered her mouth and nose.

The woman sitting next to her wore the navy uniform of Canyon Pointe's paramedic squad. Her short, dark dreads were held back by the strap of her clear goggles. She waved a penlight in her rubber glove-covered hand and frowned at Harri. "You gonna give me any more trouble while I examine you?"

"She won't." The super who had saved Harri's life sat on the opposite side of the gurney.

She would have flipped him off if he didn't have her pinned to the thin white sheet covering the even thinner pad. Instead, she shot him a dirty look. "Smart ass."

He grinned back.

The paramedic grabbed Harri's chin and turned her head back toward the flashlight. Harri winced as the brilliant whiteness forced her irises to contract and dilate. Spots danced in her vision by the time the woman was done.

"The good news is you didn't get any acid in your eyes, but there's irritation from the smoke and fumes. The ER will prescribe you something." The paramedic's nametag read "Jones" or "Jonas." Between the spots and her watery eyes, Harri couldn't tell.

"You can let her go," Jones or Jonas announced.

The super's warm grasp on Harri's wrists disappeared. The human contact was more comforting amid the chaos than she wanted to admit.

Jones or Jonas frowned again. She traced a finger horizontally across Harri's throat. "That isn't a burn."

Harri shivered. The line digging into her skin. Desperately needing air, but unable to draw a breath.

"Someone tried to strangle her while I helped the other victims of the fire," the super volunteered.

Jones or Jonas' frown was going to leave deep, permanent marks if she didn't change her expression. She scribbled something on a clipboard. "You're a lucky woman. You've got some superficial chemical burns and a little blistering, but nothing you can't take care of at home. The ER docs will do a more thorough once over at the hospital to make sure there hasn't been more damage to your throat and lungs than smoke inhalation."

The paramedic stood abruptly. "I'll grab an officer to get your statement about your assailant." The woman jumped out of the ambulance and disappeared into the people mulling outside.

Harri swiped at the tears trickling down her temples from the eye irritation. "You shouldn't have told her." God, her voice sounded as bad as her eyes and skin felt.

The super appeared genuinely perplexed. "But that man in the park assaulted you."

He couldn't be that naïve, could he?

"Did you turn him over to the police?"

He shook his head. "After I dropped you off here, I went back to the park. He was gone, so I came here again to check on you."

That didn't make sense. From the damage to the car, Crazy Jim should have been in too much pain to get far. And why the hell had he attacked her? He had sounded more lucid than he ever did while on his meds. Maybe the fumes from the fire had set off a hallucination.

Harri ran her fingers over her neck. Nope, definitely not a hallucination from the thin abrasion across her throat.

"Did everybody get out of City Hall?"

The super nodded. "I only needed to rescue the people trapped on the fifth floor."

He sounded terribly young. She took a closer look at him.

Acid holes covered his hoodie and jeans, yet the warm brown skin beneath appeared undamaged. The nasty smell of melted plastic accompanied his ruined shoes. She'd wager his feet were as uninjured as the rest of him. None of his clothing was new. In fact, it appeared to be second or third hand prior to the recent damage.

Her gaze drifted back to his face. She recognized the design of the neon yellow and lime green spandex he wore as a mask. It was the same pattern as the outfits Aisha's law firm had provided at the city's annual bicycle event for charity last year. Her best friend had claimed it was a good way for both of them to meet men after their respective divorces. Harri had never quite forgiven Aisha for making her look like an unripe citrus fruit in front of the most prominent members of their profession.

However, the tight-fitting bicycle tops and pants would have looked damn good on her super from the lines of muscle that peeked through the tears of his clothing. Even with the mask, she could tell he was young. Too young. Very early twenties at the most, and she sincerely doubted that. She stared at his face.

"Who are you?" she finally asked. "Really?"

The sudden fear in his eyes cut her to the core. His irises were pale hazel, nearly gold. Beautiful eyes, but cautious. They were eyes that had seen too much suffering.

Harri's normal irritation with superheroes evaporated at his vulnerability. "Are you legal?"

"Uh . . ." His tongue swiped across his top lip, and he glanced at the open doors of the ambulance bay. She recognized his behavior all too well. She'd seen it too many times in the runaways and foster kids she'd encountered when she'd interned with the city's juvenile court judge one year while in law school. He was about to bolt.

"I won't tell anybody." Harri reached over and grasped his hand. "Are you registered? As a super?"

His entire body twitched.

"I want to help you," she whispered hoarsely.

"No." His words were even softer than hers. "No, I'm not registered."

"Are you eighteen?"

"I don't know for sure." His fingers trembled in her hold. "I think I'm older than that."

How could anyone not know his own age? She squeezed his fingers gently. "What about your family?"

He refused to meet her eyes, giving her a sharp shake of his head.

Nothing intrigued Harri like an enigma, and this kid had puzzle written all over him. No birth certificate would explain why he hadn't registered with the federal government. If he had collared Crazy Jim, she could have cut him a deal. Especially since his first concern was the safety of the civilians.

"Do you want to be a registered superhero? I can help you with that." She squeezed his fingers gently.

He shrugged, and his body tensed.

She needed to change the subject before he flew off in a panic. "When you were inside City Hall, did you see a big, tall guy dressed in black and wearing a mask wandering around?"

"Is he the guy the cops are saying did this? Professor Venom?"

Harri shook her head. "The guy who did this claimed he was Professor Venom, but he wasn't. I know Venom. Did you see anybody matching my description?"

The super considered her question for a moment. "I saw a guy dressed in black in the alley behind City Hall when I was flying someone across to the police building. I got a glimpse, but he definitely wasn't short and skinny compared to the dumpsters. Since I was above him I didn't see his face, so I can't tell you if he was wearing a mask." He shrugged again. "Sorry, I was more worried about getting everyone out on the fifth floor."

Harri felt a tickle in her throat that quickly developed into a coughing fit. She'd been right. This afternoon's generic promise-of-destruction letter aside, the man who had attacked her couldn't have possibly been Arthur Drallhickey. Too tall. Too muscular. Too effective. And Arthur wasn't fast. An elderly woman with a walker had been the one to capture him after the park bench incident.

Arthur may have been totally incompetent as a supervillain, but he was consistent. Which meant polite threatening letters and the mishap with his acid mixture that left him pants-less when he was apprehended. So why the hell would someone impersonate him to do this?

If it hadn't been for this threadbare superhero sitting next to her, she would have died in today's fiasco. Patty and her baby could have died, which added to the sick feeling in her gut. Quite simply, she owed the kid. Twice. Four times if she counted Patty and the baby.

Harri's coughing eased. She yanked off the oxygen mask. "I need to find my assistant first, then we need to get you out of here. Stick with me. No matter what." He'd been seen by too many people, not to mention the news crew filming from their helicopter. She had to get him away from City Hall before the feds showed up. There's no way in hell he could pay the fines for unlicensed superhero acts. If she was going to cut him a deal, she needed to be the one to bring him in.

"I don't think you should be getting up, ma'am. The paramedic said you needed to see the ER doctors to check your throat and lungs." But the super made no move to stop her as she climbed off the gurney.

"It's Harri. Harri Winters." She shook her index finger in front of his nose. "If you ever call me 'ma'am' again, I'll sue those jeans off your ass. Got me?"

"Yes, m—" White teeth shone against his tan skin. "—Harri. I'm El Pájaro."

"'The Sparrow'?" She shook her head. "Kid, we have got to get you a better name."

—◆—

True to his word, El Pájaro stuck by Harri's side as she searched among the emergency vehicles and evacuated staff for Patty.

A loud crash shook the street as the fifth story collapsed onto the fourth, sending up a gigantic plume of smoke, dust, and ash. The various fire squads continue to pump special oxygen-robbing foam onto the inferno from ladder trucks. Her nails dug into her palms. So much for the restoration work on City Hall.

She didn't know who she could sue on this one. Even if Arthur had been responsible, he didn't have any money either. This was a first—a broke hero and a broke villain. That left FEMA and the state emergency fund, which meant sticking it to the taxpayers yet again. She swallowed her anger and kept searching anyone with a head of blond curls.

They finally found Patty sitting on the curb a block away, another emergency tech tending her. Second-degree burns covered her right forearm.

Harri dropped to the concrete next to her assistant while El Pájaro stood guard over them. "Is the baby okay?"

Patty gave her a weak smile. "Yeah, she's kicking up a storm right now." She hissed as the tech prodded her damaged skin. "I'm fine, too. Thanks for asking."

"She was very concerned about you," El Pájaro interjected. "She fled her own treatment to search for you."

"Oh, I'm well aware she uses her grumpy behavior to hide her marshmallow interior." Patty beamed at him. "Thank you for saving us."

"De nada."

Patty leaned closer to Harri. "Did I hear the guy in your office right? Was that really Professor Venom?"

Harri snorted. "If it was, then I'm a Victoria's Secret model."

"There he is!"

Every muscle in Harri's body tightened at the all-too-familiar shout. Shouting she was often on the receiving end of. "Shit," she muttered.

Mayor Quentin Samuels bounded out of the crowd, two police officers at his heels. "Arrest him!" He jabbed the blade of his hand in the direction of El Pájaro.

Harri forced herself to her feet. "What are you blathering about?"

"Him!" Samuels always compensated for his lack of height by doubling the decibel-level of his voice. Another sharp hand motion in the direction of the kid. "Eye witnesses place him here when the fire started."

"But I—" the kid started.

Harri held up her own hand to silence her super. He'd say something stupid and ruin his chances of getting registered properly.

"The perpetrator was in my office, and it wasn't him." Her smoke-damaged voice added a certain gravitas to her statement.

"Really?" Samuels crossed his arms. His smug expression set off warning claxons in her aching head. "So who started the fire?"

Dammit. If she said it was Professor Venom, Arthur would get charged for the arson. And even if he was annoying, he was also innocent this time. God only knew who else on the fifth floor had heard the imposter's claim besides Patty, who was smart enough to keep her mouth shut now.

Harri matched Samuels' stance. "I'm not sure. He was dressed in black with a mask. All I can tell you is he was a big guy with a deep voice. Will security be able to retrieve the camera footage?"

"Possibly," one of the officers offered. He glanced over his shoulder. "They're not using water, but that foam can still short out the DVRs if they're hit directly."

From the glare Samuels shot the officer, his assistance wasn't appreciated. The mayor turned back to El Pájaro. "I want to see your hero license."

Harri inserted herself between them. "He's just a kid trying to help, and I already lectured him on the need to get a city license." She wasn't going to mention his lack of federal registration unless Quentin brought it up. "I've granted him immunity on the license violation in return for his assistance and cooperation." She crossed her fingers behind her back and prayed the kid had taken her previous hint to stay quiet.

"You can't do that!" Samuels spluttered.

"I can negotiate any settlement that will benefit the taxpayers." She pointed at what was left of City Hall. "We've got a hell of a mess. I want the asshole who did this to pay for it."

"Maybe it should come out of your salary," he sneered. "For not reporting the intruder. Or a legitimate threat. I already know you received one from Professor Venom in this morning's mail." Samuels could be a sniveling weasel, but snooping through her office correspondence?

"You read my mail? That's bullshit," she said quietly. "And you know it."

"Why didn't you buzz security when Venom showed up in your office?"

Anger overran her fear and worry. "First, I don't know who the guy was. I didn't see his face. Second, I didn't call security because my office was on fire, and I was busy trying not to die. Third, what exactly are you insinuating, Mayor Samuels?"

"You're either incompetent or in league with Professor Venom."

Harri straightened her back and deliberately violated Samuels' personal space, forcing him to step back. "If you knew about the attempted extortion, why didn't you notify the police?"

Scarlet flooded his face as he spluttered for a full thirty seconds. He could look down at her, but barely. He wasn't much taller than she was. Finally, he shouted, "You're fired, Winters!"

Harri ignored the fine spray of his saliva that hit her face and stepped closer until she was nose-to-nose with the mayor. Something about her tight grin must have scared him because he leaned as far away as he could without actually moving his feet.

"Sorry, but I already quit." She glanced over her shoulder. "Come on, El Pájaro. Let's make you rich."

Chapter 3

"Make me what?" the kid asked.

"Rich," Harri said.

She glanced down at her assistant, who sat open-mouthed and stared back at Harri. "I'll call you later, Patty. Come on." She gestured at El Pájaro. "Let's get out of here." She stomped away from the mayor.

Once they were away from Samuels, and the police didn't follow them, El Pájaro grabbed Harri's arm, gently but with a firm grasp. "Where are we going?"

"My car. We need to get out of here. Fast."

He slipped his arm around her waist. "Okay. Hang on."

"Not like that," she hissed. "You're in enough trouble as it is."

"So are you," he said. "The guy who started the fire is still out there as well as the one who tried to strangle you."

"Another reason I want to go. But I'm more concerned about you dodging the feds. And the news ghouls, so we need to leave quietly. Lose the mask."

"But—"

Harri grabbed his arm and pulled him behind a fire truck, narrowly avoiding Ted Meadowfield and a cameraperson from Action 12 News!

The jerk only descended from the anchor chair for big splashy stories that didn't require actual journalistic skill to report. City Hall being destroyed yet again, in "an epic battle between good and evil" as Ted would call it, was a ratings goldmine, and he wouldn't miss it for anything.

"A mask makes you conspicuous as hell, even without the garish colors," Harri hissed as he let her drag him into the narrow alley behind the truck. "We need to blend in." She released him.

With a sigh, he pushed back his hood and stripped off the mask. "Better?"

"Um . . ." For a moment Harri could only stare. She knew he'd be a looker, but . . . damn. Thick black hair, tawny skin, high cheekbones, a strong chin and nose—all good, but it was his eyes that elevated him from ridiculously handsome to achingly beautiful. They were large, almond shaped, and that curious amber hazel she had noted before, almost golden. "Yeah, but I'm not sure it makes you any less conspicuous. Pull your hood back up."

"Where's your car?"

"Parking garage. Next door."

He shook his head. "Not a chance. There's cops everywhere. The whole complex is locked down."

"How do you know that?"

He pointed upward with his thumb. "Got an aerial view."

"Let me think." The adrenaline rush was starting to wear off, and all she could think about was how badly she wanted a shower, a stiff drink, and some ibuprofen. "What's your name, by the way?"

"El Pájaro."

"No. Your real name." When he hesitated, she gave him the most sympathetic look she could muster. "I've already seen your face, and if I'm going to represent you, I need to know your secret identity."

The internal struggle still played out on his features.

"I'm your lawyer. You're my client. I'm ethically obligated to keep your secrets." She laid a hand on his bicep. His incredibly solid bicep.

"I don't have money for a lawyer," he said, a panicked look on his beautiful face.

"Kid, you saved my life. Twice. I'll waive today's fees. What's your name?"

He considered this for a moment, then said, "Reyes."

"Reyes?"

"Reyes García," he finished reluctantly. "Rey is what I usually go by. Only my mom—" His voice choked slightly. "—only she called me Reyes."

Harri nodded, deciding to wait until another time to ask about his mother, but she suspected Mom hadn't been in the picture for a long time. She patted his very solid bicep and smiled. "Thank you, Rey."

He smiled back, his teeth dazzling and perfect.

Harri heard a loud growl. Then another. Both seemed to come from the kid. "Is that your stomach?"

"Yeah," he said, embarrassment lending a deep rose to his cheeks. Her estimate of his situation made her angrier at Samuels's treatment of him.

"Where do you live? Near here?"

He nodded. "In the old hotel next door to the Canyon Building."

"That whole block is condemned."

Rey shrugged. "I'm not the only one there." His stomach growled again.

Tattered clothes, no family, squatting in an abandoned building—Harri was getting a picture, and it was breaking her heart. "Okay. We swing by your place, you pick up your stuff, we get you something to eat, and then we come back for my car. If we still can't get to it, once the sun goes down, you fly us to my house. No more condemned hotels. You're staying in my guest room for now."

"I don't need any help." His tone was defensive, but under it, Harri could hear the need. And loneliness. "I can't pay you back for any of this."

"Yeah, sweetie, you do need help. I think you've needed it for a while. And I owe you for my life. Twice. There's no comparison." She peeked around the corner of the building. "Come on, we've got to get out of here before the police change their mind and decide to follow the mayor's order to arrest you."

"But I didn't—"

"I know you didn't do anything wrong," she muttered. "And we're going to keep it that way."

Trying to look casual, they slipped back into the crowd. In their torn, dirty, and acid-burned clothing, they fit right in with the parade of fleeing downtown workers. Harri patted her handbag, thankful for her coffee craving. At least, she still had her wallet and keys. And her parking garage ID. With City Hall a smoking ruin—again—it would take that idiot Quentin Samuels at least a couple of days to process her termination.

A few blocks past the chaos, as they crossed River Street, Rey took her hand and said, "Stick close. It's not a great neighborhood."

"No kidding," Harri said.

He led her through blocks that became more decrepit as they walked. The area on the northeastern fringe of the central business district next to the river was slated for redevelopment if city leaders could ever agree on what they wanted it to be. While the politicians and planners battled, a few developers, including Quentin Samuels' brother Reginald, quietly bought up everything they could.

A few businesses hung on, a few property owners tried to keep up appearances, a few shabby apartment buildings still housed the working poor, but a cloud of decay and inevitable gentrification hung over the narrow streets.

Many of the condemned properties like the Canyon Building, former head-quarters of Canyon Industries, had historic significance. Much lip service was paid to preservation as the neglected buildings continued to fall apart. The developers claimed they were diligently boarding up windows and removing squatters, but what they were really doing was waiting for an untended camp-fire or dropped cigarette to do their site clearing for them.

The entire block where the Canyon Building sat was boarded up and sur-rounded by chain link fencing covered in ominous signage about trespassers being prosecuted. But the street people knew as long as they stayed clear of the occasional city inspector, nobody cared if they lived there.

Harri hated to admit it, but she agreed with the condemnation order. The Canyon block was an eyesore. "I don't know why you super guys can't fight in this neighborhood instead of always smashing up the high rent area."

Rey smiled, but it was a sad smile. "Because nobody but Jatz'om Kuh cares about this place. At least, not the way it is now. Nobody wants to come here. Not even the supervillains."

"Jatsom . . . who?"

"Jatz'om Kuh. You know, the Ghost Owl?"

"Yeah, him I've heard of. But I've never heard the other name."

Ray shrugged. "A king from Mayan folklore. His name translates as some-thing like 'owl who strikes'. Some of the older folks in the neighborhood call him that."

"You ever seen him?" Harri couldn't help being intrigued. The myth of the Ghost Owl was what a super should be—assisting those who couldn't get jus-tice any other way.

"Once," Rey said. "When I was little. I told him I could help him. He smiled and said 'maybe someday, kid, but not now'."

"And then what? He vanished?"

"No." Rey grinned at his recollection. "He opened a man hole cover and said 'Lesson One—always know your exits. Lesson Two—never let anyone see you use them'. And then he dropped into the sewer."

Harri laughed. "I thought he was supposed to be able to dematerialize at will."

Rey shook his head, still smiling. "No, he looked pretty solid. Hasn't been around as much lately, though. And the rest of the supers never cross River Street or MLK Drive if they can help it."

"Yeah," Harri sighed. "Until this area finally gentries, and then I'll have to find money to help rebuild it every time some supervillain has a hissy fit."

"Uh . . . no, you won't. You quit, remember?"

"Shit. I did, didn't I?" What the hell had she been thinking?

"But in case you change your mind, they fired you first," Rey added.

Harri glared at him. "Well, aren't you just a little ray of sunshine?"

His smile grew sadder. "That's what my mom used to call me."

Before Harri could pull her foot out of her mouth, he pointed at a hole in the fence. "Here. We go in here and then down the alley and a quick flight up."

Harri had assumed he meant stairs, but he meant the other kind of flight. He grabbed her by the waist and zoomed up to the fourth floor before she could object.

"That's a handy little shortcut," she said as she peered around the gloomy space. "Warn me next time, okay?"

"Sorry. There's no other way in. The staircase collapsed. It's why I picked it. So nobody can steal my stuff."

"People steal from you? Seriously? I assumed you had super-strength along with the flight abilities." Especially the way he'd been hauling her around all day.

He shrugged again. "Yeah, but addicts steal from everybody, and they're way more scared of withdrawal than they are of me. It wouldn't be right for me to pound them. Life's already doing a pretty good job beating them up. They don't need me piling on. It's better this way. Hang on, let me get the lights on." He fumbled with something, she heard a whining sound like a swarm of mosquitoes, and then a soft white light filled the small space.

"What was that noise?"

"It's an emergency lamp. It's got a wind up thing to charge it if the regular batteries run down. I can't afford batteries, but I can wind it a lot faster than most people."

"Yeah, I bet." Harri looked around the room. She had expected it to be a mess, but it looked like an army barrack. Or a monk's cell. A narrow iron bed, neatly made, including hospital corners, sat against one wall. A plastic laundry basket lay near the foot of the bed, holding a pile of clean but tattered clothing, carefully folded. There was a small desk and a plastic chair. The floor was clean, thanks to the broom hanging in the corner.

But all this was merely a backdrop to the books. Rey had built a bookshelf with bricks and boards that covered an entire wall. Several hundred worn books, paperback and hardback, sat on the shelves.

He saw Harri staring at the books. "I'll need to come back for my collection. I can fly those out at night." He paused a moment. "If it's okay to bring them with me."

"Of course, it is," Harri said. "Where did you get them all?"

"Around. You'd be amazed what people throw out. And the library sale is always good. The final day, they practically give books away. And the librarians all know me so they hold back the novels they think I'll like."

"They know you?" A superhero who collected books and hung out with librarians? Most of them just liked to hit things and get their pictures taken.

"I used to spend a lot of time there. When I was younger. I didn't have anywhere else to go during the day. It was kind of home and school at the same time. The librarians used to bring me sandwiches and stuff." His stomach growled again. "Sorry."

"Not a problem. Get what you need, and then let's go eat." She couldn't tear her attention away from his collection. It had a little bit of everything, and a quarter of the volumes were in Spanish. Classics like Dickens, Cervantes, and Homer. Religious texts. Sci-fi. Mysteries. Hell, he even had Nora Roberts.

He pulled off the acid-burned hoodie and t-shirt. "I need to change. These clothes are trashed."

Harri glanced at him, then tried not to gasp at the sight of his chest, bare except for a small stone pendant hanging on a leather cord. She whirled around to give him some privacy. *He's perfect. He's the most perfect, beautiful man I've ever seen. Wait until Aisha sees him.*

Thinking about Aisha—instead of about how much she wanted to peek behind her and see if Rey's bottom half looked as good as the top—gave her something to talk about. "I have a friend who does entertainment and intellectual property law. Her firm represents supers. With merchandise licensing deals, publishing contracts, that sort of thing. There's a lot of money to be made if you're registered and working in the system."

"Uh . . . that's gonna be a problem," he said. "I don't have a birth certificate.

Which means I can't prove my immigration status or get a driver's license or do anything. I can't even get a job. I'd work if I could."

"And saving lives isn't working?" she asked.

"Not if you don't register with the government." He paused a moment. "If you don't register, then you're just a vigilante."

Harri felt her stomach drop. She'd been quoted saying that exact thing on the evening news and in the paper. "You know who I am?"

"Sure. Everyone does. You're the lady who sues superheroes."

"And you still rescued me?"

Rey laughed out loud. It was the first time Harri had heard him laugh. Even his laugh was beautiful.

"You never sued me. That's one advantage of being poor. You can turn around now."

Harri turned, relieved that he was clothed again. She wouldn't have been able to take her eyes off his chest if he hadn't covered it.

"Seriously though," he said. "I would have rescued you even if you had sued me."

"Why?"

A shocked expression covered his face. "Because it's the right thing to do."

Harri laughed. "Rey, honey, you are too good to be true. Most supers around here would have cheered when I hit the pavement."

His expression transformed from shock to anger faster than he flew. "I'm not like those guys."

"No kidding," Harri said. "Come on. Let's go eat."

———•———

Rey packed a small duffel bag with his remaining clothing and a couple of books before he took Harri to a little Mexican place down the street. At least, she assumed it was Mexican until she scanned the menu. The restaurant featured food from throughout Central America. This place served the real stuff, not the molten cheese-covered platters and watered down Tex-Mex that Americans generally thought of as south-of-the-border food.

It wasn't quite dinnertime, so the place was empty. When they walked in, the older woman behind the counter smiled at him and started chattering away in Spanish, gesturing for him to sit. Rey was clearly a regular. A couple of younger, dark-haired women peered out of the kitchen and started giggling when they saw him.

"What's good?" Harri asked.

The young waitress who'd brought them water and chips stared longingly at Rey. She looked about sixteen and obviously had a big crush on him.

"All of it," Rey said. "Marta's the best cook in town. I usually just let her pick."

"Sounds good." Harri scanned the menu for alcohol. "They got a liquor license?"

Rey shook his head. "Can't afford it and don't want it. This way they keep the drunks out."

"It can wait." Harri looked up at the waitress. "Load us up. I'm buying."

The girl still stared at Rey, oblivious to Harri.

He smiled at the waitress, a gentle big-brotherly smile. "Anna, tell Marta to send out some plates. Whatever she wants."

The girl giggled, nodded, and scurried back to the kitchen.

"She likes you." Harri said. "A lot."

Rey shook his head, as his face flushed. "No. Anna's just a friend."

Harri smiled. Beautiful, well-read, and bashful? Aisha would go nuts for this guy. Nabbing him as a client might finally get her that partnership. Maybe the old farts who ran her firm would finally be convinced Aisha deserved to be more than a token minority hire.

Before Harri had time to comment, the food began arriving. Platter after platter of the freshest, most wonderful Latin American cuisine Harri had ever eaten—ceviche, followed by thick pupusas stuffed with cheese and meat and vegetables, with the main course consisting of a perfectly roasted chicken, fried plantains, and rice and black beans.

Harri managed a few small platefuls before she was full. But Rey? The kid could eat, that was for sure. Whenever she saw him hesitate about eating a more expensive dish, like the ceviche, she reminded him she was paying and urged him on. After packing away enough food to last Harri a week, he sat back with a groan. "I kind of got carried away there. It's so good. Usually I put the brakes on so I don't bankrupt Marta, but you wouldn't let me."

"Marta lets you eat for free?"

"She claims she doesn't, but she gives me way more than a normal portion. I pay her when I can. The rest of the time I wash dishes, do odd jobs. She likes having me around. Keeps the thieves away, she says."

The dinner crowd was starting to file in. All the women ogled Rey, while the men stared, obviously not happy having to compete with him for attention. It was time to leave. Harri forced several bills on Marta despite her protests. In a high-end café in the nicer part of downtown, that meal would have cost at least twice what Marta charged Harri. She made sure to leave a decent tip for their love-struck waitress.

Despite Harri's crappy day, the excellent meal and good company made for a pleasant walk. By the time they were within a couple of blocks of City Hall, it was dark enough for Rey to do a quick reconnaissance flight despite the floodlights around the still-smoking ruin.

He was shaking his head as he landed. "Cops everywhere and the garage is blocked. Nobody's getting their car out tonight."

Harri's shoulders sagged. While she understood the CPPD's need for a thorough investigation, she wanted to get her Honda before Samuels realized it was still in the employee section of the city garage. She didn't put it past the asshole to have her vehicle towed. "Then we fly. Let's get a little further away from all the action before we take off."

After ten minutes of walking, she gave Rey directions, and they flew the rest of the distance to her townhouse. For the additional five minutes it took to get home, Harri clung to Rey, her eyes shut, willing herself not to vomit her wonderful dinner all over him.

They landed in the park across the street from the complex, acutely aware, in a way she hadn't been that morning, how much nicer it was than downtown or the Canyon Block. *We work there and debate their futures, but none of us actually live in those neighborhoods. What's that say about our commitment to this city?*

She didn't have time to wonder any further. Rey pulled her behind a tree and pointed toward her tiny front porch, which was shrouded in shadow. She hadn't bothered turning on the porch light since she was usually home well before sunset this time of year.

"Somebody's there," he whispered.

"You can see someone? I can't see anything."

"Enhanced eye sight," he whispered. "I've got great night vision."

"Can you see who it is?" She tried to push her fear back down. Not here and not now. *Please let me get a glass of wine and a shower before anybody else tries to kill me.*

"Stay here." He crept toward the house, staying in the shadows. After a moment, Harri couldn't see him at all.

She heard a feminine yelp of fear, then Rey's voice. "It's okay, Harri. You got another house guest."

After checking for traffic, Harri jogged across the street, each step on the pavement reminding her of the burns on her legs. On the porch, Patty sat in the single wicker chair, munching on a fast food burger from the streetlight's reflection on the waxy paper in her lap.

"I lost my keys in the fire, and I can't get into my apartment." she said around a mouthful. "Can I stay here tonight?"

"Of course you can," Harri said, crouching next to her. "Did you have the ER doctor check out your burns?"

"Yeah, but that's not the worst part." Patty sounded as if she were on the verge of crying. "I got fired. Quentin fired me after you stomped off. He said I helped you and Professor Venom burn down City Hall."

"He can't do that!" Harri shook with the force of her rage. Her keys slipped from her nerveless fingers and landed with a clatter on the porch. "You're a civil servant. There're procedures."

"He did it anyway." Patty focused on her burger. "And Aisha said to call her when you get a chance."

"Aisha?" Harri snatched her keys off the concrete, the wound on her calf protesting as she stretched the damaged skin. "When did you talk to her?"

"After you left, I realized I'd lost my purse in the fire." Patty shrugged. "Not that I could have gotten my car out of the garage with the lockdown. I tried to call you first, but I kept getting your voicemail, so I called Aisha, but she hadn't heard from you either. She offered to pay for a hotel, but I figured you'd be home soon."

"What about your car keys?"

A sad laugh burbled out of Patty. "My spares are sitting in the apartment I can't get into. All I need is a night on a couch until I can get my new apartment keys from my landlady tomorrow morning. Aisha and I only know each other through you, so I understand why she didn't want me at her place. And I didn't feel right about her paying for a hotel room."

Harri snorted. "Trust me, the hotel offer is Aisha being kind. Her parents are in town for the week. You don't want to be at her place right now."

With the City Hall disaster all over the news, Aisha must have been frantic. Harri fished her phone out of its side pocket on her purse. She'd been so focused on Rey, she completely forgot to call. Yep, three missed calls on her crappy burner phone that she hadn't heard ring. The phone didn't ring about half the time and had a tone quality similar to shouting from the bottom of a well. But she wasn't wasting money on another smart phone after losing the last one to a purse snatcher.

"Wait a minute," Harri said. "If you don't have your purse, how'd you call anybody?" She jabbed a finger at the Burger Chateau atrocity Patty nibbled on. "And how'd you buy that?"

Patty swallowed her bite. "Well, um . . ." Embarrassment vibrated in her voice. "Please don't be mad until you hear his side of the story."

"Who's story?"

Patty turned toward the evergreen hedges that separated Harri's entrance from her neighbor's. "Arthur, it's okay to come out."

No. Harri groaned. *It couldn't be.*

The acne-scarred face with its accompanying huge nose poked around the end of a branch full of needle-sharp leaves. Professor Venom himself, hiding in her hedge and wearing a sheepish look. Arthur Drallhickey waved lamely at her. "Hey, Ms. Winters."

Chapter 4

Harri whirled to face Rey. "You knew he was there."

He nodded. "Patty said she wanted to explain the situation to you. He's definitely not either of the men who tried to kill you earlier, and he promised to behave himself." From Rey's tone, he'd already threatened to do something to Arthur if he tried anything, though Harri doubted the kid would follow through unless she or Patty were in mortal danger.

And Arthur Drallhickey hardly qualified as an irritant, much less mortal danger.

Pounding started between Harri's eyes. "Why are you here, Arthur?"

"It's not his fault, Harri," Patty protested. "He found me crying after the mayor—" She gulped hard. "After Samuels fired me. Arthur took me to the ER, let me use his phone, and then he drove me over here."

"And bought you dinner?" Harri's attention flicked between her secretary and the supervillain wannabe.

Arthur's chin lifted. "Pregnant women need regular sustenance. And I wasn't thrilled Ms. Ames' misfortune was caused by someone claiming to be me."

Harri glared at him. "You still haven't answered my question."

Arthur straightened his skinny frame. "During our ride to your home, Ms. Ames told me you are no longer employed by the city. Therefore, I wish to hire your services to clear my name."

If Harri's day hadn't been so crappy, she would have laughed in the guy's face. Instead she rubbed the aching spot between her brows. "How do you expect me to clear your name? Did you forget about the two million dollar extortion letter you sent me? Nice piece of evidence for the district attorney, by the way."

"That was a year ago," Arthur said, his voice rising an octave.

"No," Harri said. I mean the one I received today."

Arthur shook his head, looking panicked. "I didn't send you any letter. I've gone straight. Like Judge Inunza ordered. You can ask my probation officer!"

Harri crossed her arms. "You really expect me to believe that?"

"Yes," Arthur squeaked. "Ms. Winters, I didn't have anything to do with this. I swear. You gotta help me."

"No, Arthur," Harri said. "No, I don't. I don't do criminal defense law, and I don't work for free."

"I have money," Arthur said, in a small voice.

"Really?" Harri asked. "You got four figures for a retainer? You have any idea how much a criminal defense costs?"

Arthur stared at his sneakers. "No. I had a public defender."

"You aren't charging me," Rey said.

Harri turned to glare at him. "That's different. You save lives. He . . ." What had Professor Venom really done besides stripping old paint from some park benches?

"No, it's not," Rey insisted. He waved a hand at Arthur. "He needs your help more than I do. He's looking at serious jail time if he's charged. Maybe he could do a trade, like I do with Marta. Legal services for . . . I don't know. There must be something he can do."

Harri held her hands up in defeat. God, this kid was really too good to be true. Looks, smarts, superpowers, and a healthy sense of morality. So different from the arrogant jerks she normally dealt with.

"I'm not debating this on my front porch. Everyone inside." *And hopefully, there're still a couple of bottles of wine in the pantry.*

Harri unlocked the front door and her strange little group trooped inside after her.

— • —

Aisha Franklin winced at a particularly atrocious snore from her father. He sprawled across her couch, ostensibly to watch the baseball game, but he hadn't made it past the second inning. Mom had stomped off to bed shortly after dinner.

Whatever was going on between her parents was getting worse. The only saving grace of them sniping at each other was they were too distracted to nit-pick her life.

She tried to concentrate on the novel she was reading. As much as she'd rather switch the channel to the local twenty-four-hour news, the minute she touched the remote Dad would wake up and chastise her for interrupting the game. Another loud snort and grumble from him would have impressed a grizzly.

Her attempted distraction wasn't going to work. The last update on the internet news sites merely said the fire at City Hall had been doused, and the alleged arson was under investigation. She'd feel so much better if Harri would call. At least, Harri's secretary had confirmed she was alive.

Aisha powered off her tablet and headed for the kitchen. With Mom and Dad asleep, it should be safe to go out on the balcony and indulge in her vice.

She slipped through the sliding glass door. The night air still carried a hint of spring warmth. She slid open the compartment under the gardenia planter and pulled a cigarette from the pack. Harri would kill her if she knew, but sometimes, a woman had to make allowances when her parents were visiting for a week.

No sooner had Aisha taken her first puff when her phone vibrated in her pocket. Before she pulled out the device she knew it would be Harri. The woman was psychic.

Aisha thumbed the icon. "Hey! Are you okay?"

"I'm fine." Harri normally had a throaty voice that attracted the opposite sex until they did something to piss her off, but now, she sounded like she'd swallowed glass.

"Bullshit. Patty already told me what happened."

There was a soft sigh. "Okay. I'm not fine."

The cigarette smoldered between Aisha's fingers as Harri relayed the details of the City Hall disaster and her rescuer. "Oh, yeah, and to top off my shitty day, I got fired."

"I heard. This new super really calls himself 'The Bird'?"

"It translates as 'The Sparrow'," Harri shot back.

"To-may-to, to-mah-to."

"Bite me. Seriously, I want him to talk to you. He's got a ton of marketing potential. Sweet kid, with an inspiring back story, and amazing powers. And he's gorgeous. Absolutely beautiful."

Aisha flicked the ashes from the tip of her smoke. "You said he's not registered?"

"No, but I'll take care of it. Girl, once you see him, you'll understand. Money maker. I guarantee it. And you bringing in such a cash cow may be the tipping point you need with the partners."

"Really? You're going to combine 'cow' and 'tipping' in the same sentence?" Aisha took one last drag of her dying cigarette before she crushed the butt in the planter. For Harri to wax poetic about any super was unprecedented. What the hell. This new super couldn't possibly make things worse for her at the firm.

But she wasn't about to let her best friend off the hook for not calling right away to verify she was okay. "He's apparently so gorgeous you forgot how to use your phone. It's been a while since you've even noticed the opposite sex. You sure it's only the couch he's surfing?"

"Don't go there. We're twice his age."

Aisha chuckled. "Nothing wrong with a little cougar power."

"He's a client," Harri spat at her. "We don't sleep with clients."

Maybe she'd pushed a little too far. "Just teasing, girl."

"Sorry. It's been . . . a bad day."

"That's the understatement of the century."

"Besides, he's not sleeping on the couch. He's sleeping on the futon in my office."

Aisha perched on one of the cheap plastic chairs she bought last summer. Cal had offered to let her have the good redwood furniture during the divorce, but she hadn't wanted any reminder of him in her condo. "I get Patty sleeping in your guest bedroom, but why's he on the futon? Your couch is way more comfortable than that damn futon."

"Because I'm not letting a supervillain wannabe anywhere near my files."

"Uh, Harri, I think you left something out." Aisha reached for another cigarette.

There was a loud slurp at the other end of the line. "Professor Venom has hired me to clear him of the City Hall arson. He says he had nothing to do with it."

Aisha took a deep drag on her second cigarette. This whole situation kept getting weirder. "The skinny guy with the Cyrano nose? Professor Paint Remover? What's he doing at your house?"

"He refuses to go home. He claims his place has been bugged, and someone's been watching him, but it's not the police. Although by now, the police are probably watching his place, too, thanks to the asshole who torched City Hall while trying to frame him."

"You're not a criminal defense attorney," Aisha reminded her. "He's in deep shit."

"No kidding. This is way over my head. He'd be better off with a public defender."

"So send him home."

Harri sighed. "I tried. But Patty and Rey were giving me these 'can we keep him' looks so I caved. Which is why I'm sitting on my back porch with that bottle of Bitch wine you gave me for my birthday."

Aisha snickered. "Why, Harriet Winters, I do believe you've gone soft since your fortieth. Bringing home stray heroes and sheltering villains? You've always said supers are only as good as the cash in their pockets. Which neither of these guys have."

"Yet," Harri pointed out. "Don't have it yet. But Rey's got the potential to make piles of cash. For both of us." Another pause. "You know, you could say screw it to Dewey & Cheatham and join me."

Aisha stared at the park next to her building. Maybe her best friend had breathed in too much toxic gas during the fire. "In running your little superhero/supervillain bed and breakfast? I'll pass for now."

"Think about it."

"Give me a sec." Aisha clamped her lips around the filter of her cigarette and thumbed through her calendar. She pulled the smoke from her mouth and said, "The answer's still no, but I'm open at two tomorrow afternoon. Bring your super by then. And don't drink that whole bottle of wine by yourself tonight."

Another loud slurp. "Too late. And don't lecture me, Miss I-need-to-stop-smoking-again. You've had two while you were talking to me."

"I hate you."

Harri chuckled. "I hate you, too. See you tomorrow."

Aisha thumbed the icon. She hadn't wanted to point it out to Harri, but the Action 12 News! helicopter had gotten a couple of good shots of her El Pájaro's rescues. Not to mention Harri flipping off the camera team. While she loved her best friend dearly, Harri didn't get how necessary good relations with the media were.

And defending a villain? Maybe Harri had been hit on the head by falling debris.

But yeah, this El Pájaro might be the ticket she needed for that corner office.

———— •◆• ————

When Harri's rolled over the next morning to turn off the alarm, her body reminded her of yesterday's trauma. Her muscles hurt even worse than the acid burns. From the stirring in the rest of the house, she needed to get a quick shower before going to work—

No job. It was a weird feeling. She'd been employed constantly since high school, but she couldn't dwell on that. There were three people who needed her expertise, and she needed to organize things to help them.

The aroma of bacon enticed Harri as she strode toward the kitchen. When she entered, meat sizzled in her frying pan while Rey stood at the counter. She couldn't call what he was doing to the eggs whisking because his hand moved faster than an industrial-strength electric mixer.

Patty sat at the antique maple breakfast table, her injured arm extended above the surface. Arthur was carefully wrapping the burn with clean, loose gauze.

"Morning, Harri!" Patty's smile was the same bright greeting that started every morning at City Hall.

"Where'd you get the gauze?" Harri asked. "I used up everything I had last night. And the food—where'd the food come from?" She sure as hell didn't have anything to cook in her refrigerator.

"Ms. Ames needs her dressing changed every twelve hours." Arthur concentrated on securing the gauze with medical tape as he spoke. "And would you please explain to her that she needs to see her own doctor? Second degree burns are prone to infection. A serious infection while pregnant could be dangerous to both the mother and the baby."

Harri took a deep breath, prayed for patience, and propped her hands on her hips. "That doesn't explain where the medical supplies and food came from."

Rey grabbed one of her hands and pressed a steaming cup of coffee into it. "Since Patty needed more bandages, Arthur and I picked up some groceries, too. You want toast with your eggs and bacon? Or would you prefer an English muffin?"

"Rey offered to cook while I tended to Ms. Ames's arm," Arthur added. "We thought it was the least we could do for your generosity, Ms. Winters."

"Um, okay. Toast is good." Never in her wildest dreams did she imagine a superhero and a supervillain making her breakfast together. She took a sip from her cup. Rich flavor tempered by a splash of milk coated her tongue. She stared at the men. "This is wonderful."

"I hope you don't mind my presumption, but Jamaican Blue Mountain is a personal favorite," Arthur murmured.

"And Patty told us how you take it," Rey said.

"Thank you, gentlemen." Harri took another drink. "Mmmm." She could have a caffeine orgasm from this cup alone, but other matters had to take precedence.

Arthur patted his patient's hand. "There you go, Ms. Ames."

She beamed at the supervillain wannabe. "How many times do I have to tell you? It's Patty."

Arthur blushed and busied himself with cleaning up the medical supplies and packaging.

Over Rey's fluffy eggs, crisp bacon and toast with extra butter, Harri issued marching orders. "First of all, Arthur, you need to drive Patty and me down to the employee parking garage to retrieve our cars."

Patty waved her fork. "Uh, fire. No keys, remember?"

"Crap. I forgot." Harri turned back to Arthur. "Okay, then, drop Rey and me off at the garage before you take Patty back to her place. And makes sure she calls her doctor."

"Yes, ma'am," he said.

Patty stuck out her tongue at Harri.

Harri ignored her. "Rey, you and I are going shopping. You need a haircut and suit before we meet with Aisha this afternoon."

"Who?" He looked bewildered. "Why?"

She jabbed her knife in his direction. "Because we're going to one of the biggest, most powerful law firms in the state. Image is everything with these assholes, and I want you to look the part of one of their clients."

"But—"

She held up her index finger. "No, 'buts'. You need to trust me on this."

"Okay." But he didn't look convinced.

"After my doctor says I'm perfectly fine, what do you want me to do?" Patty's raised eyebrow dared anyone at the table to argue with her.

Harri hesitated. She didn't want to stomp on Patty's pride by bringing up the father of her baby in front of Rey and Arthur. But dammit, the sperm donor should be shouldering his share of the responsibility, considering Patty had lost her job this close to her due date.

Instead she said, "Come back here. Use my desktop and pull the forms for superhero registration and licensing."

"And the form for my grievance? I'm not letting Mayor Samuels get away with this."

The ferocious look on Patty's face made Harri glad she hadn't brought up the baby daddy subject. "Yes. That, too. I didn't want to add to your stress by bringing it up."

"My stress is just fine," Patty snapped. "It's everyone treating me like a china doll that's—" Her face crumpled. "I'm sorry, Harri. You were nice enough to put me up last night, and I get all bitchy—" She angrily swiped at a tear that escaped.

Harri laid a hand over Patty's. "Don't worry about it. If you're half as sore as I am, it's justifiable bitchiness."

Arthur cleared his throat, his face growing pink. "Why don't you let me drive you on your errands, Ms.—" A glare from Patty made him shake. "P-Patty? You can make out a grocery list on the way, and I'll help you make dinner here tonight."

The supervillain soothing her secretary's wounded ego? What was the world coming to? Life couldn't get any more complicated right now.

Through the exchange Rey watched everyone between forkfuls of his breakfast, but didn't offer any words of wisdom. He knew when to stay quiet, which would make Harri's job a lot easier.

No one said much else as they finished their meal. They cleaned up, and gathered their things. Her three houseguests trailed behind Harri as she strode to the front door. She barely swung the door open to be blinded by a white spotlight.

"Harriet Winters? Ted Meadowfield, Action 12 News! Care to comment on Mayor Samuels' accusation you've turned to supervillainy and you're in league with Professor Venom?"

Chapter 5

◆ ❖ ◆

Harri stared at Ted for a moment, unable to move. Then she registered the camera that went with the spotlight. She held up her index finger. "One second, Mr. Meadowfield." She slammed the door shut and leaned against it.

"Okay, the boys need to go out the back door." She stared at Rey. "Don't let them see you."

Rey nodded.

"Can you guys create a diversion?"

Arthur's eyes widened. "Are you asking me to use my talents for good?"

Oh, brother. "Yes, Arthur, I need you two to create a diversion so Patty and I can get to your car without the news crew following us. But nothing too property damaging, please."

"Shouldn't I go with them?" Patty asked.

Harri shook her head. "No. Quentin wants a media event. Let's give him one."

Patty smiled. Like a shark that smelled blood.

Harri waited until Arthur and Rey were out of sight, then took a deep breath and opened the front door again. "You were saying?"

Ted looked at the cameraman. "Bob, are we taping?"

Bob, pudgy and thirty-ish, nodded.

Ted stuck a microphone in Harri's face. "Mayor Samuels has accused you and your assistant of being in league with Professor Venom in his plot to destroy City Hall. What do you have to say about that?"

"Mr. Meadowfield, you know I can't comment. All media requests are handled by the city's PR director."

Ted shook his head. "Nice try, Harriet. You're not a city employee anymore. My sources say you got fired."

Not even trying to be professional and addressing her as "Ms. Winters." And being called her given name irritated her further. The jerk didn't realize he was admitting Samuels was his source. This was too good to be true.

"I also cannot comment on personnel decisions of the city."

"Fine." Ted grinned, obviously thinking he had the upper hand. "If you won't talk about Professor Venom, then how about the new super who rescued you and several other city employees?"

No way in hell was she letting Ted get the scoop on Rey. Not only because she hated the newsman, but because he'd get the story wrong. Nella Lopez, his long-suffering producer, was nowhere in sight, which meant Ted was off his leash. "No comment. And I didn't get fired. I quit."

Ted's grin turned downright oily. "Look, I already have the footage of this guy catching you in mid-air. Give me the exclusive."

"Ted, you need to get off my porch. Now."

"The mayor is already saying he thinks you're behind the City Hall attack. If you don't want me to start saying the same thing—on air—you'll give me an interview. I have a lot of power you know. If I tell everybody you've gone villain, you're done for."

"Are you blackmailing me, Ted? Seriously?"

Ted smirked. "I'm repeating what the mayor is saying."

Harri's glare escalated into what Aisha called "the look of death." She stepped forward. Ted stepped back and almost fell off the porch.

"Get this on film, Ted," Harri growled. "I think you and Quentin might want to educate yourselves about the basics of defamation law before you throw around baseless accusations. And I'm pretty sure the jury in my lawsuit would have no trouble finding actual malice on your part considering you tried to shake me down on camera, dumbass. Or did you forget you're rolling?"

Ted made a slashing motion, but Bob kept taping.

"Turn off the camera," Ted squealed.

"Nella told me when you go free range like this I have to tape everything," Bob said.

"You're fired," Ted said.

"No, I'm not," Bob shot back. "Nella's my supervisor. Not you."

Realizing she had an open channel to the news producer, Harri took another step toward Ted, forcing him to retreat to the walkway. "Gee, Ted, maybe you should be reporting about Mayor Samuels's failure to provide adequate security to City Hall employees. Or about how he illegally fired my assistant. Who is devastated."

On cue, Patty began to cry, in loud shuddering sobs.

"Who the hell is this?" Ted asked, his voice panicky, as he peered around Harri at Patty. "Nobody told me the girl was pregnant. Nobody told me there'd be crying."

Bob caught Harri's eye, gestured with his head toward Ted, and mouthed, "Sorry."

Harri looked at the Action 12! van parked behind the crew. Arthur crouched next to the front tires, frantically gesturing. *Draw it out.*

"Ted," Harri said. "This isn't baseball. This is news. There's always crying in news. It's bad enough you tried to blackmail me for an interview. You sure you want to also be on camera intimidating a traumatized pregnant woman who was nearly killed yesterday afternoon—" Patty wailed even louder. "—and has been illegally fired from her job, with unsubstantiated allegations that she's a supervillain? Seriously? How well do you think that'll play with the advertisers? How will that look on your clip reel? Tom Brokaw would never have done that."

Ted's national news anchor aspirations were well known—and widely mocked.

"Kill the camera!" Ted, now completely out of his depth, turned on Bob and a very young woman, probably an intern, who was fiddling with the lights.

Harri glanced over at Arthur, who pointed toward a sleek silver Corvette parked next to the van.

Harri nodded, trying not to laugh. Ted's Corvette.

While Ted bickered with Bob and the intern, Rey picked up the Corvette and—careful not to damage anything—leaned it, like a domino, on the hood of the news van. It looked like Ted had tried to drive over the top of the bigger vehicle.

Arthur pulled an ancient metal gas can out of the hedge lining the park, but Rey shook his head. Harri could tell they were arguing. After a moment, Arthur nodded. Rey stuck his fingers in the corners of his mouth and whistled before he and Arthur disappeared into the foliage.

Rey's whistle had the volume and stridency of a freight train. Ted spun around and saw his Corvette, perched on the hood of the news van. With a strangled cry, he dropped the microphone and ran toward his beloved sports car.

"Sorry," the young intern said to Harri. "We had no idea he planned to ambush you. He's such an asshole."

Bob snorted, still taping but it was Ted's antics at his car's position. "What Meadowfield lacks in brains, he makes up for in hair and teeth. TMZ's gonna love this. I'm not on the clock, and he's too stupid to realize I'm not using the station's camera. This footage is mine."

"Were you the guy I flipped off yesterday?" Harri asked.

Bob looked over his shoulder, and his expression turned sheepish. "Yeah, sorry about that. I didn't realize you were trying not to get killed."

"Why were you guys even there?"

Bob shrugged. "Ted said he'd gotten a tip that something big was happening at City Hall." He chuckled. "Nice bit with the car."

"Did the new super do it?" the intern asked. "Is he as cute as the paramedic said?"

Harri smiled. "He's cuter. And I have no idea what you're talking about."

Bob sighed, finally lowering the camera. "I better go call a tow truck before Ted has a stroke."

"Are we good?" Harri asked.

"Yeah, we're good. If you need any promotional video of your super, let me know." He fished a business card out of his pocket and handed it to Harri. "I freelance on the side."

She nodded and tucked the card in her purse.

Ted was sobbing into his phone when she and Patty turned the corner on their way to Arthur's car.

—•—

At the knock on her office door, Aisha looked over her reading glasses to find Stuart Cheatham. There was only one reason for him to be standing in her doorway since he couldn't see her ass or legs from that position. "Did you need something?"

Stuart oiled his way into her office and sat down. The grandson of Matthew Cheatham, founder of the firm, Stuart wasn't even a lawyer after failing the bar five times. He had a position as the firm's so-called development manager and a trust-fund. He used the latest management buzzwords and double speak, but under his expensive tailored suit beat the heart of a two-bit con man.

Aisha detested him and everything he stood for. Stuart had far more power than his position entitled him to, so she did her best to not let her feelings show, which had been particularly challenging during the latest partnership review.

"As you know, the partnership committee is committed to dynamic employee development," he said with a smarmy smile on his face.

Aisha imagined throwing her stapler at his head. Imaginary Stuart grunted and collapsed sideways out of his chair. Real Stuart continued to leer at her. She clutched her pen more tightly and tucked her other hand under her thigh to reduce temptation.

"Yes," she said. "That's what they say. What's the word on my dynamic employee development?"

"Well, the partners take into account due consideration of all factors, which includes examining core competencies and drilling down to the best practices for our clients." He continued to smile at her. Stuart was nowhere near as handsome and charming as he thought he was. She suspected that the "Stuart Stare," as the support staff called it, was motivated by Stuart's belief that his attention was a gift no lady could resist, a gift he graciously bestowed upon the female gender.

Her stapler was a few inches away.

"Stuart," she said, smiling back in a way that made her face hurt, "I can't stand the suspense. What's the word? Am I going to make partner finally?"

His smile disappeared, and he began to squirm in his chair. "These are always hard decisions, especially when it comes to management visibility—"

"You sonofabitch," Aisha said, her voice barely more than a whisper. "You're screwing me over again, aren't you?"

"Now Aisha, that attitude of yours doesn't help."

"And what attitude would that be, Stuart?" Aisha asked through gritted teeth.

"I don't want to say entitled—"

"No," Aisha said. "Go ahead. Say it. In what way do I act entitled?"

"Partnership is never a guarantee, you know. You have to put in the work."

Aisha laid down her pen before she lunged over her desk and jammed it in his eye. "I have put in the work. Ten years of it, in fact. On an eight-year part-ner track. In what way have I fallen short?"

"There was all that drama with your divorce," he said, refusing to meet her eyes.

"What drama?"

"Well, crying all the time is hardly professional," he said, his voice sullen.

"Crying all the time? I let a single tear slip in a meeting. That wasn't with a client. One time. The day my husband served me with the papers."

"I'm not here to do an employment review, Aisha." He scowled at her. "And attacking me won't help you. I'm doing you a favor, you know. So you aren't surprised in the staff meeting tomorrow." He stood up to leave.

Aisha took a deep breath. She had no hope of salvaging this if she pissed off Stuart. "I'm sorry," she forced herself to say. "I thought I had it this time." She took another deep breath. "So who got the partnership?"

Stuart stared at his expensive shoes. "Uh . . . Travis. They gave it to Travis."

"Travis Beckham?" Her heroic effort to keep it together exploded. "That smarmy little shit? He's only been here for three years."

Stuart let out a dramatic sigh. "I knew you'd get like this. They said you'd be happy for him, but I knew you wouldn't be."

"Why, Stuart? Why would I be happy to see my partnership go to a less qualified candidate?'

"Well, he's . . . like you."

Aisha started laughing, but there was no humor in it. "Are you kidding me? The black folk stick together—is that it? He didn't get the partnership because he's qualified. Or because he's black. He got the partnership because his father is the plastic surgeon who keeps Dewey's trophy wife looking good." She left out the part about what an ass-kissing little schmuck Travis Beckham was. Not to mention the paralegals hated him because he expected them to do all his work.

"That is totally unfair, Aisha. Travis is a qualified, hard-working—"

Aisha shook her head, willing herself not to assault Stuart. "Well, at least I finally know what the partnership committee thinks of me."

"You're overreacting." He smiled at her. "You know how much we value you around here."

She stared at him for a long moment. "Yeah," she said. "I guess I do. I think I finally get it." And it's not like she didn't have options. Maybe this El Pájaro guy could save her, too.

—•—

Harri had worried there might be some problems getting her definitely-not-new white Honda sedan out of the parking garage, but it all went fine. The cops were gone and the middle-aged security guard at the gate didn't even glance their way when Harri flashed her ID badge at the card reader. As she'd suspected, the termination process was going to take a few days to work its way through what was left of the city bureaucracy.

Which meant she probably still had remote access to her files and e-mail on the city government backup servers. Patty could copy everything when she and Arthur finished running errands and got back to the townhouse.

"Do you know anything about computers?" Harri glanced at Rey sitting in her passenger seat.

"No, but Arthur does."

"Really?" Harri snorted. "I thought his specialty was chemistry."

"Have you actually talked to him, Harri?"

Another glance showed Rey's earnest expression. "No. Why?"

"He's got three doctorates. Chemistry, mathematics, and computer science."

"So he has a beautiful mind. So what?" She flipped the left turn signal and pulled into the turn lane.

"You should give him a break. He's not a bad guy. When we were talking after you and Patty went to bed, he admitted he's more a fan, than anything else. He said Professor Venom was an 'homage to super culture.' I said 'what culture'?" Rey laughed. "By the way, he's more scared of you than me. I told him he should call you Harri, and he looked like he was going to pass out. He said, 'Oh, I couldn't do that. She's too mean.'"

Even Harri had to laugh at that. "All right. I am—on a provisional basis, mind you—willing to give him a break. If he's so smart, why didn't some university or the government snag him for research?"

The left arrow light turned green. Harri headed west on Summer Drive.

Renaming the street had been a little eff-you from the Canyon family to the Winters nearly a century ago.

"Some big company did, but his boss took credit for Arthur's work. When he protested, his boss framed him for embezzlement. He wasn't charged, but he hasn't been able to get another job."

Crap. That explained Arthur Drallhickey's antisocial bent, and why he was so adamant about clearing his name. And if someone was trying to frame him again . . .

"Did he say how he knew his phone was bugged?"

Rey chuckled. "I may not have one, but even I know a modern phone is a mini-computer." His laughter died. "Arthur said he found spyware on both his home computer and phone. Patty suggested his computer mojo might be the skill he can trade for his legal fees."

"Good idea. She's a sharp kid."

"Arthur's already half in love with her, I think." Rey paused a moment. "There's no . . . father on the scene?"

Harri winced though Patty wasn't in the car. Thank god, Arthur had taken Patty to her apartment to meet her landlady to get the locks changed and obtain new keys.

"She refuses to talk about him. Says he's out of the picture and won't be back." Harri glanced at Rey before turning her eyes back to the street. He looked straight ahead, a million-mile stare on his beautiful face. "You aren't attracted to her, are you?"

"Hmm? Sorry. No. She's very sweet, but not my type. She . . . she reminds me of my mother."

"She was on her own?"

He shrugged. "As far as I know. I don't know a lot. When I'd ask, she'd say she'd tell me when I was old enough. But she died—" His voice tightened. "She died when I was little. All I have is this." He pulled the pendant out of his shirt, the one Harri had noticed the day before.

At the next red light, Harri inspected the small stone carving. She couldn't recognize the stone, a sort of mottled gray-green with a blue streak in the middle, but it was intricately carved with some sort of design that had been worn away around the edges and softened with time.

"Do you know anything about what this is?" she asked.

Rey shook his head. "Only that it's old, and my mom told me never to take it off."

"And you never have?"

"I took it off twice," he said, his voice barely more than a whisper. "Once on purpose and once by accident. Never again."

A horn honked behind them.

"Green light," Rey said.

Harri waved at the guy behind her and stepped on the gas.

"Where to now?" Rey said.

Happy to let him change the subject, Harri said, "First a hair cut, then the suit."

"I've never owned a suit. I have no idea what to get."

"Neither do I," Harri said. "But I know a guy."

— • ● • —

"Fine," Jeremy said over the phone speaker. "Bring him in." He sighed. "The place is empty. Nobody wants to come downtown. Typical post-super non-sense. Where are you?"

"Outside your salon. I figured I should call first." Harri pulled the cell phone away from her ear in anticipation of the shouting. Rey tugged her suit sleeve and pointed at the doorway.

"Why do I even bother with you?" Jeremy said as he opened the glass door. "I'm hanging up now."

Harri stuck out her tongue and tucked her phone in her purse. "You love me. And not just because I'm letting you in on the ground floor of an amazing opportunity."

Jeremy sucked in a breath and gave Rey the once over. "Good Lord, is this El Pájaro?"

"He needs a stylist." Harri frowned as Jeremy's question sunk into her brain. "How do you know his name already?"

"My superpower is digging up dirt. I know everything about everybody." Jeremy smiled and ran his fingers through his short blond hair, ready to flirt despite dating his assistant manager. "Mother Nature's done most of the work already." He held out his hand. "I'm Jeremy. And I don't need to know your real name. I know how careful you guys are about that."

Rey took his hand. "Nice to meet you."

"Thank you for saving Harri. I'm quite fond of her, despite her deplorable lapses in scheduling etiquette." Jeremy shot her another dirty look. "And her failure to let her friends know she was fine after a supervillain attack."

"Things were a little chaotic last night." She didn't want to get into the subject of her multiple houseguests. "In addition to the haircut and shave, he needs a good suit. We're going to meet Aisha, see if she can help with the IP and licensing side of things."

Jeremy nodded. "When's the meeting?"

"Two o'clock."

Jeremy's eyes widened. "El, honey, why don't you go inside? Tell the kids you're my new client, and I'll be right in."

Rey looked at Harri. At her nod, he entered the salon.

Jeremy turned on Harri. "Two o'clock? Are you out of your mind? You want some kind of magic makeover montage? A little gay pixie dust to make him look great?" He glared at her. "I don't appreciate being reduced to a stereotype, you know."

Harri sighed. *You're ambushing Jeremy like Ted ambushed you. What did you expect?*

"Honey, I'm not reducing you to a stereotype. You're the best damn stylist in town, you're one of my best friends, and El Pájaro needs our help. You've seen him. This kid is a potential goldmine. He's the real deal. And not just the super powers. He's a good guy, in every way. But you know I can't take him to the stuffed-shirt, old boy law firm in tattered clothes and that scruffy hair cut. Are you gonna help me help him?"

"Well, of course, I'll help" Jeremy said. "But I'm not a miracle worker. We've got about four hours, and with that shoulder to hip ratio, he'll need some tailoring to get a suit that fits properly. I'll do what I can. You still get the family discount at Grandma Harri's department store?"

Harri nodded.

"Good. Let me make some calls. I'll get them to bring some stuff over. Who the hell came up with that moniker though? 'The Bird'? Really?"

"He did, and it's 'The Sparrow.'"

"Only in Spain, Harri, dear." Jeremy cocked his head, and his expression turned super-serious. "Before I go launch Hurricane Jeremy, how are you? Really?"

Harri shrugged. "I'm okay. Some burns. Lost my job. But on the bright side, I've got my first private practice client."

"You're so full of shit. I saw the news. You almost died." He pulled her into a tight hug.

She bit back a squeal of pain when he accidentally brushed the burn on her shoulder.

Jeremy released her. "I'd lecture you about needing to process it, but I'd be wasting my breath. You're as bad as Grandma Harri." He gestured at the glass door. "After you, my dear. Time to do some magic."

Harri sucked in a deep breath as she pulled on the door handle and a blast of the salon A/C hit her. She prayed she hadn't oversold her and her friends' abilities to Rey of making him rich.

Because what little was left of her career was riding on him.

CHAPTER 6

Aisha tried to concentrate on the licensing contract for a Seismic Shift hair product line. Why the public bought into the thick blond hair above his Lycra cowl she'd never know. He wasn't the first superhero to wear a hairpiece, but she'd seen his bills. Shift paid more per month on his fake hair than she had on her BMW payment.

The intercom on her phone set buzzed. She jabbed the button. "Yes?"

"Um, Ms. Franklin, your two o'clock is here." The new receptionist's voice shook.

"Thank you. I'll be right there." Aisha always tried to address people by name, but she never bothered to learn the young receptionists'. If Stuart's antics didn't drive the support personnel out of the firm within two months, the office manager's crap did. And this girl sounded so nervous already, she might leave before the week was out.

And this was only her third day.

Curiosity over Harri's super quickened Aisha's steps, but she wasn't prepared for the sight that greeted her.

The man who towered over Harri could have stepped out of a magazine. Thick blue-black hair, conservatively cut but with enough on top to run your fingers through. His grey suit fit perfectly, leaving just enough to the imagination. Square jaw. Straight nose. White, white teeth against caramel skin. This sure as hell wasn't the barrio waif Harri had described on the phone last night.

It was his eyes that made Aisha stop breathing. They were a warm, golden hazel, and they locked onto her with the intensity of a laser beam.

She became acutely aware of a pain in her chest, and she drew a giant lungful of air. Nearly every female in the firm, and a couple of males, stood in the reception area or peered around corridor corners, all staring open-mouthed at her potential client.

Just like she was.

"Hi. You must be El Pájaro." Aisha held out her palm.

When he took it, an electric charge shot across her skin and down into her belly. She hadn't responded like this to a man since before her divorce. *We don't sleep with clients.* She chanted Harri's words in her head. *We don't sleep with clients.*

Even worse was the smirk on Harri's face.

Belatedly, Aisha realized she still held El Pájaro's hand and quickly dropped it. "Why don't we go back to my office?"

El Pájaro gestured toward the hallway behind her. "After you, ma'am."

Ma'am. She swallowed her wince and forced a smile. "This way." At the rate she was hiding her real emotions today, she'd tear a facial muscle or crack a tooth.

Harri and her super followed Aisha to her office. Once they were seated, she closed the door, grabbed a clean legal pad, and dropped onto her office chair.

Pulling out her attorney objectivity took some effort, but if she seriously wanted that corner office, El Pájaro was definitely her ticket. She looked at Harri. "Jeremy?"

She shrugged. "We needed the best."

Aisha nodded. Jeremy could pull off miracles and had since they were kids. She turned back to El Pájaro. "Harri tells me you're not registered."

He shook his head. "I don't have the money for the fee. Much less the required insurance."

Aisha looked at Harri, who also shook her head. "Haven't had the chance to start the paperwork yet. Ted Meadowfield showed up on my doorstep first thing this morning."

Grabbing a pen, Aisha started her to-do list. "Did he get any film of—" She turned back to the superhero/GQ model seated across her desk and tried to keep her composure. "Can I call you by something other than 'The Bird'?"

"It's 'The Sparrow,'" Harri said.

"Not in Mexico," Aisha shot back.

Harri obviously started to say something about Aisha accompanying her father on archeological digs in Central America, then realized they were in front of a client. She gave the slightest of nods to El Pájaro.

When he opened his mouth, Aisha held up a hand. "I don't want to know your full name since you're not technically my client yet."

"Rey." His sweet, sexy grin would be her undoing. "With an 'e.'"

Aisha swallowed hard. "Okay, Rey, with an 'e'. From what Harri told me, you don't have regular employment either."

"No, ma'am."

She waved her pen at him. "It's not 'ma'am'. Call me 'Aisha.'"

"Okay, Aisha." His pearly whites flashed again.

Another one of his smiles and she'd have to change her panties. Her fingers clenched around her pen. *Please, God, don't let him be a telepath.*

She cleared her throat. "Powers?"

"Flight, strength, speed. My senses are better than most people, but I don't have x-ray vision or anything like that."

"Indestructibility," Harri added.

Aisha glanced up from her notes, and Rey's cheeks were flushed. "Is that true?" she asked.

"Sort of."

His expression as he turned toward Harri bordered on desperate. She laid her hand on his forearm. "You can trust Aisha. Just like you trust me."

His gaze locked on the floor, and he tugged a leather thong with a tiny carved stone from beneath his shirt.

Aisha leaned over her desk to examine it. This close, he smelled as good as he looked. She wondered for a moment what his skin would taste like if she kissed his neck and felt her face heat again. Sitting back, she said, "It looks like jade. Is it some sort of talisman?"

He shrugged. "I don't know. My mother said never to take it off, but the two times I did—"

Harri patted his shoulder. "If you're in trouble, Rey, we need to know."

His words came out in fits and pauses. "When I was little, I supposed to be getting a bath. I dragged my feet, and she lectured me. I got mad—" He sucked in a lungful of air. "I took it off. That was the night she got killed."

Rey swallowed hard. "The second time was during that flooding near the causeway a couple of years ago. I rescued some people trapped in their cars. I was so filthy, covered in mud, afterwards I . . . I snuck into the Whitechapel Country Club to shower. Someone had left a locker room window cracked open." He grasped the amulet tightly in his fist. "I had this on a longer thong then, and accidentally pulled it off with my shirt."

He blew out a harsh breath. "Something attacked me in there. A few minutes later. Something with claws. I've never met anyone as strong as me until that . . . thing. The claws sliced right through my skin. It's the only time I've ever been hurt that I remember. I managed to get away from it, but barely." He shook his head as if to clear the memory. "I shortened the thong so I couldn't take it off by accident again." He tucked the stone back beneath his shirt and straightened his tie.

Guilt niggled at Aisha for forcing him to relive the obvious traumas, but she had to know what she was dealing with. In a soft voice, she asked, "Do you have any idea who it was? Was it some supervillain? Or a superhero who thought you were cutting in on his action?"

That disconcerting gaze of his bore into her. "It was more of a what than a who. I don't think it was human. It looked like a weird cross between a wolf and a monkey. Believe me, I know how crazy it sounds. But I've kept the stone on, and I haven't seen the creature or anything like it since that night."

Aisha had been dealing with supers all her professional life, but an alleged non-human assailant hit the top of her freak-o-meter. That was comic book stuff. It didn't happen in real life. Especially not by taking off a magic necklace. There had to be something about the stone. Or maybe a device inside it.

A glance at Harri revealed a frown on her best friend's face. So it wasn't just her.

"We need to keep that a secret," Harri said. "No need to advertise that you've got your own flavor of kryptonite."

Forcing yet another smile, Aisha tried to project reassurance. "No problem. For anything I line up that requires a photo, we'll stipulate that the shirt stays on." A pity because she really wanted an excuse to see him topless.

"Are you crazy?" Harri exclaimed. "His poster alone will break all of Farrah Fawcett's sales records."

Aisha tapped her pen on the legal pad. "What about a clause that if the necklace is visible, it has to be edited out in the final product?"

Harri frowned. "Then they'll know it's significant."

Aisha shook her head. "Not if I tell them it's a copyrighted image, and they'll have to pay a huge extra licensing fee if they leave it in. But discretion is huge in the side markets if you want to work with supers, and it's all word of mouth recommendations. All it takes is one unauthorized leaked photo and you're out. Plus, if we design his outfit properly it will only be an issue in shirt-less photos." She felt her face get even hotter.

Down, girl.

His eyes widened. "Does this mean you'll help Harri represent me?"

Her genuine smile at his earnestness lifted her mood for the first time to-day. "I'm definitely leaning that way. Let's get through the rest of my questions first."

After another half hour, excitement of another kind tingled along Aisha's nerves. Harri was right. This super was a literal gold mine. She'd never repre-sented any hero with this much potential. A rags-to-riches back story, a range of superpowers, intelligence without arrogance, physical beauty—he had it all.

Aisha set down her pen and pad. "Now for the hard part. I'm all for cultural heritage. One set of my grandparents met on the Selma march. The other on the Freedom Rides. But I want to make you accessible to more than the His-panic demographic. Which from a marketing perspective is not a bad place to be, don't get me wrong. With a few tweaks, you could have much broader ap-peal. We need to change your moniker to something a little more mainstream."

She waited for the inevitable blow-up. And waited. And waited.

"What exactly did you have in mind?" he asked.

Good. He wasn't going to fight her on this. At least not yet. Harri on the other hand . . . the stubborn scowl Aisha knew far too well appeared on her friend's face.

"He doesn't need to—" Harri began.

Aisha cut her off. "That's something we need to brainstorm. We don't need to make any decisions right now. How about the three of us meet for dinner?"

"We were going to cook for Harri. You're more than welcome to join us." Color flared in his cheeks as he turned to Harri. "If that's all right."

She grinned. "Yes, it's fine." She winked at Aisha. "What did I tell you?"

"No wine tonight. This is business." Aisha waggled her index finger at Har-ri. "We also need to design a proper uniform for him."

Harri frowned. "Something that will hold up. I don't want him hit with an indecency charge because a flame thrower burned off his unitard like that poor schmuck a couple of years ago." She bit her lip, thinking. "You know . . . what's-his-name—"

"Skyball," Aisha said dryly. Thank goodness, he hadn't been her client.

Harri snapped her fingers. "Exactly. Everyone called him Freeball after that. And that's my point. In this business, one unplanned wardrobe malfunction and nobody takes you seriously anymore."

Aisha shut down the image Harri's words painted in her mind. She needed to get her libido under control if she was going to represent the man in front of her. "There's a couple of specialists I can contact who've designed for Cobblestone. I'll make some calls."

Harri climbed to her feet. "Sounds like a plan." She leaned closer. "And my offer still stands if you want to get out of this mausoleum. Think how much fun we'd have."

Aisha chuckled. After her encounter with Stuart this morning, the idea was tempting as hell. But reeling in Rey would definitely change the minds of the partners about her contributions to the firm. Not to mention starting a new firm when she had all the debt Cal had helped her wrack up and then dropped on her during the divorce meant she needed a more stable source of income.

For now anyway.

She waggled her index finger at Harri again. "I know how much trouble you'd get me into. My mom is right. You are a bad influence."

Harri smiled. "Aw, Betty meant that as a compliment. Dinner's at seven." She looked at Rey for confirmation.

He nodded, then flashed Aisha one more beautiful smile and held out his hand. "Thank you so much, Aisha. I feel really good about this."

She took his hand and again felt that electric spark. "So do I." They gazed in each other's eyes for a moment longer than socially acceptable and she saw his cheeks flush.

So she wasn't the only one who felt the heat between them. Which would make resisting temptation even harder. *Damn it. I finally get my golden ticket to partnership and it's attached to the first guy I've wanted to sleep with since Cal left me. Wonderful.*

As Aisha walked her guests to the reception area, sounds of arguing echoed down the hall. She rounded the corner to find two uniforms flanking a plainclothed officer who waved his badge in the face of Howard Dewey, the firm's senior partner.

The second the detective spotted Aisha, he pulled out his handcuffs. "You're under arrest."

No, not her.

Harri.

Aisha stepped between the detective and her best friend. "Wait a minute. Where's your warrant?"

"What's the charge?" Harri added.

The detective dug into the pocket of his cheap suit and flung the paperwork at Aisha. "Harriet Winters is wanted for domestic terrorism under the 1947 Supervillainy Act. Specifically, the arson at City Hall yesterday."

Aisha snagged the wadded form before it struck her. A quick skim sent a sinking feeling through her stomach.

Harri shoved past her. "That's a bunch of goddamn—"

Aisha pinched her arm. "Shut up, girl. Don't say another word."

Common sense must have landed in Harri's brain because she clamped her jaw shut.

The detective stepped closer, and the smell of garlic and meat made Aisha's eyes water. "Get out of my way before I arrest you for obstruction of justice."

Aisha stood nose-to-nose with the officer despite his rank odor. "I better not see a mark on my client when I reach the station, or I'll slap a police brutality suit on you so fast it'll make your grandbabies' heads spin."

She turned to Harri as the metal snicked shut around her friend's wrists. "Let me know if he doesn't Mirandize you."

"Oh, believe me, I will." From the evil look on Harri's face, it was a good thing she was cuffed. Otherwise, the cops wouldn't know what hit them.

Rey started to follow Harri and the policemen, but Aisha grabbed his arm. "Stay with me. You can't help her right now."

The expression on his face was a mix of fury and sorrow. "But she—"

The firm's doors swung shut. Even with the initial excitement over, half the staff and attorneys remained in reception and stared at her and Rey. Aisha lowered her voice, too aware of their audience. "You can't help her," she repeated. "Let me do my job. Please. Trust me." When the tension didn't leave his body. "For her sake, do it my way."

His curt nod reassured her a tiny bit.

"Franklin," Dewey spat. He was a big man, in his early sixties, and he tried to tower over her, but it didn't work when she had on stilettos. His balding head shone under the overhead inset lights. "Why are you representing a supervillain?"

Aisha struggled to maintain her composure, but she was as pissed as Rey. "Harri Winters isn't a supervillain any more than I am."

"I will not have this firm's name sullied. We only represent superheroes." Dewey stared at her, his gaze cold and reptilian for a moment. He was friendly and warm when the situation required, but calculating and ruthless when it didn't. Aisha steeled herself. She possessed a similar ability to quickly shift emotional gears, allowing her to navigate Howard's moods more easily than her colleagues, but she never took their surface cordiality for granted.

Until Dewey poked the top of her sternum.

Howard Dewey actually poked her. With a terrible realization, she knew who had alerted the cops to Harri's location. This wasn't only Stuart's bullshit, and the argument here in reception had been for show. She was never going to make partner, no matter how much money she brought in.

A decade's worth of rage boiled to the surface of her psyche. "We represent people fighting the good fight. Isn't that what you told me when I interviewed here?"

He must have realized he'd used the wrong tactic. A charming smile appeared on his face. "Why don't you come to my office? We can discuss this unfortunate incident like civilized people."

"There's nothing to discuss. I need to get down to the police station and see about freeing my client." She turned on her heel and headed toward her office for her purse and keys.

She made it two steps before Dewey said, "Don't make a decision you'll regret, Aisha."

Her rage turned to ice as she pivoted to face him again. "Harri Winters is a good person who's being framed for Quentin Samuels's political gain. I am going to represent her whether you approve or not."

Dewey's face turned a brilliant shade of crimson. "If you take her on, you'll never make partner."

A bitter laugh erupted from her throat. "You were never going to make me partner, and we both know it."

"Maybe it's because you don't have the balls for this job," he sneered.

"Thank god for that!" She swung her arm to indicate the entire office. "It means I'm not thinking with them. And I'm damn tired of licking yours."

There was a collective gasp from their audience.

The snake Dewey truly was appeared in his eyes. "You're fired, Franklin."

"Don't bother exerting yourself on the paperwork. I quit."

She whirled and marched back to her office. A quick rip and the notes about Rey were shoved into her purse along with her reading glasses and her flashdrive with her ongoing cases. She examined her office. No pictures. No mementos. Nothing to show she had any life at all outside of this godforsaken law firm.

Returning to the reception area, Stuart and Travis stood in front of the doors. Both men had their arms crossed.

"Hand over your purse, Aisha. We have to search you before you leave." Stuart's smarmy smile said how much he was enjoying this. Travis had the grace to look slightly disturbed. Dewey stood to the side and watched the proceedings. The bastard never did his own dirty work.

"You're not touching, Ms. Franklin." Rey's smooth voice reassured her as much as his body heat against her back.

"And who's going to stop us?" Stuart taunted.

For the first time in years, her old self-confidence surged through her. "Gentlemen, I'd like you to meet our city's newest superhero, Captain Justice." She took a step closer to the two attorneys. "If I were you, I wouldn't get between him and his falsely accused foster mom."

Stuart paled, and Travis turned a sickly avocado.

"We-we-we still can't let you leave with firm property." Sweat beaded on Stuart balding pate.

"I don't have any firm property. My computer's on my desk. Have fun figuring out the password." When they didn't move, she smiled. "You have until I count to three to get out of my way before Captain Justice moves you for me. One . . ."

Both Stuart and Travis shot worried looks at Dewey.

"Two . . ."

The sound from Rey sounded suspiciously like a jaguar growling.

"Thr—"

Both attorneys bolted for the right hallway. Doors slamming echoed against the drywall.

With Rey at her back, Aisha strode out the doors of Dewey & Cheatham, feeling free for the first time in years.

CHAPTER 7

◆ ━━ ◆ ◈ ◆ ━━ ◆

"Captain Justice?" Rey stared at Aisha from the passenger seat of her BMW as they headed for the downtown police station.

"Sorry." Aisha glanced at him. "It was the first thing that popped into my head."

"No worries. I kind of like it." He cleared his throat. "But about Harri being my foster mom . . ."

Aisha sighed. "Sometimes a good bluff can get you out of tight situations. I wasn't about to let those assholes have my notes about you."

"So you lied to protect me?"

Damn, Harri was right. This guy really was too good to be true. "If it bothers you that much, I understand if you don't want me representing you."

"No. I—"

She glanced at him. He actually appeared grateful.

"I'm not upset. I've never had anyone put themselves on the line for me since my mother died. You and Harri have both done it, and you barely know me."

His admission floored her. She'd always had Harri watching her back, then Jeremy when Harri had dragged him into her fold. She couldn't imagine someone like Rey not having anyone.

Aisha swallowed the sentimentality threatening to overwhelm her. "When we get to police headquarters, let me do all the talking. You're my new assistant. *Comprende*?"

"Yes, ma'am."

She shot him a glare. "What did I say about calling me 'ma'am'?"

"A legal assistant wouldn't call his boss by her first name, Ms. Franklin," he said coolly.

Maybe representing Captain Justice would work out after all.

━ ◆ ━

By the time Aisha arrived at Interrogation #1 with Rey at her heels, she wore her bitch scowl. She ignored the detective and strode over to Harri. "Did they hurt you?"

"No."

"Miranda?"

"Yes."

"Don't worry, counselor," the detective snapped. "Your client hasn't said a thing."

Aisha turned her attention to him. "I want to talk to the ADA assigned to this case."

"I'm here," came an all-too-familiar voice from behind her.

Shit. Her day just kept getting worse. She pivoted to face the doorway.

Calvin Johnson met her careful gaze. The gray sprinkled along his temples gave him a distinguished air. Otherwise, her ex-husband looked as handsome as he had the day they met twenty years ago.

But the old feelings didn't tug at her like they had any other time she'd run into him over the past two years. Now? Now, she only felt tired.

His attention turned to the woman handcuffed to the table. "How's it going, Harri?"

"Your accommodations are just fucking wonderful, Cal." God help anyone Harri gave that nasty smile to.

He nodded before turning back to Aisha. "Let's talk outside."

"Rey, stay with Harri," she said over her shoulder as she followed Cal into the hallway.

When the door clicked shut, she said, "You've got nothing, and we both know it. Why the charges?"

He ran a hand over the tight curls on his head. "I've already had that argument with the DA. He says she's withholding information about the real culprit, Professor Venom, which makes her, at the minimum, an accessory."

Aisha crossed her arms. "Based on what evidence?"

He cocked his head. "You know, don't you? You're fishing."

"You still need to provide any and all evidence to defense counsel."

"Dammit, Aisha," Cal muttered. "You're an IP attorney, not a defense lawyer, and you're in over your head. I can give you the names of some people who do defense work."

"Are you refusing to cooperate with my request, Mr. Johnson?"

His exasperated sigh was her reward. "Two administrative assistants at City Hall heard a masked man dressed in black announce himself as Professor Venom when he entered Harri's office. Not only did she fail to provide that information to an officer at the scene, she fled."

"All hearsay, and you know it. And she didn't flee. She was traumatized by two attempts on her life."

Cal rocked on his heels. "Two attempts? What are you talking about?"

"Look, I can talk her into cooperating if you tell me what the hell is going on."

Cal learned closer and lowered his voice. "I don't know what Harri did to piss off the mayor, but both he and the DA are gunning for her. My hands are tied."

Politics. It always came back to politics. "What are they willing to do?"

Cal shrugged. "Conspiracy with the minimum sentence."

Aisha felt her jaw drop. "That's still a felony. She'll lose her license."

He shrugged again. "Sorry. Best I can do."

"She's got no priors, Cal."

He simply stared at her through his wire rims. They weren't giving him any room to maneuver, which was pretty damn odd.

"Fine." Aisha clenched her jaw and stalked back into the interrogation room. She pointed at the detective. "You." She pointed at the door. "Out."

He left with a huff of his rancid garlic breath.

She repeated the deal to Harri.

"Fuck, no!" She rattled the handcuff. "You've got to get me out of here. Someone's setting up both me and Professor Venom."

Aisha planted her palms on the table. "We need help. Neither of us are defense attorneys. And someone's trying very hard to get you out of the way. Too hard."

Harri blinked. "What are you talking about? What else did Cal say?"

"It wasn't just the assistant district attorney." Rey entered the conversation. "Aisha's boss said she was fired if she represented you."

Harri stared at Aisha. "You'll never get that partnership if you stay here."

"I wasn't getting it anyway." Aisha chuckled and straightened. "I don't have a dick. So I quit." She sobered. "You need to consider giving the police a statement about Professor Venom."

"I'm not throwing my client to the wolves to save my own skin," Harri snapped.

Aisha held up both palms. "Didn't think you would, but as your current counsel, I've got to present all your options. I'll relay your rejection of their deal, and see about bail. If the DA doesn't drop the bullshit, you'll need someone who specializes in defense."

She headed for the door, but with her hand on the knob, she looked back at Harri. "By the way, since I'm unemployed, is that offer to be your partner still open?"

—⋅●⋅—

Harri lay on the hard narrow cot and stared at the concrete ceiling of the holding cell. She supposed she should be grateful they hadn't put her in the general population, but privacy didn't improve the accommodations. She wasn't getting any sleep tonight, she knew that much.

Aisha had made a heroic effort, but, according to Cal, the district attorney Mike Michaels intended to fight bail on the grounds Harri was a flight risk. A flight risk! She snorted and curled on her side trying to get more comfortable.

If only people knew how very little money she actually had. Grandma Harri had tried to leave her namesake the bulk of her estate, but Harri's feckless father—or more accurately, he and Harri's grasping step-mother—had fought for control of the estate trust and won. While it was true Grandma had gotten a little eccentric toward the end, she hadn't been mentally incompetent when she'd revised the will to make Harri her sole heir. Grandma had simply known how quickly her son and his new wife would piss through the money if they got it.

She hadn't been wrong. Dad and Laura had taken their remaining assets with them when they drove the Porsche off a cliff with a big bag of coke in the glove box.

All that was left was the scholarship endowment up at the University and the nest egg in the safe deposit box. And Harri had sworn that she wouldn't touch that hidden money unless it was absolutely necessary.

Like maybe right now.

Harri groaned and rolled over again. This cot was cruel and unusual punishment.

Fortunately, Aisha had managed to set up an in-chambers bail hearing with Judge Inunza first thing in the morning, and, considering how well Inunza liked Cal's boss, Harri would be out in time for breakfast. They had no evidence against her. Nothing. At best they might get her on minor obstruction for not immediately ratting out Arthur, but it's not like they had tried to formally question her before her arrest. She couldn't be convicted for withholding evidence nobody had asked her to give.

Judge Burgess, Quentin Samuels's golf buddy, had been the judge on the arrest warrant. Harri smiled. Inunza had spent his teenaged summers caddying at Whitechapel Country Club, in the not-so-old days when a brown kid named Pablo could aspire to carry the clubs but not actually swing them. He had zero patience with the local old boy golf network. He'd grant Harri low bail out of spite to piss off Burgess and Quentin. And Mike Michaels who, Harri remembered, had gone to prep school with Burgess.

In a city this big, you'd think we wouldn't all know each other.

Much to her surprise, she yawned deeply. Maybe she would get some sleep. It had been a busy day after all. Being strip searched and deloused had really taken it out of her.

At least I know I don't have cooties. She burst into giggles at the thought, which quickly escalated into guffaws.

Her cell door buzzed. Why would someone come to get her after lights out? She sat upright, suddenly wide awake, her laughter gone.

A dark figure lunged inside her cell. In the dim light from the hallway, she had time to register paramilitary clothing and a black face mask.

Just like the asshole who'd set City Hall on fire.

In a fluid motion, the figure spun her and shoved her face-first on the cot.

"I don't want to hurt you," a hoarse male voice whispered in her ear.

Harri felt a large gloved hand grasp the back of her skull.

"Don't move. My partner has to believe you're comatose. I need your help," the voice whispered. "Keep Patty safe. Please. And the baby."

Holy crap! Was this guy the unknown sperm donor?

"I will," Harri breathed back.

"Thank you." He slid his fingers around her wrist as if checking her pulse. "I'm supposed to be giving you an aneurysm. Don't move until you hear the cell door lock."

"Security camera?" Harri whispered.

He grasped her skull again. "We took care of it. Nobody will check on you until the morning shift change. I'll make sure your lawyer gets here before then."

She felt his weight lift off her and, as instructed, didn't move until she'd heard the lock click. She counted to a hundred to be safe before she carefully raised her head.

An aneurysm? The guy must be a super. Patty's baby daddy was a super. *And he was sent here to kill me.*

Fear uncoiled from her belly and spread through her. She shook with the weight of it. Not only for herself, but for her assistant, too. She shook inside the jail cell she wouldn't be in if some serious procedural corners hadn't been cut. *What the fuck have I gotten us into?*

Harri curled up into a tight ball on the cot and waited for morning.

Chapter 8

A loud, harsh buzzing ruined the best dream Aisha had in a long time. It had been about Rey and had reached the X-rated part. *He's a client. Don't go there.*

She groped for her phone and hit the answer button. "What?"

"Is this Aisha Franklin?" a gruff male voice said.

She glanced at the screen. Unknown number. "Yes. Who is this?"

"You need to get to the jail before the seven a.m. shift change. If you have some official muscle, bring it. She's okay for now, but she won't be if you don't get to her first. Don't let them know you know anything."

She rolled upright, her heart hammering and cold sweat on her skin. "Who the hell is this?"

"The guy who was supposed to kill her." He hung up.

Aisha, now wide awake, reached for the light switch. It was after three-thirty and she definitely wasn't getting back to sleep after that phone call. Official muscle? She had Rey, but the caller had definitely said official. His insinuation was it shouldn't be somebody affiliated with the Canyon Pointe PD.

That left one person. And Harri was going to be even less happy about this.

She had an email with his new number. She found it and punched the digits on her phone, praying he'd answer.

"Lewis," a gruff voice said after the third ring.

"Eddie? It's Aisha."

"Aisha? What the hell? What time is it?"

"Almost four. Harri's in trouble."

He sighed. "What did she do now? And why isn't she calling me?" He sighed again. "Okay, stupid question. She wouldn't call me for help if she was on fire. It's been two freakin' years since the divorce and she still hasn't spoken to me."

"She's in big trouble, Eddie, and I need your help, or I wouldn't be calling."

"That thing with City Hall?"

"Yeah," Aisha said. "They've arrested her on suspicion of supervilliany. She's in jail."

"What? In jail? What the hell happened?"

"It's a set up. Shut up and listen. We don't have a lot of time."

Aisha filled him in. Eddie had been a city cop, a detective, but had left in the aftermath of the divorce for a job with the FBI. He had been recently transferred to the local FBI office, something Aisha wasn't sure Harri knew yet. And even with a murder attempt and a conspiracy to frame her, Harri wasn't going to be happy to see him.

All business now, Eddie told her to get to the jail as soon as she could and he'd meet her there. If they couldn't get her bail, Eddie would call in some favors and get her transferred to federal protective custody.

Aisha made a second call to Harri's house. Thankfully, the three waywards had listened to her and stayed there for the night. She told Rey what was going on and that the three of them needed to stay put for now.

Trying to quash her fear, Aisha stumbled to the bathroom to get presentable. *Get your head in the game and get to work*, she told her reflection. *You've got a new job, remember?*

But could she save her first client?

— ◆ —

"What's he doing here?" Harri hissed when her ex-husband strode into the courtroom. The embarrassment couldn't get any worse. She still wore her jail jumpsuit and handcuffs as she sat with Aisha on a bench, waiting for the judge.

"What did I tell you?" Eddie said as he approached. He rolled his eyes. "Nice to see you too, Harri. Don't take this wrong, but orange really isn't your color."

"Bite me." She turned to Aisha. "My . . . uh, visitor called you?"

Aisha nodded. "Which is why I called Eddie." She shot a glance at the officer who escorted Harri from the jail, and she lowered her voice. "We can't trust the locals. At least not until we know what's going on."

"And you expect me to trust him?" Harri glared at Eddie.

"This isn't about your marriage. You're in deep shit, girl, and I need every shoveler I can get."

Eddie snorted back a laugh, then glared at the jail officer escorting Harri. The woman had the sense to blanch and not make a smart-assed comment about her prisoner.

"Where's Rey?" Harri asked. "And Patty? Is she okay?"

"Rey's babysitting the kids at your place."

Harri nodded, relieved. Nobody would get near Patty if Rey was there.

Judge Inunza's secretary came out and escorted them into the judge's chambers. Inunza was sipping coffee and looking over a stack of paperwork. Cal sat in one of the chairs in front of the judge's desk, accompanied by the district attorney himself.

Mike Michaels was a much better politician than a lawyer. He'd once been a gifted prosecutor, had made his name on the notorious Canyon family murders even though he'd lost, but he hadn't been in a courtroom in fifteen years. Now, he spent most of his time lunching with political supporters and sneaking out to play golf.

Harri almost felt sympathy for Cal having to work for the jerk. Almost. Cal wasn't a bad guy, but Harri's loyalty was all to Aisha, and she hated Cal on principle even if Aisha didn't.

She glanced at Eddie. Solid, plain, broken-nosed Eddie who'd wanted nothing more than three kids and a secure pension. Harri would never admit this to anyone in a hundred million years, but she hadn't spoken to him since the divorce more to avoid feeling her own guilt over how things had ended than any residual anger over his leaving her for Sarah.

Harri understood why he'd left even though she pretended she didn't. Eddie hadn't changed. He was the guy he'd always been. Stable. Husband and dad material. And Harri had once wanted to be a mom. Or least she thought she had, in a vague someday sort of way.

But she kept finding excuses and finally her biological clock started ticking too loudly to ignore. Eddie gave her an ultimatum—now or never. She chose never. He chose Sarah. She liked to claim that he'd traded her in for a younger model, but she knew in her heart that wasn't true. He'd chosen the life he'd always wanted over the life she'd hoped he'd drift into.

Inunza looked up from the paperwork and smiled at her, his dark eyes twinkling.

Harri felt the tense icy knot in her gut begin to melt.

"Hey, Harri," Inunza said. "I haven't seen you in my courtroom in a while. Never expected to see you in this role."

"Neither did I, Your Honor," Harri said. "How's Carol?"

"Good. Panicking over Paul's college applications, but that's to be expected. Mike," the judge continued, without missing a beat. "This case is a flaming load of bullshit, and we both know it. You got nothing. I'm releasing her. Without any bail and with an apology. And if you bring me one more case with such a blatant lack of evidentiary support, I'll file a complaint with the Bar. I'm not Burgess. I'm not part of your campaign staff. And make sure to pass that same message on to that weasel Quentin when you see him."

"But—"

Inunza pointed his index finger at the DA. "Not one more word, Mike. Not one."

"I'll go over your head."

Inunza looked at Mike over his reading glasses, his dark eyes unreadable. "Really? Best of luck with that. The folks over at the court of appeals don't like this political crap of yours any better than I do. And if you disobey me again, I'll hold you in contempt."

The judge turned to Aisha. "Ms. Franklin, if they continue to bother your client, come see me, and I'll make sure the district attorney becomes well acquainted with the full range of my particular set of superpowers." He nodded at Eddie. "Agent Lewis. Why are the feds taking an interest?"

"Only to ensure the civil rights and safety of Ms. Winters. We've been made aware of certain . . . irregularities in how this case has been processed."

What little blood remained in Mike Michaels' face drained away. His skin looked like slightly moldy cottage cheese.

"Do tell," Inunza said. "Which irregularities, of course, would be highlighted in public court documents should the district attorney not release Ms. Winters immediately."

"But Ms. Winters will need to be taken back to the jail for exit processing. It will take at least two hours—" the DA protested.

Inunza cut him off with a look. "No, Mike, it will not. The officer will uncuff her right now, Ms. Franklin and Mr. Johnson will go fetch her belongings, and you, Ms. Winters, Agent Lewis of the FBI, and I will wait here for them to return."

The judge smiled at Harri again. "No offense, kiddo, but you got jail stink and so will your clothes."

"Yes, your Honor, I'm well aware. Nothing a hot shower and dry cleaning won't fix."

"I'm sure the district attorney would be happy to pay for the dry cleaning." Inunza raised an eyebrow as he glanced at Michaels.

The DA merely nodded. He had enough sense to know he'd lost this round. Harri wondered if he had known about the murder plot. Michaels was a slimy character, but murder? She couldn't imagine either him or Quentin Samuels actually capable of plotting to kill her. Someone else had to be pulling their strings.

Who the hell had she pissed off enough they wanted her dead?

———•———

While Harri showered off the jail stink in her own bathroom, Aisha admired Arthur's handiwork. The supervillain wannabe had been busy since Harri's arrest.

"I hacked into the city servers. They've got everything on the cloud." Arthur gestured at the personal laptop Aisha let him borrow. "Least secure place on the planet. I copied everything with hers or Patty's name on it. I also checked her personal laptop and found the same malware that was on mine. It's on Patty's phone and home computer, too. Somebody's been watching all of us for a while."

Aisha frowned. "How did you find the spyware?"

"Patty complained how slow Ms. Winters's laptop was when she was downloading her legal forms yesterday." Arthur shook his head. "After I did some basic clean-up, it was still dragging, so I did some digging."

"Did you clean out the spyware?" Aisha asked.

Arthur shook his head. "I had a different idea. If I scrape her laptop, they'll know we're on to them. If she doesn't mind buying another computer, I can make sure it stays clean and we can use the dirty one to try to . . . I don't know . . . set up the bad guys. Feed them what we want them to know."

Aisha smiled. "Now that's some supervillian plotting. Except using your powers for good."

Arthur smiled so wide Aisha worried the top of his head might fall off. She was really starting to like him, in spite of herself. If he had clearer skin, a better haircut, maybe put some weight on him, Patty might like him even more.

No one could miss his shy, admiring looks at Harri's assistant when he thought no one was looking. Maybe Aisha could finagle Jeremy's help.

Harri walked into the dining room in a t-shirt and jeans, rubbing her hair with a towel. "I'm fried. But at least now, I can stand my own smell. We need to be thinking about office space."

"I know. Neither of our places is big enough to set up even a temporary office." Aisha shivered at Arthur's revelations. "And we need a secure place to meet clients, but that's expensive as hell."

Harri threw the towel over her shoulder. "I'm open to suggestions."

Patty and Rey's arrival with lunch saved Aisha from dealing with the money issue, even if it was a temporary reprieve.

"Oh, my god. I love Marta's place," Patty exclaimed as she pulled out aluminum food containers from the bags they brought in. She elbowed Rey. "Tell them what your friend said."

He glanced at Aisha and blushed before he turned to Harri. "We ran into Miguel, who watches the Lechuza Building for the owner. He said they'd be willing to offer you office space cheap." He cleared his throat. "That's assuming you ladies are interested."

Aisha watched Harri. "I think it's time we have the talk."

"Let's take our lunches out to the patio." Harri sauntered over to the refrigerator and pulled out a couple of bottles of water.

"You don't have to leave on our account," Arthur protested.

"It's not personal, sweetie," Patty said. Arthur's cheeks turned red at her endearment. "The attorneys need to talk strategy without the clients freaking out. It's part of their superpower of seeming to know all the answers." She grinned at Harri and Aisha.

Harri raised one hand to her forehead while still holding the water bottle. "Egads, Aisha! Our secretary has innocently revealed our secrets to the evil supervillain."

"Cut it out," Aisha said, trying not to laugh. "You're going to scare off our only clients."

She grabbed hers and Harri's lunches, utensils and napkins, not to mention her pad and pen, before following Harri out to her mini-patio. Harri pushed the sliding glass door shut and joined Aisha at the little table.

They stared at each other for a long moment.

"Well, you know my trust fund went over the cliff with Dad and Laura and the big bag of coke," Harri said. "At least most of it."

Aisha wrote "Assets" and "Liabilities" on the top of the page.

Harri groaned. "You would head right for the bottom line."

Aisha tried to look sympathetic. "I know how much you hate talking about money. I know it makes you anxious. But we need to be honest with each other, face reality, and talk numbers."

Harri blew out a deep breath and jabbed at her enchilada. "If I had any money, I wouldn't have had to live with you and your parents."

"Would you have preferred foster care?" Aisha tapped her pen against the legal pad. "Besides, the judge wouldn't have declared you an emancipated minor if you didn't have some money."

Harri shook her head. "After college and law school, all I had left of the Winters' fortune was the family discount at the Winters flagship store downtown and a lifetime membership at Whitechapel Country Club, which I never use because I hate the snobs there."

She waved her fork. "I own the house and my car free and clear. And my student loans are almost paid off. Only about twenty grand to go."

Aisha raised an eyebrow. "Only? What happened to the education account Grandma Harri set up?"

Harri shrugged. "Think about it. Books and expenses for undergrad and law school, not to mention room and board."

"But you and I both worked—"

"Not to rub it in your face, but you got a discount because your dad was a professor here at the time."

"Sorry." Aisha grimaced. "That must have been a pile of money. Too bad you couldn't have applied to be a Winters scholar."

"No shit. I doubt Grandma ever thought her own granddaughter would be a low-income female, but I was automatically disqualified from participating under the terms of the endowment. No family members. And that stupid endowment is part of the reason why people think I'm still rich. The University is always bugging me for money. 'You already got it,' I tell them. 'It's called tuition.' Bastards."

Aisha raised her hands. "Sorry. I forgot what a sore topic it was." She paused a moment. "You got any cash?"

Harri shrugged. "Some. I've got about $25,000 in an emergency cash fund Dad and Laura didn't know about because I had the safe deposit key. And there's my 401(k). Other than that, no."

Aisha shook her head. "We aren't raiding our retirement accounts. Either one of us. No way."

Harri sank down in her chair, looking relieved. "I'm sorry I'm so weird about money. I just . . . I don't want to ever feel that powerless again. Like I did when I was a kid. Never again."

Aisha reached over and squeezed her hand. "Girl, I know. I was there when Mom and Dad rescued you from that social worker. I'm sorry you had to go through all that. If I'd known—"

"You were a kid just like I was. And it's not like I told you. I didn't tell anybody how bad it was." She watched the squirrels playing by the pin oak trees in the shared green space between the buildings for a moment before her attention returned to Aisha. "What about you?"

She looked away, embarrassed as hell. It wasn't until this moment she realized she expected Harri to front the bulk of their new venture. "You don't want to know."

"Hey, I showed you mine. Now, show me yours. I'm sure you've got plenty of money. You worked for a big law firm."

"As an associate."

Harri snorted. "Making more than me I bet."

Aisha shook her head and blinked to clear her blurry eyesight.

"Please tell me you have some money."

Harri's panicked expression added more guilt to the pile. Aisha cleared her throat. "I have a 401(k) like you. And my Beemer is free and clear. The condo . . ." She trailed off and refused to meet Harri's eye.

"What about it? You have a mortgage, right?"

"Two," she whispered. "I'm already upside down on my condo from the divorce, but now that I quit—" She took a shuddering breath. "Cal was still working his way up in the DA's office, and we never saved anything because he wanted to pay off his student loans as soon as we could. Actually, he wanted me to pay them off, since I didn't have any, and I was working for Dewey and making more money, and I . . . I didn't contest the divorce. I signed what he gave me. I had to cash out his share of the condo, it was at the top of the market, and I thought I'd dig myself out when the partnership came through." She buried her face in her hands and in a muffled voice said, "I'm an idiot. I know. I know."

"You're not an idiot. Don't call yourself that. Cal's a shithead. So help me, I'm gonna kick his ass next time I see him."

The fierceness in Harri's voice made Aisha look up and giggle despite her stinging eyes. "You sound like my dad. My mom still thinks Cal was the best thing that ever happened to me, and I squandered it."

"Squandered it? He dumped you." Harri jabbed her fork in her remaining enchilada. "Because you couldn't have a baby."

"Eddie left you for the same reason," Aisha said.

Harri's cheeks turned bright pink. "Not exactly." She chopped the enchilada into tiny bits. "Eddie asked me to make a decision, and I said I wasn't ready to be a mom. He didn't start sleeping with his teenage assistant while I was in emergency surgery because I nearly bled to death from an ectopic pregnancy."

"Mina was twenty-two."

"Close enough," Harri muttered.

"You told me Eddie left you for Sarah."

"I lied, all right. He barely knew Sarah when I told him I didn't want a baby. He didn't leave me for her. He left me for himself. So he could have the family he always wanted."

Aisha sat back in her chair and stared at Harri. "Why are you only now telling me this?"

"Because I thought you'd—I was throwing away something you'd had taken from you and you were so sad I didn't want to . . . I didn't think you'd understand." Harri poked at the bits of enchilada, not meeting Aisha's gaze. "Besides what business do I have being anybody's mother anyway?"

After everything the two of them had been through together, she never dreamed Harri would hide something as big as this.

"God," Aisha finally said. "This really is like a marriage. Maybe we need couples therapy."

Harri started laughing. "Where did that come from? Girl, I love you, but not that way. Can't we just be friends?"

Aisha threw a crumpled napkin at her and laughed too. "No, dummy. I mean we need to be totally honest with each other. We need to be able to talk about money and the future and what we're trying to do here."

Harri stirred the mess she'd made of her enchilada. "And I'm the idiot who threw away a good thing with a great guy because of my hang-ups about my rotten childhood."

Aisha tapped her pen against her pad to draw Harri out of her maudlin thoughts. "Unfortunately, you're the financially solvent idiot. I can't really bring anything to the table."

Harri snorted. "Besides, you know, the actual expertise we need to do the job. And the industry contacts. You are aware that the super community hates me, right?"

"Hate is a strong word."

"How about despise? Detest? Abhor?"

Aisha sighed. "Fine. You aren't popular with the heroes and villains. But the villains don't like anybody, and the heroes' creditors actually like you a lot. Nobody dared to sue supers until you went after them."

"Mwa-ha-ha-ha-ha!" Harri chortled. "My evil plan has been achieved. The cheap bastards now have to pay their bills like the rest of us."

Aisha leaned her head against the palm of her hand. "We really need to work on that attitude of yours. Not everyone is as laid back as Rey or willing to jump at your command like Arthur."

"Yeah, yeah." Harri waved her fork in the air. "So where are we?"

"Not broke, but not well-capitalized." Aisha looked up from her legal pad. "Any chance you'd be willing to mortgage your townhouse?"

Harri leaned back in her chair, crossed her arms, and stared at her little two-story place. "Let's save that as a last resort."

Aisha frowned. "We already know we can't afford downtown rent."

Harri shrugged. "Want to go look at Rey's friend's place?"

"Not really." Aisha shuddered. "It's not the best part of town."

"We may not have any other options right now," Harri pointed out.

"All right." Aisha held her hands up in surrender. "We'll look." She hesitated for a second. "There's something else we need to discuss."

"You mean the target on my back," Harri said softly.

"Yeah. Arthur found spyware on your computer and Patty's phone."

"I . . . heard that part of your conversation with him," Harri admitted.

"I'm beginning to think the mugging at the grocery store last month wasn't a random purse snatching. And—" Aisha watched her best friend, judging her reaction. "I asked Eddie to do some checking. Quietly."

Harri swore under her breath.

Aisha waited for her to come to the right conclusion, but a knock on the glass interrupted Harri's fit. Aisha waved for Arthur to come out, but he merely pushed the sliding door back far enough to poke his head through.

"Ms. Franklin, would you mind if I take a look at your phone?"

A chill ran through her. "Yeah, go ahead, Arthur." She rattled off her password.

Once he closed the door, Harri said, "Why would they be watching you?"

Aisha cocked her head. "Really?"

"Never mind." Harri scrubbed her eyes. "I'm blaming it on sleep deprivation."

They gathered their trash and went back inside. From the grim looks on the three people sitting around Aisha's phone on the dining room table, the news wasn't good.

"You've got to be kidding me," she said as she crossed to the sink to rinse her containers.

"The good news, if you can call it that—" Patty scowled. "Your phone wasn't hijacked until you were driving to the city jail yesterday afternoon."

"In other words, after I was arrested," Harri growled.

Aisha stared at her best friend. Worry prickled her skin. "In other words, someone at Dewey & Cheatham is in league with whoever's trying to kill you."

CHAPTER 9

— ◆ —

Aisha pounded her fist on top of the snooze alarm. Her second morning of self-employment and she had to get up even earlier than normal. Dad was going home.

Without Mom.

She sat up with a groan.

Mom and Dad had planned to fly together to Portland this weekend to visit LaShun and her family, then drive back to Atlanta in a rental car. But by the time Aisha got home from lunch with Harri and her crew of misfits, Mom was on her way out the door. Refusing to let Aisha drive her, Mom took a taxi to the airport to fly on to Portland alone, no doubt to commiserate with LaShun about whatever it was she thought Dad had done this time.

The soonest Dad could get a flight back to Atlanta was a nine-thirty this morning. He wanted to be at the airport two hours early, they had a half hour drive to get there, and they needed time to talk, so she was crawling out of bed at five.

When she strode into the kitchen, Dad was waiting. He handed her a mug of coffee. "Here, baby girl. I'm sorry you had to walk in on that scene yesterday."

"Thanks." The last thing she wanted to discuss was her parents' marriage without caffeine first. Actually, she didn't want to discuss their marriage at all. "You want eggs?"

He smiled. "I'm cooking. You relax. You've been taking care of us all week."

Aisha sat at the tiny kitchen table and watched her father. Steeled with another few sips of coffee, she finally asked, "What's going on? Really? Why is Mom so angry at you?"

"Oh, you don't need to worry—"

"Yes, Daddy, I do need to worry. Mom is . . . I've never seen her this furious before."

He brought her a plate of scrambled eggs and some toast. "You want jam?"

Aisha nodded. "Yes, please, but don't change the subject. Are you and Mom splitting up?"

"No!" Jam jar in hand, he sat down at the table with her. "No," he said again, but with less conviction. "I don't know."

Aisha shoved her shock down. Time to be the dispassionate questioner. Nothing would shut Dad down faster than drama, and Mom had grown increasingly dramatic of late. "Did you do something to cause this?"

He sighed. "I got old. But not as quickly as your mother. And I'm not sure she can forgive me for that."

Aisha spread blueberry jam on her toast. Mom had always struggled with the fear that one of the young students who idolized their Professor Franklin would eventually turn his head. No matter what he said or did to prove his love, the anxiety remained.

She pushed her eggs around on the plate and then gave up in favor of the toast. They ate in silence, until Aisha asked the question she was dreading. "Did you have an affair with one of your students?"

Dad tossed his fork onto his plate. "Aw, baby girl, not you, too. It's bad enough LaShun keeps getting her all wound up, I don't need you joining the chorus." He glared at her. "No. Of course, I didn't. And I never have. I wouldn't. I made a vow to your mother, and I've kept it."

"But Mom doesn't believe you, is that what's going on?"

Dad sighed, his eyes shiny. "I guess. I try to tell her how much I love her, but . . ." He rose, scraped his half-finished breakfast into the garbage disposal, put his plate in the dishwasher, and sat back down. "I'm so damn tired of not being trusted. It grinds away at you. I love your mother, but—" His hands clenched.

Aisha took a deep breath to steady herself and finished his sentence. "But you're not sure how much longer you can keep loving her when she treats you like this."

Dad nodded, then blew his nose with a crumpled paper napkin. "Yeah. Because she sure as hell doesn't love me anymore."

"Oh, Dad." Aisha grabbed his hand. In a heartbeat, she realized Jeremy was right about her mom. "I don't think that's it at all. Despite all her feminist rhetoric, Mom has not handled aging very well. She's angry at time, not at you."

"But she can't yell at time." He gave her a sad smile. "When'd you get so wise?"

Aisha laughed. "Actually, the wisdom is Jeremy's."

"Oh, for heaven's sake!" Dad laughed. "Don't tell her she was psychoanalyzed by him. Don't tell him he was right either. You'll never hear the end of it from either of them."

"Yes, sir." She grinned.

Dad's laughter died, and he cleared his throat. "Did you tell your mother what really happened at work?"

Aisha's grip tightened around her coffee cup. "She didn't give me a chance to."

"Good. Don't. At least not yet. I'll keep your secret. You know what you're going to do?"

The relief at not getting a lecture actually felt good despite the early hour. "Yeah. I'm going into practice with Harri."

Dad laughed again. "Oh, your mother's going to love that. On a shoestring no doubt?"

"Well, yeah, but we've got this amazing client—" She felt her face flush at the image of Rey in her head. "Harri and I can get second mortgages on both of our places if we have to—"

"Third mortgage, baby girl. You got the second mortgage to buy out that jerk ex-husband of yours. Don't think I don't know about that. Every time your mom goes on about what a mistake it was to divorce Cal, I want to find him and kick his ass."

Aisha laughed at the image he presented. "You know he really respects you."

"Well, goody for him. The feeling's not mutual. Glad-handing sack of shit."

Aisha laughed harder. "That's what I almost called Stuart Cheatham on my way out the door."

"Don't you dare take after me, young lady. When they go low—"

"—we go high," she finished for him. The memory of her confrontation with Howard Dewey struck her in the gut like a fist, and she abruptly stopped laughing. "Oh, God, Dad. They never meant to make me partner. They just strung me along all these years."

"You gonna sue them?"

Aisha shook her head. "I don't know. I know I should fight the good fight and think of all the other women I could help, but—"

"But they'll ruin you if you try." Dad squeezed her hand and released it. "This client really that good?"

Her face burned. She prayed her father wouldn't notice. "Yeah, he's really that good."

"One of those superhero fellas?"

"Yeah, but really super. Not just a big guy in tights." She sipped her coffee to keep from saying anything really embarrassing.

Dad shook his head. "Why do they all wear those damn things? Can't they fight evil in pants? Hell, my grandfather didn't wear tights while fighting Nazis. Today's supers are as bad as those men ballet dancers your mother is always hauling me off to see. It's unseemly, showing yourself off like that. Give this one trousers, will you?"

Aisha buried her face in her hands as she laughed so he couldn't see how mortified she was. Worlds collided in a horrible way. Her father could not be talking about her object of lust's private parts. That cannot happen. "Yes, sir," she said as she tried to control herself. "Trousers it is."

———— •●• ————

On the drive to the airport, he signed over all his travelers' checks to her. "Won't be needing these. So much for the cross-country get-to-know-each-other-again road trip."

"Travelers' checks?" she asked, keeping her attention on the heavy traffic. "They still make those things? Why not use a credit card and ATMs?"

"Because I'm an old man and this is what I know. Don't be a smartass." He stuffed the signed checks into her purse. "And I've got some cash too."

"But—"

"Don't argue with me. I got it, and you need it. Unless you're planning on running this law firm out of your kitchen." He stuffed the cash into her purse next to the checks. "You need more money, you let me know."

"But, Dad—"

"But nothing. I'm helping you. Let me do this. You've never needed my help before."

"That's not true," Aisha spluttered. "Not true at all."

"Yes, it is. Even when you were little. Not like LaShun. Or your brother."

"Like Martin's ever needed help—"

"Hah. Shows what you know. You are such a middle child, baby girl. You always made good choices, and I never had to worry about you like I did the others, so you got ignored."

"Good choices? That's not what Mom says." Aisha checked the rearview mirror and moved into the turn off lane for the airport.

"Huh. Since when do you believe her?"

"Well, since never," Aisha conceded.

"She doesn't like your choices because they're not her choices. Not like LaShun, who consults her on everything. And don't make that face. I love your sister as much as I love you. But I can't talk to her. She's her mother's child, just like you're my child."

"Who's Martin the child of?"

"Both of us. Which is why he's so good at playing us."

Aisha joined in with her dad's laughter as she pulled up in front of Terminal Two. "It's Del Oro right? The commuter flight into O'Hare?"

He nodded. "Only way I could get there on such short notice."

She sighed in exasperation. "Dad, you know you could have stayed a few more days."

He shook his head. "No. You have things to do with your new practice, and you don't need to get sucked any further into this thing with me and your mother."

"But LaShun—"

Dad reached for her hand and squeezed it. "LaShun loves the drama. You don't. Your mother's going to do what she's going to do. She always has. Nothing I can do, but wait and see where I fit in."

She popped the trunk, and they both climbed out of her car. He pulled his suitcase out of her BMW, and they hugged goodbye for a long moment. Aisha felt the tears rise to the surface and pushed them back down.

"I'll be fine, Aisha. I love you. Now go start your new life." Her father kissed her cheek one last time before he disappeared into the crowd.

Harri pounced on the phone at the first ring.

Aisha had sent her a rather terse text last night telling her she had to take her dad to the airport in the morning. Harri checked with Jeremy, but he hadn't heard a thing from Aisha since Marvin and Betty arrived on Sunday. Jeremy spent the rest of the call pouting about how his party planning efforts had gone to waste if no one was going to show up to his dinner Saturday evening.

"That was a quick visit," Harri said. "I thought they weren't going to Portland for a few more days."

From the whistling over the receiver, Aisha was on her balcony, smoking again. "Mom left for Portland last night. Dad left for Atlanta this morning."

Harri groaned, but she wasn't surprised. She had witnessed Betty and Marvin's relationship up close and knew things had never been quite as wonderful between them as Aisha liked to believe. One good thing about growing up with a coke-head father—you lost all illusions about the existence of the perfect family.

"Oh, shit. I'm sorry. They give you a reason?"

Aisha sighed. "The usual. She doesn't trust him. He claims he's innocent."

Harri, unsure how to respond, finally asked, "Do you believe him?"

"Yeah." Another sucking inhale before Aisha said. "Yeah, I do."

Not the time to nag about the cigarettes, Harri reminded herself. "For what it's worth, I believe him, too. No offense to your mom, but she can be kind of . . . rigid about stuff."

"He gave me some money for our firm and promised me more if we need it," Aisha added. She took another drag on her cigarette. "Mom doesn't know I left the law firm, so I'd appreciate it if you didn't mention it to anyone until I give you the all clear."

"Uh, it's a little too late."

"You told Jeremy."

"Sorry."

"Well, the cat's out then." Another deep inhale. "I'm sorry. I don't want to talk about the parents anymore. Still want to check out the space Rey mentioned?"

"If you don't think it's right for us to look right now, we can use my townhouse temporarily. Hell, all of our clients and our secretary are living with me."

"Patty's still at your place?"

"Yeah. For now." Harri leaned back against her pillows and twisted her ponytail around her finger. She'd retreated to her own bedroom to get some breathing space. "She's scared to go home, but she pretends she's staying to keep me from killing anyone. Arthur insisted Patty stay so Rey could protect us both, and Rey guilted me into letting Arthur stay since our supervillain wannabe still has a BOLO out for his arrest."

Rustling came through the phone receiver for a moment. "Well, we're going to need enough space for our offices, a conference room, a workspace for Patty, and a file room. Oh, and a space for Arthur."

Harri still wasn't sold on the idea of Professor Venom as their IT guy, but for some reason both Aisha and Rey seemed to really like the little weasel. "Fine, but how are we going to handle the BOLO on Arthur? I need to keep my distance from him. Besides you get along with him better. Maybe he should stay with you."

"Oh, no. I just got rid of houseguests, remember?"

"But you've got attorney/client privilege, and I don't with them trying to pin accessory on me."

"Shit," Aisha muttered. "It would be better if he turned himself in. Let me call Cal, since I'm apparently now doing our defense work, and set something up. How do you think Arthur would react to this plan?"

———— •◆• ————

"You want me to what?" Arthur squeaked.

"Turn yourself in," Aisha repeated. When she arrived at Harri's townhouse, she discovered Harri had chickened out and left presenting the plan to her.

"But I'm innocent!" The color in Arthur's face emphasized his acne.

I really need to take him to Jeremy. "I know, Arthur," Aisha said instead, desperately clinging to her patience. "I believe you. Otherwise, I wouldn't be offering to represent you. But Harri can't be your attorney because she's been accused of being your accomplice. If you want someone else—"

"Got the affidavit from Arthur's probation officer!" Patty charged into the kitchen. She had the paper in one hand and a hot pink laptop under her other arm.

Harri frowned. "Where'd you get that laptop?"

"We needed a clean machine. I had it drop-shipped here. Arthur's already ensured the bad guys can't hack this without some serious know-how." Patty glared at Harri. "The money came out of my baby fund, so I expect to be reimbursed by Winters & Franklin, especially the Winters portion, since it is now my work computer."

Harri held up both of her hands. "Yes, ma'am."

Aisha faced the former supervillain wannabe again. "Well, Arthur?"

He turned pleading eyes toward Patty. "What do you think?"

"Sweetie, if Aisha can save Harri's ass, she can save anybody."

Arthur nodded as if that's what he needed to hear. "All right, Ms. Franklin. What do I need to do?"

Relief threaded through her. "First of all, do you have a suit at home?"

"It's already upstairs in the spare bedroom closet, pressed and ready to go," Patty said firmly.

"How?" Harri looked askance at their secretary.

"I had Rey fetch it while you were in jail." Patty grinned impishly. "I figured we may need it."

Aisha grinned back. "Yeah, we're definitely keeping you on the payroll."

"Plus a raise," Patty countered.

"You're living here. What more do you want?" Harri grumbled.

"I'll give Aisha a list of my demands," Patty answered primly.

Harri buried her head in her hands. "When did I lose control of this situation?"

"Three days ago." Aisha laughed.

Even Arthur smiled at her rejoinder.

⎯⎯ ● ⎯⎯

Ninety minutes later, Aisha and Arthur walked into police headquarters.

Cal was waiting for her with a different detective, as they'd discussed on the phone. Unfortunately, he was her only contact in the district attorney's office.

Cal smiled. "I was surprised to get your call. Why didn't you tell me you left Dewey & Cheatham?"

She smiled back, shook his hand, and ignored his question. Despite a population of five million people in Canyon Pointe, everyone knew everyone in the legal community, and gossip traveled faster than Ultramegaperson.

Instead, she said, "I thought it was better to bring Mr. Drallhickey in as soon as possible and get this cleared up."

The detective gave Arthur an appraising look. "This is the guy?"

"Yes." She'd cautioned Arthur to keep his mouth shut unless she told him it was okay to speak. He was obeying. He remained silent, his face chalky white with fear.

They led Arthur and Aisha into an interrogation room and got right down to business. The detective handed Arthur a sheet of paper. "The letter sent to city attorney Harriet Winters on the day of the City Hall attack."

Aisha intercepted the letter before Arthur touched it. The language tracked with what Harri had told her. "How did you get this?"

"It was provided by the city," the detective said, already looking uncomfortable. He knew where she was going because she'd bet he'd asked the same question.

"Seriously? That's the best you can do? Provided by who?"

The detective looked at Cal, but neither man answered.

"The problem I'm having is this letter allegedly from my client was delivered to Harri Winters' office on the fifth floor of City Hall. The same floor that burned and collapsed onto the fourth floor three days ago according to the witnesses I spoke with." She smiled. "This letter looks remarkably intact."

The detective squirmed. "Well, it's not the original. It's a scanned copy."

Aisha smiled. "No kidding. And apparently scanned with a time machine. If this is a copy of the same letter delivered directly to Ms. Winters by sealed envelope, not twenty minutes before her office was set on fire, then how exactly did 'the city'—" She made air quotes with her fingers. "—obtain this document?"

"Well . . ." The detective looked at Cal again. "She's got a point." He looked back at Aisha. "We got it from the mayor's office."

"Really. How very interesting. So then in fact, the mayor's office did receive warning of the attack, but never bothered to notify the police or evacuate the building." While she spoke to the detective, she fixed her icy gaze on Cal. "This letter is a fake. As my ex-husband will tell you, my specialty is intellectual property and entertainment law, and I could shred this in a courtroom. Would you two like to try again?"

Cal attempted to salvage his dying case. "That's a separate issue," he said. "Mr. Drallhickey still wrote a threatening letter to a city official that was delivered immediately prior to the attack."

"Can I speak?" Arthur's voice came out in a squeak. He looked at Aisha. She nodded.

"I didn't write that letter. It's not how I word stuff." He looked at Aisha. "Can we show them?"

She pulled a folder from her brief case and handed Arthur copies of the two prior letters he had written.

He spread the papers out for Cal and the detective. "First, the letter you have is laid out differently than these. See?" He pointed at the discrepancies. "I use a template for my correspondence. All my letters look the same. Your copy is different. And the language?" Arthur shook his head and swallowed. "I'd never call Ms. Winters a—" His voice dropped to nearly a whisper. "—bitch."

"Why is that, Arthur?" Aisha asked.

"I respect her too much."

"Any other reason?" Aisha prompted.

Arthur nodded. "I'd be too scared. She can be really mean, sometimes."

At this, the detective snorted back a laugh.

Cal glared right back at her. "You've only proven he has priors pulling the same stunt, Aisha."

She pulled the third paper from her file. "You're right, but your own office cut a plea deal with Mr. Drallhickey for criminal mischief based on his actions after the second letter. Here's the affidavit from my client's PO that he has adhered to the terms of his probation."

Cal glanced at the affidavit. "That doesn't provide an alibi for Professor Venom's whereabouts at the time of the attack."

Aisha pulled out another sheet from her folder. "A copy of Mr. Drallhickey's receipt from Java Joe's for the time in question. If you'll note the time on the receipt is the same time the alleged arsonist walked by Ms. Winters' assistant, a Ms. Patricia Ames." Thank goodness, Arthur was as anal about things as he was.

"And here's her affidavit." She presented him with the last document in her folder. "Give it up, Cal," she added. "You have no case and you know it."

A uniformed officer stepped in and whispered something in the detective's ear.

"You sure?" he asked.

The uniform nodded and looked at Arthur. "It's him. The recording quality's not great, but it's him."

Aisha raised an eyebrow as the uniform left. "Recording? Do tell."

With a sour expression on his face, Cal said, "We have the security DVR for the coffee shop across the park from City Hall. It shows him sitting in there during the attack. He didn't leave until everyone else rushed out to see what was going on, which was after Harri fell and was caught by the mystery super."

Aisha felt a tickle down her spine at the mention of Rey. "So, then, you can't prove Mr. Drallhickey was in City Hall wearing a muscle suit and stilts and throwing acid at people?"

The detective shook his head, but he didn't look as pissed as Cal did. "We have witness statements describing a much larger man than Mr. Drallhickey."

"I assume we're done here?" Her attention swiveled between the two men.

"Well, there's still the issue with the letter—"

"Which we've already established I could shred with no criminal defense experience whatsoever. If you'd like to charge my client, then charge him. If not, we're leaving." She stood up. "Come on, Arthur."

"Aisha," Cal said in his charming voice. "Mr. Drallhickey does have a history of these sorts of acts."

Aisha raised her eyebrow again. "He melted paint off four benches in Founder's Green."

"That's still vandalism."

Aisha raised an eyebrow. "What was your community service during probation, Mr. Drallhickey?"

"M-melting the paint off the other eight benches in the park and then painting them," Arthur said. "Dale, the-the guy who runs public works asked that I be assigned to him at my sentencing."

The detective guffawed. "Sorry," he said, when Cal glared at him.

"I believe we're done then."

"Oh, Aisha, I forgot to tell you yesterday—"

She paused with her palm on the door handle. "Yes?"

"Mina's pregnant with twins."

A brittle smile on her face, her head roaring, she made a lame comment to the effect of that was great news and let Arthur lead her to the car. She managed to get the car started before she burst into tears. Arthur, totally out of his depth, patted her on the arm and called Harri for help.

CHAPTER 10

When Harri saw Aisha's number on the caller ID, she smiled at the salesman. "One moment, please. I have to take this." She walked down the store aisle. "So how'd things go?"

"M-M-Ms. Winters?" Arthur sounded panicked.

"Arthur? What the hell? Where's Aisha?"

"She's . . . uh . . . crying. Like a lot." His voice rose an octave. "I don't know what to do."

Rey appeared at Harri's shoulder. "Aisha needs help? Where is she?"

Harri held up a finger again. "Arthur, where are you?"

"Parked in her car outside of police headquarters."

Aisha's muffled voice said, "Give me that!" Then came a clunking noise of the phone hitting something before Aisha said a little more clearly, her voice breaking, "That little bitch is having twins."

"Oh, honey," Harri said, her heart sinking. She didn't need to ask which little bitch Aisha referred to. Obviously losing to Aisha twice in as many days had tweaked Cal's ego. "Okay. Just breathe. You want me to kick his ass? I will. I'll call your dad, he'll fly back to Canyon Pointe, and we can both kick his ass together."

"No. I-I got so pissed I wanted to punch him!" Aisha sniffed. "Where are you?"

"At the computer store."

Rey reached for the phone. "I have to help her."

Harri jerked her hand away and glared at him. "Not with this. This is girl stuff. Lady plumbing."

Rey's eyes widened and he moved away. Quickly.

Harri shook her head. Men were men, even the super ones. They'll face down destructo-rays and crazed minions, but ovaries scare them to death.

She put the phone back to her ear. "Sweetie, I'm so sorry. But you need to get it together and get out of there. Do you want Cal to know he got to you? Have Arthur drive you home."

Aisha took a deep breath. "You're right." She took another ragged breath. "Arthur's off the hook by the way."

"Well, that's good news," Harri said. She nodded at Rey and gave him a thumbs up. He edged closer to her again.

She turned her attention back to the conversation. "Can he drive?"

The trumpet sounds of Aisha blowing her nose came through the receiver, followed by a sniff. "My BMW? Not a chance in hell. It's my only asset, remember?"

Harri smiled. "Other than the expertise and industry contracts."

"Yeah. Other than those."

"Is Arthur willing to go back to his place?"

The vague sound of a discussion, then Aisha said, "He pointed out if you're shopping for computers, you believe him. So, no."

Harri sighed. "Go back to my place. Drink some wine. I won't even give you shit about . . . the other thing." Harri knew Aisha would kill her if she let Rey know about the smoking.

"What about the office space? We were going to look at it today."

"I called the real estate agent who's handling the leasing. We've got an appointment tomorrow morning at nine a.m."

"Okay. We'll see you back at your house."

Harri thumbed the button to end the call. She looked up at the superhero who was barely restraining himself from flying to Aisha's rescue. "Let's get our shopping done."

Once home, Harri spread her loot across the kitchen table in front of Arthur.

He looked up at her. "The burner phones are an excellent idea."

"How much did you spend?" Aisha eyed her suspiciously.

"The phones were a steal," Harri replied. "The salesman threw them in with the two laptops since they were discontinuing that model." She turned back to Arthur. "Patty gave me the specs you suggested for her computer. I hope I bought what you think we'll need."

He smiled at her. "This is great, Ms. Winters. We shouldn't have anymore problems with spyware."

"You kids need to get your toys off the table." Patty made shooing motions. "We need room for dinner." And like a little pregnant general, she started issuing orders.

———— •◆• ————

From the discussion over dinner, Harri had to release her lingering suspicion and agree with Patty and Aisha's assessment there was no way Arthur could have been involved in the City Hall attack. He was just about the worst supervillain who'd ever lived. Especially when she tasted his chocolate mousse.

"Oh, my god," she said around a mouthful of the concoction. "This is incredible!"

"Nothing a little chemistry can't handle." He blushed even harder when Patty piled on the compliments.

"What about the formula you used on the park benches?" Aisha asked.

Arthur's explanation went over Harri's head, but he puffed up with pride when he finished his speech with "And it's non-toxic."

Aisha laughed. "Honey, if you're a bad guy, toxic is supposed to be part of the package." She swiped her finger around her bowl to get the last bits of mousse.

"I think you should brand it as a green paint stripper," Patty said, smiling at him. "Try to sell it online or at Costco or something. You'd make a fortune. The public works guys still rave about how good it worked on the park benches."

Aisha nodded while sucking the chocolate off her finger. "That's a good idea. If the formula is unique enough, you can patent it. I could help you file the application."

Arthur's face fell. "I don't have the money for that either."

"Patenting and producing the paint remover would cover the fees for your criminal defense and the application," Harri said. "Especially if you come work for us as our IT guy."

"And we can take an equity share in the paint stripper business in lieu of a fee," Aisha added. "Our investment will be in legal services."

Patty clapped her hands gleefully. "Yay! We get to keep the gang together."

Arthur beamed at her.

Harri shot Aisha a dirty look, but Aisha was so busy sharing a scorching soul-gaze with Rey, she didn't even notice. *I need to keep an eye on that.*

"All of this is contingent on you giving up being a supervillain, Arthur," Harri said sternly. "I'm not going to tolerate any extortion, vandalism, or anything else from you. You step out of line, and I'll drag your ass downtown myself."

He looked Aisha, who gave him a smile and a nod. "Like I told the assistant DA today, I've gone straight. Last year, my public defender told me you were the person who talked the DA into reducing the charge against me to criminal mischief. I won't let you down, Ms. Winters."

"It's Harri, Arthur. You can call me Harri."

Chapter 11

Aisha parked her BMW behind the brick red minivan across the street from the old Canyon Building. She noticed a shiny new black Suburban parked at the other end of the block. While the dirty and dented minivan blended in with the other vehicles in the Northeast Side, her Beemer and the Suburban stood out like the proverbial sore thumbs. It wasn't just the suspicious looks from the tattooed kids lounging against the wall of the bodega at the corner. She could feel eyes on her from the condemned buildings cordoned off by six-foot-high chain-link fencing.

The Canyon Building loomed over the block like a tattered vulture. It had been an imposing building in its prime, the headquarters of Canyon Industries, and a gray granite Art Deco temple to capitalism. Now it looked like a haunted castle. Hotel Canyon, next door, where Harri said Rey had been squatting, wasn't in much better shape.

Until twenty years ago, Canyon Industries had been the primary employer for this section of the state until the last scion of the Canyon family and majority shareholder, Tim Canyon, was charged with the gruesome murders of his wife and four-year-old son. After a lurid eight-week trial, the former billionaire had been acquitted, but the reputation of the man and his company were shattered. With the stock in freefall, he liquidated what assets he could and disappeared. The Canyon Building, in fact the entire block, had simply been abandoned when the extended family blew the rest of the assets in proxy fights over the failing company.

The murders had been the subject of much speculation among the students when Aisha and Harri had been in law school. No subsequent arrests were made regarding the deaths, and general community consensus was Tim Canyon had gotten away with murder despite his claims of innocence during the trial. The Discovery Channel ran a special on the twentieth anniversary of the unsolved murders a couple of months ago. According to the quasi-documentary, Tim Canyon was rumored to spend most of his time drinking away his fortune somewhere in the Caribbean.

"Working in the 'hood," Aisha mumbled. "My mother will be so proud."

Somebody rapped on the driver's side window. Aisha yelped and jumped in her seat.

Harri grinned at her through the glass.

Aisha rolled down the window and glared at her partner. "Don't sneak up on me like that."

"Sneak? I parked right behind you."

Aisha rolled the window up and climbed out of her car. She and Harri joined the rest of their little Scooby gang and an unknown woman in a business suit on the sidewalk. Aisha couldn't help another worried glance at the teens on the corner.

Why did I let Harri talk me into looking at this place?

Rey sidled closer and whispered, "Don't worry. Once they see you're with me, they won't give you any trouble."

She wished she shared his conviction, but her body wasn't invulnerable like his. Neither was her car. She didn't want Harri to take the brunt of the start-up costs for their little venture, and her Beemer and condo were the only assets she had left.

But then, she also hoped spending time with Rey would make him less attractive, but no such luck. If he'd fart, pick his nose, or have really smelly socks, it would help. There had to be something wrong with him.

Something other than him being a client and twenty years younger than she was, because those inconvenient facts didn't seem to be cooling her ardor one little bit.

"Hi! Julie Belafonte! Canyon Point Commercial Realty!" The agent pumped everyone's hand vigorously. She didn't wait for an answer before she launched into her pitch.

"The Lechuza Building is owned by Lechuza Holdings. Of course, it's a little bit of a fixer-upper." Her hands darted around as she talked, showing far too much bling on her fingers and wrists in this section of the city for Aisha's comfort. "I assure you the structure is solid, though I'm sure you'll want your own inspector to take a look, and the entire building's available. The officer for their U.S. interests will meet us here. He's running a teensy bit late."

The agent was too blond, too bouncy and too enthusiastic for nine a.m.

Aisha rubbed her scratchy eyes. She wouldn't be this grouchy if she'd gotten more than a couple of hour's sleep. The reality of her situation had caught up with her after leaving Harri's place, and she'd spent most of the night smoking on her balcony.

In her peripheral vision, she caught a middle-aged man exit the bodega. The teens clustered around him and pointed at Harri and the real estate agent.

"Uh, Rey . . ." Aisha elbowed him at the same time the man yelled, "Yo, Garcia!"

The rest of their little group realized what was going on, and the real estate agent's fake tan turned a sickly yellow.

Rey flashed Aisha a smile. "He's a friend." He walked over to meet his so-called friend.

Except the man eyed Rey as suspiciously as the kids on the corner had. She didn't think it helped that Rey wore the new jeans, shoes, and polo shirt Harri had bought him while his so-called friend's attire was threadbare, though clean and neat. The two exchanged rapid-fire Spanish she didn't think she'd understand even if she stood close enough to hear the full conversation, but she definitely caught the word *abogadas* when Rey pointed to Harri and her.

Finally, the man's expression lightened. They clasped hands, and he accompanied Rey back to the office building.

"Everyone, this is Miguel Esperanza." Rey went through the rest of the introductions with a sincerity any politician would envy. "Miguel is a general contractor. He's the one who suggested we see this place. Perhaps he could assist us as we go through the building. Help us with a rough estimate?"

The real estate agent's face wrinkled with distaste, but Harri smiled and said, "Sure."

Aisha suppressed her own humor at the agent's reaction. It was sweet Rey was looking out for everyone's interests. They would need someone reasonable to build out the office, and Miguel obviously needed the work.

Harri was right. Rey really was too good to be true.

— •◆• —

Aisha turned off her old phone and shoved it into the zippered bag full of tampons. The damn things really needed to go into the trash now that they were officially useless, but she hadn't wanted Mom to question why perfectly good feminine products had been thrown away.

No, she hadn't wanted to deal with her parents asking any questions about the latest test results from her doctor. If she ignored the results, then there was hope, even though she knew deep down she was fooling herself.

Especially since she turned forty-one next year.

Was that the real reason she was attracted to Rey? One last chance at a baby?

She sighed. No, it wasn't. Though he was definitely handsome, he was also gracious and kind to her. Things she hadn't gotten from the opposite sex in a long time.

But her chance at motherhood was over regardless of her feelings about him.

Aisha stuck the bag back into her purse and set the purse behind the door to the stairwell. No one would see it immediately to steal it, and since her phone had the same spyware Arthur had found on Harri's computer, the cotton would block the microphone. She definitely needed to have a heart-to-heart with her best friend about how much trouble they were in.

Aisha entered the large second floor suite, leaned against a dirty window and watched Harri poke around. Patty and Arthur had cornered the agent downstairs, asking pointed questions about wiring and plumbing. Rey and Miguel had gone upstairs to check the status of the other three floors. It was the first time the two women had been alone since the craziness had started, other than their lunch discussion over finances, and Harri wasn't saying a word.

"Are you that pissed at me for calling Eddie?"

"What? No!" Harri jumped and whirled to face Aisha.

"Really?"

Harri brushed back a strand of hair that had escaped from its ponytail. "Yes. Maybe. I don't know." She crossed her arms.

"Well, that covers the entire gamut of reactions," Aisha said dryly.

"I'm sorry. If I stay mad at you, I don't think about someone trying to kill me. Multiple times in less than forty-eight hours." Harri hugged herself more tightly. "If I think about that, I'll lose it. And if I lose it, I'm no help to Rey and Arthur."

"Given the circumstances, it's okay to lose it. You wouldn't be human otherwise."

Harri snorted. "No one expects a lawyer to be human."

"C'mon, girl. You're overdue for a freak out. And we've seen each other at our worst."

"Yeah, when you made me wear those godawful lemon-lime bike shorts! Did you know Rey was using a pair as a mask when he saved me?"

"Oh, god. Please tell me you're joking." Aisha slapped a hand over her mouth.

"I wish!"

They both chuckled.

"Well, you know I won't drag you to another firm charity function," Aisha said.

"Except our own. Then it's margaritas for everyone." Harri strolled over and leaned against an abandoned desk. "You sure you want to stick with me through this mess?"

"You know who Dad would quote."

Harri chuckled again. "You know, for someone whose specialty is Mayan history, the professor is a little too obsessed with Lincoln."

"That was for you and Jeremy." Aisha shook her head at her father's idiosyncrasies. "LaShun, Martin and I got Frederick Douglass."

She took a deep breath. "There's something else you should know. Dad called me last night to let me know he'd made it home okay. He asked me if your situation had anything to do with the fake cable guy who appeared at my door while I was trying to bail you out of jail the day before."

"What?"

"I checked with my next-door neighbors. Mr. and Mrs. Brinkman didn't have any unscheduled visits, and they said no one else in the building had either. You know what busybodies those two are."

"Marvin's overreacting. With everything that happened with your grandparents when he was little—"

Aisha nodded. "That's the point. Dad learned to recognize surveillance when he was a kid. He's pretty sure the guy bugged my place, but this is beyond the old-school stuff he knows. He told me to watch my back, and drag your ass down to Atlanta with me if things get too hot here."

"Shit," Harri muttered. "We're going to have to assume that Patty's place has been compromised, too."

"And Arthur's. Which brings me to another suggestion." Aisha braced herself. Harri valued her personal space. "I'm going to put my condo on the market."

"You said the mortgages were upside down."

"The market's starting to pick up," Aisha said. "And the Brinkmans mentioned some friends were looking for a good deal before prices got out of control."

Harri waved as if to dismiss the idea. "We've got Grandma Harri's rainy day money."

Time to be brutally logical. Aisha held up her right index finger. "One. I'm not letting you foot the entire bill. Two." She held up her middle finger. "If the guy in your cell the other night and my mystery caller is Patty's baby daddy, then he's going to be in deep shit with his boss for not carrying out his mission."

"You're assuming he's not dead already." Harri's tone was as bitter and scared as Aisha felt.

"Exactly. Patty needs as much protection as you do, and Rey can't be at her apartment and your townhouse at the same time." Aisha sucked in a lungful of dusty air and added her ring finger to the other raised digits. "Which brings me to three. We all move into this building. It's big enough. Arthur can wire it out the wazoo for security, and Rey's got us all in one place to keep an eye on everyone."

"Having us all in one place will make it easier to kill us." Harri's voice turned sour.

"They, whoever 'they' is, is trying to pick you and your support team off one at a time already. I won't get a friendly phone call from the next assassin." Aisha shivered. Dad's revelation had shaken her as much as Baby Daddy's warning. For all she knew, a sniper could have her in his sights this minute. But she couldn't abandon her best friend no matter how scared she was. "And I also think we need to give Jeremy a heads-up."

Harri blew out a harsh breath and stood up. "I'd have to sell my place, too, to make this work." She grinned. "You sure you want to be roomies again? This won't be like stealing my pizza."

"Or stealing my condoms?" Aisha grinned back.

"I only stole your Real Property notes," Harri huffed. "Speaking of which, we need to look into zoning for dual commercial/residential."

"I'm sure the owner will be happy to assist with that, Ms. Winters."

Aisha squeaked at the stranger's voice, and she whirled to face the stairwell. It was almost a relief to see Harri jump higher at the intrusion.

The man who strolled in was definitely not from this neighborhood. About six foot with a trim build under his navy business suit, a full head of silver-flecked red hair, pale skin with a dusting of freckles, almost boyish features if it weren't for the heavy lines around his eyes and mouth.

While his face and body could have been anywhere between thirty-five and fifty, his dark eyes showed a man who'd seen far too much.

He inclined his head toward Aisha. "Ms. Franklin. I'm Tim Canyon."

"Timothy Mitchell Canyon?" Harri's eyebrows slanted to emphasize her skeptical tone. "Former owner of the property across the street."

"'Fraid so." He tilted his head. "And you're Harriet Matilda Winters, sole heir to the Winters fortune."

"You ever call me 'Harriet' again, and I'll rip your balls off."

Most men either got pissed or scared when she threatened their manhood. His expression was amused.

"'The mouse with the mouth' is your nickname down at the courthouse."

Aisha's skin prickled when he turned back to her. "You're the quiet one. The snake in the grass who watches and waits for the perfect moment to strike. Dewey & Cheatham were fools to let you go."

Figures he'd use the ugly nickname she'd picked up in law school. Aisha lifted her chin. "Like they had a choice in the matter."

"I'm just saying they should have offered you that partnership." Despite his unassuming looks and laid-back manner, something was off about this guy. The picture snapped into place. The wide stance, the angle to keep her, Harri and the exits in sight, reminded her of Eddie, but he didn't give off a cop vibe.

"And you're the billionaire who got away with murder," Harri shot back.

He ignored her challenge. "I think we can help each other, ladies."

"How so?" Harri's fingers brushed the dust into a little pile on top of the desk though she kept her attention locked on him.

Canyon pulled a device from his suit jacket and placed it against the wall.

With a click and a hum, the metal impaled itself into the crumbling dry wall. A red light on top blinked. He grinned. "In case they followed you here, they won't hear anything."

"Like what?" Aisha asked.

"They were so busy trying to frame Ms. Winters and Arthur Drallhickey individually they haven't realized you are already working together. They will figure it out eventually, and when they do, your pet boy scout, El Pájaro or Captain Justice or whatever he wants to call himself, isn't going to be a big help."

Aisha's blood chilled. This guy knew too damn much about them. And the discussion about Rey's new moniker hadn't gone beyond their little group. "I think you underestimate him."

Canyon spread his hands. "I'm not insulting the kid. I'm talking sheer experience. These people have been taking down supers for years. The ones that won't play ball with them anyway."

"What are you talking about?" Harri demanded.

"The procedural shortcuts that ended with you in jail, Ms. Winters. Those same procedural shortcuts were used to deprive me of my reputation and a majority of my property." A scowl marred his face. "Among other things."

"Harri! Aisha!" Rey's shout echoed through the building.

"Second floor!" Harri called back.

"What do you want from us?" Aisha hissed.

Canyon's expression brightened again. "Like I said, I'll cut you a very good deal on this building in return for a . . . personal favor. I can also throw in a little money for the renovations and a lot of extra security measures." Canyon rubbed his chin. "I'd like one concession. Would you be willing to hire Miguel Esperanza and some of the other folks in the neighborhood to do the work in this building?"

Harri folded her arms over her chest again. "Depends on this personal favor of yours."

Aisha bit her tongue to keep from laughing at Harri's bluff. The sheer fact that Miguel was homeless and a friend of Rey's meant Harri had already decided to bring him into her save-a-stray program.

"Fair enough." Canyon poked a button on his device. The red light blinked off, and he pulled it from the wall and slipped it back into his pocket as Rey appeared in the stairwell doorway.

Canyon inclined his head to Rey before he continued talking. "I believe your grandmother bought you a lifetime membership at Whitechapel Country Club, Ms. Winters."

Harri grimaced. "And?"

"Call and set a tee time for ten-fifteen a.m. for you, me, Ms. Franklin, and Mr. Garcia."

Whitechapel? Was he insane? Aisha tried to rein in her anger. "What are Rey and I? Your token color?"

Canyon grinned. "Actually, yes. You will be our colorful distraction. Everyone at the club will assume you and Ms. Winters are attempting to prove a point after the events of the last four days." Again, he spread his fingers in fake modesty. "When in fact, I'm the one playing them."

"What do you mean?" Harri said.

"Let's just say there's a certain satisfaction in cutting the deal that will bring our mutual enemies down right under their noses."

Canyon strode toward the stairwell, but stopped short of Rey and pivoted to face her and Harri again. "By the way, Ms. Franklin, that was an interesting trick with your tampons. I'll have to remember it. But next time, remember to disable your phone's GPS, too."

He slipped past Ray with a nod to their client, whistling, of all things, a Barry Manilow tune.

Aisha rushed over to the stairwell door and retrieved her purse. Sure enough, the zipper on her supply bag was open. She checked her smartphone's settings. The GPS had been turned off.

Chapter 12

"Everything okay?" Harri asked. Aisha was staring at her phone.

She looked up from the device. Worry dug lines in her forehead. "Yeah," she said out loud, then she mouthed, "Arthur's plan."

Great. Just great. Harri wanted to hit something. Once again, they'd have to wait and have their conversation far away from their bugged phones. What the hell had Canyon done to Aisha's phone that bothered her?

During Harri's teen years, Marvin had taken her to his gym and taught her how to box. The ring had been far more successful in helping her deal with her rage at her parents than any of the therapists she'd been dragged to by every other adult in her life. Maybe she needed to dig out her gloves and pick up the sport again.

"Who was that?" Rey pointed in the direction of the departed Canyon.

"A big problem," Harri growled.

"I thought you researched the owner." Aisha's frown said she was rethinking the idea of using the upper floors as apartments.

"I did," Harri snapped.

Dammit! Aisha bringing up the subject of everyone living here had saved Harri from talking her partner into the concept because she had the same damn worry about whoever was spying on them. Assuming the mysterious "they" were the same people who wanted her dead.

"Um, Miguel asked me to get you," Rey said. "He wanted to run a few ideas about the upper floors past you."

Harri took a deep breath and nodded sharply. Distraction would be a good thing.

Before she put a fist through the plasterboard.

Miguel started his tour on the fifth floor. The top two floors were split into single offices on either side of a long hallway. Judging by the dust on the hardwood, these floors hadn't been used in years.

"The floors are solid which is the best news. You could knock most of these walls out." Miguel pointed at the ones as he spoke. "They aren't load bearing.

There's a few support columns that would have to stay, but you could open these floor up into larger office space."

"Or residential lofts?" Harri said as she glanced at Aisha.

"Yeah." Miguel nodded. "You could do that. This whole area's been rezoned for mixed use, so all you'd need are building permits and a certificate of occupancy." His expression darkened. "Not that the city would let you. The mayor's got plans for this area."

Harri smiled. "I've got friends in the permits office. They'd speed us right through to piss him off."

Instead of brightening at her suggestion, Miguel appeared alarmed. "Were you planning to sublet these lofts?"

"Actually, we were discussing living here ourselves," she said.

The contractor visibly relaxed. "Would that include Rey?"

"Yes," Harri said. "For as long as he wants to, anyway."

They made their way downstairs. Other than the fact, she was irritated Tim Canyon managed to hide his ownership of the building, this plan could work. The business space on the first floor needed updating, but it had four offices, a nice sized open area, a small break room, and a bathroom. It even had a tiny reception area out front separated from the main office by a door and a frosted glass partition.

After Miguel answered a ton of questions, Harri felt confident he knew what he was doing. He clearly had extensive experience with commercial contracting. But she suspected he wasn't licensed. That would explain what he was doing down here scrounging for work in this area of the city.

She smiled at the real estate agent. "I love this place—"

"But we need to discuss it first," Aisha interjected.

Julie smiled at Harri as if she were trying out for a beauty pageant. "The owner has already called me. He said since you're an old friend of the family, he's willing to cut you a deal for the entire building."

Old friend? Well, that was one way of putting the ancient rivalry between the Canyon and Winters clans.

Harri stopped herself from saying the thought aloud. If she hadn't been able to discover who owned the building, maybe Julie had no clue of who she worked for. But hell, if Canyon was willing to lower the price . . .

"Tell you what, Julie, I've got a tee time tomorrow morning with your boss."

The real estate agent's smile fell.

"If we can work out a deal at the golf course, I'll make sure you get your full commission."

The beauty pageant smile returned. "That would be great, Ms. Winters." She held out her business card. "Just let me know what you decide."

Before Harri could say anything, Aisha said, "We will, Ms. Belafonte." But the glare she shot Harri could have melted steel.

Once the building was locked up and Julie departed with a cheery wave, Harri found herself eyeing Miguel as he sized her up.

"Rey, why don't you go down and say hello to the boys?" the contractor said. "They haven't seen you in a few days, and Francisco wanted to return the books he borrowed from you."

For the first time since Harri met him, suspicion crossed the super's face. She couldn't help laughing at the incongruity.

"Don't worry, Rey." She patted his arm. "Miguel's going to lecture me about how I'd better not corrupt you because he regards you as a son."

Once the super sauntered down the sidewalk toward the bodega, the contractor chuckled and shook his head. "Was I that transparent?"

Harri held up her forefinger and thumb. "A teensy bit."

She dug into her purse and pulled out some cash and her keys and handed them to her assistant. "Patty, you and Arthur take my car. You know Marta's, the place Rey took you to pick up lunch the other day?"

Blond curls bobbed, and excitement shone in her eyes. "The same variety as last time?"

"Yeah. We'll meet you back at my place—"

"No. Go to my condo building," Aisha said. She fished a business card out of her purse and scribbled something on the back.

Harri stared at her partner. What the hell was Aisha up to?

"What?" She shrugged as she handed the card to Patty. "That's the code for the pool area. It's too nice of a day not to have a picnic. With Marta's cooking, we'll end up splayed over Harri's furniture in food comas if we don't do something different, and we have too much to do today."

"Sounds good to me." Patty and Arthur headed for Harri's Honda.

Miguel chuckled again. "I see I'm not the only one with transparent motives."

Aisha turned to the contractor. "Don't worry about Rey. He's the first person I've ever met to trigger a maternal instinct in Harri. And she thinks she owes him for saving her life."

"He could use a mother's touch." Miguel's expression grew sad.

"How long have you known him?" Harri asked.

He hesitated, and suspicion flared in his eyes.

"Please talk to us, Miguel. He's our client, and he wants to go legit so he can help people. If he's in trouble . . ."

Miguel nodded as if coming to a decision. "His mother Maria was still nursing him when I first saw her. She was more a friend of my Beatrice than me. That was about the time Mr. Canyon lost his family."

Curiosity tugged at Harri. "And how do you know Tim?"

"Beatrice used to work for the Canyon family. Her grandmother was their household manager back when Old Jack Canyon ruled the city." Miguel waved at the building across the street. "My wife sort of inherited the position when her grandmother retired. I couldn't argue. The money was good."

"What happened to Maria?" Aisha asked quietly.

The sadness didn't only return to Miguel's face. His whole body seemed infected.

"She was very secretive. I know she was originally from Honduras. She had a green card, but was afraid to use it. She'd take the most menial of jobs in order to be paid under the table to avoid leaving a trail. The one time she confided to Beatrice, Maria said she feared that enemies of Rey's father would kill them both."

Aisha frowned. "Granted my knowledge of Honduran history isn't the greatest, but most of their civil unrest has happened after Maria brought Rey to the United States. Could his dad have been older? Part of the Chinchoneros?"

Miguel shrugged. "Maybe. Or he could have been a Sandinista or Contra fleeing Nicaragua, or even someone who simply crossed the wrong person. Either way, she was paranoid when it came to Rey's safety. She wouldn't even let him go to school when he was old enough. He always went with her to work."

"Then how did he learn to read?" Harri asked. "He's got a better book collection than I do."

He chuckled. "I think he was born knowing everything. What he didn't know, he learned in the library. Rey's the one who taught my youngest to read when the teachers said he was incapable of being educated."

Harri glanced at Aisha. If someone asked her, she would have sworn she saw stars circling in Aisha's eyes. Maybe she needed to rethink everyone living together under the same roof.

But getting Rey situated was the more important task at the moment. "What happened to Maria? Rey said she died when he was very young."

"He was about seven when—when—" Miguel took a deep breath. Harri pretended not to see him wipe his eyes.

"The police said Maria was stabbed," he continued when he regained his composure. "But Beatrice was the one who found her body when she did not come to our house for Labor Day. Maria always came for holidays so Rey could play with our own children as well as our nieces and nephews."

Miguel sucked in another harsh breath and released it. Harri wanted to hug the poor man. After all these years, the event still shook him.

"Beatrice said it looked as if a wild animal had mauled Maria. And Rey disappeared. Toys, clothes, everything was still there. I feared his father had killed her and taken him. The police didn't care. We searched and searched for him, but all we could do was bury her. I didn't see Rey again until three years ago. Shortly after we lost our house."

Something about his story didn't make sense. "Why did the morgue release her body to you and Beatrice?"

His smile was as sad and bitter as his words. "She lied and said she was Maria's sister. Neither the city nor the county officials wanted to deal with the expense of burying a poor, murdered Latina."

"Do you still have Maria's death certificate?"

He shook his head. "If I do, I wouldn't know where to look. But I can tell you she was buried at St. Raphael's cemetery."

Harri smiled. "Actually that helps a lot."

———— •◆• ————

The first official staff meeting of the Law Office of Winters & Franklin took place around a table under an umbrella at the Fiesta Place Condominiums pool. Aisha focused on eating her plate of flautas and dirty rice while Patty and Arthur argued her case against Tim Canyon with Harri.

She dipped a chicken flauta in guacamole. Harri was right. Marta's food was incredible. She'd be lucky if she didn't gain fifty pounds if they actually rented the Lechuza Building. Economically, it made sense for their start-up boutique firm, but if word got out their landlord was an accused murderer, their business would be dead before they began.

Surprisingly, Canyon hadn't touched the wad of benjamins and the traveler's checks in Aisha's purse. It wasn't like she'd had a chance to take the cash Dad had given her to the bank with the chaos her life had become.

"This isn't only about Tim Canyon," Rey finally said. "Miguel and his family need the work!" He turned to Aisha. "You of all people know what it's like being the wrong skin color in this city."

She blinked. "You expect me to back you up playing the race card?" She jabbed a finger in the direction of the other three people sitting around their table. "I expect that shit out of them, but you?"

Rey folded his hands together. She recognized the move. Harri made it when she was pissed and wanted to hit something. However, she wouldn't bring down an entire building if she lost her temper.

"Miguel lost his business and his house when Miss Beatrice had cancer," Rey began quietly. "He couldn't even give her a proper funeral. She was buried at the county's pauper cemetery in an unmarked grave. Domingo and Emilio are incredibly smart and hard-working. They would go to college if they could afford to. Not to mention, Javier and Francisco need a real home. It's one thing for me to be squatting at that hotel. But two little kids . . ."

Dammit, Rey was worse than Harri and her crusades. Aisha laid down her flauta, her appetite gone. As screwed up as her own family could be, Aisha knew she could rely on them. It made her sick that these people had nothing and no one to go to for help.

She glanced around the table. Was the same worry going through Patty's mind? She kept rubbing her belly.

Arthur angrily stabbed his fork into his cabrito. "For all we know, Canyon is the one spying on you! I lost the trace in a Singapore bank's server."

Harri shook her head and spooned more salsa into her gordita. "If he's that bad, why did he want us to hire Miguel?"

"So he could spy on us," Patty offered.

"Miguel would never do that!" Rey raised his voice. "And I will not have you or anyone else insult his integrity." He turned to Harri. "And going to Whitechapel is a bad idea."

"Whatever attacked you there isn't going to again as long as you take precautions," Harri said. "Not to mention, it'll be broad daylight."

"Canyon was put on trial for killing his wife and son," Patty said.

"And declared not guilty by the jury." Harri nudged Aisha's knee with the toe of her shoe. "You haven't said much, little Miss Snake-in-the-Grass."

"Call me that again, and I'll call you by your full name for the rest of your life, bitch," she said. She sipped her can of diet soda. "I think we should go through with the meeting at the country club, then make our decision from there."

Patty, Arthur, and Rey stared at her with appalled expressions. Harri waited quietly for her reason.

"I don't like the fact he knows too much about us, stuff he couldn't have gotten without bugging us, but why did he admit it? If he wanted to mess with us, Canyon could have as easily called in an anonymous tip on Arthur before our meeting with the police yesterday." She met each of their gazes. "Rey, I know you're looking out for your friend, but Canyon could be using him. I have no doubt Canyon's playing a game, but we're not going to find out what it is by sitting on our hands."

Harri gave a single decisive nod. "Then we're settled. Tomorrow morning, the three of us will piss off the local Powers That Be. That leaves this afternoon and tonight."

Aisha recognized the look on Harri's face, and worry prickled underneath her skin.

"Rey and I are going out to St. Raphael's and see if we can find information on his mom. Patty needs to go back to my place and—"

"I'm not resting," their assistant snapped.

Harri grinned. "I'm not giving you time off before your water breaks. I need you to call Whitechapel and ask for a ten-fifteen tee time, finish putting together the rest of Rey's registration, then file your complaint against the city."

Patty's eyes narrowed. "You mean file my complaint, then finish Rey's paperwork."

"Fine." Harri laughed. "Whatever order you prefer. Just get it done. Aisha, can you take Arthur with you and start pricing equipment and furniture?"

Aisha stared at Harri. "What happened to making a decision after golf tomorrow?"

Harri shrugged. "We're still going to need the furniture and equipment regardless of whether or not we rent the Lechuza Building." She hesitated a moment. "And can Arthur stay with you tonight?"

Shock and a little disappointment shone on the former supervillain's face.

Dammit! Harri could be so fucking insensitive at times.

"You think Canyon's right about Arthur's theory the same person is trying to set you both up?" That should appease the poor man.

"Wait! What?" Arthur's wide-eyed stare switched between her and Harri. "He said I was right?"

"Yeah, I do. But we also need to stick to a semi-regular routine so we don't tip them off." In other words, Harri didn't want the poor guy around Patty though the girl wasn't seeing anybody.

Aisha wanted to laugh until an ugly suspicion occurred. Did Harri really think she'd be stupid enough to make a pass at Rey?

Okay, maybe she had been dreaming about him every night. And he was young enough to be her son. And sleeping with a client was a stupid, stupid move.

She prayed she had enough cigarettes in her secret stash to get through the night.

St. Raphael's was the oldest Catholic church in the state. Its white-washed limestone exterior reflected the early afternoon sun and made Harri glad she wore sunglasses as they pulled into the parking lot.

The cool, shaded interior of the church was a lot easier on the eyes. A few white votive candles flickered and burned in their red cups before the cross on a side altar. Otherwise, nothing moved.

Rey tapped her shoulder and pointed to a sign on a door that said "Office". She marched over and knocked.

"Come in!"

She opened the door to find a bespectacled priest kneeling before a copier and peering at its innards.

He looked up at them. "Is it too much to hope you're the service people for this blasted contraption?"

"'Fraid so, Padre," Harri said.

He climbed to his feet and brushed futilely at the white paper dust on his black slacks. His dark hair was speckled with gray, but his smile made him look nearly Rey's age. "Father Gabriel. How may I help then?"

"We're looking for any information you may have on a Maria Garcia. We were told by an old friend that she was buried here."

The priest blinked, and a salt-and-pepper eyebrow rose above the rim of his glasses. "Could you narrow the search down a bit?"

"I'm looking for my mother's grave," Rey said.

The priest's expression turned sympathetic. "I understand that, my son, but I need a little more to go on with such a common name."

"Could you cross-reference it with who arranged the funeral and burial?" Harri asked.

"Now, we're getting somewhere." The priest sat at the desk. The keys of the computer clattered as he entered some information. "What's the last name?"

Harri gave him what little information Miguel had relayed.

"Here we go. Plot 53 in the southwest section." The priest pulled out a brochure and marked the spot on a map of the cemetery.

"I hate to ask, but do you have any documentation regarding Ms. Garcia on file?" She couldn't bring herself to say "death certificate" with Rey standing nearby. "We're trying to locate other relatives. I'm trying to establish Mr. Garcia's identity. He doesn't know who his father is, and in shuffling around over the years, he lost his birth certificate."

The priest's expression turned sour. "That depends on whether my secretary managed to scan them before she broke her leg. Otherwise—" He jabbed an accusing finger in the direction of the broken copier. He banged on the keyboard some more.

Harri crossed her own fingers.

"Bingo!" Father Gabriel grinned as the printer whirred to life. "My secretary's predecessor even had a copy of the death certificate in the file." He sobered and winced. "And I didn't ask for your ID."

She showed him her driver's license and handed him a business card. "I recently left my position with the city, but the cell number is correct if you need to contact me." After this, she needed to ask Patty to order business cards for the new firm.

The priest held up an index finger. "Just one moment, Ms. Winters." He tapped out more keystrokes, and he nodded. "And there's your license." He pulled the papers off the printer and checked them before he smiled and handed the brochure and the sheets to her. "Thank you for your cooperation."

"Thank you for these, Padre. You have no idea what this means." She saluted him with the stack.

"Thank you, Father." Rey bobbed his head.

The priest motioned toward the side of the church. "Go to the end of the parking lot and make a right for the main entrance to the cemetery. God be with you."

Once they were in the car, Harri handed the papers to Rey. "That went better than I expected."

Rey was silent. She glanced at him. A tear trickled down his cheek.

"Hey, if you don't want to go to her grave, we don't have to."

"I do," he said. "What's the saying? I need closure."

She started the car and headed in the direction Father Gabriel had instructed.

Rey released a deep breath. "Take the first left. Can I ask you a question without you claiming it involves women's plumbing?"

"'Women's plumbing'?" A quick glance revealed a wry smile on his face.

"That's what you said when Aisha called you, crying, yesterday."

"And?"

"What happened between Aisha and her ex-husband? You're the one who said I need her expertise, and I don't want to accidentally say the wrong thing to her."

Oh, crap. Aisha hated looking vulnerable to anyone. She'd probably threatened Arthur with bodily harm after the poor schmuck witnessed her breakdown. The hard part was Rey really believed in doing the right thing. If he were any other guy, she would know he was looking for a way to get into her best friend's pants.

Harri sighed. "You remember Calvin Johnson, the ADA in the interrogation room when I was arrested?"

"Yeah."

"That's her shithead ex-husband. He and his new wife—" Harri couldn't keep the growl out of her voice. "—are having twins."

"And that's . . . bad?"

"Yes . . . no . . . well, not for them. I hate the bastard, but he does love that little twit he dumped Aisha for, and they'll be good parents I guess. But . . ." Oh god, how did she explain this to Rey? Aisha will be furious for Harri blabbing.

"Basically, Cal got pissed because Aisha beat him in his own legal specialty. Twice. Being a mother is something she always wanted and if you tell her I told you this, I'll—" *You'll what, Harriet? Kick his ass? He's a freaking superhero. All you'll do is break your foot.*

"If you tell her I said anything, I'll . . . be very disappointed."

Rey smiled. "That actually matters quite a lot to me. I would never want to disappoint you. Make a right up here."

"Aisha has always wanted kids, and she can't have them. Cal wouldn't even consider a surrogate or adoption." Harri guided her car through the turn. "So he had to rub the twins in her face. Don't let her know you know, okay?"

He nodded. "Okay. Not a word from me. Um . . . not to change the subject but pull over up here."

Harri parked her Honda at the spot he indicated. They both got out, and she followed him to the small stone marking Maria Garcia's grave. When she saw the year of Maria's death, she tried not to gasp. Her suspicions of Rey's age about the time of Maria's murder matched what Miguel had told her. How the hell had he survived for so long on his own?

She glanced at him. If he wasn't a super, he would have been dead. Another statistic of the streets.

"You okay?"

Rey nodded. He knelt in front of the gravestone. With trembling fingers, he brushed some dry grass clippings out of the etched letters. "I should have brought her flowers."

"We can bring some out tomorrow if you want." Harri wanted—needed—to ask him more about his childhood, but here, at his mother's grave, the pain was too raw, and she knew her curiosity would have to wait. She squeezed his shoulder, but stayed silent.

After a few moments, he stood and nodded. "Thank you. I've never been here before. I . . . I should have come before this and not left her all alone."

"Don't go there," Harri said, fighting back her own tears. "She's in your heart and your mind, not in the ground. These markers are for us, not for them."

He threw his arms around her and hugged her.

"Aw, kiddo, now you're gonna make me cry," she said, as she patted his back. Yup, her feelings were still—oddly and uncharacteristically—maternal. How could she and Aisha respond so differently to him? "Come on. We need to get back to work. You ever been to the county records office?"

"No," he said, sniffing back tears. "Am I in for a treat?"

Harri rolled her eyes. "That's a way to describe it, I suppose."

They walked through the rows of gravestones to the parking area. A black SUV with dark tinted windows parked over in the next section of markers. The vehicle pulled away when they approached and drove slowly down the drive to the exit.

Rey grabbed her arm and held her back. "You see that?"

Harri nodded. "Yeah. Somebody you know?"

He shook his head. "I should have told you about this sooner."

Harri looked sideways at him. "Told me what?"

"I think I'm being followed. I always lose them. It's not hard to do when you can fly."

Her conversations with Arthur and the spyware he'd discovered sprang to mind, and her stomach tighten. "Why didn't you tell us this before?"

"I didn't want—" He glanced in the direction the SUV had traveled before he turned back to her. "I know you think Arthur's being paranoid, and I didn't want you to think I was, too."

Harri frowned at him. "You've got more credibility with me than Arthur does. You know that, right?"

"Yeah, but I do believe him. He said he's seen the same vehicle parked in front of his apartment building. I never told him about my encounters, but he described the same vehicle we just saw."

Harri glanced around, feeling suddenly exposed. Anybody could be hiding behind one of the huge old trees shading the cemetery. "Let's get out of here. Now. We need to compare notes on this with everybody else."

Maybe she needed to start taking Arthur a little more seriously because her gut said there was something to both men's stories. There was more to this than the two attempts on her life.

But what the hell was the connection between the three of them before the damn attack on City Hall?

⎯ •◆• ⎯

Aisha drove while Arthur summed up the numbers on the calculator app of his phone.

He rattled off the total. When she remained silent, he said, "Well, it's actually not too bad."

"No, it's not that." Even though it was. She never realized what all went into running a business. Arthur suggested some things she hadn't thought of, though he made a point of leaving the negotiations to her. She'd been spoiled while working at Dewey & Cheatham. So many little things were taken care of that she didn't have to think about.

"I'm a little sleep deprived after the last few days, and I need some caffeine," she said. "My treat. It's the least I can do after all your help this afternoon." She pulled into the coffee shop she often stopped at on her way to work. Where would she go for her morning hit if they moved to the Northeast Side?

Arthur followed her into the coffee shop like a small child who thought he was in big trouble.

Aisha got her usual, a large no-fat, no-whip mocha with sugar-free peppermint syrup. Harri called it "pixie barf," but then she had no sense of adventure when it came to her taste buds. Arthur ordered hot chocolate. With extra whipped cream.

Like Patty drank these days.

Aisha resisted the smile that threatened to erupt on her face. Arthur had it so bad for Patty. Eight months pregnant—most men would run away, screaming, but Arthur was in love.

Worst supervillain ever.

They found a table.

"So, Arthur, now that you're in the clear, you don't need to work off your legal fees."

His face fell. "Oh. Yeah, I hadn't thought about that." He stirred the whipped cream slowly into his drink. "Uh . . . can I work for you anyway?" His cheeks flushed and he said, in a rush, "I mean you'll still need your computers and phones set up and make sure you've got a good back up system and the right software and—"

"Whoa there!" Aisha said, holding up her hands. "We can't pay you a lot, at least not yet, but we could definitely use the help." She took a sip of her coffee. "Like Harri said, we can only make this work if you're done with the supervillain thing. We can't represent superheroes if a villain handles our IT."

Arthur nodded. "I'm totally done with that. I'm . . . it was stupid and I wasn't, you know, any good at it anyway, and besides I need to . . . I have responsibilities . . ." He took a sip of his hot chocolate. His face got even redder. "Or at least I'd like to."

"Yeah, I kind of figured. She's all alone. She needs somebody."

Arthur stared out the window for a long moment and then deflated in his chair. "Oh, who am I kidding? She's so beautiful and sweet and kind. What would she want with me?"

"You're here, aren't you? That puts you about twenty miles ahead of the baby's biological father." She exhaled, trying to release her own hang-ups. "And practically every other man I've ever met. Most men don't fall for pregnant women."

He looked up at her, misery etched on his face. "They don't?"

"No. Generally, they run in the opposite direction. Unless they did the impregnating. And even then . . . well, like I said, baby daddy's out of the picture." She patted his hand. "Cheer up. She likes you. I can tell."

Arthur sighed. "As a friend."

"Keep showing up. You'd be surprised how well that works over the long haul."

She took a long look at him, really looked this time. He was so skinny, it made his nose look bigger than it actually was. And the acne could be dealt with. If he filled out a little, got a better hair cut, saw a dermatologist—he'd never be handsome, but he had a nice smile and a good heart. Patty could do a lot worse. Hell, she had done a lot worse.

"Harri and I have a friend, a stylist," Aisha finally said. "Maybe he can help us with a little makeover. Make it more obvious to Patty what a catch you could be."

"You'd do that for me?"

"Absolutely. We can make this our little project. Show her you're boyfriend and daddy material."

"Daddy." Arthur smiled down at his hot chocolate. "I like the sound of that."

Aisha shoved her own emotions back down. How many Arthurs had she ignored in her life because she liked the picture Cal Johnson presented? The power couple with the two-point-two kids, a dog, and a white picket fence. Hell, now, she didn't even have a hamster.

Time to change the subject.

She cleared her throat. "So, Arthur, there's something I want to talk to you about. You said you were being watched as well as bugged. How did you know? Besides the spyware, I mean."

The poor guy's nerves were back. He glanced around the café. "There's this big black SUV with tinted windows always parked nearby no matter where I go."

Fear flooded her mind. "A big Suburban? Windows tinted so dark you can't see who's in the vehicle?"

He nodded, then he paled. "You saw it, didn't you? Where?"

"Parked at the end of the Canyon Block while I was waiting for you all at the Lechuza Building this morning."

Arthur's hand shook, and hot chocolate sloshed out. "Have you seen it before? Has Ms. Winters seen it?" He set down his cup and wiped off his hand.

Aisha shook her head. "No, I haven't, and Harri's never mentioned it to me. Which, by the way, she did say you could call her by her first name."

"I-I don't feel that's appropriate. Especially if I'm working for you both."

One more little crisis on top of her pile. Maybe she couldn't do anything about the damn SUV right now, but she could help him with Harri.

"Here's a secret about my ferocious little business partner. She's basically marshmallow fluff disguised as a porcupine. All that hard-ass stuff is the surface. It's . . . armor. She had a really tough time growing up. Very deprived."

Arthur shook his head, confusion all over his sharp features. "But she's a Winters. They're rich."

"They were rich. Her mom died when she was little, but her dad was a drug addict, who not only pissed through the family fortune, but managed to steal Harri's trust fund, too. If my parents hadn't taken her in, she'd have spent her last couple of years of high school in a foster home." Aisha took a sip of her mocha. "Don't you dare tell her I told you that. But if you don't stand up to her, she'll run you over."

"But she's so, so . . ." He stared out the window.

"She's Harri Winters. Of course, she's intimidating. But believe me, if she likes you, she'll move heaven and earth for you."

"Except she doesn't like me," he said forlornly.

"But Rey and I, and especially Patty, do like you. Between the four of us and your kick-ass computer skills, we'll change her mind. Hell, it's changing already if she told you to call her Harri."

Arthur's cheeks flushed a deep red.

She'd pushed him as far as she dared for now. "Anyway, you ready to head home?"

He shook his head. "Not a chance. I don't want to be at my apartment alone if they come for me."

"Whoops. No. I meant my place. You're staying with me tonight, remember?"

Arthur stared down at his hot chocolate. Now, his ears matched the rest of his face. "She hates me, doesn't she? That's why you took over my case, right? And she doesn't want me in her home?"

And they were back to square one. "Arthur, honey, I took over the case because Harri realized she's a witness and ethically can't represent you. Because of that, she doesn't have attorney/client privilege with you and could be forced to testify about anything you told her.

"Also, Harri's got a small house and two other house guests at the moment." She smiled. "Besides, I've slept on her couch before. You can't tell me that thing's comfortable."

Amazingly, his ears didn't catch on fire. "Can we collect my computer and things from her place? That way, I can work on the trace again."

She sighed. "And here I was leaning towards a quiet evening with pizza and TV."

"I don't mean to be a bother." He stared at his cup again.

"I'm trying to get you to relax a little." She laid her hand over one of his. "We've all had a rough few days."

And she had a bad feeling things would get worse until they knew what, or who, they were dealing with.

———•———

Harri and Rey had a frustrating visit to the county records office. The Lake County commissioners had graciously offered to house various city departments until City Hall was repaired. This resulted in two levels of government now being at a near standstill rather than just one. If the records office was any indication, the temporary transition was not going well.

"Who needs supervillains when you have politicians," said the older woman at the counter when Harri commented on the chaos. Harri had met her before but couldn't remember her name.

"No kidding. I'm glad I'm out of it," Harri said.

"I heard about that," the clerk said.

"I think everybody heard about it." Harri grimaced at the reminder of her arrest.

The clerk eyed Rey. "So is this him?"

"No comment," Harri said with a smile.

The clerk nodded and smiled back. "I'll see what I can do to speed up the birth certificate search." She glanced around before she handed Harri a business card and whispered, "My direct line. Call after one tomorrow."

"Now what?" Rey asked as they walked back to the parking garage.

"I'll go over the paperwork Patty has been prepping this afternoon," Harri said. "How's your golf game?"

"I've never played before," he said with a rueful expression.

"That's not what's important tomorrow." She hesitated. While she didn't want to denigrate Rey's friend, she had to ask. "How long has Miguel been working for Tim Canyon?"

He was quiet for the elevator ride to the floor where they left her car. The doors parted before he said, "I don't know. I didn't know he was until this morning."

They reached her Honda. She unlocked it, and they climbed inside.

"I'm worried." She turned the ignition. "Tim Canyon was far too interested in you. His ownership of a building so close to where you and Miguel's family are squatting isn't a coincidence."

"You think he's behind the people watching all of us," Rey said, giving voice to her own ugly suspicion.

"I think he's connected to this mess somehow." It was getting damn hot in the car. So much for spring in Canyon Pointe. She cranked up the A/C.

"He also seemed very interested in you," Rey commented. A wry smile tilted his mouth. "Since your families run in the same circles, he may confide more to you."

With all his naiveté, Rey's observation took her by surprise.

"Maybe. Let's play tomorrow by ear."

All the way home, Harri found herself searching for black SUVs.

Chapter 14

At ten-fifteen the next morning, bile rose in Harri's throat when she spotted Mayor Samuels and DA Michaels with Judge Lester Burgess in the group teeing off ahead of them. She didn't recognize the fourth man, but whoever he was, he took a long, hard look at her from behind his shades.

"You selected this slot on purpose," she whispered to Canyon. "How'd you know it'd be open?"

Aisha demonstrated the proper form to Rey while their foursome waited for their turn. Harri wanted to stalk over to them and smack them both. It wasn't hard to miss her super staring at her best friend's ass as she swung the golf club.

"I hacked the reservation computer and cancelled Ted Meadowfield's ten-fifteen."

Harri slapped her hand over her mouth, but couldn't stop her rush of laughter.

Canyon looked pleased with himself. "I thought you'd like that after the way he ambushed you at your townhouse."

Her eyes narrowed. "How'd you learn about that?" She'd called Nella at Channel 12 after the incident with Ted to complain, but the cameraman Bob had beat her to it. The news producer had even offered to act as a witness if Harri and Patty sought a restraining order against Ted.

"I hacked the TV station's e-mail, too." No hint of remorse at all on Canyon's face.

"Why?"

"Originally, to stay one step ahead of Meadowfield myself."

"Now that, I can understand." And she really did. Ted had nabbed the anchor seat based on his coverage of the Canyon murders, and he was still riding that single accomplishment into the ground.

Despite their conversation, Canyon stared at the men in front of them. "By the way, setting up those additional appointments online to look at other office spaces was a nice touch."

"So you are spying on us?" Anger boiled in her gut. The rollercoaster ride of her emotions this week alone was going to give her acid reflux.

He looked at her. "After the attempts on your life, it's good to know you're taking precautions."

"It's not 'precautions,'" she retorted. "We haven't made a decision about renting at the Lechuza Building. This outing is supposed to be a negotiation."

"Fair enough. Let's go." However, he looked terribly amused instead of annoyed.

She and Tim picked up their bags, climbed into a cart, and slowly followed Aisha and Rey as they walked down the fairway.

"So, now that we're here, ruining Ted's morning, why golf?" she asked. "Why here? And why are we using a golf cart? I can walk faster than this."

"Because this cart is rigged so no one can hear our conversation."

"Like your little box from yesterday?"

He nodded.

"That still doesn't explain why you're spying on us."

Another terribly amused expression appeared on his face. "Technically, I found out about the plot against you because I was spying on your watchers."

"And why were you spying on these mysterious watchers?"

"Do you even know why you're being targeted, Ms. Winters?" He stopped at the green and cut the electric engine.

She paused getting out of the cart and stared at him. "If I knew that, I wouldn't be playing Twenty Questions with you."

He met her stare. "You're tenacious and thorough. Admirable qualities in a public servant. But you're getting too close to things that Corvus doesn't want anyone to know."

"Corvus? What the hell is a Corvus?"

"The folks in the black SUV. Which hasn't been around the Canyon Block much lately since Rey's now living with you, but they're not gone. Trust me."

Harri nearly fell out of the golf cart. "You know about that?"

"You think you're the only ones being followed? No. We go way back, Corvus and me." His smile wasn't exactly comforting. More like the smile of a crazy person.

"Who are they?"

"On paper, they don't exist. They are a special division of the NSB. Or maybe I should say super, to be more accurate."

The NSB, aka the National Superhero Bureau, handled registration, licensing, and fines of supers at the federal level, but Harri had never heard a whisper of this Corvus.

"What do they do?"

"A lot of questionable things in the name of national security." Tim pulled himself out of the cart. "I used to do business with them. One of my best customers. Until . . ." The smile evaporated, replaced by a haunted look.

"Until?" Harri prompted.

"They wanted me to come in-house. Be their private designer. I didn't know they were into black ops until they wanted me to make some seriously scary stuff from technology I'd developed to help people." His voice tightened. "To help my son." He bent to line up his shot and when he stood up, anger had replaced the haunted expression. "He was born deaf. I wanted to help him hear. They wanted super sensitive surveillance bugs. I said no. They didn't like that answer."

From the awful look in his dark eyes, she knew immediately. Eddie had been one of the first beat cops on the scene. He wore nearly the same ugly look the night he came home after the murders.

"They killed them because you said no," she choked out. "And they framed you for it."

Tim gave her a tight nod. "We need to look like we're having fun." He tapped the ball with his putter, and it rolled into the cup. "I want to expose them, Harri. I want you and your partner to help me do it."

"Expose them how?"

"I've already written a tell-all manuscript. I have the documentation to prove everything I know. I want you and Aisha to get me a media deal."

"If what you say is true, they'll kill you."

"Not if I'm already dead."

Harri grabbed his arm. Corded muscle tensed under her fingers. "I won't help you commit suicide."

Tim shook his head. "I'm not committing suicide. I want help faking my death. Right before the book comes out. Let them see how a frame job feels.

You transfer any money after your fees to an offshore account. And you'll never see me again." He nodded at the club in her hand. "Your shot."

Barely noticing what she was doing, Harri hit the ball. It sailed over the cup and right into the water. Even upset, Tim played better than she did.

They climbed back into the cart. "There's two little problems," Harri said. "No one's going to believe you about this Corvus. Even with evidence. You're a disgraced would-be murderer."

He didn't bat an eye at her statement. "And the other?"

"The slight illegality of committing fraud."

"Who am I defrauding?"

"Well, your life insurance company for one thing," she spluttered.

His bitter laugh echoed over the water hazard as they drove around it to the next hole. "You mean the policy my insurer dropped when they were forced to pay my wife's after my acquittal?"

Harri tried to ignore the looks Aisha and Rey shot their way. "All I'm saying is you merely have to disappear. Fall off the grid. You don't have to fake your death."

"You're right. No one will believe Tim Canyon, but they'll believe a respected superhero."

"I'm not involving Rey in this mess," she hissed. Hell, they hadn't even had a chance to register the kid yet.

"I wasn't referring to Mr. Garcia."

"Who then?"

"I was thinking more like Jutz'om Kuh."

"The Ghost Owl is an urban legend," she sputtered.

He chuckled and he climbed out of the cart. "So's Tim Canyon these days."

"How do you know the Ghost Owl really exists?" she called out.

Tim ducked to look at her. A wicked expression twisted his features. "Because I'm the Ghost Owl."

CHAPTER 15

Harri climbed out of the cart and stared at him. The concept was so ridiculous that after a stunned second or two, she burst out laughing. "You are not. If you're the Ghost Owl, I'm Joan of Arc."

Tim smiled as he teed up the ball. "You know, I can see you leading an army. Why do you think it's so impossible for me to be the Ghost Owl?"

"Because you're . . . it's like discovering Richie Cunningham is really Batman."

Tim laughed, too. "Richie Cunningham? Seriously? What? A super can't have freckles, boyish charm, and geek appeal?"

"You're not as charming as you think you are," Harri said. But she couldn't help noticing how his eyes twinkled when he smiled, how the weight of the years dropped off him when he laughed.

He's a potential client, Harri reminded herself, *and he's probably part of the group trying to frame me, and oh my, look how adorably tight his bottom is when he swings that golf club.*

Her cheeks grew hot.

He turned back to her and grinned. "If I'd known golf made you blush, I would have invited you a long time ago."

"Shut up," she answered.

"No, I get it. I'm a blusher myself," he said. "It's the curse of the redhead. But you're too olive to be a reflex blusher, so I'm hoping it's because you're attracted to me. Have dinner with me tonight."

"What?" Harri tried to think about cold water splashing her face. Icy wind. Snow. "You're hitting on me?"

Tim shrugged. "Yeah, I think I am. It's been awhile, so I'm probably not doing it very well."

No, you're doing it fine. She looked to Aisha for assistance, but Aisha and Rey had wandered down the fairway, off in their own little world, oblivious to Harri and Tim's conversation. "But, I still don't know if you're plotting against me. In more than the usual . . . you know . . . trying-to-get-in-my-pants sort of way."

Tim laughed again. "I was hoping my big reveal would leave you trembling in awe, but I'm going to need to prove my case, I guess. Wine will help. And ambience. Come on. Let me take you out for a nice meal."

"You are so not the Ghost Owl," Harri said. "You're not broody enough for one thing."

He grinned. "You should have seen me ten years ago. This is the warm and fuzzy me."

Harri snorted and took her shot. Right into the water again. Tim had gotten it onto the green in one, like he had at the last hole. "The Ghost Owl doesn't play golf."

"Well, when he's working, he doesn't," Tim said. "But everybody needs a break now and then. And I feel pretty good today. Minimal pain."

"Pain?" She shoved her club back into her bag and climbed into the passenger seat.

Canyon drove toward the balls. Apparently, they weren't really playing by any golf rules she knew. "You asked about the golf cart. When I got started, I had a shitload of money and a burning need for revenge, but no actual superpowers. Gizmos and gadgets will only take you so far. My knee cartilage disappeared right along with my fortune. On bad days, I have to use a cane. So I take it easy when I can."

"You're an inventor. Can't you build some sort of exoskeleton thingy to take care of it?"

Tim grinned. "I could, but what I really need is a double knee replacement. However, I can't afford the time off. What with thwarting evil plans for world domination and all."

They played through several more holes. Now that she was paying attention, Harri could see the stiffness in his gait, how he pulled himself to his feet with the frame of the golf cart, the occasional wince.

She couldn't look at him while she set up her shots. Doing so would destroy what little concentration she had left. Everything whirled through her head. Was Canyon even telling her the truth? Or was this some elaborate fantasy of his?

Aisha and Rey had given up after the third hole. All three times at tee Rey had launched the golf ball so far out of sight it was probably in orbit. Aisha had grumbled something about golf being stupid shit for rich white folks before she and Rey headed to the clubhouse.

For the next nine holes, Tim kept the conversation casual, but Harri noticed that he never let the foursome ahead of them out of his sight. And he made sure they saw him. Quentin even waved once.

"What a pompous bag of shit," Tim said as he smiled and waved back. When Quentin swung and missed the ball for the third time, Tim grinned at Harri. "I think we're making him nervous."

"Who's the fourth guy?" Harri asked. "The one who keeps eyeballing me?"

"He's with Corvus. Talent recruiter."

Harri gasped. She glared at Tim and hissed, "You bastard. That's what you're up to? You're handing them Rey?"

Tim sighed heavily. "Of course not. They already know about Rey. I wanted to send the message that I know they know. And look closer at the fourth guy. You've met him before."

The guy was about six-feet tall, broad and solid. His bald head shone under the morning sun. Harri felt her stomach drop. "Oh, shit. Is that the guy from City Hall? The one who claimed he was Professor Venom?"

Tim nodded. "Yeah. But you know him from somewhere else. In fact, he canceled another appointment with you so he could do his Professor Venom imitation."

"Another . . ." Harri chewed her lip, thinking, and was shocked to realize it had only been five days since City Hall was attacked. It felt like another lifetime. "I didn't have any appointments that day."

"Not even a deposition?"

"Seismic Shift," Harri whispered. The hot blood drained from her face. "His lawyer rescheduled." She turned to Tim as fear and rage washed over her in alternating waves. "Seismic Shift is the one who tried to deep-fry me with acid?"

Tim nodded again.

"You asked me here today because you wanted him to see me alive and well, didn't you?"

"And with me. I know a few secrets about Shifty myself. Seeing the two of us together will make him even sloppier."

"None of this makes sense." Harri tightened her grip on her club. Even with a busy Saturday morning at the country club, there were fewer people on the course right now than there had been in City Hall. Fewer witnesses than when Shift had tried to kill her.

"I don't know anything," Harri said, the panic growing inside here. "I knew his hair is fake. He wouldn't kill me over that, would he?" She glanced at Tim. "He's vain, but come on!"

Tim smiled. "No, I doubt that's it. You have his financial records, right?"

"I had them," Harri said. "They burned up in the City Hall fire." She wasn't about to admit Patty had scanned the financials, Arthur had retrieved them from the off-site servers, and she had copies at home.

"In Shift's records, you ever run across the name Darryl Bloch?"

Harri chewed her lip, thinking. "The name sounds familiar." She tried to visualize the paperwork in her mind. "Some kind of training consultant I think?"

"More like Shift's secret identify. And the man who murdered my family."

Everything blurred. If Tim was telling her the truth . . .

"Oh, my god. What have I done?" she whispered. Aisha, Patty, Rey. Even poor Arthur. They were all in danger because of her.

Harri's knees buckled and Tim caught her and helped her over to the golf cart. She stared at his lined face. "Are you really the Ghost Owl?" she murmured.

"I really am," he said in a soft voice. "Still want to have dinner with me?"

Harri felt hysterical laughter begin to bubble up. *Seismic Shift tried to kill me, and the Ghost Owl's asking me on a date.* The world has officially gone mad. "I never said I'd go in the first place."

Tim took her hand and gave it a gentle squeeze. "So say you'll go now. We need to make a few more public appearances. And I need their eyes on me tonight so Rey can help Miguel with a project."

Miguel she understood, but Rey? Had he been lying to her this whole time? No. *No,* she told herself more firmly. She wasn't that bad of a character judge.

"Who will guard Aisha and the kids?" she murmured.

"Your ex-husband. He's a little more than he seems, too."

"Eddie's a super?" Okay. Brain will explode in three . . . two . . . one . . .

"No. But he has significantly more training than the average cop or FBI agent. Those National Guard training weekends? Let's just say Eddie was in the advanced class. And he wasn't a student."

Harri sat for a long moment, numb. The party behind them caught up. They needed to keep moving. "I don't want to play golf anymore. Can we go to the clubhouse now?"

Tim smiled at her. "Sure. I know it's a lot to take in. Let's see how Aisha and Rey are doing."

— ·◆· —

"I don't trust him," Aisha said over her lunch. Tim had told them he'd pick up the tab so out of spite she'd ordered the lobster salad and the most expensive bottle of champagne in the place. "I know you trust Miguel, and Miguel trusts him, but what's he up to?"

Rey was wolfing down a burger the size of a hubcap. "I don't know," he said between bites. "But he's on our side. Miguel is one of the best people I've ever known. He says I should trust Tim, so I'll give him the benefit."

She shifted in her seat and their feet tangled for a moment. The alcohol was making her tingly and if they weren't in public, she'd have a hard time resisting the urge to throw herself across the table at him. Maybe the champagne wasn't such a good idea. "So Miguel is really a general contractor?"

Rey nodded. "Yeah, he had his own business when I was little. A nice house with a pool in a good neighborhood. When the economy went bad and his wife got sick, the lack of work and the medical bills wiped him out. This job would let him get an apartment. Javier and Francisco back in school."

"But what's in this for Canyon? If he and Miguel are that tight, why doesn't he help him?"

Rey sighed, set the burger down, and wiped his hands on the napkin. "You're assuming Tim still has money. If he did, do you really believe he'd live on the Northeast Side?"

"How do you know that's were he lives?"

Rey shrugged. "How else would he have gotten to the Lechuza Building so soon after Miguel called him?"

"Where specifically?"

Another shrug. "I'm not sure." Rey forked a seasoned potato wedge in his mouth.

Heaven forbid if Whitechapel had anything as mundane as French fries.

"Which is part of the problem. Canyon knows everything about us, and we don't even know where he lives."

Rey gave Aisha an appraising look. She could see the wheels turning behind his beautiful face. "Did you ever wonder how I happened to be at City Hall to save Harri and Patty?"

"I . . ." Aisha's fingers tightened around her fork. "Now that you mention it, why were you there?"

"Miguel. When we were looking at the Lechuza Building, he admitted Tim told him to find me as fast as he could because something was about to happen at City Hall, and I needed to be there, or people were gonna die."

Aisha's own mental wheels were now turning. Things had been so crazy the last few days, she and Harri had never wondered about Rey's involvement. But if Tim . . .

"Honey, that makes him even more suspicious."

"But if he hadn't—"

"Yeah, but think about it. How did he know what was about to happen?"

Doubt clouded Rey's golden eyes as Aisha's words sank in. "Well, he . . ."

Disappointment replaced the doubt in his expression. "Either he's been tracking the people who did it, or he's the one who planned it. But why save Harri? I don't have any question that someone was trying to kill her. Twice. If getting rid of Harri was Tim's plan, then why send me in?"

"I don't know," Aisha said, reaching across the table to take his hand. She couldn't help it. He looked so forlorn. "And that's the problem. I know you want to trust him. I want to trust him, because we sure as hell need the help. But we don't have enough information."

He started to rise from the table. "And Harri's alone with out there with him."

Aisha pulled him back down, or rather he let her. "In broad daylight, on a crowded golf course, at the country club where she has a lifetime member-ship. Carrying a bag of steel clubs. And she's monumentally pissed off at the moment, which—believe me—makes her a force to be reckoned with. Plus, she's got a can of mace on her keyring. Even with the size difference, I'm pretty sure she could take Tim Canyon in a fight. Besides he has bad knees or hips or something. Did you notice the limp?"

"Yeah," Rey said. "Knees, I think. Miguel says some days Tim needs a cane."

"So, relax, she'll be fine." Aisha said.

"But—"

"If you go charging out there in full super mode, all you'll do is tip our hand. We need to play him right back." Aisha knew Rey could pull her arm right off, but he yielded to her gentle touch, his fingers twined in hers. For a moment, their eyes met, and the heat spiked again.

No, no, no. Don't go there.

Her body ignored her. She abruptly dropped his hand and looked away, trying to regain her composure. Harri—decidedly non-maternal Harri—had gone right into mommy-mode with this guy.

Whatever Aisha was feeling for Rey, it wasn't maternal.

"Excuse me."

Aisha and Rey pivoted their heads in the direction of the well-oiled voice.

The dining room manager bestowed a smarmy smile on them. "I apologize for interrupting, but there is some concern about . . ." He adjusted his tie, and looked away. "About your membership status. This dining room is for club members only."

Aisha, relieved to have something to distract her from Rey, slid into ice queen mode. "And their guests."

"And who would you would be guests of?"

Aisha mentally licked her chops. *Try and throw me out of this place, you officious prick. Go ahead and try it.* "Tim Canyon and Harri Winters."

"Uh . . ." The manager's smooth demeanor evaporated. He knew he was in trouble. Even broke—and in Tim's case, disgraced—their family names still packed a social punch in Canyon Pointe. And more specifically Whitechapel, the center of the city's society. "And where would they be?"

"Here," Canyon said as he and Harri strolled up to the table. "Is there a problem?"

Harri plopped down in a chair and inspected Aisha's salad. "Mmm, yummy, is that lobster?"

Aisha, still impaling the dining room manager with her glare, handed Harri a fork. "Yes, it's lobster."

Harri took a huge bite of the salad.

The manager gave the former billionaire a relieved smile. "No problem, Mr. Canyon." He backed away from the table. "Ms. Winters."

Harri gave him a disinterested wave as he scurried off. "Boy, the stahn-duds here have really slipped. In the old days, Muffy and Biff would have freaked out before you even had a chance to look at the menu. God, I hate this place."

"She said, with a lifetime membership and her mouth full of lobster." Aisha shook her head. She loved Harri, she really did, but sometimes, she wanted to smack her.

What Harri failed to understand was that the place she so casually eschewed had never once questioned her right to be there. Harri's father was a coke head for God's sake, and the Winters fortune was gone. Dad was a nationally recognized writer and distinguished historian, her grandparents part of the Civil Rights Movement's inner circle, and Aisha still had to prove she deserved to sit in the dining room.

Canyon slid into the seat between Harri and Rey. They didn't seem to notice his grimace. Her dad had the same expression when he waited for his arthritis meds to kick in.

"Seriously, though," Harri said, a worried look on her face. "Were they awful to you? If they were, I'll make sure that manager gets reamed a new butthole."

"No," Aisha said, her anger fading. One of the things she loved about Harri was her uniform mercilessness to jerks, regardless of their social or super standing. "The manager had the good grace to look embarrassed."

Harri nodded. "Well, he'd better be. He should be grateful he's not dealing with Gran. She used to threaten to have people crucified on her office wall—"

"So she could laugh at their suffering," Canyon finished. "Your grandmother is a legend around here. Like some kind of vengeful goddess."

Harri sighed. "I really miss her." She smiled at Canyon. "Imagine what she'd do to Seismic Shit."

Aisha watched them grin at each other. She didn't recall Harri looking at Eddie like that, even during their wedding. *So we don't sleep with clients, huh?*

"Seismic Shift?" Rey asked, taking care to pronounce the superhero's name correctly. "What's he got to do with this?"

"Long story," Harri said. "We'll fill you in on the ride home. Rey, go with Tim, okay? Miguel needs your help with something."

"But—" The last thing Aisha wanted was Rey alone with Canyon. Not that he couldn't take care of himself, but still . . .

Harri gave her a warning look. "Trust me. He'll be fine. I have . . . news." She frowned at Canyon. "You sure you want me to tell her?"

Tim nodded. "I'll take care of the check and meet you outside. I want to make sure your car is clean."

"My car is clean? What the hell is going on?" Aisha whispered as Tim walked away. Yep, definitely a limp though he tried to hide it. "I still don't trust that guy."

"I know. Let's talk in the car," Harri said, her attention on someone across the dining room. "Too many . . . ears around here."

Aisha followed her line of sight. Judge Burgess led the way to a table with a good view of the golf course. Mayor Samuels and DA Michaels followed. Bringing up the rear was—

Well, this was the first time she saw Seismic Shift without his hairpiece. The bald look wasn't an improvement.

Chapter 16

Harri pulled on her black dress and took a look in the mirror. *This isn't a date.*

After talking with Aisha—or more accurately sitting in the passenger seat and getting yelled at by Aisha—she was no longer fully convinced that Tim was the Ghost Owl. She had a little evidence, but it was far from clear and convincing.

But he has a really nice smile.

With a disgusted snort, she grabbed her makeup bag and turned her attention back to the mirror. She hated supers on general principle. Rey was the one exception, and that was because he was still unspoiled.

All right, sort of unspoiled. He'd been rather secretive about the errand he needed to run with Miguel tonight when she not-so-subtly asked him to keep an eye on Arthur and Patty while she was out. Then Aisha butted in and insisted she had to go with Rey, which ruined any chance Harri had of questioning him further.

Even worse, both Aisha and Arthur insisted he stay with Patty tonight since Harri would be out, and Rey would sleep at Aisha's so he didn't wake anyone if he came home late.

Harri pulled her hair into a loose bun and examined the effect.

On the surface, their plan sounded logical, but both Aisha and Arthur were letting their hormones run the show. Not like her cynicism when it came to Tim Canyon. However, Patty could physically take down Arthur if he misbehaved. And Aisha wouldn't deliberately hurt Rey emotionally.

Deep down, Harri didn't want Rey to turn into the other supers like Seismic Shift, Cobblestone, or Ultramegaperson. They and a host of other so-called heroes and their ridiculous foes fought their stupid epic battles, and then left the mess for the puny mortals to clean up.

Maybe she shouldn't have pushed Rey into registering. The heroes were as bad, if not worse in some ways, than the villains. Regular people got hurt, they died, lives were ruined, while that pack of self-important schmucks strutted around in their silly outfits, oozing faux-humility, and making overwrought speeches about good triumphing over evil.

And they didn't do crap to eliminate crime—regular old garden-variety crime—which flourished because the cops were too busy dealing with death rays and crazed minions and elaborate plots to do any actual policing.

She'd ban the whole lot of them, if she could, the Ghost Owl included.

Which would give Tim more time for a social life, whispered a teenage fragment of her mind. "This is not a date," she growled at her reflection. "It's a business meeting. Goddammit."

The doorbell rang. She slipped into a pair of high heeled pumps, grabbed her purse and wrap, and headed downstairs.

Arthur and Patty had gotten to the front door before her.

"Hey, Tim," she called, paying too much attention to her efforts not to break her neck on the stairs. "Ignore my houseguests." Then she saw who was standing in the doorway.

"What are you doing here?" she growled.

Eddie grinned at her. "Whoa! Harriet Matilda, look at you. Heels and everything."

She raised an eyebrow. "Call me that again and all the commando training in the world won't be enough to keep your balls attached to your body."

Eddie laughed and held up a pizza. "I'm the babysitter for your staff this evening while you go out on your super date."

"It's not a date," Harri snapped as Arthur closed the door.

Patty giggled. "Are you wearing perfume?" She made a show of sniffing. "You are actually wearing perfume."

Harri ignored her assistant and glared at her ex-husband. "Who the hell contacted you?"

"Your new boyfriend."

Eddie's grin made her want to actually kick him in the nuts.

The doorbell rang again, saving Harri from further embarrassment. She pushed past the men and pulled open the door. "My hero. At last. Get me the hell out of here."

Tim grinned. "Wow, and I haven't even plied you with alcohol yet."

"Hey, that's my ex-wife you're talking about," Eddie said.

"Key syllable in that sentence is 'ex'. Good night, everyone." She started to pull the door closed, but Eddie grabbed the edge.

"You two need any condoms?"

Harri flipped him the bird and charged down the sidewalk to the vehicle parked at the end.

Behind her, Eddie and Tim exchanged words before her front door closed once again.

She whirled to confront her so-called date. "There wasn't anybody else you could call beside Eddie?"

"Nope." No explanations. No apology.

Why the hell didn't this type of behavior bother her with Tim the way it had with her ex-husband?

She took a good look at the man standing before her. This time the suit was soft gray, worn with a muted sage green shirt that set off his dark eyes. For the first time she realized they weren't brown, but a deep indigo blue. *God, he looks good.* Then she noticed the cane. "Are you okay?"

"I overdid it a little today," he said, opening the passenger door of his car. "Waiting for the vitamin I to kick in."

"Vitamin I? Do I even want to know?"

"Ibuprofen."

She climbed into Tim's aging Mercedes. It was old enough to look like he had a penchant for classic cars. More likely, he couldn't afford to replace it. Harri knew from hard experience what it was like to be broke but still look like you were rolling in old money.

Harri had squeaked nearly three hundred thousand miles out of Gran's old Jaguar with the Chevy V-8 engine. Everyone thought she was a spoiled rich girl during college and law school, but she was living on ramen noodles and peanut butter. She could have sold the car for a little money, but then she wouldn't have had the option of living in it if things got really bad.

By the time Dad and Laura had died, they'd pawned everything of value in the Winters mansion, except the Porsche and the Jag, along with mortgaging the property to the hilt, so Harri lost that too. If it hadn't been for Betty and Marvin Franklin giving her a place to stay and helping her get herself declared an emancipated minor, she would have ended up in foster care.

Harri knew all about shabby gentility and could see the signs in Tim. His fortune was long gone and he was merely riding on its fumes. *Well, great. We can all be broke together.* So much for the financial help he'd promised. Thank God for Gran's secret nest egg.

Stop it, she said to her inner voice. Sure, she depended too much on Aisha working her mojo and getting Rey a ton of offers. But if Harri had to use Tim Canyon to get their little firm back on track, then by God, she'd do it.

He chose Nolan's, the venerable high-end steakhouse that was the favorite of the city's ruling class. More back room deals had been brokered in Nolan's dim interior than in City Hall. The steaks were huge and perfectly cooked. The whisky was premium. And they had a peanut butter pie that Harri had dearly loved since early childhood, when Gran would bring her here for Sunday dinner.

Once they were seated and served their drinks, Tim said, "We've met before you know. Once when we were kids."

"I don't remember that," she said.

He shook his head. "I was twelve, so you must have been around five. I only remember it because the day before I'd caught your grandmother and my grandfather . . . in a private meeting." He raised an eyebrow and sipped his whisky. "If you get my meaning."

Harri started laughing. "That's even harder to believe than the . . . other thing." She wasn't stupid enough to mention Tim's extracurricular and very illegal activities in public. "Gran and Jack Canyon? They hated each other. Their feud was legendary."

"In public maybe."

"Ewww," Harri said. "Please don't tell me we're cousins or something." *Please don't*, the teenage part of her brain whispered, *because then we couldn't*—Harri started coughing and reached for her water.

"You okay?" Tim asked.

"Fine," she said, her face hot. "Are we family?"

Tim laughed. "God, no. I don't think anything happened between them until after my grandmother and your grandfather passed away. They had to be in their late fifties when I walked in on them. It was in his office in the Canyon Building on a Saturday afternoon. I tore out of there and they found me in the reception area. Grandpa hemmed and hawed a bit, then your grandmother said, 'Aw hell, Jack. He's old enough to know what we were doing. Give him a twenty and tell him to keep his mouth shut.' Then she gave me another twenty and winked at me and said if I ratted them out she'd skin me alive."

It was Harri's turn to laugh. "Okay, that does sound like something Gran would say." She took a careful sip of her whiskey. She knew she should be grilling him for information about what he was up to, but it had been so long since she'd been on a date with a man she actually liked, and she wanted to enjoy it. Despite all the trouble she was in.

If I'm about to get killed, I'm getting the peanut butter pie for dessert.

But this wasn't a date. If her suspicions were correct, this was a diversion so Rey could complete his mysterious errand. And she wasn't going to tell Tim that Aisha had said "as if" when Harri told her she needed to stay with Arthur while Rey did his thing. Whatever Rey was up to, Aisha was with him. She'd keep the kid out of trouble.

I hope.

Harri and Tim settled into normal small talk until their dinner arrived. Once, the waiter flitted away, She leaned over the table.

"Why is you-know-who so interested in Rey?"

"From what I've been able to discover—"

"You mean hack their computers?" She took a bite of her filet mignon.

Tim merely smiled. "They originally wanted to recruit him. When he helped you escape their third assassination attempt on you at City Hall, they moved up their timetable and changed his status to capture or kill."

The bite of beef slid down her throat like a rock. "What do you mean 'third' assassination attempt?"

"Your mugging a few weeks ago was not a mugging."

Nausea replaced her appetite, and she stared at her plate. "That was an average everyday purse snatching."

"Have you seen Crazy Jim lately?"

The acid in her stomach could give Arthur's formula a run for its money. "No," she whispered.

"Don't tell Rey he put one of Corvus's top wetworks men in the hospital." Tim calmly buttered a roll.

"Jim was my mugger?" she squeaked.

"Valentine Delante, AKA Crazy Jim, specializes in strangulation." Tim took a bite of his roll.

The lawyer part of her brain put everything together. "This plan has been going on longer than a few weeks. When this Delante failed to kill me, they brought in their bigger guns."

Tim nodded as he chewed, though his dark blue eyes twinkled.

"This isn't funny," she hissed under her breath.

He swallowed and openly grinned. "Your description of Darryl is." He abruptly sobered. "As long as they don't bring in Black Death, we have a fighting chance."

"Black Death? Didn't that go out of style in the Middle Ages?" Making jokes kept her from puking alcohol all over her lovely steak and green beans.

"He's a super." Tim took a sip of his whiskey. "But I haven't been able to discover his true identity. I'm beginning to think they don't even keep him in the unofficial records. Supposedly, he can kill with merely a touch. The results look like a heart attack in an autopsy."

"Fuck," she muttered. "I've met him."

"You what?"

She'd barely registered the switch between incredulous to deadly in Tim's expressions when he yelled, "Get under the table!"

He jumped to his feet and kicked his chair back. His cane slashing through the air at a figure in black tactical clothing and a black face mask. Screams and shouts filled the air.

Harri ducked under the white tablecloth. She desperately searched through her purse. It was a tiny clutch! Had she left her keys at her townhouse?

Relief filled her when her fingers closed around the mace canister. At the same moment, something grabbed her hair and pulled her from beneath the table. She dropped her purse, but tightened her grip on the canister.

She looked up at her assailant. He wore the same face mask as the man from City Hall and the one who'd attacked her in jail. She screamed in rage and sprayed the mace. The figure gasped, and his fingers loosened enough for her to pull free. She lunged for her steak knife, but her attacker got there first. He backhanded her hard. She stumbled into another table before landing on her side.

Through the stars she saw, her assailant stalked toward her.

Get up! Get up! Get up! her inner voice screamed.

Too late. He pulled a much larger knife from his belt and grabbed her hair again.

Before Harri's attacker could strike, Tim was on him. He fought with graceful precision, everything on the tables a weapon. Tim scooped up Harri's dinner plate. Her barely touched steak and green beans flew through the air.

Holding it like a discus, Tim slammed the edge against the masked man's throat. With a gurgle he fell back. Tim struck him hard across the side of his face with his cane, and the man dropped.

A second assailant tried to drop a garrote around Tim's neck, but wasn't fast enough. Tim ducked and spun jamming the head of the cane into the man's gut. As he doubled over, Tim followed through as if his cane was a driver and the bad guy's head was the golf ball. Their assailant flew into a third, and thankfully vacated, table.

Tim helped Harri to her feet and dragged her toward the door.

Another man dressed in black appeared. He had what looked like a cattle prod in his gloved hand. Tim dove toward him, but the man was faster. He kicked Tim in the knee. Tim grunted and dropped. His assailant swung at Tim's head, but he blocked the blow with his cane. The move was a feint. The man jabbed her date with the cattle prod. Tim collapsed, convulsing on the floor.

The third man turned toward Harri. "Your turn, bitch."

Everything seemed to slow down. She'd dropped her mace when she'd been slugged. The other patrons who hadn't made it through the kitchen doors huddled at the back of the dining room. They weren't going to be any help. To her right, a wine bottle sat on an abandoned table.

Harri grabbed the bottle and swung. Her attacker laughed and knocked the bottle out of her hand with the cattle prod. She backed away and bumped into something.

The dessert cart. With panic fueled strength, she grabbed the cart and spun it around as her attacker lunged at her and jammed it into his legs. He stumbled and dropped the prod.

"I'll make you pay for that," he snarled as he pulled a collapsible baton out of his boot.

Harri picked up the closest thing, which happened to be a pie, and hurled it at him. *Seriously, dummy? A pie? You're hitting an assassin with a pie?* her inner voice said in total disbelief.

It was a perfect shot. Right in the face. Harri dove for the cattle prod, expecting to feel the man's hand on the back of her neck at any moment. She heard a gasp and then a strangled cry.

"Peanut butter? You fucking bitch. I'm allergic to peanuts!" Blinded by the pie and wheezing with panic, the man frantically patted his pockets, looking for something.

Harri didn't wait to find out what it was. She jammed the prod into the man's gut and pulled the trigger. He jerked and collapsed in a convulsing heap.

She ran to Tim. Strength fueled by adrenaline and raw panic pulled Tim to his feet and half-carried, half-dragged him out of Nolan's into the cool night air.

Aisha guided her car in the direction of the flashlight shining in the recesses of the parking garage for the Lechuza Building. Even though the sun set later in the spring, the waning light emphasized the haunted feeling in the old Canyon district.

She turned to Rey. "If your bird-sense starts tingling, fly out of here, and head straight back to Harri's."

He chuckled. "My 'bird-sense'?"

"You know what I mean. If there's trouble, leave."

"Not without you and Miguel."

"This is not a discussion," she snapped.

Rey remained silent, but his jaw muscle twitched as he stared through the windshield. His too-good-to-be-true crap was starting to gnaw on her last nerve. Of course, he'd ignore her. She hadn't had a client yet that listened, much to their and her everlasting regret.

And that's exactly what Rey was. A client.

Miguel waved them toward a corner in the back of the garage. A series of concrete partitions sat nearby.

When she parked and they climbed out of her BMW, Miguel handed the flashlight to Rey. The older man fished around inside a nearby toolbox and pulled something out that looked like a portable Geiger counter.

"Give me a moment. I need to make sure there are no tracking devices or bombs." He swept the wand portion of the device over every nook and cranny of her baby before he gave a satisfied nod. Apparently, the contractor was as paranoid as Canyon.

Miguel put away his equipment and retrieved the flashlight from Rey. He pointed at the concrete partitions. "If you would stack those around and over Ms. Franklin's automobile—"

"Whoa, whoa, whoa!" She shifted between the men and her vehicle. "You are not getting a scratch on my car." Any nick would kill its resale value. She hated putting her baby up for sale as it was, but their fledgling law firm needed every cent she and Harri could scrape together.

Miguel scowled at her. "For what we need to do, Ms. Franklin, I don't want my sons involved. Watching your car on the street is one thing." He pointed at a nearby maintenance door. "Moving heavy equipment is another. And Tim doesn't want to give your opponents the opportunity to harm you."

There was more to his meaning than the actual words. When had her life changed from getting the best licensing percentage on a superhero's action figures to spies and espionage? As much as she distrusted Canyon, she nodded.

Rey made short work of hiding the BMW by stacking the partitions like Legos around and over the vehicle. Unless someone with super-strength or the ability to stretch their body or make themselves microscopic came in here, no one could get to her car.

Including her.

Aisha glared at Rey. "Not a scratch."

He smiled that devastating smile of his. "I promise it will leave the garage in the same immaculate condition in which it arrived."

Miguel unlocked the maintenance door and picked up his toolbox. "This way."

She followed him into a cramped stairwell. The door slammed shut behind Rey with an ominous clang. "Is that locked?"

"Of course," Miguel said. He handed the toolbox to Rey before he turned and trudged down the steel lattice-work steps. "We don't want the unsavory elements finding this place."

She grimaced and prayed that one of her heels didn't get caught on any of the openings. With no more health insurance, she couldn't afford a broken ankle. "How do I know you and Canyon aren't the unsavory elements?"

"Aisha," Rey hissed in dismay while Miguel laughed good-naturedly.

"Oh, I was definitely suspicious of Tim Canyon as well, Ms. Franklin. My Beatrice worked for his family since she was a little girl. As if the murders and rumors weren't bad enough, she spent more and more time at his home after the trial. I thought they were having an affair." Another laugh, but this one was bittersweet. "She told me the truth the day she was diagnosed with cancer because she knew Tim needed more help than she could give."

He stopped abruptly on another landing, and Aisha ran into him. Both Miguel and Rey steadied her.

"What's wrong?"

"Please be very quiet." Miguel unlocked another door and whispered something she couldn't catch. Inside the door, the flashlight shone on a modern intercom unit, but the wiring around it was from her grandparents' time.

Miguel placed his free hand on what looked like an ancient breaker switch. "I want you to understand something, Ms. Franklin. For years, my wife was the only one who knew the truth about Tim. And after she died, there was only me. It says something about his regard for you and Ms. Winters that he has brought you into his confidence." He threw the switch.

Aisha gasped as light flooded the basement. The scene was something from the news reports and documentaries on supervillains' secret lairs. Odd machines and carefully labelled chemicals. Work tables and tools. Exercise equipment and a small sparring ring. Except . . .

The mannequins on the far side of the room drew her. They stood on a raised platform. Her heels clicked as she crossed the smooth concrete. It couldn't be.

She stared up at the, well, she couldn't call them costumes. Her nephew Devon had worn a replica of the middle outfit for Halloween because it was the only known togs caught on camera. Her hand rose and covered her mouth.

Timothy Canyon was telling the truth. He really was the Ghost Owl.

Holy crap! They were standing in the infamous Owl's Nest!

"*Dios.*" Ray whispered the word in prayer from her right.

She looked up at him. "You really didn't know?"

He shook his head as he continued staring at the uniforms. "I . . . suspected. But Tim saying it in his car and seeing the proof are two different things."

"As I said, Ms. Franklin," Miguel said as he approached them and stood on her other side. "Until today, only my wife and I knew."

"And Corvus," she said.

He grinned. "No, they don't."

The muscles on her face tightened. This whole situation was getting deeper, and she didn't like the smell. "He told Harri that they tried to recruit him."

"They tried to recruit Tim Canyon, the inventor." White teeth flashed under Miguel's thick salt-and-pepper mustache. "They also tried to recruit the Ghost Owl, the vigilante. They have not deduced they are the same man. They have tried repeatedly to track Jatz'om Kuh to no avail." He waved toward the mounds of metal and plastic in the room. "And until today at Whitechapel, they believed they destroyed the inventor."

"What kind of game do you two think you're playing?" Aisha said. "These guys have tried to kill my best friend more than once."

"One we intend to win, Ms. Franklin. Seismic Shift and the others won't protect this city. The Ghost Owl is getting too old." Miguel looked up at Rey. "That, *mi amigo*, is why I suggested Tim take you under his wing." He laughed at his own bad joke. "He needs a successor. Someone who cares about the people the same way he does."

"Why didn't you tell me?" Rey asked softly.

"We were going to when this was ready." Miguel waved about the room. "When Ms. Winters escaped Corvus's efforts and then decided to help you get licensed, they moved up their time table to recruit you or kill you."

"Kill me?" The same raw fear she'd seen on Rey's face in her old office appeared now. It made him look far too young.

"No one's going to kill you, honey." Aisha laid her hand on his upper arm. He trembled beneath her touch.

She turned back to Miguel. "Do they know where he's staying?"

He shook his head. "Other than Ms. Winters' home the last five nights, no. They've triangulated within a square mile of here, but my boy evades them."

She looked askance at Rey. A ghost of a smile flitted across his face. "That explains the black SUVs and the drones."

"Drones?" This whole situation sounded more and more like something out of a big budget thriller.

"The men following me on the ground couldn't keep up." His grin widened. "Neither can the drones."

"The jammers Tim has scattered through the city have helped," Miguel added. "But as I said, Rey's public rescue of Ms. Winters and the others from the City Hall fire has changed things."

Aisha filed that information away, but Corvus trying to track Rey worried her more. "How long has this been going on?"

Rey twitched, and the same uncomfortable expression he had before he showed her his jade pendant appeared.

She jammed her fists on her hips. "Rey, how long have they been following you?"

"Since I can remember," he said softly. "Mama and I were always moving. Never stayed in one place for very long."

If his token hid him from most surveillance, maybe . . . "Did she have a pendant like yours?"

He nodded.

"What happened to it?"

"Th-this is hers. She put it on me before she pushed me out the window. Before . . . the monsters killed her." He looked so guilty Aisha wanted to hug him.

"A pendent?" Miguel interjected. "The carved jade one you used to wear as well?"

"You've seen it?" Aisha asked.

"*Sí.* I didn't think about it when we—" He plastered on an obviously fake smile. "We're not here to reminisce. We've got work to do. Come, let me show you."

Aisha let his change of subject go. Harri had already informed her Miguel and Beatrice had been the ones to pay for Maria Garcia's funeral. If they had been the ones to clean out the Garcias' apartment, Miguel might have some more documentation to track down Rey's relatives.

But Miguel obviously was worried about upsetting Rey further.

"How are you two going to move this equipment without being seen?"

"Through the Cold War tunnel system." Miguel bade them to follow him to what looked like a submarine hatch from the same era, but he held his hand to a palm reader that was definitely from this century. The little device whistled, and the light at the top shifted from red to green. "Tim and I have already disassembled everything in the old Nest. We need to bring it over here. Unfortunately, we are not in our prime any longer and need the extra muscle." He clapped Rey on the shoulder.

The wheel spun quietly, and the latch retreated with the slide of metal on metal. Miguel yanked on the hatch and it opened with a pneumatic hiss. Stale air seeped into the room. The opening was pitch black until he reached in and flipped another switch.

Yellow bricks and white-washed concrete formed a passage large enough for two automobiles to sit side-by-side. Old-fashioned incandescent bulbs were covered by wire cages. Rey stepped over the threshold, but Miguel grabbed his arm before he could go further.

"Let me go first." He eased past Rey. "I need to disable the alarms and traps."

"Traps?" Aisha squeezed next to Rey.

Miguel pointed to a small blackened object about twenty yards ahead. "Unless you want to be fried like the fatter rats, then yes, I go first."

He placed his palm against another reader to his right. This time he spoke a password. The electrical hum she had assumed came from the ancient light fixtures disappeared.

"Okay," she drawled. "You definitely go first."

The tunnels split, converged, and zigzagged in the general direction of the Canyon building. Or they might have gone in the opposite direction. She wasn't quite sure because she paid more attention to the obvious lasers and electrical grids.

"I will program the security system with your prints and voices before we leave," Miguel assured them as he pointed out the not-so-obvious security measures like the knock-out gas nozzles and the steel bars that slid out of the walls.

Finally, he opened another hatch. This room was much larger, and there were obvious marks on the floor and walls where items might have once rested. Two hand trucks stood next to a series of neatly stacked boxes on the right. Large sections of machinery lay scattered on the left.

Aisha helped Miguel with the boxes, but in the end, Rey ordered them to stay in the new Nest so he wouldn't worry about accidently hitting them with the quarter-ton of equipment he carried each trip.

Once she was sure Rey was out of earshot, she turned to Miguel. "What's the deal about the pendant Rey's mom wore?"

"She didn't have it on when Beatrice found her. Nor was it in her personal effects when we claimed her body from the morgue. I'm glad Rey had it all this time," he said quietly. He removed items from one of his boxes, pulled out a Phillips screwdriver, and started attaching pieces together. "We found the one Rey wore in the bathroom tangled in one of his shirts when we . . . cleaned out their apartment. I knew it was important because he started to take it off to swim with my boys, and Maria started screaming at him. It was so unlike her."

"So these stones hide them." Aisha tapped her fingernails on the work table as she tried to put the puzzle together. "Maria could have been a super trying to get the hell out of the mess in Central America."

His refusal to meet her eyes said a ton about his emotions. "Or his father could have been a super with one of the militant groups."

"That's against the Geneva Convention."

"So is rape. Given Maria's fear, she may not have had a choice in getting pregnant." Miguel pointed toward his toolbox. "I need a number ten Allen wrench."

Aisha recognized the dodge, but she handed him the appropriate tool anyway. Maybe searching for Rey's family wasn't such a great idea after all.

After she silently counted off sixty seconds, she said, "Miguel, Rey listens to you. If you think he's in danger, he'll get the hell out of here."

Miguel set aside the wrench and stared at her. "Of course, he's in danger. This Corvus group may have killed Maria. But between you, Harri and Tim, the boy has a fighting chance. You plan on hiding him in plain sight. It will be harder for them to do something, no?"

"Yes, but—"

"If your plan works, Rey will save this neighborhood. Will save all of us. There was a time I could afford to bury a stranger. But five years ago, I couldn't bury my own wife. All that could change with your help." He swiped at the couple of tears that escaped, and Aisha pretended not to notice.

Rey came in with another armful of equipment, saving her from releasing her own tears. "I've got one more load."

"That's great, honey." She made a show of checking her watch. "Why don't we call it a night after that? It's five till nine." She almost added, "And I'm starving," but stopped herself in time. She didn't know the meaning of the word, compared to what Miguel and Rey had been through.

Once Rey headed back down the tunnel, she looked at Miguel. "Do you still have any of Maria's personal effects?"

He shook his head. "I still have lots of boxes from before, but if Beatrice kept anything, I wouldn't know which one to start looking."

She smiled. "Don't worry about it." She glanced at the tunnel. "Maybe it's for the best."

—— •◆• ——

Aisha handed Rey some cash for their take-out, telling him she needed some extra toiletries since he was spending the night at her place. What she really needed was a new pack of cigarettes to get her through a night in her condo without jumping him. With his super hearing, her battery-operated boyfriend was not an option.

As he strode into Marta's, she turned toward the convenience store next door. And immediately spotted the black SUV across the street.

Maybe her conversation with Rey and Miguel was too fresh in her mind. Lots of people bought that type of vehicle at an enormous discount when the auto manufacturers got into trouble during the economic downturn. Even though it sat under a streetlight, she couldn't see through the tinted windows. She quickly memorized the license plate number.

No such thing as the Boogeyman, she told herself sternly.

Except a boogeyman had warned her he'd been ordered to kill Harri.

Pretend you don't see them.

She yanked on the door handle for the store and walked inside. Toothpaste, toothbrush. Shampoo and body wash that smelled more masculine than her favorite pomegranate-scented brands.

The handful of men in the store checked out her legs and ass, but otherwise didn't bother her. Good to know she could still rock it at forty. The two Hispanic women ignored her. The Asian woman dressed in black leather at the magazine rack though . . .

Aisha's skin tingled as she passed her. Something was off but she couldn't place why. Dad always said to trust her gut. Right now, her gut was filled with icy fear.

She reached the counter and asked the clerk for her favorite brand of menthols. The monitor on the shelf above the check-out showed the leather-clad bitch behind her. The bridal magazine she held wasn't convincing cover. Not with the plain platinum wedding ring on her left hand.

Once Aisha's purchases were rung up and paid for, it was all she could do to not run from the store.

Rey was standing by her BMW with their dinner when she came out. Something must have shown on her face because his smile faded.

She forced one of her own. "Let's go home. I'm exhausted."

He picked up on her silent signal and climbed inside her car. Once she slammed her own door and reached for the seatbelt, he murmured, "What's wrong?"

"The woman in the black leather."

He glanced over Aisha's shoulder. "She's putting on a helmet." He snapped his own buckle into place and watched from the passenger side mirror. "Now she's climbing onto her motorcycle."

The distinctive low-pitched kick and hum of a bike followed Rey's words. Aisha shifted her car into gear and backed out. The black-clad rider peeled out of the parking lot and onto the side street.

So why did that icy ball remain in her gut?

"What is it, Aisha?" Concern colored Rey's voice. "What happened?"

"Nothing." She gave a short laugh. "With everything that's happened, I'm jumpy." In her rearview mirror, the black SUV remained parked at the corner and was soon out of sight.

She still couldn't relax. The feeling of impending doom continued. She rolled down the front window to let in the night air. No help.

Focus on the case, girl.

"Would you like to go to your mother's grave tomorrow to pay your respects? Harri said you wanted to take some flowers to the cemetery, and she hasn't had a chance to take you back."

He hesitated for a moment before he said softly, "Yes."

More silence filled the car. She reached over and grasped his hand. "I know how difficult this must be for you, but now that we have a copy of her death certificate, I should be able to find your birth certificate."

"I thought Harri was going to do that."

"I'm trying to make this easy on both of you." Aisha glanced at him. Rey watched her intently. "Harri was pretty young when her mom died, too."

"Oh."

A sigh escaped her, and she returned her attention to the street. Two people she cared about had the worst possible childhoods. She didn't want to know the details of Rey's, but she had to. If he had a criminal record, even a juvenile one, it would make obtaining his license difficult, if not impossible.

"There's no way to make this easier, honey, but I have to ask. What happened to you after your mom was murdered? Miguel said you disappeared."

For three red lights, he didn't answer. Finally, he said, "I did what she told me to do. I ran."

She waited for more, but there was only silence. "From what? The men in the black SUVs?"

"No," he said. "At least, not that time." His fingers tightened around hers, to the point of pain. If she could take away the emotional agony he was feeling…

"I heard her screams. I was so afraid."

"It wasn't your fault. You were a little kid."

"So I did what she told me. I ran, jumping from roof to roof. These things came out of the shadows and chased me."

His pulsed hammered beneath her touch. She considered pulling over, but he might not continue his story if she did, so she kept her eyes on the road.

And her mirrors. There was a black SUV three cars behind her.

"All I could hear was the scrape of claws on concrete and metal as they followed. I reached a warehouse at the edge of the lake. There was nowhere else to go. The monsters with claws surrounded me. I-I decided it was better to jump and drown than let them do to me what they did to Mama."

More silence. The freeway entrance ramp was coming up in two lights. She changed lanes. After the count of three, the SUV switched lanes, too.

She couldn't stand it anymore, though she didn't know how much of her tension was from Rey's story or their possible tail. "So you jumped?"

"Yes." A bitter laugh erupted from him. "It was the first time I flew. I didn't know how I did it. I couldn't control it. Just floated over the water most of the night. Near dawn, I crashed into the mud flats on the other side of the lake."

"And?" She checked her review mirror as they climbed the entrance ramp to the Lakeside Freeway and breathed a sigh of relief when the SUV continued on the boulevard.

"Some fishermen found me and took me to the local sheriff's office. While they were arguing about who to call, I slipped out a service door. I've been on my own ever since."

"What did you eat? Where'd you sleep?"

"Trashcans and any safe cubbyhole I could find." He shook his head. "It's amazing what people throw away in this country."

Another dark SUV appeared behind them. She gently pulled her hand out of his. "Can you read the license plate on the black SUV two cars behind us?"

He looked over the seat and rattled off the number.

Her heart splashed into the icy liquid in her gut. It was the same SUV she'd seen at Marta's.

"Aisha?" Rey's voice was no longer a scared kid's. He sounded stern. In command. Like Captain Justice.

She jammed down on the accelerator and cut into the next lane. "It was parked across the street from Marta's. I think your old buddies are following us."

"The monsters or Corvus?"

"Does it matter?" She swerved around a semi and nearly rammed a pickup. Another quick lane change triggered a series of honks from the vehicles she cut off. Another jerk of the wheel, and she was in front of the pickup she almost rear-ended.

"They're gaining," he said. "We need to get off Lakeside."

"We need the cover," she shot back.

"Innocent people will get hurt," he growled.

Her heart was trying to climb out of its icy bath in her stomach and back up her throat. God help her, he was right. Her knuckles tightened on the steering wheel. She was so out of her depth.

"Take the causeway," he ordered.

"Are you insane?"

The driver's side mirror exploded, and she shrieked.

"Fewer people on the causeway this time of night," Rey said. "I can protect you. I can't protect everyone on Lakeside."

The two raised roadways cut across the shallowest, narrowest part of the lake. Two miles long with no way to get off unless she wanted to swim.

Another ping and the rear window shattered. So much for the resale value.

Maybe the swim wasn't such a bad idea.

The BMW's engine whined as the tachometer needle approached the red line. She changed lanes again. Behind them came the scream of metal on metal.

"What the hell?" she muttered.

"There's two of them now."

A quick glance in the rearview mirror confirmed Rey's assessment. Tires screeched as she whipped onto the causeway exit at the last minute.

"Did we lose them?"

"No." He unbuckled his belt and twisted in his seat.

"What are you doing!"

"Trust me. I've got a plan."

She winced as his fingers pried a corner of the roof up and out. He peeled the metal back until the entire sheet ripped off the car with a shriek. It clanged and bounced across the asphalt, but the diversion only slowed their pursuers for a moment.

"What do we do now?"

"Do you trust me?"

"What?" She glanced at him.

"Do you trust me?

She nodded.

"I'm going to unbuckle your seatbelt."

"What!" She jammed down on the accelerator, racing down the causeway over ninety miles an hour. She wanted to look at him, but she didn't dare take her eyes off the road.

"They don't have any air support, and someone's going to get hurt at this rate." His warm fingers touched her hip, and the safety device loosened. His foot nudged hers from the pedal. "Crouch on the driver's seat."

"Why?" But she found herself kicking off her heels anyway. His hand replaced hers on the wheel as she pulled her feet beneath her on the seat.

White teeth flashed under the passing lights. "Ripping off my attorney's legs when we exit a speeding car isn't good PR."

Oh god, he was really going to do this.

She squeezed her eyes shut. Hard muscle surrounded her. Harsh wind ripped her breath away and roared in her ears.

When she could breathe again, she dared to open her eyes.

In time to see her beloved Beemer ram into the causeway's barrier far below them. The newly minted convertible tumbled. Once. Twice. And flipped over the concrete to be swallowed by the ebony waters below.

"Ah, fuck." She groaned. "I left my cigarettes in the car."

CHAPTER 18

Thankful Tim hadn't opted for valet parking and praying the goons from the restaurant hadn't brought along any friends, Harri poured Tim into the passenger seat of his Mercedes, fished his keys out of his pocket, and climbed into the driver's seat. The car screeched out of his side street parking space. She stared in the rearview mirror. No headlights behind them.

Harri stuck to the darker side streets. Nobody seemed to be following. Instinctively she drove towards her place, but about a mile from Nolan's she began to shake with delayed shock. Pulling into the darkest street she could find, she stopped the car and sat for a moment, trying to catch her breath, then turned to check on Tim.

"Are you still alive?"

He groaned. "Mostly. Where are we?"

"About five blocks north of Edison and Commerce."

Tim shook his head. "Not your place. They'll be waiting."

Harri gasped. "Oh, God. We have to get Patty and Arthur out of there."

Tim nodded. "I'll call Eddie. Both our phones are clean."

"Except mine is somewhere on the floor with my clutch back at Nolan's."

He reached into his pants pocket with a wince and pulled out a cheap flip phone. Eddie must have been waiting for his call because Tim started talking almost immediately. "They hit us at Nolan's." He listened a moment. "We'll live . . . Time for plan B." He weakly turned his head to Harri. "Eddie's moving them somewhere safe for now."

Harri could hear the pain in his voice. "We need somewhere safe to go, too. You need a doctor."

"No doctor," he rasped.

"Then where?"

He didn't answer. Harri shook him, a little more roughly than she intended. He moaned, but didn't otherwise respond.

Harri felt the panic bubbling up and fought it back down. *Think, think, think. Where to go . . .*

Not Aisha's condo. Besides, she was with Rey, and God only knew where they were. The Lechuza Building was an option, but she didn't know if Tim had those keys on him. And to get to the offices, she'd have to take either Commerce or Lakeside, which were main streets where they were more likely to run into trouble. But she couldn't stay here. Deciding it was better to keep moving, she started the car and drove down the dark street.

Inspiration struck within a block. She could get to Jeremy's salon through the alleys that zig-zagged next to Commerce and park in back. He'd converted the second story of the building into a loft when he decided to move out of the Franklins. The salon would be closed, but Jeremy might be home. Harri pulled over again, found Tim's clean phone in his pocket, and called Jeremy.

"Pick up, pick up, pick up." The phone rang but nobody answered. She left a message in case he was screening calls. "It's me. Call me right back at . . . oh, shit. I don't know the number on this phone. But don't call me on my phone. It may not be safe. I'm—" She was about to say "on my way," then realized Jeremy's phone might not be safe either. "I'm heading out of town for a few days. I'll be in touch."

Ten minutes later, she was a block from Jeremy's, and Tim was still out of it. Harri killed the headlights before pulling into the dark alley that led to an even darker alley behind the salon. Jeremy had built out several covered parking spaces for the loft that customers didn't know about. The parking area was dark and secluded and hard to find if you didn't know it was there.

It was also a great place for an ambush, she realized as she coasted under the deck that made up the roof of the parking area. Hopefully, whoever was after her didn't realize that. Harri felt dizzy with relief when the only thing she saw was Jeremy's MINI Cooper. *Please be home, Jeremy, please.*

"Tim, wake up." She shook his arm. "Can you walk?"

He groaned again. "It hurts."

"I know, honey, but we need to get inside."

"Leave me alone," he whined.

Time for a different tack. "You are the Ghost Owl," she hissed. "Get your sorry ass out of this car, you miserable excuse for a superhero."

It worked. He mumbled something that might have been "bitch," pushed open the car door, and carefully swung his legs out. Harri hurried to his side of the car. She crouched and put her arms around him. "Put your weight on me. It's ten steps to the door."

Using the car door and leaning on Harri, Tim pulled himself into a standing position. "Give me a second," he wheezed. "Kinda dizzy here." He took a couple of deep, ragged breaths. "Where's my cane?"

"No idea. Back at Nolan's, I guess." She pulled his arm around her shoulder and they slowly hobbled to the door. Now that the immediate danger was past, she became acutely aware of Tim's warmth pressed against her and the smell of his skin. She hadn't been this physically close to a man since her divorce.

Jeremy didn't count.

And Tim could barely walk, and people are trying to kill them. Not the best time for romance.

If only he didn't smell so good.

She kicked Jeremy's door a couple of times. There wasn't a bell. There wasn't even a door knob on the outside. It looked like a service door. Jeremy didn't like to advertise where he lived. He reserved his social butterfly persona for work.

"Please be here," she muttered. It occurred to her that it would have made a lot more sense to leave Tim in the car until she knew for sure Jeremy was home. With a growl, she kicked the door again.

A spot light came on and an intercom crackled. Intercom? When the hell did he get an intercom?

"What's the password?" she heard Jeremy say through the intercom.

"Password? Are you insane? Open the goddamn door." She shifted Tim on her shoulder and he groaned. She couldn't hold him up much longer. "We're bleeding out here."

The door opened. Jeremy stood in the dim light with a drink in his hand. "Sorry, darling. I had to make sure it was you. You know how I treasure my privacy." He noticed Tim and his breezy demeanor abruptly departed. "Inside. Now."

Jeremy pulled Tim's free arm over his shoulders and shoved his cocktail into Harri's hand. "We're going into the salon. How many?" he asked as he led them through a door.

"Three," Tim gasped. "Left knee's gone."

"He also got zapped with a cattle prod and hit his head pretty hard when he went down. What the hell happened here?" Harri stared around the salon in shock. Work stations were tipped over. Several of the leather styling chairs were slashed. The frosted glass reception counter was smashed along with the front door, which was now covered with a sheet of plywood.

"Had a couple of unexpected visitors myself." Jeremy steered Tim into a spa room. "Help me get him on the table."

"We need to get him to a doctor."

"Not yet," Jeremy said. "Doctors ask inconvenient questions. I need to see what we've got first. I've been putting Gingersnap back together for years. If it's worse than I can handle, we'll need to come up with a cover story."

"You've—what the hell is going on?"

Jeremy smiled at her. "Let's take care of your boyfriend first, okay?"

"He's not my boyfriend," Harri said in a weak voice.

"Too bad," Jeremy said. "I always thought you'd be perfect for each other. You know about him?"

"Maybe," Harri said. "Do you?"

Jeremy chuckled as he lifted a medical bag out of a cabinet. "Maybe." He pulled out a large orange pill bottle. "Harri, be a dear and get me some water from the break room fridge."

"What's that?" She nodded toward the pill bottle.

"Pain meds. I used to keep liquid morphine around for these occasions, but it's been a while since I needed it." He smiled at her again. "Harri, sweetie, I'll spill all my nasty little secrets. I promise. But right now we need that water. And grab the blue packs from the freezer. I'll need those too."

"Right." Harri scurried out of the room, the task keeping her panic in check. It was hard enough wrapping her brain around the idea Jeremy knew Tim. But he also appeared to know about the Ghost Owl. The matter of fact way he was tending to Tim suggested this wasn't the first time Tim had shown up at Jeremy's door battered and bleeding.

And the salon—there'd been a big fight here. The pile of bloody towels in the break room sink indicated casualties, although Jeremy didn't appear to be one of them. She grabbed a couple of water bottles and the ice packs and hurried back.

"Thank you," Jeremy said, some of his breeziness returning. He'd cut Tim's pants leg open revealing the swelling and misshapen knee, and had already bandaged Tim's chest where the cattle prod had burned him.

Harri stared down at Tim's bare chest and gasped. So many scars . . .

Jeremy placed two of the ice packs on each side of Tim's knee and gave the third back to Harri. "You're getting a hell of shiner, girl. That eye's gonna swell shut if you don't apply that one to your face. I'll tend to you as soon as I get him fixed up." He handed Tim some pills. "Time for your medicine, sweetie."

"What is it?" Tim asked, his voice thick with pain.

"Vicodin." Jeremy opened a water bottle and handed it to him. "It's going to take a few minutes to kick in, but I have to look at that knee now. Sorry in advance."

Tim, his face grim, nodded. He swallowed the pills with a couple of gulps of water and slumped back onto the table.

"Harri, dear, hold Timmy's hand. This is gonna hurt like hell. Here's a towel."

"A towel?"

"For him to bite down on to muffle the screams."

"I won't scream," Tim said.

"That's what they all say." Jeremy smiled. "Ready?"

Harri shoved a corner of terrycloth in Tim's mouth.

He grunted loudly through the towel as Jeremy probed his swelling knee. The inventor-turned-vigilante squeezed Harri's hand hard enough to hurt and stared into her eyes. Harri gritted her teeth and stared back.

"Sorry, doll," Jeremy finally said. "Ice and ibuprofen won't get it done this time. When he kicked you, did you feel something pop?"

Tim's face was the color of milk and covered in sweat. He spit out the towel. "Yeah. That's bad, right?"

"Yeah," Jeremy said with a sigh. "That's bad. Surgery bad. You still seeing that orthopedist? The one over by Lakeside Hospital?"

"Yeah," Tim said. "Oh, hey. There's the Vicodin. Now I feel it. Yay, drugs." He gazed up at Harri with a goofy grin on his face. "So, how's our date going? Having fun?" Before she could answer, he turned to Jeremy. "You shoulda seen our girl take out the bad guy with a pie. That she threw at him. I never took anybody out with a pie. She's a badass."

Jeremy patted his hand. "That's nice, Timmy. You go night-night like a good stoned boy and let the grown ups talk."

Tim, his eyelids fluttering closed, waved his middle finger at Jeremy and grinned. "Nighty-night."

Jeremy covered him with a couple of blankets, dimmed the lights in the room, and pulled Harri out into the hallway. "Come on. Your turn. Let's go in the break room. I don't want to leave him alone down here."

"He needs to go to a hospital," Harri said.

"Darling, that was a professional hit team that came after Tim Canyon. He's not going anywhere until I know we can protect him. He'll be okay for now. Eddie's calling in some reinforcements." Jeremy pulled out two glasses and a bottle of bourbon and poured them each a very stiff drink.

"We need to warn Aisha and Rey," Harri said.

"Eddie's tracking them down. Don't worry. Rey will keep her safe. It will take more than a Corvus hit squad to take him down. That kid is . . . unique. And powerful."

With gentle fingers, Jeremy examined Harri's swollen cheek and eye. "Good. Nothing broken, but you'll look like hell for awhile." He handed her back the ice pack. "I'm guessing you have some questions."

"Yeah, but I'm not sure where to start." She pressed the gel pack to her face, sank back into the battered leather sofa, and stared at him. "You have this whole secret life I don't know about."

Jeremy chuckled. "Not my whole life. Only an interesting corner of it."

"What happened here tonight?"

"Some bad guys came calling. We took care of them."

"We? You aren't a super, are you?"

"Honey, we're all super in our own ways. But my only alter ego is The Lady Jaye, and she was never a secret. You know I coach the youngsters coming up, right?"

Harri sipped her drink and nodded. She knew from long experience that she needed to let Jeremy tell the story his way. If he wanted to detour into his drag queen mentoring activities, there must be a reason for it.

"Our special guests were expecting a swishy, middle-aged hairdresser. And like many hyper-masculine men, they assumed I would be a pushover. Which I am not."

"No kidding," Harri said, taking another healthy sip from her drink. Jeremy had been the scourge of the schoolyard bullies. He wasn't a big guy, but he was fast and believed there was no such thing as fighting dirty. Particularly if you were smaller or outnumbered.

"Well, we had a scheduling conflict so instead of meeting my students on the regular night, we met tonight." He chuckled again, his eyes twinkling with malevolent glee. "Instead of the aforementioned swishy hairdresser, our gentlemen callers got me plus six fit young queens. In a room full of scissors and straight razors. And those girls can fight. Well, you know. We all can. It's not a job for the timid."

Despite everything that had happened to her in the last few days and her throbbing headache, Harri laughed until she cried. "Oh, that must have been epic." She stopped laughing abruptly. "What did you do with the bodies?"

"We didn't kill them. They're under—shall we say—protective custody, while Eddie and I figure out what to do with them."

Harri's eyes widened. "You're holding them? Where?"

"My other place of business. Very secure." He smiled. "Which leads to your next burning question—how do I know Tim Canyon?"

"Well?"

"First of all, don't hate on Aisha. I know how big attorney-client confidentiality is with you lawyer types."

"What does she have to do with this?"

"I provide certain . . . services to superheroes."

Harri waved a hand to encompass the salon. "Like grooming?"

"When was the last time you saw me cut anyone's hair, Harri?"

"You still do mine and Aisha's."

Jeremy crossed his arms. "I haven't done hers in years, and when was the last time you were in here?"

"When I bought in Rey the other day."

"Uh-huh, and the time before that?"

Harri stared at the tips of her shoes. "Dammit, I haven't even had enough alcohol tonight to deal with this mess, much less deal with your tiptoeing." The side of her face was starting to ache from the cold, and she laid the gel pack aside. "What does Aisha have to do with anything?"

"She asked for my help designing Rey's costume."

Harri's head jerked up. "She what? Why didn't she go to one of her professional hero designers—"

At Jeremy's mocking expression, Harri took a large swallow of her bourbon. "Is that the reason for your warehouse?"

"Yes, it's been my side hustle for quite a while thanks to Aisha."

"W-why didn't either of you say anything?"

"Really, girl? As much as you hate supers, and as much crap you give, well, gave Aisha for working at Dewey & Cheatham all these years?" He swirled the contents of his own glass. "Which, by the way, I'm glad you got her away from those little shits. They were killing her soul bit by bit."

"And you know about Tim's extracurricular activities?" She took a sip of her drink.

"Know? I helped create the Ghost Owl."

Harri spit out her bourbon and began coughing. "You . . . what?"

"When I met Tim, he looked like a SWAT cop. No style. Nothing super about him. Except for all those amazing gadgets of his. Which I soon found out were based on owl anatomy." The dark liquid in Jeremy's glass sloshed dangerously close to the rim as he waved his hand in his enthusiasm. "Amazing creatures, owls. Stealthy and lethal and fraught with mythological import. Style to burn. And so the Ghost Owl was born."

"You came up with the idea for the Ghost Owl? Is that what you're telling me?"

Jeremy nodded. "Tim had the gadgets. What he lacked was the persona. I helped him build it."

"So, you . . . what? Designed his costume?" Harri chugged her bourbon and started to cough again.

"Not his costume," Jeremy said in an offended tone. "They aren't costumes—well, mine aren't at least. I design tactical wardrobes. Form and function. And I help supers fine tune their chosen persona."

"That's what you do for the local drag queens!" Harri stared at him.

"It's not as different as you'd think. Do you have any idea of the textile science involved in producing natural looking cleavage? Falsies only get you half the way there."

"But, I mean . . ." She looked around the room, trying to dig the words out of her brain. All the fear-induced adrenaline was gone, and the bourbon added to the crash. "They're . . . it's . . . you know what I mean."

"What? You think drag queens and superheroes have nothing in common? Au contraire. Think about it. It's all about the persona. It's all about creating a vivid image to trick the eye into not seeing the real person behind the mask."

"Okay. When you say it that way, it makes sense." Harri was moving past shock and into numbness. *My ex-husband is a commando, my assistant is gestating a possible super baby, and one of my best friends helped create the Ghost Owl. What's next? Can things possibly get any weirder?*

Her stomach growled. "You got any food in here? I didn't get to finish my dinner."

Jeremy nodded and headed toward the fridge. "Here's some leftover mu shu pork from lunch. But we ate all the pancakes. Sorry. Ooh, and some lovely smoked salmon spread and crackers. Our party crashers ruined our post-coaching nosh. Bastards."

Harri grabbed the cardboard container out of his hand and finished up the mu shu pork in less than a minute. She didn't even bother to heat it in the microwave. Jeremy nibbled on his crackers and salmon goo, watching her.

Her immediate hunger sated, Harri asked, "Do you have a lot of supers you design for?"

"A few." He smiled, the please expression of a parent who was proud of his child. "But the Ghost Owl is my masterpiece. Most of them now only care how they look on TV. No appreciation for the subtleties. With the Ghost Owl, Tim and I created a mythic figure, an old school hero in the best way possible."

"Old school hero is right." Harri sighed and shook her head. "He was amazing tonight, but look at him now. He can't do this any longer."

Jeremy shook his head. "No, *he* can't. On the other hand, the Ghost Owl persona doesn't have to be Tim."

Harri stared at Jeremy as the parts of various conversations clicked into place. "Rey. That's why Tim is interested in Rey."

She rose to toss the mu shu box in the trash. Every muscle and joint reminded her she qualified under the Age Discrimination Act. So much for Rey making them all rich. The Ghost Owl had bled Tim dry and would do the same to Rey, except the kid was already broke. "Does this have anything to do with the mysterious errand Rey had tonight?"

Jeremy looked at his watch. "Yes. Miguel needed help moving the Owl's Nest."

"Of course. The Spanish word for owl is *lechuza*. Like my new office building."

"Bingo." Jeremy grinned. "Now you're getting it."

"And your other place of business? Is that being moved to the Lechuza Building, too?"

Jeremy snorted. "Hell no. That place is a dump. My very nice, nearly new warehouse space is on the other side of town."

"Aisha mentioned something about getting in touch with the person who designs for Cobblestone. Is that you?"

His face wrinkled in disgust. "Cobblestone? That spandex nightmare? Please. I do have standards, you know. His designer, whoever he or she may be, is a hack."

"Why didn't you tell me?" The plaintive whine in her voice would have annoyed the hell out of her if it came from someone else, but the fact that Jeremy and Aisha hid something like this made her feel like the odd woman out.

He shook his head. "Harri don't act stupid. It doesn't become you. Supers are a unique clientele. Confidentiality is paramount. As is security. With what I know about my clients, it's safer for all concerned if I keep a low profile. I protect my identity as carefully as Tim does."

"So nobody knows about Tim?"

"Beyond our immediate circle? No. Nobody knows Tim is the Ghost Owl. Nobody."

Despite Jeremy's assertions, Tim's comments on the golf course about making sure Corvus knew Harri was under his protection didn't quite add up. "I don't think he keeps it as secret as you think. From the way Seismic Shift glared at us at Whitechapel, he knows Tim is the Ghost Owl."

"Seismic Shift? What's he got to do with this?"

"He's not one of yours?"

"Hell, no."

"Actually, I'm glad." Harri yawned. "Sorry. I probably should have poured the bourbon on top of the food instead of the other way around."

"It's been a busy day." Jeremy spread the last of the smoked salmon goo on a cracker. He held it out to Harri. "Want it?"

"God, no. Eat it. What do you know about Seismic Shift?"

"That hair isn't real," he said with a grimace. "I'd bet my salon on it."

Harri chuckled. "From the way the sun was bouncing off his scalp, I don't think he has a follicle left."

Jeremy laughed. "Why am I not surprised? All I can tell you is he's more of a diva than Ultramegaperson." He turned serious. "From some hints Timmy dropped while stoned, I think he designed some of Shift's tech."

This woke Harri up. "Tim works with him?" *I want to trust Tim Canyon, I really do, but I still don't know what he's up to. The whole exposé thing could be a scam.*

Jeremy shook his head. "Not that way. His day job is being an inventor. He's made a lot of stuff for other supers over the years as Tim Canyon. But he saved his best gadgets for the Ghost Owl. I can't imagine he'd ever let Seismic Shift know he and the Ghost Owl are the same."

The same jolt ran through her, the one she got during a deposition that said she was close to the truth. "Is there any reason Shift would be scared of Tim Canyon?"

Jeremy stared into space, thinking. "Tim? Well, he does know some of his secrets. Like, Seismic Shift isn't a totally natural super. He's augmented."

"Augmented?"

"Yeah." Now, Jeremy yawned. "If I have to stay up and play nurse to Gingersnap, I'm making java. You want some?" He stood and crossed to the coffee maker.

"Yeah. Tell me about Seismic Shift. I was supposed to depose him about the Lake County Retirement Home last Monday."

"You mean the day of Professor Venom's attack on City Hall?" Jeremy pulled out the pot and filled it from the faucet. "The one I saw on the news? The one where you nearly plummeted to your death? That day?"

Harri winced. "I'm sorry I didn't call you."

"But you called Aisha." Jeremy flung his free hand in a dismissive gesture. "Now I know where I rate."

"Hey, you're getting to view Rey in his skivvies if you're designing for him," Harri huffed. "I think that makes us even."

Jeremy's eyes glittered as he poured the pot of water into the maker's reservoir. Between seeing Rey nearly naked and Jeremy's urge to gossip, she had him.

"Well, Shift stomps his foot and causes pinpoint earthquakes, right?" Jeremy tossed the premeasured packet of ground beans into its slot and hit the "Brew" switch. "Except that's not all him. On his own, he can shake the furniture around, maybe knock the guy in front of him off his feet. Tim made him some kind of gadget to magnify the effect, something with sound waves I think. I don't understand the science, but basically without Tim, Seismic Shift is an overgrown toddler pitching a fit. Needless to say, old Shifty doesn't want that getting out."

That put a different spin on Tim's story from the golf outing.

"Tim said he wanted Shift to see me alive and well and under his protection. From the context, it sure sounded like he was talking about the Ghost Owl, not Tim Canyon the inventor."

Jeremy opened the cupboard and pulled out two mugs, a puzzled look on his face. "He said that? But you still haven't answered my question. What's Seismic Shift got to do with this?"

"He's the one who started the fire at City Hall while pretending to be Professor Venom. And according to Tim, he's a talent scout for Corvus."

The two mugs slipped from Jeremy's fingers and shattered on the tile floor. "Shift works for Corvus? He's an ass, but . . . I thought he was still on our side. If they flipped him—"

For the first time that evening, Jeremy looked truly afraid. He ran his shaking hands through his short blond hair. "We need to find your boy. Big trouble is coming."

CHAPTER 19

—◆—◆—◆—

Aisha peered over Rey's arm. Far below them, the three SUVs on the causeway that had been chasing them didn't stop. Their lights winked out, and she lost them in the darkness.

However, other vehicles screeched to a halt. Like tiny ants, people poured out and ran toward the spot where her BMW had flipped over the concrete partition and into the inky waters of Lake Del Oro. From the direction of the city, sirens wailed.

"Turn your face into my chest and keep your hands between our bodies," Rey murmured in Aisha's ear.

"W-w-why?" She tried to get her shakes under control. In all her years working with supers, no one had actually tried to kill her.

"Three drones incoming, and I don't want you to get frostbite," he said.

She did as he said and squeezed her eyes shut. The last thing he needed was her screaming in his ears.

Rey's flying maneuvers were worse than the time LaShun, Harri, and Jeremy talked her into riding on the Space Fighter rollercoaster. His climbs, dives, barrel rolls, and loop-de-loops would have brought up her dinner if it weren't already sitting at the bottom of the lake along with her car.

Finally, he slowed, paused, and gently tried to set Aisha on her feet. Her knees decided not to cooperate. They were too busy turning to jelly. Rey caught her before she collapsed.

"It's okay to open your eyes, Aisha," he whispered.

She blinked. Lights spread out beneath them. "Wh-wh-where—" She looked up at Rey. The stylized neon scarlet and gold eagle sign of Del Oro Bank framed his dark, wind-blown hair. They were on the roof of the bank's headquarters.

Sixty stories straight up.

"You want to sit down while I call Harri?"

Aisha nodded. He helped her over to a concrete ledge that surrounded the industrial A/C units. His phone started ringing, and he answered it.

The night was so quiet up here. No screeching tires or squealing metal.

Oh, god. If Rey hadn't been with me, I'd be dead. She buried her face in her hands.

A touch on her shoulder brought her out of her post-adrenaline shakes. "Aisha, Harri wants to speak with you."

Her hand still trembled as she took the little, cheap phone from Rey. "Hey, girl."

"Are you okay?" Harri's worry carried over the line.

"Define 'okay.'" Aisha gave a weak laugh. "I'm intact. Rey had to do some fancy flying, and my toes are freezing."

He dropped to his knees in front of her. The warmth of his skin on hers as he checked for frostbite felt better than she'd ever admit to Harri.

"We had our own problems tonight."

Acid swished in Aisha's stomach while Harri told of her interrupted date. But the fight at Nolan's gave Aisha something to focus on besides Rey's hands massaging her feet.

"Was the attack focused on you or Tim?"

"Both. We're someplace safe, and Eddie got Arthur and Patty out of my place." She hesitated. "Don't go home tonight, Aisha."

"We won't," she promised. "We'll regroup in the morning. We all need to get some rest in order to think straight." She laughed. "The worst thing out of all of this is my cigarettes went into the lake with my car."

Harri chuckled. "Good. Keep your head down. I'll call you after I talk to Eddie in the morning."

Aisha clicked off Rey's phone and handed it back to him.

His golden eyes reflected the bank's sign. "You really shouldn't smoke. It's not good for you."

"I don't need a lecture right now from the super boy scout," she snapped. At his hooded gaze, guilt rushed in. "Sorry, I don't know what to do right now. I can't get us a hotel room because my purse is with our dinner and my Beemer at the bottom of Del Oro. Everyone I trust in this city is on the run, too."

"We can't put Miguel or Marta or any of their children in danger either." His jaw muscle twitched as he considered their options. "Do you trust me?"

She nodded.

He stood and scooped her up in his arms. "I can't provide any food, but there's one place we can stay Corvus hasn't found yet."

———— •◆• ————

"It's okay to open your eyes," Rey said.

Aisha did, but there was nothing around them but shadows. "Where are we?"

"My place." Rey set her on her feet.

She still wobbled a bit. The second flight wasn't as bad as the first, but he did a lot of zigzagging to avoid anyone seeing them.

"Let me wind my light—"

"No!" she said more sharply than she intended. "I don't—" She sucked in a deep breath, wishing desperately for a cigarette. "They've seen you and me at the Lechuza Building. We can't take the chance they're patrolling this area."

The largest shadow stayed close to her. "You sure there isn't someplace else you can go? These men are after me—"

"Honey, stop. Just stop with the self-recriminations." She reached out, and warm, solid muscle met her palm. "They weren't only after you. They've already framed Tim and killed his family. They tried to frame both Harri and Arthur. Therefore, I'm as much a problem to them whether you're involved or not."

Rey's chest vibrated under her palm with his laugh. "That's the first time you haven't referred to Tim by just his last name."

"Yeah, I guess it is." She sagged, and Rey's hand covered hers. "This whole alleged conspiracy sounds like something out of those stupid comic books. I guess I looked at the whole industry as nothing more than glorified cosplay."

"Cosplay?"

Damn. In some ways, he seemed wiser beyond his years, then he would say something incredibly naïve like that. "People who dress up like their favorite heroes and villains."

More of Rey's deep laughter. "I always thought the real heroes looked rather ridiculous." His laughter died abruptly. "I'm going to have to wear one of those stupid costumes, won't I?"

"Yep." Aisha giggled. "In fact, I have an appointment set up with a designer for you on Monday morning, but now—" She shivered at the memory of those men shooting at them on the causeway.

"Let's get through tonight and tomorrow first." Rey pulled her close.

She shouldn't be enjoying this, but his hug felt pretty damn good.

"You take my bed—"

"No, I—"

"It's okay." He stroked her back. "I'll be right here in the room."

"It's not that." She swallowed hard. "I don't want you to let go of me." She felt more than heard the catch of his breath. "I'm sorry. This isn't helping my big, tough lawyer image, is it?"

"I-it's not that." One heartbeat passed. Five. Fifteen. "I like you more than a super should like his attorney, and I don't want you thinking I'm trying to take advantage of you."

"And here, I was afraid you'd think the same about me," she whispered. She froze in place. Not from the shock or the flying, but afraid to break this . . . thing . . . between them.

Finally, Rey said, "Let's go to bed."

He led her to the dim outline by the rear wall, and lifted the blankets. She climbed between the sheets softened from years of use. He slid in after her and curled around her body. Neither of them were small people, but the full-size bed didn't seem half as crowded as her old king-size bed with Cal.

Despite the emotional and physical aftermath of the attack, despite the fact Rey could kill her with the flick of a finger, Aisha felt safer laying on this bed with Rey in the abandoned hotel in the crappiest part of town than she had in a very long time.

—⋅●⋅—

The ringing of a phone jerked Harri awake. She blearily looked around her.

She was in one of the spa rooms of Jeremy's salon, sprawled out on one of the relaxation recliners. A throw covered her, and she pushed it to the side. The ringing stopped with a beep.

Tim lay on a nearby massage table, snoring softly. Jeremy must have gone upstairs and to bed.

The phone started ringing again, and she realized the sound was coming from Tim's pants. Reaching in his pocket to answer was probably not a good idea. Coffee first sounded much better, maybe after a little more shut-eye.

Bang!

Harri sat up at the noise from the main section of the salon. It was followed by the low hum of male voices. Tim snorted and shifted, but settled back into sleep. She slipped on her shoes, crept to the door, and eased it open enough to peek through the crack.

The only person within her line of sight was Jeremy's assistant manager and boyfriend, Leonardo. He caught sight of her and flicked his fingers in her direction "Zzz. Zzz. Zzz."

She took the hint and closed the door. A few seconds later, Leonardo came in with a drink tray and steaming cups from the café down the street and a bag that smelled of bacon.

"How are you feeling, Harri?" He set down the bag and handed her one of the coffees before he peered at her face.

"I've had better dates," she remarked before she took a sip. Black with a splash of cream. She couldn't fault the men's hospitality.

"I'll let you in on one of Gingersnap's secrets." Leonardo pulled the other cup from the tray, and tossed the cardboard aside. It landed on a pile of towels He lifted Tim's head and waved the steam vent under the inventor's nose. "Rise and shine, Timmy."

Tim bolted upright. Leonardo jerked the cup away just in time to keep the inventor from hitting and spilling it.

"Works better than smelling salts every time." Leonardo flipped back his blue-streaked black hair and winked at Harri.

"Gimme," Tim demanded.

Leonardo handed him the coffee, then reached into his pants pocket and pulled out a key chain anchored by a bright blue rabbit's foot. "Matching VW behind the building for your use. Jeremy already hid Gingersnap's car at another queen's house. You're driving until the Vicodin's out of his system."

Harri gratefully accepted the keys, but her stomach lurched as last night's events poured back into her brain. "We don't have anywhere to go."

Leonardo pulled a folded slip of paper out of his other pocket. "Directions."

"Where?" She frowned at the barely legible scrawl on the page.

"Harri, honey, my job is to run this place." He waved his hand. "I don't ask, and Jaye doesn't tell. It's safer for all of us that way." He pulled her into an abrupt hug. "I am sorry he and Gingersnap pulled you into their shit."

She patted his back. "No, I'm sorry. I think I may have dragged them into my problem."

Leonardo leaned back and eyed her. "Then I'm trusting you to get them out."

Harri nodded. If she said anything, she'd start crying from the stress. And the last thing she wanted or needed was to end up a weeping damsel-in-distress in front of the Ghost Owl.

Leonardo squeezed her again and released her.

The muffled sound of a phone broke up Harri's maudlin mood.

"Gingersnap, your pants are calling you," Leonardo said in a sing-song voice.

Tim scowled at the hair dresser as he pulled out his phone. "Yeah." His scowl turned to a worried expression, and he glanced at Harri. "It's your ex. Says he needs to talk to you."

Damn. It'd been two years since their divorce, and she'd spoken more to Eddie in the last week than she had in the last month of their marriage. She took the phone from Tim.

"It's me."

"Harri, I'm sorry for doing this. I tried your phone, but you didn't answer. Have you seen the news this morning?" Eddie sounded awful. Like he had when a buddy had been killed in the line of duty.

Oh, God! Harri sat on the recliner she'd slept in. "Who—" She swallowed the huge lump threatening to choke her. "Who did we lose?"

"I don't know if we did yet." Car noises, metal grinding, and men shouting in the background nearly drowned out his voice. "Witnesses say Aisha's car flipped over the side of the causeway last night. I'm with the retrieval team recovering it out of the lake. The divers haven't found any bodies."

Harri bit her lip. Aisha and Rey were safe. At least, they were last night. But she couldn't be sure Eddie's phone wasn't bugged, too.

She needed to say something though. "Are you sure it was Aisha's BMW?"

"Yeah, the plates match," Eddie said. A car door slammed, and the background sounds were muffled. "Arthur said she was with your assistant last night. Have you heard from either of them?"

"No." Her chest hurt so bad. Despite all their problems, she'd never out and out lied to Eddie. What the hell had she been thinking when she took Rey to Aisha?

"Do you have your assistant's number?"

"Y-y-yes."

"Can I please have it, Harri? Your staff wouldn't let me have it without your approval, and the dive team found Aisha's phone in her purse." Eddie wasn't getting mad. In fact, he was being incredibly patient. Like he would with a crime victim.

Or he knew someone was listening in. He was being too careful about not saying Rey, Patty or Arthur's names.

If things had gotten bad after she talked to Aisha last night, if Corvus was hunting them, she and Rey would have hidden somewhere safe. The only question was where.

"Eddie, was a black Suburban chasing them?"

His breath whistled through the signal. "Yeah, and witnesses reported shots fired from it." A pause, then he added, "Your assistant is like your new boyfriend, isn't he?"

"Let me make a couple of phone calls—"

"Harri, I can't help you if you don't tell me what the fuck is going on," he growled.

"I'll tell you everything, but if they were being chased, my assistant may have ditched their phone as a precaution." How far did she go in this conversation? Would Eddie even trust her?

She glanced at Tim, and he nodded. "I know you don't believe in Bigfoot, but do you believe in Jatz'om Kuh?"

Another long pause. She was half-afraid he'd hang up, but he said, "Fine. We'll do it your way."

"Thank you," she murmured. "Keep the kids safe. I'll talk to you soon." She ended the call and handed the phone back to Tim.

"Now what?" he asked.

She held up the car keys and jingled them. "We follow Lady Jaye's trail of breadcrumbs, Gingersnap."

<h1 style="text-align:center">CHAPTER 20</h1>

A ringing phone pulled Aisha out of a very pleasant dream. She cuddled in bed with Rey. Except a very hard chest was under her arm.

Reality jerked her upright.

Rey.

The people shooting at them last night.

Her Baby plunging into the lake.

Rey pulled his phone out of his pocket. "Hello?" He looked at Aisha and mouthed, "Miguel." He listened a bit more. "Are you sure it's okay with her?" Another pause. "All right."

He thumbed the button to end the call. "Miguel's got an exit plan to get us out of the Canyon Block." He shook his head. "I feel like I'm in a spy movie."

Aisha stared at her bare feet. "I hope it doesn't involve a lot of walking."

"Some, but we'll take care of it." Rey grinned at her. "Don't worry. I'll carry you for now." He stood and rifled through the worn clothing in the clothes basket at the foot of the bed. "I'm just glad I left a few things here."

She turned away as he changed. Despite their admissions last night, she didn't feel right about watching him. Instead, she focused on his book collection. Harri was right. It was enormous.

"Ready." Faded, torn jeans covered his lower half. Equally worn t-shirt and hoodie covered his torso. Not much they could do about his brand new athletic shoes.

Once again, he scooped her into his arms. He floated gently down to the first floor and headed down a tunnel from the quasi-abandoned hotel to the Canyon Building. From there, he floated down an elevator shaft.

"This is a little better than last night's evasive maneuvers," she whispered. Despite her lowered volume, her voice still echoed up the shaft.

"Sorry. I didn't mean to scare you."

"You weren't the one scaring me, honey," she said dryly.

From the deep set dark eyes and high cheekbones, the young man waiting for them with a flashlight by the elevator doors at the bottom was one of Miguel's sons. He carried a bundle of cloth and a worn pair of athletic shoes.

"Hey, Dom." Rey set Aisha on the dusty floor before he clasped the other man's hand and shoulder-bumped him.

"Dude, I swear you get into the weirdest trouble." Dom nodded to her. "These are for you, Ms. Franklin. Don't take too long."

She accepted the bundle. Both men deliberately turned away so she could change.

Dom switched to Spanish. "Here's some money for the bus. Julio will take you in his truck to the bus stop on Washington. Take the Number 5 to Downtown, then take the Express to the Northside Mall. Go to Victoria's Secret. Dad said a friend of hers will meet you outside the back door."

"Who?" She asked in the same language.

Both men jerked and looked at her. She tugged on the last shoe, wiggled her toes, and said in English, "Don't make assumptions about *gringas*." She grinned. "Who's meeting us at the mall?"

Dom shrugged. "Dad didn't tell me. Just said you'd know them. He's not happy about me being this involved. The men that have been following Rey and Ms. Winters are following him now." He waved. "This way."

She and Rey followed him through a maze of tunnels. They were the same concrete and ugly yellow brick as the ones between the old and new Owl's Nests, but dust, cobwebs, and animal droppings were everywhere. The last tunnel ended with steel rungs embedded in the wall.

Dom led the way. When he reached the door set in the ceiling, he knocked a specific pattern. The door rose up, and he climbed out.

Aisha blinked her eyes at the brightness. They were in a storeroom. Rey followed her, and a woman lowered the door and screwed the seals back into place. When the woman straightened, Aisha recognized her as the proprietress of the bodega.

She held out her to hand. "Celia Benevides. Welcome to the neighborhood, Ms. Franklin."

Aisha laughed and shook the woman's hand. "Thanks." She tugged at the too large waistband of her borrowed jeans. "Are you responsible for clothing me?"

Celia shook her head.

"Those are my brother Emilio's." Dom laughed. "Dad and I figured he wouldn't mind."

Rey groaned. "What did he do this time?"

"Came home late singing *West Side Story* songs at the top of his lungs." Dom shook his head. "Dad's paranoid the idiot's going to knock up his girlfriend."

"And as much as Ms. Franklin would love to hear our neighborhood foibles," Celia interjected. "Julio's waiting in the back, and we don't need the assholes after Rey to get suspicious."

She beckoned Aisha and Rey to follow her. Past the tiny office, Celia opened and peeked outside before she waved. "Hurry."

A forest green garbage truck sat in the alley. The passenger door was already open. "The driver waved frantically. "C'mon."

Rey lifted Aisha into the truck.

"Stay down." The driver pointed at the blanket on the floor.

Aisha curled up on it as tight as she could manage. Rey squeezed in beside her. The situation made his bed last night feel pretty damn roomy.

"Clear?" Dom called out.

"Clear," Rey replied. The door slammed shut and Julio shifted the truck into gear.

"Sorry, but this may take a little while and it's uncomfortable as hell." Julio didn't look down as he spoke. "Miguel said it was imperative we stick to our regular routine."

"De nada," Aisha said. "We really appreciate your help."

Julio's mouth twisted into a sour grimace. "There's been a big debate about you and Ms. Winters moving into the Lechuza Building. Some of us think you're trying to get a jump on the gentrification for this neighborhood."

She laughed. "No, we were just trying to find some office space we could actually afford. Contrary to popular belief, neither of us are rolling in dough."

"But she's a Winters," Julio protested.

"And she has even less money than any of the Canyons."

Julio roared with laughter. "Welcome to the neighborhood, Ms. Franklin."

"It's Aisha."

"Aisha." He nodded, then the truck ground to a halt. "How much do you and Ms. Winters know about city workings?" He pulled a couple of knobs.

She had to wait until the grinding gears and the metallic banging stopped before she could even hear herself. "Harri knows quite a bit. She used to be a city attorney."

Julio looked down at her, his eyes narrowed. "So she's one of the assholes messing around with the abandoned buildings and not fixing the enormous potholes?"

The truck lurched into motion again. Rey cushioned Aisha's head with his arm as best he could.

"Actually, just the opposite. It's one of the real reasons she was fired," Aisha said.

Julio's expression turned contemplative. "The idiot news guy with the bad rug on Channel 12 said she was helping a supervillain. Professor Snake or something like that."

"Oh, he did, did he? When was this?"

"Thursday or Friday night." Julio shrugged. "No, Friday night because my wife ordered pizza."

Anger curled through Aisha. In other words, two days after she'd cleared Arthur. That wasn't the only strange thing going on. "Julio, why are you collecting garbage on a Sunday?"

"We're behind schedule for this end of downtown between the fire at City Hall and some lady who committed suicide on the causeway." Julio scowled. "Boss said if my team didn't complete our route today, we'd be fired. Not even getting overtime for this."

"What's the union say about this?"

Julio's expression was a pretty good imitation of her niece Jada's preteen disgust.

Aisha shook her head. "I'll talk to Harri. See what we can do to help you."

"I think you need to look out for your own skin right now, Ms.—" His mouth quirked. "Sorry, Aisha."

The garbage truck made three more stops before Julio said, "I think it's safe for you two to get off the floor. No black SUVs around, and the bus stop is coming up."

The truck ground to a halt right as Aisha poked her head over the dashboard.

"Thanks, man," Rey said.

"Yes, thank you, Julio," Aisha added.

"Go on. Get out. The bus is coming." Julio made shooing motions.

Rey pulled on the door lever and jumped out before he lifted Aisha from the cab. Julio gunned the garbage trucks engine, and it jerked into motion with a noxious cloud of exhaust trailing behind it. They jogged the few yards to the tiny bus stop shelter. No one else was there this time of day on a Sunday. Everyone already awake was at church services.

The two bus rides were uneventful. Unfortunately, it gave Aisha plenty of time to work up a head of steam about the loss of her car and the crazy path she was now on.

"You okay?" Rey whispered. The express bus out to the mall was fairly full, folks headed to work from some of the uniforms since the shopping center opened at noon.

"No," she whispered back. "I don't know where we're going or who we're meeting."

"Trust Miguel."

She looked into Rey's golden eyes. "I have a hard enough time trusting the people I know."

"You trusted me last night." His earnest expression didn't change. Not even a flicker of an eyelash. "I won't let anything happen to you. I promise."

Like Harri said, too good to be true.

"So you're actually telling me you never thought once about copping a feel while I was sleeping last night?"

His expression turned sheepish, and he sighed. "I thought about it. Despite everything, I am human. But I wouldn't betray yours or Harri's trust in me. Just like I wouldn't betray Miguel's."

Bemusement filled her, and she shook her head. "You're killing me here, Rey."

"How so?"

"You make it really hard for a woman not to fall for you."

"Then I'll let you in on a secret." He leaned even closer. His breath caressed her neck. "I'm really a supervillain, and it's part of my evil plan to make you fall in love with me."

She couldn't help laughing. "You are terrible."

He sat up straight and grinned. "Then it's working."

We don't sleep with clients. Despite Harri's words ringing through Aisha's head, she had technically slept with Rey last night though nothing had happened. Trouble was she'd had the same thoughts about him.

The express bus pulled in front of Northside Mall, and passengers shuffled out and toward the main entrance. Aisha looked around as they tried to blend with the crowd filtering into the shopping center. Plenty of SUVs, even a few black ones, were scattered through the parking lot, but none were shiny and new, much less had the extra heavy UV coating.

Aisha grabbed Rey's hand and threaded her fingers between his. Thankfully, he didn't protest. They looked like any other couple strolling through the mall.

She had to drag him past the food court since they had to spend the money Dom gave them on bus fare. Her own stomach grumbled since it had been nearly twenty-four hours since the last time she'd eaten, which had been the blasted lobster salad at Whitechapel.

A sales girl dressed a mannequin when they reached the lingerie store. She obviously recognized Rey because she rushed to the door. When she unlocked it, another pair of shoppers tried to force their way in. The sales girl body-checked them and waved Aisha and Rey forward.

"Why are you letting them in?" one of the women complained. She had to be thirty years older than Aisha.

The sales girl smiled sweetly. "When you have a multi-platinum rap album, and my manager approves you, then you can get in early."

After she locked the door, she gestured for them to follow her.

Rey smiled and shook his head as they headed for the back of the store, and out of sight of the still fuming older lady. "Really, Paloma? A rap star?"

"You've never had to help that woman fit a thong." Paloma smiled at Aisha. "Hi, Ms. Franklin. My mom's Marta. I hear you've been frequenting the family restaurant lately."

No wonder Miguel didn't want to say who was doing what. A twinge of guilt jerked Aisha's conscience.

"Is this going to get you in trouble with your boss?" she asked.

"I *am* the manager," Paloma said with a wink. She led them through the store room and out the back door. "Your ride is behind the dumpster." She pointed to her right. "And, Rey?" She waggled her index finger. "Ms. Franklin isn't invulnerable. Remember that before you pull any stupid stunts."

"Yes, ma'am." He gave her an impish grin.

After the door slammed shut, Aisha looked up at him. "Should I ask?"

Dark pink flushed his face. "I accidentally broke her wrist when some idiot from her school played a prank on her."

Aisha chuckled. "I was wondering when the skeletons would come out of your closet."

He scowled at her as they headed toward the dumpster. "I thought I was saving her."

"And impressing her?" she teased.

"Maybe I have a thing for older women," he shot back.

She shivered under his intense gaze. Harri's warning echoed dimly in the back of her mind. Sure, someone had tried to kill her last night, and he saved her. Would she be as attracted to him if he was the new intern at her accountant's office?

"'Bout time you two showed up," a familiar voice said.

But Rey had already seen the black SUV. Before Aisha could say anything, he shoved her behind the dumpster and charged Harri's ex-husband.

CHAPTER 21

Aisha bolted toward the men. "Rey! No!"

Her super held Eddie by the throat. The FBI agent's loafers kicked a good foot off the ground. Rey's fist halted in mid-swing.

"Put him down. That's Harri's ex-husband."

"Then maybe I should punch him for leaving her." Rey scowled at Eddie, but he did lower and release the agent.

"Maybe I should arrest you for assaulting a Federal officer." Eddie rubbed his neck and scowled right back.

"I won't say anything if you decide to shoot Harri." Aisha worked hard to suppress her grin. "She should have told you not to bring an agency-issued vehicle like the ones that have been following us."

Eddie pulled his keys from the pocket of his olive chinos. "Actually, she did. It seemed logical they wouldn't be looking for you two in one of their own vehicles."

"One of their own?"

"The plates." He gestured at the front of the SUV. "That Miguel of yours would make a hell of an operative. He and his kids have memorized the plates of the vehicles that have been cruising the Northeast Side. One of my people made a matching fake." His gaze swept the little unloading dock. "But let's get out of here before your buddies do show up."

Harri breathed a sigh of relief when Aisha and Rey followed Eddie into the little green room in Jeremy's warehouse. Rey looked longingly at the spread Jeremy had provided for them on the table.

"Go for it, kid." She waved at the subs and side dishes.

With Rey occupied, she turned to Aisha, "What the hell happened last night? Why didn't you call me?"

"Because my phone was at the bottom of Lake Del Oro with my purse,"

Aisha snapped back. "Between people shooting at me and being chased by drones, excuse me for not making you my top priority at the time. And what the hell happened to you? The last time you had a black eye—"

Aisha's face crumpled, and Harri pulled her into a huge hug. "None of us had a good night."

"I'm so sorry. Are you okay? Is Tim okay?"

"Everyone's fine." Harri released Aisha. "Relatively speaking. Any bumps, bruises, gunshot wounds we need to worry about?"

Aisha shook her head. "Rey was incredible." She glanced at Eddie. "Maybe we should talk about this privately."

"You and Harri pulled me into this mess!" Eddie threw his hands up.

"Dammit, Eddie!" Aisha yelled. "You have no idea—"

"Here." Rey handed Aisha a plate piled high. He frowned at Harri. "She's grouchy because neither of us have had anything to eat since lunch yesterday."

Harri laughed. "She's grouchy because she hasn't had a cigarette in the last twenty-four hours." She wrapped a hand around Aisha's elbow and tugged her toward a chair. "Sit down, and tell us what happened."

Aisha still eyed Eddie warily, and realization dawned on Harri.

"He knows about Tim," she said quietly. "My ex-husband is the idiot who trained the Ghost Owl how to fight."

Aisha sank down in the plush chair. "He what?"

"Apparently, Mr. Canyon has a whole cadre of helpers." Harri shot Eddie a dirty look. "None of them have known about each other until now."

Eddie dropped in the chair on the other side of Aisha. "Canyon and Harri have already given me their versions of last night's attempts on their lives. How about you do the same?"

"You make this sound like an official interrogation," Aisha said around a mouthful of turkey sub. Rey set another chair directly across from her.

Harri eyed the two. Something was different. Neither of them had the puppy dog looks of unrequited love. No, this seemed deeper. What the hell had happened last night?

"It's not," Eddie said. "Yet." He looked at Harri.

She shrugged. "You need to tell them."

Eddie's mouth formed a grim line. "The reason the FBI set up a satellite office in Canyon Pointe was to investigate civil rights violations. Pablo Inunza reported some irregularities in sentencing among his fellow judges. When he questioned it, a masked man showed up at his house and threatened his family."

Aisha swallowed her food. "Is that what his warning to the DA was about?"

"Yeah." Eddie leaned back and ran both hands through his hair. "I'm letting you know the next thing because Harri knows, and there's no such thing as secrets between you two and Jeremy. Cal is my inside man at the DA's office."

"What?" Aisha stared at Eddie. "He wouldn't take a chance on a lottery ticket, much less with his career."

"I can't go into the details. Not yet." He gave Aisha a pleading look very similar to the one he'd given Harri this morning.

She almost felt sorry for her ex. "There's more. Miguel's been the only one associated with us who can still function publicly."

Aisha shook her head. "Corvus is watching Miguel now. Dom said his dad wasn't happy about involving him in helping meet up with Eddie. If we're using Jeremy's warehouse—"

"He can't do much more for us." Harri slumped in her chair. She hadn't realized how much hope she had in Miguel. "His salon was hit last night, Eddie got Arthur and Patty to a FBI safehouse before they ransacked my place, and an assassination team came after me and Tim at Nolan's."

Aisha stared, her hunger obviously forgotten. "Nolan's? As in the restaurant? That's way too public."

"Which is why I'm wondering what you girls are doing that's making Corvus so fucking nervous." Eddie's attention shifted between the two of them.

Harri and Aisha looked at Rey.

He shrugged. "Like I told you, they've been after me long before I met you."

Harri rubbed her forehead. "This has to be related to Seismic Shift somehow. The whole point of the City Hall fire was to cover up my death." Her hand dropped to her lap. "Oh, god. What if the collapse of the Lake County Retirement Home wasn't an accident? There was one death."

"But under the Superhero Act . . ." Horror covered Aisha's face as the same logical conclusion hit her the way it had Harri. "The National Superhero Bureau accidentally gave you proof of a criminal act which nullifies Shift's protections when you subpoenaed his records." Aisha's eyes narrowed. "And from our little golf outing, Shift is in deep with the local politicians."

"Which means your situation is tied into my case," Eddie added. "Please tell me the evidence you have didn't burn up in the City Hall fire."

"The discovery copies the NSB sent us did." Harri grinned. "But my super-efficient secretary already scanned everything and our new IT guy downloaded the information." Her grin fell. "It took me weeks to go through everything the first time."

Eddie rubbed his chin. "So how do we buy you that time?"

"Move up my debut," Rey said.

They all turned and stared at him.

"No." Harri shook her head. "That will put you in their crosshairs."

The kid shrugged. "I'm already in their crosshairs, but if they're too busy paying attention to me, they won't be harassing you."

"He's got a point," Eddie admitted.

"You're not helping," Harri snapped. "He's not one of your informants you can dangle—"

"Rey's right," Aisha said.

Et tu, Brutus? She expected this kind of shit out of Eddie. But Aisha?

"If I can borrow Patty for a couple of days, Jeremy and I could pull this off. He's already working on some uniform concepts." Aisha turned to Eddie. "Especially if you have a friend or two at the NSB who could speed through Rey's application?"

Eddie nodded. "I know someone who can as long as you don't mind if I tell her why."

"Are you going to tell her about Corvus?" Harri exclaimed. "Because that will put your contact in danger, too!"

"What about Miguel?" Worry flickered in Rey's eyes. "We can't leave him and his family on the Canyon Block, unprotected."

"All right," Harri said. "If we're going to do this, we're going to do it all the way. Miguel's going to finish the build-out for our offices. With Tim's help, we'll have security out the wazoo." She jabbed a finger at Rey. "When you're not at Aisha's events, you'll be at the Lechuza Building, helping Miguel."

She turned to Aisha. "That moves up our timetable for selling both our places."

"I know." She sighed. "That also means we're going to have to make things look normal and actually go back to staying in our homes until Miguel can get the lofts livable. Otherwise. Corvus will tear Canyon Pointe apart, looking for us."

"I can set up a protection detail—" Eddie started.

"No," Harri and Aisha said at the same time.

"No offense," Harri began. "You feds are too obvious, and I put more trust in Tim's gadgets and Rey's strength."

"If we were still married, I would be offended." Eddie rose. "I've got a couple of people who can help with the discovery review—"

Harri held up a hand. "Do they have experience dealing with supers?"

"No, but—"

She shook her head firmly. "Then no. Patty and Arthur will be covered under the firm's malpractice policy. Your people won't." In a gentler voice, she said, "Go home to your wife and kid, Eddie. Keep digging from your end. We'll call you once we know something from ours."

———•———

Two hours later, Aisha sat down wearily next to Harri at the folding table Jeremy had set up for her and Arthur to work. Aisha passed a can of diet soda to her partner and popped the tab on hers. Her fingers tapped the folder she'd brought with the drinks. She had the we-may-have-a-problem look on her face.

Regardless of whatever trouble had occurred, Harri was glad of the interruption. She couldn't read anymore financial statements or she'd explode. Rolling her head relieved some of the tension in her neck.

"Arthur, you want to go grab us some sandwiches," Harri said.

He looked up from his laptop and blinked. The former supervillain had saved the files regarding Seismic Shift, grabbed everyone's laptops, and wiped her home computer after Tim warned her ex to get everyone out of her house. Despite Eddie's bitching, Arthur Drallhickey had saved their butts.

"Patty and Rey are getting lunch in the green room, too," Aisha added.

Arthur jumped up from his chair. "I'll be right back."

Once Arthur was out of the room, Harri chuckled softly. "That was evil."

"He's not a bad guy, and you know it." Aisha's dark complexion didn't hide the circles under her eyes. How much sleep had she and Rey gotten last night? "Any luck." She inclined her head toward Harri's screen.

"Not yet." Harri rubbed her temples. "I'd say it's like looking for a needle in a haystack, but if it were a needle, I'd know what we were looking for. With this—" She shook her head.

"Have you been cross-checking any travel expenses with his personal appearances?"

"Yeah." Harri gestured at Arthur's computer. "Our new IT guy has been putting together search algorithms for us. It's still going to take a lot of good old-fashioned work." She took a drink of her own soda before she added, "You were right."

"About?" Aisha's brows drew together.

"Arthur. If it wasn't for him, we'd be royally screwed."

Aisha shrugged. "Enemy of my enemy, and all that."

Harri sat up straight. If she continued to wallow in their problems, she'd be useless. Time to change the subject. "How'd things go with Jeremy?"

"Fine." Aisha took a sip of her soda. "Fine."

Which Harri knew meant not fine at all.

"What happened?"

Aisha refused to meet Harri's eyes. "Jeremy had some mocked-up outfits available. And some sketches."

Uh-oh. "The Lady Jaye has a new sidekick? The Lady Rey?"

Aisha flushed. "No. Nothing like that."

"Can I see the sketches?" Harri reached for the folder.

Aisha held them out of Harri's reach and sighed. "These are Jeremy's preliminary designs, but we may not have the time to refine them if we're pushing for Rey's debut this week."

They must be terrible. Maybe letting Jeremy do this was a bad idea despite both Aisha and Tim's assurances. "Let me see." She held out her hand.

Aisha still kept the folder out of reach. "Just remember you said I bring the expertise to the table."

Damn Aisha and her Amazon height even without her stilettos. Harri clenched her fists. She wasn't embarrassing herself by trying to wrestle for the folder.

"Gimme!"

Aisha handed her the pictures.

Harri flipped open the folder. So that's why Aisha's so embarrassed. Jeremy had taken a photo of Rey and used software to create a series of potential hero costumes. Harri spread the shots out on the table. These outfits left nothing to the imagination.

Nothing.

"Golly gee, Captain Tourniquet," Harri said. "Those are some really tight tights. How's he supposed to sit down? Or breathe for that matter?" She glanced at Aisha. "And God help us all if he gets a boner wearing one of these outfits. He'll break the internet and get all his contracts cancelled. At least for the children's toys."

Aisha held up her hand and looked away. "Don't go there. Just don't go there. I already got enough from Jeremy, thank you."

Harri grimaced and put the last photo down. "We have to go there." *No matter how pissed off you might get. Particularly with you and Rey smoldering for each other.* "This is not an issue we can avoid. They don't wear tights merely for the ease of movement."

She glanced at the photo of Rey in a mainly white outfit. The costume set off his skin nicely, but the formfitting cloth revealed every muscle and curve. It was widely known within the industry that Redwood, despite pretending to be shocked by the claims, made a lot of money licensing the mold for a certain body part to the adult toy industry.

"Aisha, are we doing the right thing here? Are we helping Rey or ruining him?"

To her surprise, Aisha didn't lose her temper or throw her IP experience in Harri's face. She merely shook her head and whispered, "I don't know." She looked up at Harri. "Right now, I want to keep him—all of us—alive."

"You think I don't?"

"Neither of us could have anticipated the shit we're in." Aisha picked up one of the photos. "What about this one? The design's fairly clean. Red and white are on both the U.S. and Mexican flags."

Harri recognized the deliberate change of subject to avoid a fight, but Aisha was right. This whole insanity was beyond anything they were taught in law school. "What are you going to do about his assets?"

"I didn't do anything with his assets last night!" Aisha snapped.

"Whoa!" Harri held up her hands. "I didn't mean you specifically, but could your guilty conscience be any more obvious?"

"He was a perfect gentleman last night." Aisha narrowed her eyes. "And I'm really getting tired of your innuendos regarding my behavior."

Harri looked down at the picture of Rey. Had she been that hard on her best friend? She'd kept most of what she'd been thinking to herself. "I don't want you to make another mistake."

"Like you did by lying to Eddie about what you really wanted in your marriage?"

"What the hell is wrong with you?"

"I'm wearing someone else's clothes, I lost my car and my purse, and I want a shower. And I want it all without you questioning my professional ethics." Aisha glared at her.

Harri stared down at the clothes Jeremy had loaned her. She swam in the t-shirt and the knit athletic shorts fell past her knees. "I'm sorry. We've both had really bad nights. Can we call a truce?"

"All right."

"What about a name? We haven't had a chance to brainstorm."

Aisha shrugged. "Something simple, something familiar."

Harri snorted. "You won't have any problem there. They're all familiar now. Between the comic books and the actual superheroes, we'll be lucky if he doesn't get sued for trademark infringement."

"You'd be surprised how often you can work out a deal on those sorts of things. Real life supers are great marketing for the comics. If we come up with something that's been taken, we'll pitch the copyright holder on drawing a new line featuring Rey."

"My client as a comic book character." Harri scowled. "This is why I have issues with this whole racket. It's not about doing the right thing any more. It's all about sales figures!"

"I'm not the one who promised to make him rich." Aisha sat back in her chair and crossed her arms. Her scowl was back. "How do you think that happens, Harri? These folks may be heroes, but they're also big entertainment. Without the media, they're just glorified cops."

"Here's a name—Captain Media Whore."

"Very funny." Aisha relaxed a hair. "Rey's partial to Captain—"

"No!" Harri groaned. "Please, no, not Captain anything. I hate Captain.

It's so overused. And why aren't they ever promoted? Captain America is like a hundred years old. Shouldn't he at least be Colonel America by now?"

Aisha gave her a look. "He's fictional. If he was real, he'd be forcibly retired and living on Social Security."

Harri laughed. "That because there's no justice in this world.

"Why not Captain Justice?" Aisha said. "It's simple, easy to pronounce, and generic. Exactly what Rey needs to make his splash."

Harri banged her head a few times on the table. "God, please, no. That is so lame. Why not Captain Meso-America? At least it's accurate."

"So, you prefer racially insensitive to lame?" Aisha said.

"I liked 'Captain Justice' the first time Aisha mentioned it." Rey walked into the room with plates piled high with food. He was followed by Jeremy, Arthur, and Patty equally loaded. Tim on crutches brought up the rear.

"Besides," Rey said as he set the plates on the table. "If someone as lilywhite as Tim can be Jatz'om Kuh—"

"Hey!" Tim mock-glared at Rey. "If you're going to insult me, the proper term is 'ginger'."

"Actually, 'ginger' is more commonly used in the United Kingdom," Arthur corrected.

Jeremy passed around bottles of water. "Don't let Harri's white guilt influence you, Rey. It's a leftover side effect of Grandma Harri telling our girl she needs to take care of the poor and misfortunate."

"And, Rey, I like 'Captain Justice', too," Patty said as she handed out napkins.

"Hey!" Harri protested. "You're my assistant. You're supposed to be on my side."

"No," Patty said with a cross expression. "I was the assistant of city attorney Harri Winters until I was fired after she left that position. Nor has an offer been tended for me to work for the Law Office of Winters & Franklin. What I am is your client, except I'm doing all the work of representing myself in my wrongful termination."

Aisha cocked her head. "I thought you talked to her about working for us."

"Like you talked to me before hiring Arthur? A supervillain, I might add." Harri jabbed a finger in the direction of the former Professor Venom.

Then felt immediately guilty at the shamed expression on his face.

"I get shot at last night, but I'm overreacting?" Aisha stared at Harri with a mild expression on her face, which meant a bigger explosion of temper was about to go off.

Jeremy must have seen the same thing. "Stop it! Both of you!" He propped his hands on his hips. "Harri, you apologize to Arthur right this minute."

She turned to the former supervillain. "I'm sorry, Arthur."

"Now quit trying to take over everything," Jeremy continued.

"Yeah, because this is Jeremy's queendom," Tim added with a grin.

"Shut your mouth!" Jeremy waggled an index finger at Tim. "I do not need help from a cis-gendered hetero-male vigilante who had no fashion sense before he met me. We need to be working together, not ripping each other apart." He said the last with a pointed look at Harri.

"Fine." She raised her hands in surrender.

After a long moment of silence, Rey asked, "When does Captain Justice make his debut?"

"Have you narrowed down a selection yet?" Jeremy said.

"I'll leave that to my attorney." Rey rested a hand on Aisha's shoulder.

His gesture hit Harri in the gut. Professional jealousy warred with common sense. She knew how to ferret out information. Aisha knew how to put on a show that would result in revenue.

"Harri and I were leaning towards the red and white." Aisha picked up that picture with a glance at Harri.

She nodded. The fact Aisha included her meant she'd been forgiven, but this fight wasn't like either of them. Would their partnership work in the long run? Like when people weren't trying to kill them both?

"But no white in the crotch area, Jeremy," Aisha continued. "Lady Jaye may love the look, but it won't play well with Middle America."

Jeremy nodded. "The pattern's already in my computer. I need to enter Rey's measurements. Plus, I've got the material in stock." He sighed. "I suppose you want the Burt Ward treatment, too."

From the shift of Aisha's eyes, she'd be glowing red if her skin were lighter. "We have to."

"Burt Ward treatment?" Harri asked.

Tim laughed. "You remember the old Adam West Batman series?"

"I know of it." Harri's attention flicked to the others. Rey and Patty were curious, too. Aisha and Arthur looked as embarrassed as hell. Jeremy had the same shit-ass grin as Tim.

"Burt Ward played Robin the Boy Wonder, Batman's sidekick," Tim continued. "He is rather well-endowed, so between the soundstage lighting and his green costume shorts, nothing was left to the imagination."

Now, Rey's face turned dark pink with horrified fascination. "What did they do to him?"

"Strategic padding in the costume, sweetheart." Jeremy patted Rey's arm. "Aisha wants to make sure the public's focusing on the guns up here, not the one below."

Harri couldn't help it. She peeked. And she noticed Patty doing the same.

"How soon can you have it ready?" Aisha asked.

"That depends on what our next step is." Jeremy raked his hands through his hair. "Timmy and I have been talking. As much as I love having guests, this place wasn't designed as a fortress."

"Neither are any of our places," Harri protested.

"Which brings me to simply going home and continuing your lives," Tim said quietly. "Stay in public as much as possible."

Harri stared at him. "That's setting us up at targets while you're perfectly safe in your little nest."

"Well, you were planning to build out the Lechuza Building." Tim played with a carrot stick like he planned to stab someone with it. "Do you want the lofts done first?"

"No," Aisha stated firmly. She turned to Harri. "Let's make a statement as the firm that represents Canyon Pointe's newest superhero. The more the public sees us—" Her gesture included everyone at the table. "—the less likely Corvus can cover this up like they did with Tim twenty years ago."

She made sense. Harri sighed and nodded. "All right. The office is first." She turned to Patty. "Ms. Ames, would you care to join the fledgling Law Office of Winters & Franklin, where the possibility of death is way higher than anyone sane should accept, but we run the full gamut of superheroes, supervillains, and vigilantes as clientele?"

"And the best drag queen in the city!" Jeremy snapped his fingers for emphasis.

Patty raised her index finger. "Point of order—former supervillain." She winked at Arthur.

"All right." Harri couldn't help smiling. "Former supervillain and head of our IT department."

Patty smiled. "I accept your offer, Ms. Winters."

"Now, back to Aisha's question." Harri eyed Jeremy at the other end of the table. "How soon can you have Rey's suit ready?"

"How's Wednesday sound, Ms. Winters?"

After lunch, Harri was back to searching through records while Arthur worked quietly across the table from her.

He cleared his throat. "Ms. Winters?"

She rolled her eyes. "It's Harri, Arthur."

He shrugged. "Old habits, which is why you don't trust me."

She saved the notes she'd made and looked up at him. "You're right. There's some history between us."

"I know, but I think we can both agree we care about the safety of Patty and her baby."

His earnest expression reminded her too much of Rey's. "Where are you going with this, Arthur?"

"I don't think she should be staying at your townhouse."

"Because I'm obviously Corvus's primary target?"

He sighed. "Unfortunately, yes."

"I thought you were afraid to go back to your place."

"My apartment is even more poorly defensible than your townhome." He leaned his elbow on the table and propped his cheek on his fist. "I was thinking her apartment. With some help from Mr. Canyon, I could set up a security system than would more than adequately protect her."

"Are you going to stay with her?"

Arthur's cheeks flushed. "I wouldn't want to impinge on Patty's privacy."

"Actually, it would be a good idea if you stayed with her." Even as Harri said it, she realized she meant it. "And speaking of places to live, would you like an apartment in the Lechuza Building as part of your compensation?"

He blinked. "Do you mean that?"

"Yeah, it would be loads better than your—" She stopped herself from saying, "flea-infested rat trap." His address was a matter of public record while he was on probation, and it really was crappy, but all he could afford. She'd made a point of checking his location and consulting with his probation officer over the last year until work piled up over the spring. With the way Arthur had stepped up to help over the last week of total chaos, maybe she could petition Judge Inunza to expunge Arthur's conviction. "It may be one of the few perks I can throw you for a while."

A weak smile appeared on his face. "Assuming Corvus doesn't kill us all, you mean."

"Yeah, there's that."

A heavy weight settled in her head. Could she keep everyone alive long enough to find the evidence that would put Seismic Shift and Corvus away for good?

CHAPTER 22

"I don't like this plan," Harri repeated for the umpteenth time from the back seat of Eddie's SUV. The fact that Eddie had packed a bug-out bag for her before he evacuated Patty and Arthur from her house bothered her more than she cared to admit. It was too intimate.

Almost as intimate as staying with someone she was attracted to and barely knew.

"Wow. Really?" Eddie shot a glance at her in the rearview mirror. "Tim, how about I leave my ex-wife with my current wife, and I sleep on your couch?"

"Stop it, you two," Jeremy snapped. "Or I'll do Corvus a favor and shoot you both."

Harri shifted in her seat to glare at the man next to her. "Aren't you going to say anything?"

Tim's eyes twinkled. "I've been living by myself in a World War II bunker for nearly twenty years. A little company would be nice."

Harri threw her hands in the air. "You're insane!"

The corner of his mouth twitched. "That has been the consensus of everyone in this vehicle at some point over the last twenty years."

She would be in the basement of the Lechuza Building.

Alone.

With the Ghost Owl.

Despite his past, Tim didn't feel like a threat. She had a crash-course reading the subtle cues people gave off as a child living in a chaotic and often dangerous home. Her inner alert system was finely tuned, and Tim Canyon didn't set it off.

That didn't mean he was harmless. She could sense something coiled in him, like an overwound spring. But the weapon powered by that spring was pointed away from her.

For now anyway.

Despite the failure of their marriage, Eddie was looking out for her and her little crew. He vouched for Tim, and he didn't trust many people. Not to mention, Jeremy had her back, always had since middle school. Neither Eddie or Jeremy would steer her wrong on purpose.

"How's it looking around your block?" Eddie said.

Tim pulled out his phone.

Harri could see various street views flash across the screen. "The city doesn't have that many security cameras in the area."

"They don't have any," Tim murmured. "These are all mine. Nothing Corvus-looking in a five block radius."

Eddie grunted. "Between Rey disappearing and Harri pie-ing their operatives, they may have decided to back off for a bit. You sure you can manage with that knee?"

"Don't worry. We won't be taking the stairs." Tim winked at her.

"But the elevator isn't working." Harri cocked her head. "Or was that a lie when we looked at the office space?"

"Miguel didn't lie about that," Tim said. "But he's been insisting I move it to the top of the priority list." He frowned at his injured knee. "I think he won the argument."

Five minutes later, Eddie braked in the alley behind the Lechuza Building. The setting sun cloaked the tiny space in shadows. Harri popped her door open and jogged to the back of the SUV to grab her bag while Jeremy helped Tim out of the vehicle.

"Ten seconds, people," Eddie called out.

The back door of the office building swung open to show a grim-faced Miguel. No introductions, just simple nods of acknowledgment between the men while Tim hobbled into the building. She waved to Eddie as he and Jeremy sped off before she followed Tim into the building.

Miguel gave Tim the once over. "And how do you plan to get downstairs? I'm not carrying you. And she definitely can't."

"I could drag him down the steps," Harri offered. "By his feet so the bumps on his head could knock some sense into him."

"I'll use the same method I use every other time I can't manage the stairs," Tim said dryly.

"*Dios,*" Miguel muttered. "This way, Ms. Winters. I'll clean up the bottom of the elevator shaft if he falls." The contractor stalked off with an angry huff.

"Hey, Esperanza! What crawled up your ass?" The spring coiled inside Canyon was obviously starting to slip.

Miguel whirled to face them again. "I had to involve one of my sons today. I told you if that ever happened, I would quit."

Harri looked up at Canyon. His face tightened, but he said nothing. Miguel threw his hands in the air and strode away.

Dammit. Part of their insane plan hinged on Miguel's help. Harri raced after the contractor.

"Miguel! Wait!"

He stopped, but didn't look at her when she puffed to a halt beside him.

"Look…I…get…why you're angry," Harri finished in a rush. Some kind of exercise program was in order if she and Aisha were going to be in this much trouble with their first two cases. Harri gulped more air before she continued. "I'm pissed Tim pulled my ex-husband into this mess. We may not be married anymore, but I don't want his kids to lose their dad because of me. And my assistant's pregnant, too."

Hot liquid burned her eyes. Just the last couple of days catching up with her, right?

Harri blinked a few times. "I need your help. To protect Rey, if nothing else. But I can't do it alone. Please stay until we can put these bastards away, and everyone is safe."

Miguel stared at the floor for a long time. She half-expected him to flip her off and walk out.

"Using Rey is a low blow, Winters," he murmured.

"I wasn't—" She swiped at the one tear that escaped. "He's the closest thing I'm ever going to have to a child of my own. I want to live long enough to make sure these clowns don't get their hands on him, and he has a decent start in life. He's already been dealt a shitty hand. Just like your boys. But if we work together, we can make it better for all the kids."

Miguel glanced back the way they'd come, but Tim was out of sight. "But I don't want him using my sons as cannon fodder for his war against the men who killed his own boy."

"That's not what he wants either," Harri said softly. "If Captain Justice can watch over this area of the city—"

"Captain Justice?" Miguel laughed.

"Believe me, that was not my idea." She shook her head. "Anyway, you were the one who told Aisha the Ghost Owl will be retiring."

Miguel nodded as if coming to a decision. "Fine. I'll do it for Rey's sake." He relaxed a bit. "I put the boys to work this afternoon. They've cleaned out two of the third-floor offices. Your desks will be lumber planks on sawhorses and your chairs milk crates with pillows, but the building's wiring has been kept up to date so you can use your computers and keep your phones charged."

"Thank you." She held out her hand, and Miguel shook it. "We start in the morning."

— ◆ —

Tim on his crutches waited for Miguel and Harri at the bottom of the stairs. The lattice work fixture ended in a relatively small room with a door. A door with no handle. And the room was far too small for a building the size of Lechuza.

"Make sure you show her all the security measures," Miguel said. "You don't want to lose her."

"Because her ex-husband will shoot me?" Tim quipped.

"More likely my power drill will slip," Miguel said with a scowl. With his not-so-subtle threat, he bounded back up the stairs.

"You need to apologize to him," Harri said after the upstairs door slammed shut.

Tim blinked. "I didn't ask him to involve Domingo."

Okay, now she got why Aisha was peeved with her sometimes. "No, you expect everyone to help you without saying 'please' or 'thank you'. And you expect them to be at your beck and call at all hours, or to be in all places at once. Miguel's only human, or did you expect your charm would work on him the same way it worked on his wife?"

"So you're saying I'm a snob?" From Tim's expression, he wasn't sure whether to be offended or amused.

"'Fraid so, Canyon." Harri poked him in the chest. "And take it from a Winters who hit rock bottom before you Canyons did, it's the little people who are going to catch you when you fall."

"Warning noted, Ms. Winters." His amusement won the war. "But before we continue, you need to promise me what you're going to see stays a secret. For everyone's safety."

She laughed. "I knew it. You are growing pot down here. It's for your knees right? Started with personal use then you realized how much money you could make?"

Tim shook his head, still smiling. "I'm not growing pot."

"It's okay if you are. You're my client, so I have to keep your secrets."

He sighed. "I know. But I think I'd want you to see this anyway. I'm tired of keeping secrets."

"But Miguel already showed Aisha and Rey. What's the big deal?"

"They only saw a couple of the work rooms."

Harri took a deep breath and nodded. "Okay. So I'm getting the full Owl's Nest tour?"

"Something like that." He made his way to the door and touched a black panel. With a pneumatic hiss, the door swung open.

Lights flicked on automatically before them, showing a long hallway, much cleaner than the rest of the facility she had seen above. This wasn't a typical basement. It looked more like a bomb shelter. Or a military facility.

She followed him down the hallway. He stopped before a steel door with a numbered keypad and what looked like a camera. "Before we go any further, there's something I want to ask."

"I'm okay with a pot farm, but if it's a meth lab you need to find a new lawyer."

"It's not a meth lab either." He punched a number into the door pad before he leaned toward the camera.

Harri found she enjoyed teasing Tim Canyon a bit too much for just a client. Maybe she needed to listen to the lecture she'd given Aisha about Rey.

"This is a retinal scanner, by the way." A green light flashed on his face. "I'll program it for you once we're inside."

"Great." Wait a minute. She had the Ghost Owl all to herself for the night, and she wasn't taking advantage of the fact. Excitement thrummed in her blood.

Harri took a deep breath, trying to calm down. "When did Eddie start training you?"

"About a month after my acquittal." The door clicked, and Tim yanked on the handle. "He was my contact in the CPPD until he joined the FBI a couple of years ago."

Crap. Eddie disappearing for hours. The refusal to tell her where he was. She'd had a friend in accounting check his timecard, and the hours hadn't been clocked with the department. After everything with her dad, she feared the worst, and her abandonment issues took their toll on her marriage. Their fights about whether to have kids was simply icing on the cake.

She swallowed all the old regrets. "He was so fucked up by what he saw that night at your house, but then he decided you couldn't have done it. I never understood why he changed his mind."

The grim look was back on Tim's face, the one that made him look old. "He caught me one night trying to break into Burgess's condo to look for evidence of the payoff. He was so angry I thought he was going to shoot me dead where I stood, but he gave me a chance to explain. It took a while to convince him, but he'd seen enough bullshit coming out of the D.A.'s office to believe Burgess was dirty."

"And Michaels was Burgess's handpicked successor to run for the office of District Attorney." She rubbed her forehead. That was why Eddie had been so adamant about applying with the FBI. Why hadn't he said something to her years ago about the corruption? Or had he been threatened?

Harri looked up at Tim. "I need a drink. You got a bar in this bat cave of yours?"

Tim snorted. "It's not a cave. And owls are way cooler than bats."

"Whatever. You got any bourbon? Whisky? I'd settle for a joint."

"Yes, on the alcohol only." He gestured with a crutch. "Stick close. I need to disarm some alarms along the way."

"Alarms? You mean the two vault doors back there aren't enough?"

"Nope. Stay behind me."

More lights flickered on as they walked, or in his case, swung on his crutches. "Hang on." Tim stopped about ten feet down the hallway, before it made a sharp turn to the right, and pressed his palm against a glass panel built into the concrete wall. It flashed green after a moment and a small steel panel next to it slid open. Tim leaned close and in a clear voice said, "Timothy Mitchell Canyon."

Harri stared in wonder. The man had more security than Doctor Magma's secret lair. For an instant, she wondered if she were entering the den of a super-villain as Arthur had suggested.

The glass panel flashed green again. "It's coded for my palm print and voice. Come on. It's safe now."

"So, what would happen if somebody came down here and didn't pass the test?"

Tim grimaced, as he led her down another dark hallway, this one shorter than the last. "You don't want to know. It's messy."

"Yikes." Harri said in a soft voice. "And I thought I could fight my way out of here with a can of mace and a few well-aimed kicks."

"Eddie told me about your kicking skill. Testicles, right?"

Harri tried to laugh, but it came out as a strangled squawk. "In your case I'd go for the knees first. Then I'd kick you in the balls."

Tim nodded. "Sound strategy. So, how about dinner?"

"Oh, my god. Buy me a drink first."

"Done." He stopped in front of another steel door. "One last scan. Take my crutches and step back, okay? This one will get confused if you're too close." He stood still, as a beam of blue light swept over him. "Biometrics," he said. "It recognizes my shape. I have to recalibrate it weekly to take into account my hair growth, subtle changes in weight, that sort of stuff. Very hard to fake this one."

"And if somebody doesn't pass?"

He pointed upward. "Electrical field. Stuns the shit out of you—literally—and leaves you incapacitated for hours."

"Like the damn cattle prod the Corvus asshole carried?"

"Yep, now please be quiet." Tim balanced on one foot and tapped the button that looked like a standard doorbell. There was a short hum Harri felt more than heard.

He twisted the latch and waved for his crutches. She handed them over. Lights blinked on inside as she followed him into a rather large workspace with a couple of tables full of what looked like computer parts, tools, and other assorted bits.

"Don't let Arthur see your toys." She whistled. "You may end up with a new roommate."

"Smart one, there," Tim answered. "He's not a lousy villain from lack of talent, that's for sure."

Harri laughed. "He just lacks the megalomaniacal spark the best ones have."

"Home, sweet home." Tim hopped around to face her. "What do you think?"

Harri pivoted to take in everything. The room had none of the gloomy ambience of a cave, or even a basement. It was a workspace. Two large supply cabinets separated the gym area to her right. A couple of punching bags and mats dominated the area. It was rounded off by a treadmill, a bench, and a rack of free weights.

"My living quarters are back here." He led her to a wooden door beside the free weights and opened it. "After you."

Passing through the doorway, Harri found a small cheerful apartment, simply furnished, and well organized. The only problem was no windows. "This looks like an IKEA ad."

"It should. That's where I got everything. Without any natural light, I figured I'd better go for bright and happy. And they're geniuses at small spaces." He gestured at an eye-searingly red sofa. "Have a seat."

Harri sat down, staring around the room. *The Ghost Owl shops at IKEA.* Laughter erupted from her in great whooping gasps until tears ran down her face.

Tim dropped next to her on the couch, close but not touching, until the storm passed. "It's a lot to take in, I guess."

"You think?" Harri stared at him. Wrapping her head around her landlord being the Ghost Owl was easier than the idea of ex-husband training the Ghost Owl "You got any tissues?"

Tim handed her a roll of toilet paper from a bright blue magazine rack beside his end of the couch. "No. Sorry. This is the best I can do at the moment. How do you want your bourbon?"

"You got ice?"

Tim smiled. "That I've got. You want any water with it?"

Harri blew her nose loudly. So much for impressing him with her cool demeanor. "Let me get everything. You need to stay off that knee."

It didn't take a genius to find the ice and glasses. He pointed out the cabinet with the liquor. She found a bottle of decent Kentucky bourbon, and frankly, she was more than a little relieved there were only two bottles in the cupboard, the other being an unopened bottle of scotch. She grabbed the bag of pretzels from the shelf above the liquor and carried everything to the storage trunk that acted as Tim's coffee table.

He grinned. "Pretzels are a good idea. Don't want the alcohol going to your head too fast."

"It's not going to." Harri sat gingerly on the couch and took a sip of her bourbon. "Are you serious about hiring us to represent you?"

"Yes." He sipped his drink as well. She made a point of checking with Jeremy about Tim's pain meds before they left his warehouse. It was good to know Tim didn't use the Vicodin past the initial injury.

"Then we need to have a frank discussion. No bullshit." She watched him, but no twitches or tics gave him away. "You're the Ghost Owl. You're an unregistered vigilante who's practically a damn urban legend. Do you have superpowers?"

Tim grinned. "Hell, no. All I have is a burning need for revenge and a pile of money. Well, I had a pile of money. That's gone. But I don't have any actual superpowers." He exhaled and leaned back against the couch. "And I think one of the ligaments in my knee went with my money last night."

"That bad?"

Tim made a face. "Remember Jeremy mentioning his orthopedic specialist?"

"Yes."

Tim shrugged. "I already consulted with him. I wasn't joking yesterday at the golf course about needing a double knee replacement, but I can't afford it. Superheroing generally doesn't come with a great benefits package."

"Unregistered superheroing." Harri had always been secretly impressed with the Ghost Owl's refusal to play by the rules, but now that he was a client, she could never admit it to him. "Why not register? You could have made a fortune off the comic book rights alone."

Tim shook his head. "That's what's wrong with the whole mess. It's about entertainment now, not justice. About selling shit. It should be about helping people."

Harri resisted the urge to hug him. "You just said you were all about the revenge."

He reached for a pretzel from the bag sitting between them. "I was. Believe me, it's all I wanted at the start."

She plucked a pretzel to nibble. "So what happened?"

"I . . . people needed someone on their side. It was Eddie who turned me around, showed me what was happening to the city. He made me realize my tragedy wasn't just my tragedy. What they'd done to me affected a lot of people."

"When Canyon Industries closed up, you mean?"

Tim sighed and broke his pretzel in half. "Yeah, but it was more than that. The whole superhero/supervillain nonsense. Regular people were getting caught in the crossfire, but nobody seemed to care. A lot of lip service about the public good, but—"

"But the public kept getting screwed." Harri took a long pull on her drink. "That's what convinced me to join the city attorney's office."

"It's worse than you know," Tim said. "Corvus . . . they're dangerous. Big Trubble's building his own personal super army."

"Big trouble?"

"T-r-u-b-b-l-e. General Byron S. Trubble, nickname 'Big'. Corvus is his baby."

Harri shook her head. "You said they were part of the NSB. Having a military officer in charge violates the Geneva Convention."

"Trubble's retired. He headed up a Department of Defense and CIA joint black ops program, but Trubble was too extreme even for them. Think about that for a minute." He shuddered and drained his glass.

"So how is Corvus still in business?"

"Trubble's a charismatic guy. He's well-connected and clever enough to hide his supers program behind bureaucracy and paperwork. And there are still plenty of whack jobs out there who believe his patriot spiel and want to help. Particularly in the last decade or so. The-ends-justify-the-means crowd."

The ache in her frontal lobe was back, and Harri rubbed her forehead. "What the hell does he want with me?"

Tim leaned forward and grabbed the bottle of bourbon. "That's what I can't figure out. And I'm not sure he's really behind this. Trubble's an evil bastard, but he's not sloppy. I think this is Shift on his own, trying to cover up something. I think you're right about the discovery you received. At a minimum, there's something linking him to Corvus, if not evidence of criminal activity."

"The records I got from the last discovery request were the same vague shit I always get," Harri protested. "I swear I've never even heard of Corvus until I met you."

Tim motioned for her glass. She frowned when she realized she'd already emptied it.

"Then he's afraid of what you might figure out if you take a closer look," Tim said as he poured. "There's only two other things Seismic Shift is afraid of, Byron Trubble and the Ghost Owl."

"Well, that's just fucking wonderful," Harri said, clutching her drink. "Now, he knows I'm working with you. Thanks for making the target on my ass bigger." She glared at him. "This is why I hate supers. I don't appreciate being bait for your little vendetta."

He leaned toward her, his eyes intense. "Shift doesn't know I'm the Ghost Owl. Trust me. He's not scared of Tim Canyon. What he thinks I know about him is embarrassing, but not lethal. He doesn't know I know about his involvement with Corvus. Or what he did to my wife and son. Hell, I was merely the guy who kept his tech working for him. Or not working as the case may be. I licensed his sonic device to another firm through one of my dummy corporations. The dumb bastards helped subsidize the Ghost Owl for the last two decades."

"What happened to your burning need for revenge? Why are you still doing this?" She waved her glass, sloshing the amber liquid.

Tim ran his hand through his hair and leaned back with a groan. "Because the stakes got higher. A lot of people could have died at City Hall. Not just my tragedy, remember?

"And I don't want revenge anymore. I want justice. Shift is my way to get to Corvus. They have to be stopped. Trubble's creating an army of supers. Right now, they're mercenaries. Super services for the highest bidder. But Trubble's got ambition."

"He wants to be the guy in charge," Harri said. "Not a subcontractor."

"Exactly. And Rey Garcia—"

"That's why he wanted to recruit Rey." Harri set her drink on the coffee table, a sick feeling in her stomach that had nothing to do with the alcohol she drank or her lack of food. "And now he knows he can't."

"If Rey won't play ball, then he'll use anyone or everyone Rey cares about to ensure his cooperation."

"Miguel and his family?" she whispered.

"Yeah." Tim nodded. "So I totally understand why Miguel's pissed at me. And if extortion doesn't work, Trubble will take Rey apart, cut him into little pieces to try to figure out where his power comes from to see if he can duplicate it. Either way, the kid is useful to him."

"Over my dead body," Harri growled.

"That's what I'm afraid of." Tim looked away a moment before that intense gaze returned to her. "But the Ghost Owl could protect him."

Harri could feel her eyebrows climbing her forehead. "No offense, but you can't play nine holes of golf without crippling yourself. Rey can fly. I think you got it backwards." She reached for her glass.

Tim shook his head. "No. I don't. I want Rey to take over as the Ghost Owl."

Harri dropped her drink onto the polished concrete floor and heard the glass shatter. "No."

"Harri, I—"

"Look at yourself!" She waved at him as she stood. "You live underground like a rat. You're broke, financially and physically. Your family is dead. You're a pariah. You really want to dump all that on Rey? That kid's been through enough already. He deserves a shot at being something better."

"Better? Like Captain Justice? You really think that's better? You think he cares about all the money and the fame?" Tim glared up at her. "And yeah, I'm all those things you said, but that's Tim Canyon. Not the Ghost Owl."

Harri took a step back, her heart pounding in her chest. "What happened to your tell-all and your plan to fake your death?"

Tim's face flushed. "It's now become part of the same plan. We put away Shift and take down Corvus. I fake my death and disappear. Rey becomes the Ghost Owl with no one the wiser. It's the only way to protect all of us."

Harri stalked toward the kitchenette and grabbed the roll of paper towels from the counter. "Where's your damn broom?"

"In the closet to your right."

Harri dragged the broom over to the mess she'd made. "How are you so sure Corvus or Shift or anyone doesn't know Tim Canyon and the Ghost Owl are the same person?"

"Because Arthur Drallhickey isn't the only one with hacking skills." With a hiss of pain, Tim lifted both of his legs so she could sweep up the glass. "I've been watching them for a while. That's how I amassed the evidence to show their corruption. Bribes. Blackmail. Murder."

She paused in mid-stroke. There was an edge to his voice. A haunted look in his eyes. She set aside the broom and sat on the couch once again. His pain was a palpable thing.

And terribly familiar at the same time.

Finally, she said in a small voice, "I hate the Captain Justice thing."

Tim laid his hand over hers. "I suspected you would. That's part of why Miguel worries, too. Rey's a good kid. I hope Aisha's right about staying in the public eye."

"You're too used to hiding." She turned her hand over so they were palm to palm. "And if you run now, you will always be running, regardless of whether we take down the people who murdered your wife and son and destroyed your family's legacy. You stayed in Canyon Pointe for a reason."

"I'll stay long enough to make sure you and your staff are safe and to train Rey." The pain in his eyes made her heart ache. "That's all I can promise right now, Harri."

"That's good enough." She smiled at him.

Even if they managed to pull off their insane plan, she found herself wanting Tim Canyon to stay, but she didn't have a damn reason to give him that wouldn't sound selfish and self-serving.

And like Eddie, he was the type who'd want more from her than a good time.

CHAPTER 23

Aisha watched Rey while he prowled around her condo, checking all the windows and closing blinds and curtains. After last night, all she wanted was to take a shower and crawl beneath clean sheets. Thank goodness, she'd left a spare key with the Brinkmans.

Rey stalked back to the kitchen. "How long have you known your neighbors?" His eyes gleamed with intensity. He was taking this protector thing way too seriously.

"Ten years." Had it really been that long already? "I take care of their cat when they're out of town, and they collect my mail and keep an eye on my place when I'm gone."

Except she hadn't taken a vacation since the divorce. She couldn't afford it. And now, she didn't even have her BMW to sell. Her phone call with the insurance company this afternoon had been a nightmare.

Mrs. Brinkman had cooked for her after Cal moved out, complaining no man wanted a woman with no meat on her bones. While Harri had made cracks about helping bury Cal's body, Aisha had no doubt Mrs. Brinkman would have gleefully poisoned her ex-husband first.

Aisha opened the refrigerator door. A dozen eggs, a wilted head of lettuce, and the box of baking soda to keep everything smelling fresh. She should have taken Dad up on his offer to cook for the few days he was here. There'd be some leftovers. But he was experimenting with Chinese cooking, and Mom hated Chinese, so to keep the peace, they'd gone out or ordered in every night. And since they left, she and Harri had been taking care of their little gang through Marta.

The freezer didn't yield anything better than her refrigerator. Two frozen pizzas for her once-a-month munchies. And even those wouldn't be happening anymore.

Rey's hand closed over hers. "Why don't you run a bath and relax? I'll take care of dinner. Would you prefer omelets or pizza?"

She looked up at him. Yep, definitely too good to be true. It wasn't his looks or superpowers. Rey was a genuinely nice person. Why couldn't she have met him before she met Cal? For that matter, why hadn't she been born twenty years later or Rey twenty years earlier?

Maybe Harri's fears were totally founded, and they were about to change Rey into something she would never again recognize.

Aisha forced a smile. "Cook's choice."

A knock on the door roused Aisha. The bath water had cooled. How long had she been asleep?

"Dinner's ready," Rey called.

"Be out in a minute."

She dried off and donned some gym shorts and a t-shirt before she headed for the kitchen, which smelled better than some gourmet restaurants. But it was the smashed phone on the floor tiles that drew her attention.

"What happened?"

Rey looked up from sweeping the mess. "Believe me, I did this under orders."

"We can't trust my landline," she hissed.

"Someone has Harri's new phone." Rey straightened and dumped the contents of the dustpan into the trash. "The one she lost at the restaurant last night. They've been trying all the numbers on the contact list."

"Corvus is trying to locate us," Aisha whispered.

"That's what Arthur thinks." Rey shrugged as he returned her broom and dustpan to the pantry. "Or they're trying to download spyware. Anyway, he said he'll replace all of our phones with more burners when we meet at the Lechuza Building in the morning."

"Where's he going to get the money?"

"Patty's fronting the funds until Harri can get to the bank tomorrow." Rey's mouth twisted like he found the idea distasteful. Aisha didn't blame him. Patty had to be dipping into her baby fund again.

"Dammit." Aisha shook her head. "I should have left Dad's money here instead of taking it to the bank."

Rey turned to wash his hands, but he inclined his head toward her little table. "Go ahead and start eating." He'd already laid out filled plates, silverware, and in her case, a glass of wine.

She sat down and took a bite of her omelet. "Oh, my god! This is incredible."

With an expression of what could be called pleased embarrassment, Rey slid into the seat across from her. "I'm glad you like it. I salvaged what I could of your block of parmesan and added a little rosemary."

"I didn't even know I had rosemary. Or parmesan." She forked another bite into her mouth. "Where'd you learn to cook?"

He shrugged. "Marta's son Rueben. I trade cookbooks for lessons when things are slow for him at the restaurant. He wants to go to the Cordon Bleu so bad he can taste it." Rey gave a little half-smile at his joke.

She didn't have to ask why Rueben hadn't gone to Paris. "Tastes to me like he could show the French a thing or two."

They finished the rest of their meal in silence. Except it wasn't the uncomfortable kind, which was really weird considering she'd known him less than a week. Once they cleaned up the kitchen, she jammed her hands in her pockets to keep from doing anything really stupid, like running her fingers through his hair.

"I need to put together my to-do lists for the next couple of days." Aisha waved at the TV. "Go ahead and watch something. It won't bother me."

He smiled. Did he know he had the most adorable dimple on his chin? "Is it okay if I read instead?"

"No problem."

— •—

Three hours later, Aisha stretched her neck and shoulders. Everything possible had been lined up so she could get started on Rey's new persona as soon as Harri had the registration number and Jeremy had the Captain Justice outfit ready. Heck, she'd even started on Arthur's patent application for his so-called paint remover.

She closed her laptop, only to realize her legs were stretched out over Rey's thighs. And he was absently rubbing her feet with his free hand.

Aisha jerked her feet from his grasp and planted them firmly on the floor.

He looked up from his book.

She covered her face with her hands. "Oh, god. I am so sorry. I'll go lock myself in my bedroom now."

"Hey." Her laptop lifted away. "You didn't do anything wrong."

"I don't normally put my feet in a client's lap," she muttered. She couldn't look at him. Hell, she couldn't even blame it on the wine. She'd only had one glass.

"I kind of liked it."

She dropped her hands and looked at him. "Don't tell me you have a foot fetish. Please don't."

"No, I like that you feel comfortable around me." Those damn eyes of his seemed to glow. "Most people are either afraid of me or they want something."

"You realize both Harri and I fall into the second category, don't you?"

Rey chuckled. He held her hands. "Harri thinks she owes me for saving her life, but she also puts me on a pedestal I don't deserve. All she's seen in her job are the supers who are trying to get out of their responsibility.

"But you . . ." He stroked her fingers. "It's more than business. You're as lonely as I am, but you're making up a whole bunch of excuses in your head to protect your heart."

"It's not my heart I'm protecting," she said softly. "You are my client, Rey. I'd be taking advantage of you."

"Have I signed anything yet? Because you haven't done anything but suggest a superhero moniker and give me your opinion on outfits. Things a girl-friend would do." The impish expression on his face made her laugh.

"Could you slice my ethics responsibilities any closer?"

"Probably." He shrugged. "You're not the only one afraid. I . . . want you, but I'm more afraid of hurting you than I am of you saying no."

What he was really saying tugged at her soul. She pulled one hand free and cupped his cheek. "No, honey, your first time should be special. It should be with someone your age. Someone you love."

One dark eyebrow arched. "Are you really going to give me the 'you need to experience life first' lecture?"

This was stupid. And wrong. And it had been so damn long since any man had treated her with simple kindness.

She looked away a moment to collect her thoughts because those damn eyes of his could talk her into just about anything. "I'm not going to lecture you. It sounds to me like you've gotten enough of those."

"Aisha . . ." He gently lifted her chin and kissed her. A kiss that was warm and sweet and innocent.

And all her reasons for saying no disappeared as surely as her car into the depths of Lake Del Oro.

Chapter 24

Three days later, Aisha stood in front of the remnants of City Hall with Captain Justice. Harri, with a little help from Eddie, had pushed through Rey's registration. With Maria's death certificate and an affidavit from Miguel swearing Maria was Rey's mother, Harri had gotten him a replacement birth certificate. There was a brief hiccup when a low-level bureaucrat at the local Hero Registration office demanded a DNA test to prove Miguel's story. But Harri threatened the power-tripping jerk with a lawsuit under the Superhero Persona Protection Act, and he quickly backed down. Having her intimidating ex-husband with her probably had more to do with the jerk giving up, but Aisha wasn't going to disabuse Harri of the notion. It would put her partner in a pissier mood than sleeping on Tim's couch had.

Eddie could never admit it, but Aisha had a strong feeling the FBI was looking into more than some civil rights irregularities in Canyon Pointe. Eddie must have a strong incentive to keep Rey and Tim on his side that went beyond the attempts on hers and Harri's lives.

Unfortunately, only Essie Morales, Channel 12's brand-new investigative reporter, and Bob, Harri's freelance cameraman friend, had come to the press conference. News cycles were fast, but in nine days, Rey's involvement in the rescues was an ancient headline. Or the worse possibility—someone was deliberately blackballing the city's newest superhero.

Aisha plastered on her best PR smile. "Well, Ms. Morales, since you have Captain Justice's undivided attention, what would you like to know?"

"Is it true Mayor Samuels tried to have you arrested as an accessory to Professor Venom's arson of City Hall?" Essie batted her big brown eyes.

Aisha had whip her green-eyed monster into submission. The intense young reporter was exactly the type of girl Rey should be dating. Except the last three nights with him had been incredible. So incredible, she needed to replace her bed's headboard when she had the funds. She swallowed hard and pushed aside the thoughts of what she'd been doing to him when he cracked it.

". . . Professor Venom was recently cleared of any wrongdoing," Captain Justice was saying.

"Do you have any leads on who did set the fire?" Morales asked.

"I'll leave the investigation to the professionals." Rey smiled that devastating smile of his. "I trust the Canyon Pointe Police Department are working hard on the matter."

Aisha's new phone beeped. She pulled it out, but Tim's text chilled her to the bone. "R—Captain Justice!" She held up the phone for him to read.

His eyes widened, and he glanced at her. She gave him the slightest of nods.

"Excuse me, Ms. Morales." Captain Justice launched himself upward in a rush of wind that sent trash and hair flying.

His speed startled even Aisha. *And that, LaShun, is why I refuse to wear a wig.*

"What is it?" Morales demanded. "What's going on?"

"It was a tip from a friend with a contact at the Canyon Pointe Airport tower," Aisha answered with the right hint of anxiety. "There's a jet coming in that lost one engine to a lightning strike, and the second engine is questionable."

Morales and Bob exchanged glances before they scooped up their equipment and ran for the station's van. The reporter paused at the passenger door. "You need a ride, Franklin?"

"I'm good." Aisha waved. The van's tires screeched as Bob whipped it around and headed for the closest freeway entrance ramp. Her smile faded, and she muttered, "You better not have caused that engine malfunction, Timothy Mitchell Canyon."

—•—

Harri swung her sledge hammer. A chunk of plaster gave way with a satisfying crack. She may not officially be part of Miguel's construction crew, but tearing out a wall to give Arthur more space felt pretty damn good, especially after the amount of paperwork she'd filed over the last two and a half days. Or the physical activity did until someone started banging on metal in the reception area.

"Get your goddamn ass up here, Canyon!" Aisha's voice. She must be back from the press conference. And she did not sound happy.

Harri set down the hammer, pushed up her goggles, and trudged out to the reception area. Miguel's oldest sons, Domingo and Emilio, paused in putting up their respective sheets of drywall. Both boys stared at Aisha like she'd lost her damn mind.

Maybe she had.

"Hey, what's wrong?" Harri strode over to the basement door where her partner pounded the solid steel.

"Your spoiled little rich boy, that's what's wrong!" Aisha struck the door one more time with her fist.

"Enough," Harri hissed. "Upstairs."

Painters poked their head around the plastic covering the doorways of the two rooms that would be hers and Aisha's offices. They didn't need to be discussing whatever Tim had done to piss off Aisha in front of people who weren't part of the firm.

Harri didn't feel the slightest bit of remorse when she wrapped a filthy hand around the sleeve of Aisha's silk suit and dragged her toward the stairs. For all of Aisha's Amazonian height, her upper body strength sucked. Nor did Harri say a word until they reached the rooms on the third floor the kids had cleaned out for them to use temporarily.

"Now, what the fuck was that all about downstairs?" Harri growled. "We represent superheroes. You do not throw a fit like that. Much less in front of non-firm personnel."

Aisha pulled her new phone out of her jacket pocket and shoved it in Harri's face. "You'd better tell me your boyfriend didn't have anything to do with a malfunction on a jet."

Harri read the text before she rolled her eyes. "You couldn't have texted me to confirm instead of screaming like a banshee in front of the help?"

"Excuse me for not having your snooty manners!" Aisha shoved the phone back in her pocket. "However, I did notice you haven't answered my question."

Harri pulled out her own phone and thumbed the speed dial.

Before she said anything, Tim said, "Is your partner still on the rampage?"

"You heard her, huh?" Harri scowled at Aisha who was pacing in those damn stilettos of hers.

"Saw her on the security cameras, too." He sounded amused by the whole thing. "Put your phone on speaker."

Harri thumbed the control.

"Aisha? I may be a shit, but for the record, I wouldn't put two hundred-twenty-seven passengers and crew in danger for a stupid-ass press conference. Feel me?"

After a moment of shock, Aisha laughed. "Boy, you are too ginger to be talking brown."

"My set-up monitors all the emergency channels," Tim continued in a less aggressive tone. "We don't have any other super in Canyon Pointe who could handle something like this, besides Captain Mojave. All I did was give Captain Justice a head start." He chuckled. "Nice play though, sending Morales out to the airport to scoop Meadowfield on the Captain Justice rescue."

"I can't take credit for that one." A rueful smile twisted Aisha's mouth. "They took off for the airport the second I told them what was going on."

"Uh-huh," Tim drawled.

Patty shrieked in the room next door.

Harri could hear Tim yelling over the phone as she raced for her assistant. But the expression on Patty's face wasn't fear.

"Oh, my god!" Patty bubbled. "You guys have to see this!" She turned her laptop toward Harri. The livestream from the Channel 12 website took up the screen.

A broadcast marked "Live" showed Essie Morales standing in front of a mass of firetrucks and ambulances surrounding a jumbo jet. Smoke drifted from the far side of the plane, but a familiar red and white figure assisted people getting out of the rear hatch.

Harri held up her phone. "Tim, are you watching Channel 12?"

"Yep. He did it." Tim couldn't have sounded prouder if it was his own kid saving people.

"He did it." Harri couldn't help grinning. She looked over at Aisha.

Her partner nodded, still staring at the screen. "We've got this."

— ·◆· —

The following Monday afternoon, Aisha dropped her phone on the desk to keep from throwing it. She'd hit another wall trying to get Rey a deal. Any deal. What the hell was going on? Channel 12's Action News! had been running

Bob's footage damn near continuously last week, but none of the networks or cable news channels even nibbled at a chance for an exclusive interview.

When she called Essie, the reporter had cut her off, saying she'd call Aisha later. Even weirder, none of her contacts with merchandisers or other media jumped at the chance to get in on the ground floor of Captain Justice. The social media response was even stranger. There'd been a ton of blowback about minority supers taking the attention away from hardworking American heroes.

The only interest she'd gotten from anyone had been from a small California company that did sleazy beefcake calendars.

And super-themed pornography, or at least that was the rumor.

Aisha, as much as she loved to see Rey with his clothes off, had turned them down.

Once Rey was licensed and he got a few news and social media mentions, they should have been fine. Sure, he was new, but he'd passed his first test with flying colors. The offers should be rolling in. Instead Aisha was cold-calling everyone she could think of and getting nowhere. Somebody was shutting her down and she had a pretty good idea it wasn't Corvus despite Harri and Tim's grumbling.

Howard Dewey, despite his icy cold demeanor, had to be furious with her for walking away from the firm like she had. Particularly if she took her clients with her.

There was a non-compete clause in her contract with the firm. They could try to enforce it against her, but they couldn't enforce it against clients who wanted to jump ship, and besides that opened the door for her to countersue for gender bias. It was easier, and far more both Howard and Stuart's style, to poison the well with the super industry instead. If they hurt Rey in the process, so much the better. As soon as he gave up on Aisha, they thought they could scoop him up.

Aisha stretched in the chair she'd brought from home. Or rather Rey had brought for her. It was more comfortable than the crate and pillow set-up. She needed a break before calling the final number on today's prospect list.

Patty had donated her coffee maker to the cause, but she insisted it had to be kept in Aisha's room so she wasn't tempted while she was still pregnant. Aisha poured herself a cup and winced at the taste of the plain black brew.

The nearest coffee shop to the Lechuza Building was fifteen blocks away, hardly within walking distance. Worse, it had no parking. Maybe she could front the funds for Rueben to open his own little breakfast bistro on the block once the money started coming in. Harri was right. The only way to keep the neighborhood from gentrifying and forcing out the locals would be to invest in making it productive and livable.

She wandered around the third floor, looking for signs of life. Harri's office was empty. She'd been spending a lot of time helping with the construction, especially if Tim Canyon was involved. He may not be able to crawl around for the wiring with his bum knee, but he drafted the design and could do the work above waist level.

When Aisha had asked Harri about what was going on with them, Harri blushed and said, "Nothing much."

When Aisha had pushed about installing security at Harri's townhouse so she could go home, her face went from pink to crimson. She mumbled something about Corvus taking Tim's inventions which meant they knew how to bypass the alarms and changed the subject.

Harri always blushed when she tried to lie, so Aisha knew something was going on. Judging by the looks Harri gave Tim when she thought no one, including Tim, was watching, Aisha had a good idea what it was. Harri was falling for Tim and was afraid of what Aisha would say after Harri's admonitions about sleeping with clients.

If Aisha focused on Harri, she wouldn't think about her own stupidity at home.

Damn.

So Harri and Tim . . .

Her partner had been right when she'd said that, as of now, Aisha had all the expertise for both Rey and Tim's legal issues. And Aisha was the one with the industry contacts, as worthless as they presently seemed to be.

Harri had her history working against her, no matter what Aisha told her to try to make her feel better. Supers didn't like her. Aisha had been trying hard not to reach the conclusion that Harri's bad reputation was as big a problem for them as Howard Dewey's meddling.

Aisha poked her head in the room Patty was using.

"I sent you today's media hits on Rey," Patty said without looking up from her typing. "There's not a lot."

Harri had gone ahead and bought their assistant an ergonomically correct chair. With her bulging belly, Patty definitely needed to be as comfortable as possible.

"What about that bank robbery Friday night?" Aisha asked. "And that family whose minivan he pulled out of the lake before they drowned yesterday morning?"

Patty shrugged and looked up from her monitor. "They got a little local traction, but nothing big enough to trigger national interest."

Aisha sighed. No doubt Howard Dewey had a hand in that, too. "We need something terrible to happen." The words were out of her mouth before she could stop them. "I'm sorry. That didn't sound quite so creepy and self-serving in my head."

"You're fine." Patty smiled. "I knew what you meant. We all thought the plane rescue would be the turning point. Right now, he's just a cop in spandex." Patty groaned and propped her feet on the ottoman Arthur had bought for her. "They like him, though. So that's good."

"Who?"

"The cops," Patty said. "They like him a lot. He doesn't make work for them like Seismic Shift and Cobblestone. No nemesis."

"Yet," Aisha said. "Somewhere out there, some maladjusted whack job is nursing his resentment. I just wish he'd hurry up with the evil plan. We need the exposure." She took another sip of coffee. "Ooh, that sounded even worse. Don't tell Harri I said that."

Patty chuckled. "Not a peep from me. You're right. Harri . . . I love her, but she's kind of naïve about how all this works. You don't make money for doing the right thing. At least not big money. She says she wants to make him rich, but then gets in a snit when we try to do that." She sighed. "It's the mommy thing she has with him. It's scrambling her brains. She still hates supers, but she cares about Rey and doesn't know how to deal with it."

Harri wasn't the only one. Aisha's face grew hot. Too bad her thing with him wasn't maternal.

Aisha took another sip of coffee. "She wants him to succeed, but not turn into the thing she hates. Is she still downstairs?"

"No. Upstairs with Miguel. Working on the condo plans." Patty shook her head. "I can't believe she wants to live up there. It's a mess."

"Is Tim with them?"

Patty gave her an odd look. "You noticed, too, hmm?"

No sense lying to the woman. Aisha hadn't met an assistant yet who didn't know more than her boss. "Yeah, I just hope she knows what she's doing."

"Like you and Rey?" Patty smirked.

Aisha sighed. "Are we that obvious?"

Patty laughed. "To everyone but Harri. She thinks she can keep you from corrupting her little boy."

Aisha cleared her throat. "So where is everyone who's not condo planning?"

"Waiting for paint to dry."

"Excuse me?"

"Seriously, they finished painting the first floor this morning," Patty said. "So don't touch anything when you leave. Arthur took Tim to his doctor's appointment, then they were going to stop and pick up equipment and wiring to finish the phone and computer lines."

Aisha grimaced. "That's got trouble written all over it. Arthur may not have it in him to be a supervillain, but he and Tim both are major minion material."

Patty laughed. "Nah, Arthur's not a minion. He's too good a guy for that." She stared thoughtfully at her laptop. "He is a good guy, don't you think?"

Aisha smiled into her coffee cup. "Very good. We're lucky to have him on the team." She'd noticed Patty watching Arthur. Jeremy's makeover was working, but it was more than that. Arthur was blossoming in his new job and in his role as Patty's protector. Tim had taken him under his wing a bit, too, and between Tim's mentoring and Rey's friendship, Arthur's supervillain days seemed far behind him.

"Yeah," Patty said, her blond curls bouncing as she nodded. "Funny how things work out." She smiled. "He's going to my Lamaze classes with me since Harri's been busy with the office stuff. He's going to be my backup labor coach. Isn't that sweet of him? Most guys are totally freaked out by babies. Not Arthur. He's gonna be a better mommy than I am."

"They call them daddies." Aisha hesitated before she added. "You okay with him taking that role?"

Patty continued to stare at her monitor, the thoughtful look back on her face. "Nobody else is stepping up, that's for sure."

"Then be grateful for the guy who is." Aisha finished her coffee. "Where's Rey?"

"Off being heroic somewhere, I guess," Patty said. "I don't keep his calendar."

"Yeah, right. Sorry." Aisha sighed. "Not your job."

Patty smiled at her. "Not that I'd mind. Rey's a sweetie." Her smile disappeared. "Not like some supers I've known."

Aisha noted her tone, but didn't say anything. She and Harri had decided it was best not to mention the baby daddy's involvement in the jail assassination attempt to Patty. The poor woman had enough on her plate.

But what would happen if Patty's baby turned out to be a super? The feds had removed more than one super kid from their home when they could convince a judge the parents' couldn't handle raising a gifted child. Would they hold Patty's single motherhood against her?

Aisha couldn't imagine doing the baby thing all alone like Patty. Her idea of children had always included a husband she adored. Well, she had neither, and for the first time, the idea didn't send her into a spiral. Maybe she was really and truly cried out over Cal and his crap.

"I've got one more call to make and then I think I'm heading home," she said. "It's been a long day already. You should head home, too. Nothing's going on, and you need to rest while you can."

Patty shook her head. "I'm waiting for Arthur to get back. Do you and Rey want to join us for dinner?"

"No, thank you." Aisha shook her head. "After the last couple of weeks, I could use a quiet night in front of the TV."

Patty's smile was sympathetic. "I totally understand that feeling."

One last call. Aisha headed to her temporary office and entered the number for the direct line to the CEO of Luxman Manufacturing.

She'd known Henry Luxman for years. He was an old friend of Dad's. He specialized in action figures, both kids' toys and fancier collectibles. The big companies might not touch a new hero like Rey, but Henry had a track record for picking winners. Plus, he trusted Aisha's judgment and wouldn't be swayed by Howard's bullshit. If she couldn't sell Henry on Rey, she might as well pack it up.

Dammit, she couldn't let either Harri or Rey down.

"Henry Luxman," he answered.

"Hey, Henry. Aisha Franklin," she said. "How are you?"

"Uh . . . let me call you back. Give me a couple minutes."

"Okay," Aisha said. A bad feeling settled with the coffee in her stomach. Henry's normally effusive voice had sounded muted, almost frightened.

Luckily, she'd been able to get a new phone with her old number after the bugged phone went into the drink with her car. Arthur made sure her new phone couldn't be compromised, though she still had a burner as a backup. So there was no reason for Henry not to have her number.

She pushed some stuff around her desk, wondering what was up with Henry, then tried to distract herself with the internet. Finally, after ten minutes that felt like ten hours, her phone rang. The caller ID showed a number she didn't recognize.

"Aisha Franklin," she answered.

"It's me," Henry said. "I'm at what's probably the last pay phone left in the city. Down at the bus station. Sorry if it's loud. I wanted to make sure it was safe."

Aisha frowned. "Safe from what? What the hell is going on?"

"You're in big trouble, sweetie. That new guy, Captain Justice, the Mexican kid, I can't help you with him."

Since when did Henry have a problem with Latinos? "For the record, he's a U.S. citizen and his mother's Honduran, not Mexican. Is this coming from Howard Dewey? They're blackballing me, aren't they? I've seen them do this before."

Henry sighed. "Like I give a shit about your old firm. There's a reason I would only deal with you, sweetheart. I told that schmuck Stuart Cheatham to blow it out his ass. I'm not scared of him or Howard Dewey."

Aisha took a deep breath. She'd called it correctly. She should have kicked Stuart in the balls when she had the chance. "Henry, Captain Justice is the real deal. This is a great opportunity to get in before everybody else does."

"No, honey, it's a great opportunity to walk away before you get hurt. You gotta cut this kid lose."

"Why?" Aisha could hear the fear in Henry's voice. "What are you talking about? I thought you weren't afraid of Dewey."

"Honey, this has got nothing to do with the law firm," he said. "I love you like one of my own kids, and your pop and I go way back. Please. Listen to me. Walk away now, before it's too late."

"Henry, what is going on?" Her stomach clenched like an icy fist. Maybe Tim wasn't as paranoid as he sounded. "Is it the people in the black SUV?"

"SUV? No, this was a . . . a super."

"Who?"

"Please don't ask me that. I shouldn't even be telling you this much. He—" His voice broke in what sounded like a sob. "He threatened to hurt Ada and the girls if I worked with you on this Justice kid. Your boy's pissed somebody off big time. And not one of the usual loonies."

Aisha took a deep breath. Panic wasn't going to help. She knew Henry well enough to know he wasn't jumping at shadows. If it were Corvus, Arthur and Tim had schooled everyone never to mention them over the phone. Even if their phones were clean that didn't mean the other guy's phone was, even a city pay phone. "Can we meet to talk about this?"

"No. It's not safe. For either of us. Please. Find some other super to help. I gotta go." Henry hung up on her.

Aisha sat in stunned silence. She'd counted so much on Rey's marketability. Hers and Harri's meager savings wouldn't last forever, even if they sold their respective homes and bunked in their offices.

Rage swept over her. She hadn't exactly been in Tim's court. Part of her didn't trust him. But now she understood his fury.

Fine. If Corvus wanted a war, she'd damn sure help Tim Canyon wage his.

CHAPTER 25

Harri bounced down the stairwell, everything in her tingling with excitement. The first floor was essentially done, and their second-hand office furniture would be delivered tomorrow.

Miguel's ideas for the lofts had been spectacular. To the point where it sounded like a better and better idea for her and Aisha to live in the Lechuza Building and sell their places. She'd prepped herself for Aisha's objections and possible solutions regarding her upside-down mortgage. Not to mention, the Ghost Owl would be providing security.

But when Harri entered Aisha's temporary office, that plan might as well have been dropkicked to the moon by Rey after she told Harri about her conversation with Luxman.

"What are our options if Corvus is blackballing Rey?" Aisha tapped her pen in a rapid-fire rhythm on a legal pad. "Because right now, all I'm seeing is we go along with Tim's tell-all."

"Corvus isn't out to get just Rey. It's all of us," Harri pointed out as she perched on the patio chair she'd brought from home.

"I still don't get what they have against Arthur." Aisha's pen snapped in two.

"He was nothing more than a convenient patsy to frame for my murder." Harri crossed her arms. She'd have to broach the subject, even though she knew Aisha would argue. "Maybe we need to go forward with Tim's plan."

"I was hoping you'd come up with something else." Aisha tossed the remnants of her pen in the trashcan beside her makeshift desk. "It's not my first choice, but I don't have a better idea either."

"Really?" Harri tried not to inject too much disbelief in her voice. This was the woman who had contingency plans for everything, including back-up bars when they went out for a drink.

Aisha stared at her. "As long as you realize that tell-all will paint a bigger bullseye on our butts. But I am not helping anyone fake their death. Not even Canyon."

"How do you feel about me running all this past Tim tonight?" She could probably get him to agree to drop the fake death part, but not if Aisha treated him like the accused murderer he was.

Aisha's eyes narrowed. "Why can't we talk about this with him when he and Arthur come back from the geek guy supply run?"

"Because the tell-all is part of his plan to keep Corvus's attention on him rather than Rey."

Aisha slammed her hand down on the plank acting act her desk. "Try again, Harriet Mathilda."

"Don't you dare call me that." She clenched her fists.

"Then don't fucking lie to me, Harriet Mathilda Winters." Aisha deliberately drawled out the hated full name.

Harri's jaw clenched twice before she ground out, "I don't want him to leave, okay."

"And you also want pump him for information?" Aisha's faux innocent expression at her deliberate double entendre shortened Harri's fuse.

She jumped up from the patio chair and planted her fists on the faux desktop. "Well, if you could get a fucking contract for our only other client—"

Aisha slowly rose, making the most of the fact she was nearly a foot taller in those ridiculous stilettos she always wore. "Don't you fucking dare lay this on me. And don't be giving me those disapproving looks about Rey if you're going to turn around and do Canyon."

"I didn't—" Harri's protest died. "Okay, neither of us should be seeing a client socially." She took a deep breath, blew it out, and held up a hand. "I promise there will be no hanky-panky with Tim. Scout's honor."

Aisha snorted. "I seem to recall you getting kicked out of our troop for telling our den mother to quit screwing your dad."

Harri rolled her eyes. "I thought she had better taste. And you have no idea of the scene burned into my retinas. There is not enough bleach in the universe to scrub out that image."

Aisha plopped back in her chair. "Fine. Just . . . be careful. Henry was seriously scared when I spoke with him. And he doesn't spook that easily."

"I will." Harri crossed her heart.

"Look, Harri, I'm not questioning your judgment—"

"Really? And the past five minutes were what exactly?" She scowled at Aisha.

"Seriously, does he have any real evidence on Seismic Shift?" Aisha's fingernails took up the tapping on her legal pad. "If we don't have something besides hearsay, best case scenario is Shift will slap a libel suit on us."

"And the worst is we all end up dead. I know." Harri considered the question, but a knock on Aisha's door interrupted her train of thought.

Patty poked her head around the corner. "Hey, you two. There's some gossip you need to hear."

"Sweetie, now's not the time—"

"Hush!" Patty held up her index finger. "Grownup is talking."

This must be serious of she's getting pissy. "Sorry. You were saying?"

Patty lowered her hand, but the other gripped the doorknob so hard her knuckles pressed bone white against her skin. "I just got off the phone with Leslie. She works in permits, and she's pushing through the residential paperwork for me. With Harri out of the way, the mayor pushed the demolition of the Canyon Block through during last Thursday's city council meeting."

"Shit," Harri muttered. "That was fast."

An ugly look filled Patty's face. "It would explain why no one's seen any of the black SUVs since Sunday morning. Those assholes are probably now disguised as the demolition crew."

"Wait." Aisha waved a hand. "Who's watching for them?"

"Mainly, Miguel's son Javier and his crew of middle school gangster wannabes." Patty smiled. "Though they're all too busy trying to impress Rey now that they have a real live superhero in their midst."

"Wait," Aisha said again. "They all know Rey's secret identity?"

Patty laughed. "Everyone knows everybody's business in this neighborhood. They're like their own village within Canyon Pointe." Her expression saddened. "When no one gives a shit about them besides the Ghost Owl, Rey, and Harri, they have to depend on each other. So, they're watching Rey's back."

"Why am I included?" Harri frowned.

"Because you're paying them, silly," Patty said. "What are we going to do about all the people still living in the condemned buildings?"

"Are you serious?" Aisha stared at their assistant. "We're barely succeeding at staying alive!"

Patty's chin lifted. "And who do you think will be dressing up as Captain Justice next Halloween? Or buy his toys?"

"Or his porn films?" Aisha buried her face in her hands.

"Porn films?" Harri stared at her partner. She couldn't be serious.

Aisha dropped her hands and looked up. "If we don't stop Corvus, that's all I'm going to be able to book for Rey."

Harri glanced at her watch. "Patty, call in an order to Marta's. We're having a firm-client brainstorming session tonight."

—•—

Aisha braked the bright blue VW at the exit of the parking garage. She really needed a car, but her insurance company was stalling since her Baby's destruction was a result of a super incident. Which left her with Leonardo's niece's car. Since the girl had been grounded for a month for smoking pot at home, her parents had no problem loaning it to Aisha.

Rey offered to come with her, but Tim and Arthur had arrived from their errands. Despite the injections for pain at the orthopedist, it was obvious Tim needed some help, and Arthur had his hands full of their equipment purchases. She alerted the guys to Harri's declaration for a meeting as she left. Besides, she'd be back before it was fully dark.

Traffic was its normal five o'clock busy, which on this end of 6th Street meant barely busy at all. But a check for oncoming cars revealed a familiar motorcycle parked in front of the bodega. The same one that had been in front of the convenience store next door to Marta's restaurant on Saturday night.

The same icy ball collected in Aisha's stomach. She automatically reached for the hands-free call button before she remembered she wasn't in her own car. Guiding the VW in a right-hand turn out of the garage, she breathed slow and deep. It might be nothing. She could call Harri from Marta's parking lot.

No. Call Miguel. If Patty was right about his younger son watching the street while Miguel and the older boys worked on the office, he'd know if this woman was a problem.

Besides, the motorcycle rider may simply live in the neighborhood, right? Technically, every time Aisha had seen the black SUV, she'd been with Miguel or Rey. So it was really nothing. She was blowing this out of proportion, right?

Except her internal reassurances did nothing to melt the damn ice in her gut.

Harri and Patty entered the newly painted reception area of what was becoming the Law Office of Winters & Franklin. The faint chemical scent of drying latex didn't detract from the restored splendor. The walls and ceiling had been rag-painted using various tones of cream to an orange-gold, giving it an antique plaster feeling. Cherry wood trim had been touched up with stain where needed and polished to a spit-shine. The colors gave the atrium the same art deco impression the building originally had a century ago when it was first built.

"Wow." Patty pivoted, drinking in the sight. "Miguel's crew does damn good work."

"Gracias." Miguel beamed as he exited from what would be the office break room. "We're leaving the drop cloths down until the furniture is delivered tomorrow at ten. Unfortunately, the carpet installers won't be here until one. Also, the letterer for the main door will be here on Friday. The first floor windows and the glass for the reception area will be installed on Saturday, and you'll be ready for your grand opening next Monday."

Harri shook her head. "How'd you get an installation team here on a Saturday?"

"An old friend cut me a deal because he's as desperate for work as I am." Miguel's thick moustache twitched.

"But bulletproof glass—"

"After the incidents two weeks ago, neither Tim or I want anything to happen to you." Miguel grimaced. "And if my men and I are going to be renovating the upper floors as you plan, I don't want them in the crossfire either."

His phone rang. He pulled it from his pocket and frowned at the screen before raising it to his ear. "Ms. Franklin?"

Harri tried to listen in on the conversation. Why the hell was she calling Miguel? She should be at Marta's picking up their dinner for tonight.

Miguel smiled and rolled his eyes. "Yes, Aisha. I won't make that mistake again." As he listened, his smile faded. "That sounds like Ms. Riley's bike." Another pause. "Qiang Riley. She's an accountant for one of the downtown firms." A third pause. "She told Celia she lives in the Broadview neighborhood."

Broadview? Why was Aisha asking about someone who lives in the older middle class neighborhood north of downtown that bordered the Canyon District? Harri motioned for Miguel's phone.

"*Un momento*, Ms. Harri wants to speak with you." He handed her the phone.

"What the hell is going on?"

Aisha sighed over the receiver. "I think I've been hanging around Arthur and Tim too much. I keep seeing this woman in black riding leathers on a Kawasaki Ninja around the Canyon Block. The last time I saw her was at the convenience store next door to Marta's right before Corvus took potshots at me and Rey. She had a wedding ring on, but she was buying a bridal magazine."

"Maybe she was buying it for a friend," Harri growled. "I seem to recall someone buying a ton of those damn things for me no matter how many times I said Eddie and I were doing a civil ceremony at the courthouse."

"Fine," Aisha muttered. "Let me get our dinner, and we'll discuss this when I get back."

"Wait a sec." Harri looked up at Miguel. "Did you want to join us for dinner tonight?"

The contractor smiled and shook his head. "I need to take the younger boys shoe shopping tonight. Javier and Francisco both went through growth spurts over the last month."

"Did you—"

"I heard," Aisha bit out. "Later." The signal abruptly died.

Harri stared at the phone for a second before she handed it back to Miguel. "What crawled up her ass?"

"Maybe getting shot at?" Patty gave Harri a wide-eyed, innocent look she didn't believe for a second.

A wry smile appeared under Miguel's moustache. "I would have to agree." He waved toward the room that would be Harri's. "Check everything in your office. Please have Aisha do the same for hers. If there's anything you don't find satisfactory, make a list and we will tackle it in the morning before the furniture arrives." He touched the brim of his cap. "G'night, ladies."

"He needs to find someone," Patty said with a wistful expression after he left. "He's trying to raise his boys all alone."

"He's done a pretty good job raising Dom and Emilio," Harri said. "I mean, look at the place!"

"It does look incredible." Patty rubbed her back.

A thread of guilt ran through Harri. Even though she had made a point to buy Patty an ergonomically correct chair for their temporary office, her assistant was three weeks away from her due date.

"Why don't you go on downstairs and put your feet up?" Harri gestured toward the basement door. "And tell the guys I said they had to cater to your every need."

"What about—"

Harri pointed at her new office. "I'll double-check the office like Miguel asked, and help Aisha when she returns with dinner. Then we'll put together our plan."

"You're the boss." Patty headed for the basement door. "But I think the next thing on the list should be getting that antique elevator fixed. Even with shots in his knee, Tim doesn't need to be going up and down these stairs. Neither do I with the bowling ball I'm carrying."

She winced and rubbed her abdomen. "I apologize, sweetie. I won't call you a bowling ball anymore."

"Yes, ma'am. I'll raise the priority of the elevator." Harri shook her head as the door swung shut behind her assistant, and she strode toward her new office. The woman was turning into her own personal Jiminy Cricket.

But Patty was right. Not only for Tim's sake, but all of theirs. She and Aisha weren't getting any younger either, and she couldn't imagine dragging boxes, much less furniture, up four flights of stairs. Rey could, but they were already abusing their relationship with the kid.

She'd already overheard an argument between him and Miguel over the contractor paying him for his time working on the renovations. They thought they covered up their disagreement by speaking in Spanish, but even with her meager skill at the language, she'd understood Rey still believed she would deliver on her promise to make him rich. And that hit even harder after what Aisha had told her about her former employer and Corvus blackballing the kid.

Harri turned the latch to her new office, ready to drink in the sight, but the splash of scarlet stood out in the middle of the room. A dozen roses sat in a clear bowl of water on top of a stool covered in pristine white cloth.

She crossed to the stool. A card had been enclosed. Her brief flare of suspicion was quickly melted as she read Tim's neat script.

Harri,

I hope you'll allow me to make up for the dinner we didn't have a chance to finish last Saturday.

Tim

Warmth curled through her. It had been a long time since someone had made such a romantic gesture.

And she immediately dismissed it. Dammit, she was old enough and experienced enough not to fall for sentimental tripe.

Harri bent over to sample the roses' aroma. But still, it would be a waste to throw out such beautiful flowers. She ran a finger over a velvety petal. Yeah, a total waste.

Dragging her attention from the bouquet, Harri circled the room. As much as she would love to refinish the original hardwood flooring, it was an expense they couldn't afford. At least not right now.

A little electric lamp sat next to an outlet. She used it to test each outlet. Arthur's toolbox remained underneath the wall socket for the big screen monitor she could use for presentations and to keep an eye on the news. Finally, she flipped the switch for the overhead Tiffany-style light fixture. After Rey had cleaned the stained glass and changed the bulbs, it gleamed brilliantly.

A shuffling sound came from the reception area. Dinner was finally here. Harri headed for her door.

"Hey, Aisha! You going to tell me what crawled up your—"

A figure wearing the same black tactical gear and mask as the crazies from her aborted dinner with Tim stood by the pile of paint supplies. The person raised their hand, but there was no weapon.

Static raised the hairs along Harri's arms. She slammed the door shut and dived behind the office wall as a bolt of electricity blew apart her brand-new door.

CHAPTER 26

Harri looked around for a weapon. Any weapon. Arthur's toolbox and the lamp were both on the other side of the non-existent door.

And what exactly were you going to do against a super with electrical powers, Harriet Mathilda?

Her best bet was to hit the jerk hard and fast, then run like hell. Too bad she didn't have any peanut butter pies to throw. And what the hell was Tim doing? Wasn't he watching the damn cameras he had all over the building?

She rose to a crouch and tried to control her breathing. Static tickled the fine hairs all over her body. A black boot crossed the threshold. She launched herself into her assailant.

They tumbled across the floor. The jerk caught her arm and shoulder in some kind of martial arts hold. With her free hand, Harri reached blindly. Her fingers found the test lamp.

She smashed the bulb over her attacker's head. The hold on her arm loosened, and she rolled over to jab the jerk with the shards of broken bulb in the socket.

The jerk jumped back and tripped over a fold in the dropcloth. They raised their hand again. Harri dived for Arthur's toolbox. The electric discharge singed the new paint where her head had been.

"Asshole!" Harri flipped open the box lid and started throwing tools at her assailant.

The jerk fended off the metal, wood, and plastic until a lucky shot with a clawed hammer hit them in the diaphragm. Harri raced for her attacker and launched her best counter move—a well-placed kick in the groin.

The asshole doubled over, and Harri seized the vase of roses. It was heavier than it appeared. She hesitated a micro-second at destroying Tim's gift. A static charge tickled her skin. There was nowhere to run this time. She brought the vase down as hard as she could.

It shattered. Electricity discharged and popped. The shock knocked Harri back and she landed hard on her ass. But her assailant shook as if they'd stuck a finger in one of the sockets. When the seizure stopped, the black-clad figure collapsed in the puddle of water formed by the heavy canvas drop cloth.

Harri slowly climbed to her feet and approached her assailant. "I hope a thorn stabs you, and you get sepsis."

Her beautiful roses were scattered across the floor. She picked up a piece of the broken vase. Not glass. Crystal. It was probably one of the last pieces Tim had kept from his family's belongings. He given it to her, and she ruined it.

She glared at the crumpled figure on the soaked dropcloth. No, it was the jerk's fault.

"You asshole!" She kicked one of her assailant's legs. "You fucking asshole!" Another kick. "First time I get flowers from a man in, like, forever, and you ruined it!"

Her third kick aimed for her assailant's head, but someone yanked her backward, and she missed.

Harri whirled, fists raised, to find Aisha. Her partner immediately released her shirt.

"What the hell are you doing?"

"That bastard attacked me!" Harri turned back to give the asshole another kick. This time, someone actually picked her up before her toe connected with her attacker's head.

"No," Rey said sternly. "This isn't how we deal with the bad guys."

"Put me down, Reyes," Harri growled. "Right this minute."

"No more," he replied.

Realizing this was one battle she couldn't win, she nodded. He gently set her on the floor.

"Who is it?" he asked.

"Let's find out," Aisha said. She crouched down next to the unconscious figure and pulled the mask off, revealing a woman with Asian features and chin-length black hair. "Shit."

"What?" Harri and Rey said at the same time.

"This is the woman I was telling you about." Aisha looked up at them. "The one Miguel said was a local accountant."

"What do we do with her?" Rey asked. "Call the police?"

"No." A malicious glee filled Harri. "I think she needs to have a little talk with the Ghost Owl and Captain Justice."

"Good cop, bad cop?" Aisha asked.

Harri smiled. "More like the superheroes will save the bad guy from their very pissed off attorney as long as she cooperates."

— ◆ —

"You sure this is going to work?" Arthur handed Harri the package of rubber fingertips he'd retrieved from Patty's makeshift office on the third floor.

"Between these and buckets, we should be covered." Harri split the package and tossed half to Aisha. "I don't think hitting her over the head again would be a good idea."

Rey had carried the woman downstairs. Using some nylon rope Tim had on hand, they tied her to a chair in a basement room he hadn't put to use yet. Harri and Aisha had removed her boots and socks and placed each of her feet in their own plastic bucket filled with water.

While they took care of the prisoner, Tim ran her picture and the name Miguel had given Aisha through the federal superhero and supervillain databases. It confirmed she was Qiang Reilly, aka Sparx, a registered superhero on inactive status. Then Tim and Rey changed.

Harri placed the last piece of rubber over their prisoner's thumb when the guys entered the room. Her breath hitched at the sight of Tim in his full regalia. It definitely offset the limp in his stride. And he'd made a point of wearing the costume with the reflective visor.

He straddled the chair Rey set in front of their prisoner. "Ladies, I know you're used to taking charge, but let me take the lead on this one." His voice was altered, definitely Tim's if you knew him but deeper. More menacing.

Harri exchanged a look with Aisha. "All right. We'll follow." She glared at the Ghost Owl. "For now."

He sighed. "Arthur?"

At least, their new head of IT wasn't dressed as his alter ego. He broke a smelling salts capsule and waved it under their prisoner's nose.

Her head jerked up, and Arthur stepped back. She struggled a bit with her bonds. The myriad of emotions that crossed her face when she recognized the Ghost Owl was almost comical.

She eyed him warily while he appeared to calmly watch her. Her attention flicked to Captain Justice standing at the Ghost Owl's right shoulder.

"Why am I your prisoner?" she finally asked.

"Actually, we're here to protect you," the Ghost Owl said mildly.

"Protect me?" Her eyes narrowed.

"Yes."

Her gaze fixed on Aisha, Arthur, and finally Harri. "From who?"

"My attorney." The Ghost Owl gestured in Harri's direction. "She was rather peeved when you tried to electrocute her tonight."

Their prisoner's face blanched. "What?" she whispered. "Where-where am I?"

"Safely in the Owl's Nest for now."

Harri could hear Tim's smile in his words.

"Here's the thing, Sparx—" he started.

Her expression could only be described as dread.

"I need you to answer my questions to my attorney's satisfaction. Otherwise, I can't guarantee your safety once you leave the Nest."

Sparx closed her eyes. "I'm already dead." She opened her eyes.

Something jerked inside of Harri. This was a woman facing her own mortality. Grandma Harri had the same look when the doctor's said they couldn't do anymore for her.

"Please, Jatz'om Kuh," Sparx said. "Kill me. You will be far more merciful than what the man who sent me would be. But I beg you to guard my son and parents."

CHAPTER 27

"What are you talking about?" Harri took a step towards Sparx. "Who sent you?"

"I-I can't tell you." Sparx's throat bobbed. "They'll kill my family."

"Did Byron Trubble give you the order to attack Ms. Winters, or did someone else?" the Ghost Owl asked.

The name triggered something in Sparx. She seemed to collapse in on herself.

"Please," she begged. Tears freely rolled down her face. "I didn't want to do it, but he said he'd kill them."

"Didn't want to do what?" Watching Sparx, Harri's own eyesight blurred.

"Kill you." Sparx sobbed. "He said it was my family or you."

"Who? Byron Trubble?" the Ghost Owl asked.

Sparx shook her head. She probably couldn't speak because she was crying so hard.

"Darryl Bloch?" the Ghost Owl growled. "Otherwise known as Seismic Shift?"

She sniffed and nodded.

"What do you normally do for Corvus?" he asked.

Sparx shuddered and couldn't meet anyone's eyes. "Corporate espionage. I usually go into a target to steal information or prototypes or to destroy research." The words spilled out, like the dam of secrets had broken inside of her.

"How many wetwork jobs?" the Ghost Owl asked.

"This would have been my first one," she said softly.

Disparate facts clicked together in Harri's brain. "You missed me on purpose."

"Yes." Sparx looked up at the Ghost Owl. "You patrol this district. I hoped to hear something at the local businesses. Someone had to know something about you. You're outside the system. I want out. Wanted out for a while. You would be the only one I could trust. It's no secret her partner represents Captain Justice, and it's no secret he also patrols this area of the city, too. I assumed

I could cut a deal with Justice to contact you." She faced Harri. "I didn't expect you to fight back."

The Ghost Owl chuckled. "Ms. Winters is five feet of rage topped by two inches of woman. She's more dangerous than Justice and I put together."

"Yes, she is." Sparx gave Harri an appraising look.

"Give us a reason not to turn you over to the cops," Harri demanded.

Sparx turned back to the Ghost Owl. "If you do, you're signing my family's death warrant."

"Why does Trubble want Ms. Winters dead?" he asked.

She hesitated. "I don't think he ordered it, but I can't prove it."

"Who normally gives you assignments?"

Sparx sniffed again. "Mostly Trubble, but sometimes Shift if Trubble is otherwise engaged. Shift is the regional director."

"So why does Shift want Ms. Winters dead?"

"He didn't say, but it seemed awfully personal."

"Would you be willing to spy for us in exchange for protecting your family?" Harri asked.

"You can't possibly . . ." Sparx's attention drifted to each of the men.

"Not just them." Harri smiled. "I've got resources of my own. You're the sixth operative sent to kill me. And that includes Seismic Shit himself."

Sparx's eyes widened, probably more at Harri's deliberate insult than her survival skills. "He left that out of my briefing."

"You help us, I won't press charges, and everyone lives." Harri shrugged. "What's it going to be?" She counted to five Mississippi before Sparx answered.

"I'll do it." For the first time, the female super actually relaxed. "On one condition."

"You don't have a whole lot of bargaining room," Harri warned.

"This is more straightforward." A tremulous smile appeared on Sparx's face. "I want you to represent me. I want to be a legitimate superhero. Not a tool for Corvus."

Harri looked at Aisha.

For the first time, her partner spoke. "That may be difficult to do. If we can't take down all of Corvus, they could smear you with your previous activities for them. And assuming we do manage to take down Corvus, they may have people outside of the organization with copies of their files and instructions to disseminate that information."

"Then I need to make sure we take both Corvus and their associates down," Sparx said.

"Any future communication with Sparx will have to go through me," the Ghost Owl said as he looked at Harri. "Corvus is keeping too close of an eye on the rest of you."

"But how can you if you don't know—" Sparx started.

"Your real name is Qiang Tranh Reilly," Arthur recited. "You live at 4976 Elmhurst here in Canyon Pointe with your twelve-year-old son Connor and your parents, Binh and Hang Tranh. You were married to Kevin Benjamin Reilly until his death in a traffic accident four years ago. Your son is autistic—"

"Stop!" Sparx's voice dropped. "Please stop."

"This gentleman is our head of IT," Harri said softly. "He used to be known as the supervillain Professor Venom, but he's busted his ass to go straight. And he's not happy Corvus tried to frame him for the fire at City Hall."

Sparx swallowed hard, but said nothing.

"You follow his example in going straight, then we'll help you." Harri crossed her arms over her chest. "But you'll have the same terms as him—one screw-up and we're done. Understood?"

Sparx nodded.

"So how are we playing this?" Aisha asked.

"We won't be able to get her family to a safe house until the last minute." Harri crossed her arms as she tried to work out the logistics. "We don't want to tip off Shit too soon, and odds are someone is watching her place tonight."

"She still needs a cover story for failing to kill you," Aisha insisted.

Harri shrugged. "Her best bet is the most of the truth. I kicked her in the crotch and smashed a crystal vase over her head. When she came to, Captain Justice was flying her home. He told her to stay clear of me, or he'd drop her from forty-thousand feet."

Luckily, Rey didn't say a word about her threat, but he did give her a dirty look.

"What about my bike?" Sparx said. "If Seismic Shit, uh, Shift is watching my house, I can't use it to get home."

"I'll take her bike to her employer's garage," Arthur offered. "It will be in keeping with Captain Justice's non-violence principles. And the garage security cameras will merely record a known associate of his."

Harri cocked her head. "You know how to ride a motorcycle?"

"I have a motorcycle license," Arthur said. "However, motorcycles are statistically the second least safe mode of highway transportation—"

Harri held up a hand to forestall his lecture on vehicle safety. "All right. One of us will follow the professor here—"

"The traffic cameras at the corner of Washington and Jefferson are currently inoperative," Arthur said. "It's two blocks from Ms. Reilly's employer. I can meet the driver there."

"Ms. Reilly, you understand you'll have to be blindfolded to leave here," the Ghost Owl. "And I want to place a bug in your phone."

"To make sure I don't double-cross you?" The wariness was back in Sparx's eyes along with a touch of disappointment.

"No, so either Captain Justice or I can get to you if Shit—" The Ghost Owl turned toward Harri. "Dammit, Winters! Now you have me doing it."

She shrugged and smiled. "If the moniker fits . . ."

He turned back to Sparx. "If Bloch realizes he's being set up. Your safety and that of your family is our primary concern."

"But if this doesn't work . . ." Sparx's face paled again.

"It has to," Harri said. "We don't have a choice but to make it work. Too many lives are riding on this."

CHAPTER 28

Harri didn't want any more of her little family out tonight. Not if Corvus was actively gunning for them again. In the end, the guys checked Sparx's motorcycle for bugs before Arthur rode out. Rey dropped off Sparx near her house before he flew to the corner of Washington and Jefferson and picked up Arthur.

In the meantime, Aisha kept Patty entertained making a final list of what the mom-to-be needed before the delivery while they waited nervously for their guys to comeback. So Harri fetched an ice bag for Tim's knee while he monitored their people.

"Either Sparx is playing us, or Corvus believes they firmly have her under their thumb," Tim said as he stared at the jiggles on his computer monitor.

"I'd opt for the latter," Harri ventured. "Single mom with aging parents. I hate to say this, but they learned their lesson with you. They need live bargaining chips."

A wry smile crossed his face. "I think that's why I like you, Harri. You don't sugarcoat the truth."

She shrugged and held up both of her hands as if physically weighing the matter. "Brutally murdered by a psychopath, or driving off a cliff coked out of your brains. Result is the same."

A few minutes after Rey reported leaving Sparx, the bug Tim had surreptitiously placed on Sparx clothing crackled to life.

"Well?"

Harri's blood chilled. It was the man who'd sprayed her office with acid. The one who burned down City Hall. The one who would have killed her if not for Rey.

"Her pet boy scout showed up." Sparx sounded genuinely pissed.

"She's still alive?" Outrage filled Bloch's voice.

"I barely escaped," she hissed. "You said he's been guarding her partner."

"How'd you get away?" Suspicion laced his voice.

"I electrocuted him in mid-air and fell, you asshole. Why do you think I'm limping?"

"Did you kill him?" For the first time, he didn't sound quite so in charge.

"I doubt it. I just got the hell out of there."

"Where's your bike?"

Sparx sighed, a world-weary, I-can't-believe-you're-this-stupid sigh like the ones Harri had to hold in during many meetings with Mayor Samuels. "It's registered in my real name, Shift. I left it at my day job. How dumb do you think I am?"

He muttered a racial slur that left Harri's mouth hanging open.

"You know, if Corvus wanted her dead that bad maybe you shouldn't have fucked up."

"What's that supposed to mean?" he said defensively.

"You set the City Hall fire, didn't you?" she accused. "Tried to make it look like a supervillain attack. You suck even more as a villain than you do as a hero."

"It would have succeeded if it wasn't for Captain Justice," he sneered.

"And now, you need me to clean up your mess before Big Trubble kicks your ass, right?"

"Shut up, bitch. I'll be in touch."

"Don't rush." After a moment, she whispered, "I hope you got all of that, Mr. Ghost Owl."

Harri and Tim stared at each other.

"She's smarter than I expected," he murmured.

"Damn, why is she wasting time as an accountant?" Harri shook her head. "She'd be one hell of a trial lawyer. She got Shift to admit to the fire."

"She tried hard enough."

One of the alarms on another screen beeped. It was followed by the sound of one of the pressurized doors opening.

"Oh. My. God. That was so awesome!" Arthur's voice echoed down the corridor.

Tim grinned. "I'd say the boys are home, June."

Harri chuckled at his joke over the ancient TV sitcom family. "Then let's see how their playdate went, Ward."

Aisha and Patty had warmed up the dinners Aisha brought back and then stuffed in Tim's refrigerator after the appearance of their unexpected guest.

The guys cleared a work table and scrounged enough chairs, so they could eat and compare notes.

"If I had a choice, I'd want flying powers," Arthur gushed. "Canyon Pointe looks so beautiful from the air." He turned to Rey. "I don't suppose I could get you to take me up again so I could snap some photos."

"Hey!" Harri rapped her knuckles on the wooden surface. "Can we deal with some more serious matters before we start renting Rey out for tourist flights?"

"Sorry, Ms. Winters." Arthur's enthusiasm deflated.

"It's Harri, Arthur." She laid a hand on his shoulder. "And I don't want to kill your excitement, but Rey's bulletproof. You aren't. And you've had our backs through this whole mess. I don't want to lose you."

His face blazed scarlet. "I-I—um—thanks."

Harri quickly laid out Sparx's conversation with Shift. "She got him to pretty much admit to the fire." She looked at Arthur. "I don't suppose any of your algorithms came up with anything?"

He nodded. "I got to thinking about your case. The death at Lake County Retirement Home?"

Harri frowned. "Yeah, but neither Eddie or I found anything on our backgrounds checks."

"That's because you didn't have access to Corvus's database." Arthur's expression turned stern, which was a weird look on him. "Tim showed me some of the backdoors he uses. The man who died in the earthquake was Linwood Baxter, also known as Eagle Forever."

"Please tell me you're shitting me." Aisha stared at Arthur. "The founder of the Allied League of Heroes?"

"It gets better." Arthur poked at his enchiladas. "He was General Trubble's mentor at the National Superhero Bureau. Reading between the lines, their falling out was due to Baxter's refusal to endorse Trubble's plan for superhero black ops. Baxter retired shortly thereafter."

"Why kill Baxter now?" Patty shook her head. "The man was a hundred years old!"

"I don't know if he was about to reveal something." Arthur shot a look at Tim. "But considering Seismic Shift's penchant for killing, it did get me thinking. I started cross-referencing high profile deaths by earthquake with activity by Shift." He shook his head. "In each case, he has an alibi. He had a public appearance at some kids' event."

"Wait a minute." Aisha waved her fork. "Was every single event related to kids?"

Arthur nodded.

"No way." Aisha shook her head firmly. "Shift hates kids with a passion only Harri could rival."

"Hey!" Harri protested.

"It's true, and you know it," Aisha shot back. "Dewey & Cheatham have an actor to attend those events. He has some sort of device to imitate Shift's powers."

"You mean tech those assholes stole from me," Tim said sourly.

"What's the actor's name?" Harri leaned forward. Her blood raced. This may be the break they needed.

"I don't know. That was something only the partners knew." A wicked grin lit Aisha's face. "Or the development manager. And I know his password."

Harri grinned back. "In the meantime, Patty and I can compare Shift's financials to these appearances."

"But how are you going to get the actor to cooperate?" Patty's attention flicked between the two attorneys. "You know damn well they'll hold a non-disclosure agreement over his head. The minute you two subpoena him, Dewey & Cheatham will be all over it."

Rey spoke up for the first time. "Perhaps a visit from Captain Justice and the Ghost Owl would be more effective in eliciting this actor's cooperation."

Even Tim's face lit up at the idea. "Then, partner, I think we need to get dressed for visiting while Aisha pulls our actor's address for us."

CHAPTER 29

When the steel door leading to the sewer system creaked, Harri jumped off the couch, snatched a modified Taser off Tim's makeshift coffee table, and pointed it at the groaning metal.

Aisha looked up from the numbers she was crunching on her tablet. "Seriously, girl? We would have heard his booby-traps going off long before now."

Harri lowered the Taser as Tim entered, followed by Rey. Brown sludge stained their superhero togs from the waist down. "Well?" she blurted. A wave of odor emanated from the open doorway that churned her stomach. She dropped the weapon and covered her mouth and nose with both hands.

It didn't help.

"Do you really want to have this conversation before we're clean?" A ghost of a smile filtered through the lower half of Tim's face shield. He shut the door and reactivated the alarm system.

"Short answer—no." Aisha's words were muffled by her own hand over her nose and mouth. Her cheeks had a distinctly greenish cast that her dark skin couldn't hide.

"Seismic Shock's body double confirmed he was at the Lesleyworld and children's hospital appearances," Rey muttered. "And if you think we smell awful, imagine having super senses." He stomped off in the direction of Tim's gym.

"Thank god, you have two bathrooms," Harri mumbled.

"Actually, three working." Tim slid off his helmet and set it aside. "It was more for convenience because of my knees than the thought I'd have this many guests. But we have the recording, and he's convinced it's in his best interest to cooperate with Eddie in the investigation." He pulled a small device from a pocket and handed it to Harri before he limped in the direction of his bedroom.

"Harri!" Arthur rushed into the living room, his laptop in hand.

"Please tell me Patty didn't go into labor," she quipped.

Confusion marred Arthur's face as he processed her off-the-cuff remark. He shook his head. "No, I finally convinced her to get some sleep."

Harri definitely owed Rey. He'd retrieved his cot from his room at the condemned hotel for Patty. No one wanted to take the chance of going home. Not even Patty. Not after the incident with Sparx.

"I traced Bloch's personal accounts." He sat next to Harri on the couch and flipped open the device. "It looks like he's setting up his own personal fiefdom in Canyon Pointe. And if Mr. Baxter was on to him, it would explain the Lake County Retirement Home. From what Tim has put together, General Trubble is too intelligent and strategic of a thinker to do anything sloppy that would reveal Corvus's existence."

"What do you mean about a 'personal fiefdom'?" Harri leaned forward and squinted at the screen since she'd loaned her reading glasses to Aisha.

Arthur tapped a key, and a graph sprang up. "First of all, he's paying the mayor, the judge, and the DA." He pointed at the graph. "A small sum each month. Small enough for it to slide under the IRS's radar." He looked pointedly at Harri. "He's been doing it since the day murder charges were filed against Tim."

Aisha rose from her chair and crossed to look at the computer over Harri and Arthur's shoulders. "That isn't much. Hell, he could claim he was reimbursing those three for golf fees at the country club."

"But the bulk of his money is going somewhere else." Arthur tapped another key. A picture of the nine-block area everyone referred to as the Canyon District popped up on the screen. Nearly all of it was flagged in red. Splotches of other colors interrupted the eye-blistering scarlet, including one spot Harri recognized as the Lechuza Building.

"Bloch bought a few of the buildings." Another tap of the key revealed five locations marked with white cross-hatching the red. "But he promptly sold them for a loss."

"Money-laundering?" Aisha ventured.

"Yeah, combined with tax fraud." Anger itched along Harri's spine. "Who owns them now?"

Arthur chuckled, the first time she could remember hearing him laugh. "I had to chase through a series of shell companies, but everything marked in red is ultimately owned by City Restoration Holdings. It is owned by Bloch, DA Michaels, Judge Burgess and the Samuels brothers."

"Bastards!" The exclamation was followed by a crack.

They all twisted to look behind them. Tim's whole body shook and his knuckles bled, probably from the fist-sized hole in the drywall.

At the agonized look on his face, Harri handed the recording device to Arthur before she rose, crossed the floor, and gently grasped Tim's hand. "Let's get these cuts cleaned up. We'll talk when Rey's out of the shower." She looked over her shoulder at Aisha and Arthur. "You two keep digging."

⎯ ⦁ ⎯

"Sit down." Harri motioned toward Tim's bed. The room was neat. Precise. For an instant, she had the uncomfortable impression Tim and Rey were simply two sides of the same coin.

The fact Tim did as she ordered without any innuendo said how shaken he was. She followed the humidity to his bathroom and flipped the light switch. It was as neat and precise as his bedroom. The full-sized cabinet between the sink and the door not only had the expected linens, but rivaled an ER. Suture kits. Antibiotics. Even a couple of IVs.

She grabbed a bottle of alcohol, bandages, medical tape, and a couple of clean washcloths. When she reentered Tim's bedroom he stared blankly at the far wall. She set the medical supplies on his nightstand and sat gingerly next to him.

Under her concern for him, a thread of anger ignited. "How much longer are you going to pout?"

His head jerked, and he turned to glare at her. "What?"

"You heard me." She grabbed his injured hand, none too gently this time, and he hissed in pain.

"You don't understand," he growled.

"Yes, I do." She opened the bottle and deliberately poured alcohol over his knuckles. The fumes stung her nostrils, and alcohol splashed on the concrete.

"What the fuck is wrong with you?" He yanked his hand away from her.

Harri screwed the lid back on and set the bottle on the nightstand. "I could say the same thing about you."

"My family died so those bastards could get rich!"

"No," she said quietly. "They died for the same reasons my parents died. Sheer human stupidity. I have a strong feeling Shift fucked up that night at your house. He simply isn't that smart. Hell, even Arthur can see it, and he's not the most socially astute person I've ever met. The rest of it comes down to our city's leaders being greedy, opportunistic assholes."

"And this wonderful insight gives you the right to torture people?"

"If that's what it takes to keep the Ghost Owl's head in the game, then yes." Harri shook her head. "These assholes have shown they're willing to kill. We can't save your family, but what about Miguel's? Qiang's?" She jabbed a finger in the direction of the living room. "I've got an assistant with a baby on the way whose life is in danger because those same assholes needed me out of the way to fulfill their plan. I'm not checking out on her, and I damn well will not let you check out either. Not now. This plan needs the Ghost Owl. If Tim Canyon wants to check out of this world, I can't stop him. But I would hope the Ghost Owl would stick around long enough to complete the job."

Tim looked away from her. She took the opportunity to gently wipe bloody alcohol from his skin with one of the washcloths.

She'd wrapped his hand in gauze and sealed it with medical tape before he sighed.

"You're right."

"Well, that makes you smarter than my ex-husband."

Tim shook his head and chuckled. "So what's the plan?"

"Let's see what else Aisha and Arthur have found." She stood and held out her hand. "Would the Ghost Owl care to join us?"

"Yes." Tim rose and clasped her palm in his. "Would it be okay if he brings Tim Canyon along for the ride?"

"As long as he doesn't whine." She grinned up at him. "There's no whining in superheroing."

— ·◆· —

When Harri and Tim re-entered the living room, Patty had joined the other three at the table.

Harri touched her assistant's shoulder. "Why aren't you sleeping?"

"Because the baby started playing bongos on my bladder." Patty shot a sly look at Rey who immediately blushed. "It was worth seeing a naked superhero."

"You what?" From the look on Aisha's face, Harri half-expected her to stab Patty.

"I was in so much of a hurry to get out of that filthy Captain Justice uniform, I forgot to lock the door," Rey mumbled.

I'm too late. Aisha and Rey are already sleeping together. Harri bit her tongue to keep from saying the thought out loud. It would make things worse, and they were in too much damn trouble right now.

Instead, she cleared her throat. "Have you crossed referenced the actor's appearances?"

Aisha shook herself out of her jealous stint and pushed her legal pad across the table. "For every children's event, a seven-figure sum was deposited in Shift's public persona account allegedly from Hi-Gel's parent company America Clean, Inc. Shift has an endorsement deal for Hi-Gel's men's hair products. But the routing number does not belong to America Clean. It belongs to *American* Clean, a private company."

"That's a shell company for Corvus," Tim said.

"What's more interesting are things happening around the world when compared to Darryl Bloch's flight itineraries," Arthur said. "These all correspond to the payments and the impersonator's public appearance."

Dinner from earlier curdled in Harri's stomach as Arthur went through his list. A government coup in Central America after a major earthquake. The death of a Chinese official who opposed the current leader's trade policies when his vacation house collapsed in another tremor. Even the landslide that led to the tragic loss of an up-and-coming young American congresswoman.

"Please, stop." Harri held up her hand to halt Arthur's recitation.

"But, Harri, there's—"

Patty laid a hand on Arthur's arm. "We get the gist, sweetie."

"Harri," Aisha said softly, concern twisting her face. "We need to deliver this to someone, but who can we trust outside of Eddie? I don't want to put him and his family in danger."

"You're right." Harri took a deep shuddering breath. "He can't do this alone. I hate to say this, but—" She swallowed hard. "Who can we trust locally?"

"You're asking if Eddie's wrong about Cal and whether my ex is dirty?"

Aisha leaned back in her chair. "He's a total shit, but I would have to say no. Cheating on me is one thing. Murder?" She shook her head. "I think you can count on Judge Inunza, too. Not to mention Eddie's old partner would know who in CPPD is clean and who isn't."

Harri turned to Tim. "You're our client. Do I have permission to say the Ghost Owl is helping us put together the case?"

He stared at the tabletop for a few minutes before he looked at her. "I know you and Aisha trust these people, but only Eddie knows the truth about me. We need to keep it that way for a while longer. At least until Bloch is in jail."

"Agreed." Harri's gaze swept the group. "Anybody else have any concerns or suggestions?"

Everybody shook their heads.

She smiled at Aisha. "I'll call your ex if you call mine."

Her partner's lips twitched. "Deal."

Chapter 30

Holding the client/staff/ex-husband meeting in the Franklin & Winters conference room the following evening had seemed like a good idea when Harri proposed it. Especially after their furniture and carpet arrived a few hours before they met.

Everyone sat at the table except Tim and Rey who propped up the corners of the outside wall. Eddie, of course, sat at the head of the table, but Harri didn't give a shit about his posturing.

Patty's presence on her right worried Harri more. Especially with the proverbial bullseye painted on her butt. But that didn't account for all of her anxiety.

She wanted to blame her nervous feeling on the tension from certain participants. Cal had been dumb enough to sit to the left of Eddie and right across the table from Aisha. But Tim's anti-surveillance devices were probably the real culprits. Their sub-audible hum bounced off the walls of their little conference room and rattled her teeth. Or it could be sheer nerves over Sparx's failure to appear. They should never have trusted her.

Harri pointedly stared at her watch before looking at her partner seated beside her.

Aisha lifted her chin. "Give her some more time. Miguel's not here yet either."

"Before you two ladies have a naked pillow fight—" Eddie started.

Harri turned her glare on him, "Don't. Just don't." The rest of the men and Patty had expressions of disgust to varying degrees as they too watched him.

Eddie raised his hands in surrender. "Sorry. Just trying to break the tension in here."

"Can we go over what evidence you two do have?" Cal leaned his elbows on the table. "I'm already in enough trouble for missing dinner with my in-laws."

"Missing dinner with my parents never bothered you when we were married," Aisha said.

"Maybe because Mina's parents don't spend the entire meal sniping at each other," he shot back.

When Rey pushed away from the corner where he stood, Harri jumped to her feet. The last thing they needed was Aisha's current—whatever the hell Rey was—beating the crap out of her ex.

"Eddie, fill them in on what you told Aisha."

He sat up straighter, all business now. "The reason the FBI opened the Canyon Pointe office is due to the high number of civil rights and criminal investigation irregularities over the last few years. Arthur and Harri's bogus arrests aren't the first."

Tim coughed "Bullshit" into his fist.

Eddie gave him a slightly sympathetic nod. "Believe it or not, your case wasn't the first either. Whoever was behind this earlier was careful."

"We know who's behind it." Tim glared at Eddie.

"Evidence, man. We need hard evidence. And right now, we've got nothing tying Corvus to this mess that's admissible in either state or federal court. You already admitted you think Bloch's off the reservation. We'd be cleaning up Corvus's mess for them." The two men stared at each other with unreadable expressions.

"What Eddie is saying is we may be taking Corvus down one corrupt superhero at a time," Harri said. Tim's attention shifted to her. The anger and pain in his eyes was almost unbearable, but he nodded his acquiescence.

"Go back a sec, Eddie." Patty rubbed her swollen abdomen. "What do you mean about the asshole behind this being 'careful'?"

"The uptick was so gradual over twenty years no one paid attention. But the higher ups in D.C. definitely noticed the surge in oddities when Samuels took office." Eddie spread his hands again. "I'm sorry I can't get into specifics since these are ongoing investigations."

"RICO," Aisha stated.

"What?" Harri's gaze flitted between the two.

Aisha's expression was peeved. She jabbed a thumb at Eddie. "He already knew about the payoffs and the property bullshit. The FBI's trying to nail Samuels, Michaels and Burroughs on RICO charges."

Harri turned back to Eddie. Her nails dug into her palms. "Seriously? You used me for a fishing expedition?"

"And you're not using me?" There wasn't any bite in his words. In fact, he appeared sad.

She crossed her arms. "I thought this was a group effort."

"I've been after Bloch for years," Eddie snapped. "You're the newb on this case, Harri."

Aisha rolled her chair back a couple of inches. Whether to encourage her to smack Eddie or to get the hell out of the way was the question.

Harri tried to dial back her anger, but blood still simmered in her veins. "Corvus has been trying to control this city for years. Every time I was shut out of a meeting, someone from Corvus was here."

"Every time?" Eddie's thick right eyebrow climbed his forehead.

"All right." She held up her hands. "Definitely, the one's with Seismic Shift. I need a warrant for the rest."

"Didn't you just tell Tim we may have to take down Corvus one super at a time?" Eddie sniped.

"People—" Tim appeared relaxed where he leaned against the opposite corner of the room from Rey, but she noticed the tension along his neck and jaw. "Eddie's right. It doesn't matter how each of us got our information. The question is do we have enough all together to bring Bloch down."

Harri stared at Tim in disbelief. They'd both worked too hard to make all the connections. He gave a slight shake of his head, and her heart sank.

Dammit, Tim being right was almost as bad as when Eddie was right. They might be able to take down Seismic Shift, but Corvus was out of reach. For now anyway. When had that become so important to her?

When she started having feelings for Tim Canyon.

Ignoring the realization, Harri sucked in a deep breath. "Here's what we've found out."

She laid out the discovery the federal government had accidentally delivered to her. That someone broke into her old desk top and removed the digital files, but Patty and Arthur had already made backups. The payments to Seismic Shift. The assassinations. The actor confirming he'd stood in for Shift's public appearances during the same times.

Tim summarized his observations and collection of information over the past twenty years, especially Corvus's involvement in local politics. Arthur backed him up with his traces on the hacking. Patty added the attempts on Harri and Aisha's lives over the past month.

The only question left was whether Cal was on board with their plans. Even if it was just to keep his mouth shut. Harri didn't have the faith in him Aisha still appeared to.

He was quiet for a long time before he said, "What else do you have?"

"Isn't this enough?" Harri snapped.

"No." He shook his head. "We have to be dead sure."

"How dead do I have to be before you can make up your mind?" She jabbed a finger in Aisha's direction. "How dead does she have to be!"

Cal slammed his palm on the table. "I've got a family to think about. You don't!"

"What about the rest of us?" Aisha said quietly. "You think I'm not worried about my parents? My brother and sister? LaShun's husband and kids?" She inclined her head toward Patty. "What about her? Or Eddie's wife? You're not the only one with babies on the way."

Harri thought Aisha was done, but she was just warming up. "What about Tim? His wife and baby are dead thanks to Bloch. What about Rey's mama? Murdered because no one else wanted to stand up to the ugly things happening in Canyon Pointe. If we don't start making this city a better place, no one's family will be safe."

Even though Cal had the grace to look abashed at Aisha's lecture, it did nothing to stem Harri's blood from sliding from simmer to boil. "Let it go, sweetie. He's only worried about his own skin."

"That's not fair, Harri, and you know it." Aisha's eyes narrowed. "His concerns are valid. How would you have felt if Rey hadn't rescued Patty from the City Hall fire?"

A flood of shame drowned her anger. "That's different."

"Is my son different enough for you to want to save, too?" Sparx stood in the doorway to the conference room in jeans and a polo, typical soccer mom attire. She didn't need her superhero costume or powers. Her expression could have killed everyone present.

Harri winced. The ugly look was aimed at her and no one else.

Miguel stood behind Sparx, but his expression was distraught. "And what about my Francisco? How are you going to save him, Ms. Winters?"

Tim pushed away from the corner, his arms dropping to his sides. "What's going on?"

"Bloch snatched the boy about an hour ago." Amid the murmurs and curse words of the rest of the group, Sparx pulled her phone from her hip pocket. "I tried to talk him out of it." Her eyes narrowed. "But I'm not giving you the recording of him admitting he's been trying to kill Winters unless I have some guarantees of my own family's safety. The minute Bloch finds out I've turned on him, he'll kill my son and my parents. So, Winters, is my son special enough?"

"Of course, he is," Aisha said. She stood.

"I want to hear it from her." Sparx voice was low, deadly . . . and desperate Harri realized.

And damn, if it didn't make her feel like the most callous jerk on the planet. "Of course, your family's important. Everybody's is." She turned to Tim. "How do we get Francisco back?"

He, in turn, faced Miguel. "Tell us exactly what happened."

Miguel's voice caught for a moment. "H-he grabbed my baby on his way home from a friend's house. Javier was supposed to fetch him, but—" Anger and fear warred for his expression. "H-he wants me to lure Ms. Winters to the Canyon Building tomorrow morning. He's using the demolition supplies delivered earlier today. The office building's already wired to blow." He clasped the female super's shoulder. "Ms. Sparx recorded the entire conversation."

"That stuff is supposed to be locked up and under guard," Eddie growled.

"Not if Samuels or Bloch paid off the police." For the first time, Cal sounded truly angry at the corruption.

"Why not use his powers? Claim it was a natural disaster?" Arthur spoke up for the first time.

Tim crossed his arms again. Harri was beginning to recognize it was his favorite thinking pose. "He can't without arousing suspicion. Canyon Pointe is too far from any of the major continental fault lines. Plus, his amplifier emits a specific signature. He had to pay off his co-conspirators to cover up Baxter's death, and we still have no idea why Baxter was a threat to him."

Eddie grinned. "So that's how you've been tracking his activities."

"Some of them," Tim said. "Arthur was instrumental in tracking down the rest. And we can compare natural quakes to Bloch's using data from the U.S. Geological Survey to prove he was the cause."

"We need to go rescue Francisco now." Rey edged toward Miguel and the door.

Tim circled the conference table to intercept them. "Do you two trust me?"

Both men nodded, Miguel hopeful, but Rey wary.

"We're going to let Bloch keep Francisco for a few hours." Tim grinned, a tight hard thing that scared Harri.

"Are you insane?" She stomped around the table, past Arthur and Patty, and glared up at him. "We can't leave an innocent little boy in that psycho's hands!"

Behind her, Cal muttered, "Oh, sure, but my kids she'll let him kill." The words were quickly followed by a grunt of pain. She didn't bother to check who had kicked him into silence, though she wouldn't put it past either Aisha or Eddie.

Tim rested his large palms on Harri's shoulders. "Trust me. I have a plan." He turned back to Miguel. "He's watching the office?"

Both Miguel and Sparx shook their heads.

"I told him I had to come to finish some work in the building tonight. Otherwise, Ms. Winters would grow suspicious," he said.

"And guess who's supposed to be watching your guy." Sparx smirked. "I'm playing Miguel's new girlfriend."

"That doesn't make sense." Harri didn't want to admit how much Tim's touch settled her racing heart. "Why wait?"

"He's having problems keeping tabs on Captain Justice," Sparx replied. "Shift's worried about getting caught."

Miguel fidgeted. "I told Shift that Rey will definitely be here in the morning since he's helping with the renovations."

"And I already told Bloch I made an appointment with you in my civilian guise tomorrow in order to take you out." Sparx's smirk widened into a full grin. "But you've pissed him off enough that he wants to do you personally. Now, I'm supposed to distract Rey while Miguel here appeals to your ambulance-chasing instincts."

Harri decided to ignore the insult. "But Seismic Shift is expecting you to go back to him today. How soon?"

"Two hours. Tops," Sparx said.

Tim's own grin widened to match Sparx. "Play your recording. I want to hear his full plan."

She thumbed the icon, then the speaker. The whole conversation rolled out. Sparx had listened to the tips they'd given her, and Bloch had no idea he played fill-in-the-blank on his oral confession.

Harri and Tim looked at each other, and said in unison, "We have him."

Eddie grunted. "There was a time we had that kind of rapport."

"You should have thought of that before you served me with divorce papers," she snapped back.

Aisha socked his shoulder. "You blew it." She turned to Cal. "Is an admission of kidnapping and conspiracy to commit murder enough to convince you?"

He nodded and leaned toward Eddie. "What do you need from me?"

"I have a list of officers I trust. But since I've been out of the force for a couple of years, cross reference with locals you trust, especially SWAT. My team will need backup if we're taking down a super." He leaned on the table, his chin resting on his fists. "The problem will be getting the kid out tonight without Bloch doing something stupid."

"No." Tim released Harri.

She didn't want him to let go, then wanted to kick herself. When had she become so needy? She'd always taken care of herself, even when she'd been with Eddie. Maybe that was part of the problem. If they'd had children, she would have needed him. There was no way she could handle even one kid by herself. Not when her sterling example of parenthood had done a header off a cliff while higher than a kite.

"We wait until Bloch leaves to meet Harri in the morning."

The enormity of what Tim said, considering what Bloch had done to his son, smacked her like a Mack truck. "You can't be serious!"

Tim turned to Miguel. "This is ultimately your call, but you know me. Hear me out before you make the decision."

The contractor nodded.

Tim turned to Sparx. "He's got Francisco in his warehouse at the docks, right? And he's rigged an ambush for Captain Justice."

Tim's statement shocked the grin off of Sparx. "How do you know about his warehouse?" She looked downright scared.

"We can't tell you yet," Harri interjected. "We've got a witness. Please trust us for a little while longer."

Sparx took a step back, her hand firmly wrapped around her phone. And they needed that phone. "If you don't tell me, then why should I trust any of you?"

"She's got a point," Aisha said.

Harri pivoted to face her partner.

Aisha shrugged. "She and Cal are the only ones in the room who don't know." She shot her ex an evil smile. "As long as Cal promises not to press charges . . ."

"Or what? Are you really threatening an ADA?"

Harri covered her mouth to hide her silent laughter at Cal's incredulous expression. To egg him even further, Tim leaned over and whispered in Sparx's ear.

She jumped back and nearly stumbled over Miguel. He steadied her, but she stared at Tim. "No freakin' way."

"Do you trust us now?" His indigo blue eyes stared into Sparx's big brown ones.

She slowly nodded, her expression still incredulous. "If anyone can make this crazy plan work, it's the Ghost Owl."

"The Ghost Owl?" Cal rose abruptly. "We can't bring a vigilante into this case!"

"Shut up, Cal," Aisha and Eddie said.

"We're only going to use him to get Francisco out of the warehouse when Bloch comes to kill me." Fear burned her throat as Harri said the words. She glanced up at Tim. "Right?"

"Yeah, and we've got to disable the charges he's already rigged across the street." He clasped Miguel's shoulder. "Feel up to helping me before you have to go back?'

Despite his sickly expression, Miguel nodded.

Eddie rose. "I can keep the demolition crew out in the morning, but there's god-knows-how-many squatters in the Canyon Block. What happens if he decides to risk using his powers when the explosives don't go off?"

"Sparx and I can get them out," Rey stated.

"And I can rig a booby-trap to take out Bloch without any police or civilian casualties," Tim added.

"Uh, excuse me?" Harri propped her hands on her hips. "Remember who's going to be at ground zero of your little trap?"

Tim shot her a mischievous grin. "I'm not about to put my favorite attorney in harm's way. Can you follow my directions?"

A snort came from Eddie's direction followed by "Good luck with that, man."

But Tim's expression was so earnest, so protective, she couldn't help saying, "Yes."

He clapped his hands. "Okay, folks, we've got a lot to do and only a few hours to do it."

———•—

Aisha followed Eddie out to his pickup to help him bring in camping equipment. The last thing she wanted to do was sleep on the concrete floor in Tim's lair for a second night, but it was the one defensible place they had.

However, six people crowded in a small space was worse than when she, Harri and Jeremy had roomed together during college. She wanted a little quiet. A glass of wine. A long soak in her garden tub.

No, what she really needed was just two minutes alone.

Or a cigarette.

And helping Eddie kept her guilty conscience off what had happened, was happening, between Rey and her.

"So when did Harri and Tim become an item?"

Eddie's question jerked Aisha out of the places in her head she swore she wouldn't go. "You know attorneys can't date clients." Amazingly, her nose stayed the same size.

"Uh-huh. So when did they start not-dating?" Eddie handed her two bed-rolls with straps.

She slung those over each shoulder. "They aren't dating. Too much baggage between the two of them." She glared at him. "A couple of tons of which is you."

"And the twenty tons of Harri's fucked up family didn't count when we were married?" He handed Aisha an air mattress before loading his own arms.

"Why do you care? You're the one who left her, or did you conveniently forget that?"

Eddie paused. "Believe it or not, I want her to be happy. But I couldn't make her happy, and I got tired of being miserable trying to please her."

Aisha leaned against the bed of his truck. She really couldn't hate him on Harri's behalf anymore because he was right. "I know. I'm sorry she wasn't honest with you. She wasn't honest with herself about what she wanted." She sighed. "I think she likes him . . ."

"But she's using the ethics thing to keep him at arms' length?"

Aisha chuckled. "Among other things. Corvus thugs attacking them on their only night out didn't help."

"Good grief." Eddie laughed and nudged the cab door shut.

As they headed back into the Lechuza Building, a shout of "Miss Aisha" came from behind them. Rey herded the rest of the Esperanza boys across the street. Everyone was loaded with backpacks and sleeping bags, their own mini Boy Scout troop.

Except they looked terribly somber for a sleepover. Either Rey or Miguel had told them what had happened to Francisco.

They reminded her that she had nothing to wear for tomorrow. And she could almost guarantee that she'd be in front of cameras for the post-flying shit news conference. Even worse, she didn't have a toothbrush. And the mints from Patty's stash only went so far.

"Eddie, can I borrow your truck for a bit?"

"Why?" Eddie's eyes narrowed.

She glared at him. "Do I really have to get into the subject of clean under-wear with you?"

Instead of the fight she expected, he dug into his pocket and tossed her the keys.

She turned to Rey and the three kids. Okay, maybe not kids. Dom and Emilio were close to Rey's age. "You boys follow Mr. Eddie inside. He and Miss Harri will show you where you can set up camp."

As they trooped through the front doors in Eddie's wake, Aisha slung her load into Rey's arms. "I've got to run home and pack a bag for tonight."

"Let me come with you."

"No." She raced upstairs to her temporary office and grabbed her purse. When she jogged back downstairs, Rey still stood in the reception area.

He frowned. "You heard Tim. It's not safe for any of us to be out alone."

"I'm just running to my condo, grabbing a few clothes, and coming straight back."

"It's not worth the risk," he said.

"Aren't you supposed to be helping Tim and Miguel disarm the explosives?"

"It'll only take us a few minutes to fly to your place and back—"

"I don't need you clinging to me! God, grow a backbone!" she snapped.

Instead of becoming angry, a hurt puppy expression appeared on Rey's face. The same expression Cal had used to manipulate her for years. For once, the anger in her didn't diminish. It grew.

She whirled away from him and charged for the front doors.

———— •●•· ————

The drive to her condo in the late spring dusk gave Aisha time to cool down, but resentment still simmered. She parked in a visitor spot close to the main door. Thankfully, no one else boarded the car during her short elevator ride to her condo. She couldn't deal with small talk. Not now.

Her place was so familiar that she didn't bother turning on the lights as she strode down the hallway to her bedroom. Though she hadn't seen anyone follow her in a black SUV or otherwise, no sense letting anyone from outside know she was here.

Oh, who was she really kidding? She didn't want a clear look at her bed. At the accidental crack in the headboard Rey had inflicted.

A shiver rippled through her at the memory. That man was addictive. Maybe more so than cigarettes, and if that was the case, she was in really big trouble.

Forcing her mind to the business at hand, Aisha tossed her new purse on the bed and reached into her closet for her small suitcase she used for business trips. As she packed, it gave her too much time to think. Had she been too harsh with Rey this evening? He meant well. It's just that Cal—

No, she couldn't go there. It wasn't fair to compare the two men. It especially wasn't fair to Rey. She just never had any male give her that much attention before. Even Dad didn't hover like that when she was a child though she'd been the youngest for seven years before Martin came along.

Aisha was reaching for the bathroom light switch to collect her toiletry bag when she heard the creak of hardwood. But she didn't make the noise.

It came from the living room.

CHAPTER 31

Aisha held her breath as a second creak followed the first. Footsteps. She'd locked the door when she came in.

Hadn't she?

She slowly lowered her hand from the light switch, thankful she hadn't turned it on and ruined her night vision. The more terrifying thought was Harri and Tim were right about all of the team watching out for each other. She had brutally rebuffed Rey's offer to come with her.

Now, her need of a little alone time seemed like a very bad idea.

Another creak. Closer than the last. Whoever was in the condo was creeping her way.

For an instant, she wanted to believe one of the guys had followed her after all, but Rey would have announced himself. Arthur couldn't sneak if his life depended on it. And she'd bet her defunct BMW she never would have heard Tim even with the arthritis in his knees that he tried very hard to hide.

Given the fact Seismic Shift had sent Sparx to attack Harri last night, her guest was probably a super dispatched to kill her.

Aisha nibbled lipstick off her lower lip. Standing in the bathroom wasn't going to help. She needed a weapon. The toilet scrubber would just exfoliate her intruder. She dropped to her hands and knees and carefully crawled back to her closet. Maybe she'd get lucky if she threw stilettos at him.

Except that crap only worked in the movies.

She let her fingers drift over boxes, slippers, handbags. Hiding in the closet sounded damn good to her inner child. Her inner adult suggested 9-1-1, but a phone call to the police or even Eddie for help was out. Her intruder would hear.

Another creak. This time, it was accompanied by the rustle of carpet. He was in the hallway.

Aisha crawled further into the closet, and her fingers brushed unfamiliar leather. Cal's golf bag.

He'd made a point of learning the sport in law school. He insisted he needed his own clubs if DA Michaels ever invited him to Whitechapel, which never happened. Then Cal conveniently kept forgetting to pick them up because he hated golf even more than she did.

She rose up on her knees, tilted the bag, and pulled out what felt like a nine iron. That should leave a good-sized welt on her unwanted guest's head, even if he was a super, then she'd be able to run for the parking garage. At least, her decision to wear her favorite Manolo Blahnik ballerina flats had been smart.

Maybe her only smart decision in the last two decades.

When she rose to her feet, her chest ached, and she realized she'd been holding her breath. Blood pounded in her ears. She peeked out of the closet.

Nothing yet.

The door to the utility room squeaked. Thank god, Dad had been distracted by his fight with Mom, and he hadn't attacked the hinges with WD-40 like he swore he'd do. It also meant the intruder didn't have super hearing or x-ray vision. He wasn't sure where she was.

Easing along the wall to the bedroom door, Aisha lifted the club over her head and held her breath again. The floor creaked again. Shuffling. The faint wheeze of breathing. Her heart tried to hammer its way out of her chest.

He was on the other side of the wall.

A shadowy figure stepped through the doorway, and she brought down the nine iron.

CLANG!

Aisha was the one who cried out when agony shot through her hands and up her arms. Her intruder flipped on the lights.

She blinked away tears to find Cobblestone grinning at her. The steel shaft had bent around his pebbled scalp and impenetrable skull. He wrenched the ruined club from her numb fingers. His shove sent her sprawling on the bed. She landed on her purse, and something crunched under her hip.

At least it wasn't the mini-canister of mace Aisha carried at Harri's insistence since her mugging over a month ago.

"Well, I should give you credit for not trying to shoot me," he rumbled. "You got any idea how many idiots have been hurt by the ricochet?"

She glared at him. "What do you want?"

"Quit yer job for yer own good."

Play dumb, girl. She tried for an air of confusion. "I already did."

"The new one," he amended.

So much for playing dumb. Now she understood Harri's irritation with supers. The dialogue never changed. Aisha sighed. "Or what?"

He crossed his arms. "Do you know what happens to someone dropped from a fourth story window?"

"Yeah, my law partner's replacement at City Hall sues your ass for the money to clean up the mess."

Cobblestone's chuckle sounded like gravel shaken in a tin can. "And here I was told yer the smart one. He left out the smartass part."

If only she could pull her phone out to record this conversation, assuming that wasn't what crunched when she landed on her purse. On the other hand getting out of this alive was pretty damn important, too. Maybe she could keep Cobblestone talking long enough . . .

"Who called me a smartass?"

He opened his mouth, but the hamster finally got his brain wheel turning. His jaws snapped shut with a crack. "Never ya mind."

"Was it Trubble?"

Cobblestone blinked a couple of times, and confusion filled his eyes. For the first time, she noticed his irises weren't a true green. The flecks of color resembled granite.

"How do you know about—" he started, but she cut him off with a wave.

Aisha sat up on the bed and pulled her purse from under her hip. "If it wasn't Trubble, then it had to be Seismic Shift."

He shuffled a bit, smashing the carpet fibers. "Aw, I wasn't gonna hurt you, no matter what that asshole told me to do."

"He told you to hurt me? Why?"

Despite Cobblestone's six-and-a-half feet in height and a half-ton of muscle beneath his nearly invulnerable hide, he looked like a little boy caught with his hand in the cookie jar. And dammit, if she didn't feel a little sorry for the guy. And a hell of a lot angrier at Shift after he threatened Sparx's kid and kidnapped Francisco.

"Cobblestone, did Seismic Shift threaten to hurt someone you care about if you didn't do what he said?"

His expression flashed from embarrassment to a fear so raw she could feel it. "Please, just quit yer job, so no one gets hurt."

Aisha pushed herself to her feet. "You're not the first person he's threatened." She laid her hand on his arm. "Let us help you. Who did he threaten? Was it your mom? Your sister?"

"A nurse. Her name's Claire." His gravelly voice became even hoarser. "She works in the kids' cancer wing at Canyon Pointe General."

The anger in Aisha's blood turned to a burning rage. Shift had an actor stand in for him at charity events because he abhorred children, but from what she'd seen, Cobblestone actually enjoyed his personal appearances. Especially if kids were involved.

"Let me guess. Shift knows you have a thing for Claire."

Cobblestone couldn't meet her gaze. "It's not like I got up the nerve to ask her out or anything, but she's really good with those kids, ya know."

This could all be an act, but just like with Sparx, Aisha's gut said he was telling her the truth.

"Would you let me help you?"

He snorted. "What could you do?"

"I've got people who can protect your friend Claire if you're willing to press extortion charges against Shift."

Cobblestone's snort turned into outright guffaws. "Who? Mr. Tighty Whitey? Even that asshole Shift would make hamburger out of him."

She swallowed her irritation at his estimate of Rey's abilities, along with a scoop of annoyance she hadn't insisted that Jeremy use more red in Rey's costume. Now wasn't the time to let personal feelings get in the way. She debated how much to tell the super in front of her.

"Not just Captain Justice," she said. "This isn't the first time Seismic Shift has threatened somebody. There's an ongoing investigation. If you're in, you don't have to worry about anyone hurting your friend."

He crossed his arms over his chest. "I ain't agreeing to anything until ya tell me who'd be protecting Claire."

"Would the Ghost Owl be sufficient?"

Cobblestone stared at her for an instant before he burst into laughter. "No urban legend's gonna work. You need a real super."

"I wouldn't lie when an innocent person's life depended on it."

"Yer serious?"

"Yes."

His face shifted and crumpled. "Thank you." He scooped her into a bear hug that was damn uncomfortable with the texture of his skin.

A loud crack interrupted the brief expression of emotion. Cobblestone loosened his grip, and Aisha turned to find most of the outer wall of her bedroom missing.

No, not missing. Rey, in his full Captain Justice regalia, held the wood frame with its crumbling plasterboard as he hovered where her window used to be. He dropped the wall, and she heard it smash and splinter on the sidewalk below.

"Take your hands off her," he ordered.

Cobblestone roughly shoved her behind him and into the bathroom. "This here's a private conversation between me and the lady, buddy. You need to leave."

"Not without her." Rey sounded possessive, menacing.

His caveman attitude sent a little thrill through her, but she needed to calm them both down before someone got hurt. She ducked under Cobblestone's elbow. "Let's ease up here, gentlemen—"

Cobblestone reached out for her and shouted, "Get back!"

At the same time, Rey yelled, "Get your hands off her!"

The speed of his passing literally sucked the air out of her. He bullrushed Cobblestone into her bathroom. It was followed by a boom and the brittle crackle of ceramic tile.

Another loud crash shook her condo. The hiss and burble of a broken water line preceded the water flowing out of the bathroom and soaking the bedroom carpet.

Aisha leaned over and peered into what was her master bath. A superhero-sized hole glared at her where the back wall of her shower used to be. Not just her bathroom either. In fact, she had a clear view into the Brinkmans' bedroom.

Mr. Brinkman was on all fours on the bed. Naked, except for a purple harness with a glittery pony's tail on his lower half, and matching bridle and ears on his head. Mrs. Brinkman wore an equally purple cowgirl outfit with strategic sections cut out.

They both stared back at Aisha before Mr. Brinkman spit out his bit and said, "Pumpernickel. Myrtle, I think we'd better call 9-1-1."

CHAPTER 32

Aisha wasn't sure whether to laugh or cry when male grunting came from the direction of her utility room. Her washing machine flew across the hallway and smashed through the wall of the guest bedroom. Rey flew in the same direction a second later.

Backwards.

She snatched her purse from the bed. Forget the suitcase. But there was no way past Rey and Cobblestone without getting clobbered herself.

As if the universe was listening, the drywall between her bedroom and the guest room exploded. Cobblestone sailed through the dust and landed on her mattress. Her beautiful ebony-lacquered custom frame shuddered for a moment before it collapsed under the super's weight.

So much for fixing her headboard.

"Through the hole," Mrs. Brinkman called out. She waved Aisha towards their condo. "Hurry."

Despite the purple cowgirl outfit burned into her retinas, Aisha knew her neighbor was right. Neither Rey or Cobblestone would listen to her right now. Stupid heroes and their need to smash things. For the first time, she truly understood Harri's irritation with supers.

Aisha plunged into her bathroom, sliding on ceramic chunks. Water from the smashed toilet arced through the air, soaking her.

Mrs. Brinkman yelled a wordless warning. Rough fingers grabbed the back of Aisha's neck. Her purse landed with a splash in her flooding master bath.

"Not so fast," Cobblestone rumbled. "Ah don't like being set up."

She clawed at his tight hold. "No one set you up! You snuck into my place!"

"But you had Tighty Whitey watching." It wasn't so much anger as fear in his voice. Whether it was for himself or his nurse friend was the question.

"Listen to me. We can help—"

A stream of Spanish invectives interrupted her attempt to negotiate. Cobblestone turned, dragging her by her neck. If she and Harri survived the next twenty-four hours, she was definitely planning a massage day at Jeremy's.

"Leave or I pop your girlfriend's head off."

"You harm her, and—" Rey started.

"Yo, Rocky," Mr. Brinkman's voice came from behind Aisha. Far too close to a desperate super.

She closed her eyes. The headlines flashed inside her lids anyway. *Elderly man dressed in purple pony harness dies in local attorney's bedroom.*

"Eat root beer!" Mr. Brinkman's battle cry made no sense, but Cobblestone yelped in pain.

Aisha's lids popped open as she dropped to the carpet. Wood and ceramic splinters jabbed her knees and palms. She looked up to find Cobblestone cursing as he tried to rub gel out of his eyes.

The label of the bottle Mr. Brinkman held caught her vision. Root beer-flavored . . . lube?

Rey seized the distraction to tackle Cobblestone, driving them both back through the hole between bedrooms, through the wall separating the guest bedroom and the living room, and through her entertainment center.

"You okay, sweetie?" Mr. Brinkman peered down at her. Unfortunately, his short stature left things dangling at her eye level that only Mrs. Brinkman should be viewing.

"I'm fine." Aisha winced at another crash from the direction of the dining room. "You and your wife need to get out of here."

"The police are on their way, and Myrtle went to pull the disaster alarm." Mr. Brinkman couldn't have timed his words better. The distinctive supervillain siren screeched its warning through the complex. "It'll still take the cops five more minutes to get here," he yelled over the alarm.

Which didn't drown out the sound of Rey beating Cobblestone over the head with Aisha's refrigerator. Thanks to all the holes in her walls, she couldn't miss the sight either.

Mr. Brinkman tugged on her arm. "Come on, sweetie. Let's get you someplace safe."

Cobblestone's indestructible skin must not apply to his internal organs. With one last blow of the mutilated refrigerator, he collapsed on the floor and didn't move.

"I think the worst is over," she shouted. "Why don't you go get—" The disaster alarm abruptly cut off. "—some clothes on?"

A snicker came from her bathroom. Mrs. Brinkman, who thankfully had thrown on a robe over her cowgirl outfit, leaned through the hole between the condos. "You might want to do what the girl said, Lester. I think you're too much man for her."

"After the parade she's had sleeping over for the past month, I think she'd handle me just fine," he retorted.

"Parade?" Aisha's gaze swiveled between her neighbors. "What parade?"

Mrs. Brinkman's expression turned mischievous. "Well, the older gentleman and the skinny boy aren't my taste. But the hot Latino? Ooo-la-la! And he looks even better in his superhero duds."

Aisha's embarrassment gelled into fear. Had she and Rey been too obvious? What if everyone in the building knew? This would be worse than Seismic Shift threatening her. She would get disbarred.

Or get her neighbors killed. Or her family.

God, how had this turned into such a mess? All because she lost her temper with her boss.

No, because some dumbass government clerk sent Harri a file she wasn't supposed to see.

Aisha climbed to her feet. Her soaked leather flats made squishy sounds. More of her belongings ruined in the fiasco her life had become.

As long as she focused on the mundane stuff, she wouldn't collapse into a sobbing ball of fear.

She grabbed Mr. Brinkman's fleshy arm, and grimaced at how brittle his bone felt under his papery skin. She guided him toward the hole in the wall.

"Mr. and Mrs. Brinkman, I need you to listen to me. This is very important. When the police interview you, you can't tell them about any of my guests." God, how she wished Eddie was wrong, but she had no way of knowing which of the officers on their way to her building this minute were clean.

"Oh, pshaw!" Mrs. Brinkman waved both hands. "We don't tattle, dear."

"Not about our friends' personal lives, anyway," her husband added.

"Though if you and Captain Justice want to do a foursome—" Mrs. Brinkman started.

"No!" Aisha forced a smile. "Not that I don't appreciate the offer, but with my new practice, I'll be moving soon anyway." Her laughter sounded strained to her own ears. "The condo association isn't going to be happy about a super-hero tussle in my unit."

A sharp breeze announced Rey's arrival. "Are you all right, Ms. Franklin?"

Good to know some of her lessons had sunk through.

She turned to him. "I'm fine." It took everything she had to keep her game face on, but he was smart enough to play stupid in front of an audience.

"Oh, please," Mrs. Brinkman blurted. "You two don't have to play dumb with us."

"And the kid might need me to back him up if that bozo Cobblestone wakes up before the cops get here," Mr. Brinkman said.

"Thanks for the offer, but I'm sure Captain Justice has things under control." Aisha flashed her media smile at the Brinkmans. Rey didn't, but she wasn't about to undermine a client in front of any member of the general public, including her neighbors.

She retrieved her sopping purse from the floor and fished out one of her new business cards. She had been right when she insisted on the extra money for the plastic-coated cardboard. "I'm sure we'll be fine until they arrive. Why don't you find a hotel? Send me the receipt, and I'll be happy to reimburse you." Another expense their fledging law firm didn't need, but a little glad-handing would go a long way.

"Aw, sweetie, you don't have to do that." But Mr. Brinkman grabbed the proffered card anyway.

"You might want to change before the police get here," she said as he climbed through the gaping hole where her shower wall used to be.

Aisha leaned over and twisted the knob for the supply line to the toilet. At least that valve hadn't been damaged in the boys' brouhaha. She straightened, soggy and dripping, and sloshed into the bedroom.

"Aisha?" At Rey's soft question and the concerned look in his eyes, the fear in her belly turned into a knot of rage.

She jabbed a forefinger in the direction of the remains of her living room. "In there. Now."

"But—"

"The neighbors don't need to hear this," she hissed.

The man who had dominated her in her bedroom shuffled down the crunching, ruined carpet like a chastised puppy. A reminder that she had no business sleeping with someone twenty years younger.

Drywall bits cracked under her shoes and dust clung to the wet leather as she followed Rey. Cobblestone still sprawled across her entryway, out cold. She tossed her purse onto the one intact chair. It landed with a *splooch* on the cushion.

She planted her fists on her hips while she contemplated the unconscious super. "We need to secure him until the police arrive. I'm not having a repeat of what just happened."

Rey whipped past her and a cold breeze pierced her soaked clothing. He was back a minute later with a length of high-tensile steel cable coiled over his shoulder. Within seconds, Cobblestone was cocooned.

She didn't want to ask, but did anyway. "Where did you get the cable?"

"Off one of the truck reels at the causeway repair site." Rey crossed his arms.

"You're going to have to reimburse the state department of transportation."

"I've had that talk already with Harri. I'm not going to be one of those assholes," he snarled. "Why are you getting pissed at me? I wasn't the one threatening to pop off your head."

"Cobblestone didn't threaten me until you started whaling on him."

"I only whaled on him because he planned to drop you out of your window."

Aisha dropped her hands from her waist and dug her nails into her palms in a supreme effort to not do anything stupid. "I'm not sure which is worse, you spying on me or you not bothering to listen to the entire conversation you're eavesdropping on!"

"Somebody was trying to kill you!"

"So now, you attack anyone I speak with?"

Rey threw his hands in the air. "That's not true, and you know it!"

"Really? It sounds like standard super behavior. I mean, none of you can just say 'Hi' or shake hands, even when you're both good guys. No-o-o-o-o. You have to pummel each other until someone is unconscious." She pointed at Cobblestone.

Rey crossed his arms again. "I get it. This is about us. You're using him as an excuse to drive me away."

"Of all the conceited—" She rammed her fingers into her hair and yanked.

"Not everything is about you. I had him talked down until you ripped off my bedroom wall!"

"You are loco! He admitted Shift sent him here to kill you!"

A loud rumbling moan made them both look down.

One granite-flecked eye peered up at them. "Can you two lovebirds leave the screaming at your couples therapist? I've got a major league headache thanks to the concussion Mr. Tighty Whitey gave me."

"Don't call me Tighty Whitey," Rey growled.

"I'll call you whatever the hell I want, Nacho Boy."

Rey muttered an obscenity in Spanish regarding Cobblestone's parentage and raised his fist.

"Stop!" Aisha poked a forefinger into his chest. "You. Go sit over there." She aimed her index finger at what was left of her couch.

Cobblestone snickered, but one look shut him up.

She crouched next to him. The motion squeezed more water out of her jeans, and it ran down her ankles and into her ruined shoes.

"Here's the deal. You tell me everything you know about Seismic Shift, Trubble and Corvus. You also pay—"

"Nacho Boy started it," Cobblestone protested.

She held up her forefinger, and he subsided.

"You both are at fault." She lowered her hand to her knee when he remained silent. "You will also pay half of my losses from your battle here tonight. In return, I'll help you get the best defense attorney in town, and Claire will be protected."

"And if I don't?" But she could tell he already made his decision.

"I file assault charges against you on top of the public nuisance charge the DA will file. If I do, we both know your nurse friend won't see tomorrow's sunrise."

"What makes you think I'm afraid of you?"

Men. They always think they have to get that last word in.

Aisha smiled sweetly. "Cobblestone, honey, the only thing more dangerous than a superhero is his attorney."

CHAPTER 33

The next morning, Aisha tapped her pen in a rapid-fire rhythm on her new desktop. Rey and Arthur had gotten bored last night. Rey moved the new furniture into all the offices while Arthur hooked up their phones.

Though more likely, Rey was feeling guilty or embarrassed about their fight in front of Cobblestone.

She was more worried about Francisco. Why didn't Sparx warn them of Shift's plan to kidnap the kid before he did it? Had she really changed sides?

Sure, Aisha had been the one to stand up for the super to Harri, but after Cobblestone threatened to pop off Aisha's head last night, all bets were suspect. The friction burns still hurt and had made sleep last night uncomfortable as hell.

She didn't have to worry about Miguel's acting abilities. The man was terrified about losing Francisco. So was she, but she trusted Tim to rescue the kid.

Funny. When this mess all started, she never thought she'd trust a man she truly believed had gotten away with murder twenty years ago.

The clock on her infected computer flipped to eight-fifty-eight. Good thing she wasn't normally a morning person. Neither Corvus nor Seismic Shift would be expecting much activity from her, assuming they were even watching her now.

No, someone would be watching her, which was the whole reason Tim and Arthur insisted she use her infected machine. So she flipped through news sites. She sure as hell couldn't concentrate on any work. Not with Harri and Miguel walking into a death trap in a few minutes.

God, she wished she had a cigarette to take the edge off, but she'd promised Rey she'd try to quit. That left banging her pen.

Which flew through the air the instant her intercom buzzed.

"Ms. Franklin, your nine o'clock is here." Patty's voice sounded as shaky as Aisha's knees felt when she stood.

She pressed the button to respond. "Be right there." And winced that her voice sounded as bad as Patty's. They all needed to up their game if they expected to pull off this insane plan.

Her new client smile firmly in place, Aisha strode into the reception area. Qiang Reilly sat on the couch, but this wasn't Sparx the assassin or even the soccer mom from last night.

A polished businesswoman in a sharp, black pantsuit and cute boots had taken her place. Her blue-black hair was twisted into a perfect chignon, and her makeup was impeccable.

I really need to ask Qiang where she shops. Knowledge that the fleeting thought was her way of masking the anxiety over what was about to happen almost sent Aisha into a fit of giggles. Or worse, hysterics.

Years of practice kept her expression from faltering. "Good morning, Ms. Reilly."

In one fluid motion, Sparx rose from the couch and mouthed the word, "Duck."

Plasterboard exploded above Aisha as she dove to the floor. Patty screamed on cue and disappeared behind her desk. The second electric bolt fried the temporary, and laughably out of date, phone on the reception desk. The third left a scorch mark on the front of the cheap plasterboard piece that poor Arthur had painstakingly assembled rather than take the chance of ruining Patty's real desk.

Ozone tickled Aisha's nose as she peered between the legs of the decorative coffee table. So far, so good. Sparx was sticking to the script.

Harri's office banged open. "What the hell is going on!" She stood there a fraction of a second too long.

Sparx hesitated.

Dammit, they were both going to blow this. Aisha rose to her knees. "Get down!"

Her shout seemed to kick the other women into gear. Sparx's next blast barely missed Harri.

The ugly smell of burnt hair filled the reception area. Sparx hadn't missed after all. Aisha clapped a hand over her mouth to keep from laughing. She would bet a year's worth of doughnuts that Sparx was retaliating for Harri bashing her over the head with the rose vase and kicking her while she was unconscious.

From the back of the office, she could hear Arthur's frantic voice as he called 9-1-1. Both Eddie and Tim insisted someone call emergency services on a tapped phone to make this look like a legit attack to Corvus.

Aisha counted silently to herself and rolled away from the main entrance. Sparx had taken one step toward the back offices when the glass exploded. A crimson and white blur whisked the super out of the building before the last of the glass tinkled to the floor.

Sucking in a deep breath, Aisha carefully climbed to her feet. "Everyone okay?"

Patty peeked over the top of her desk. "Yeah, we're fine."

From outside came the distinctive crash and boom of concrete. Since the parking garage on the opposite side of the Canyon Building from the hotel couldn't be salvaged, Tim calculated Rey could punch a few holes without setting off Seismic Shift's explosives in his pretend battle with Sparx. And if the two supers "accidentally" demolished the entire structure, Harri was sure the city could get clean-up money from the federal reimbursement fund.

Aisha tried not to wince at the second crash since their plan hovered on the edge of fraud.

Harri charged out of her office. "That bitch tried to fry me on purpose."

"Then you shouldn't have kicked her while she was unconscious," Aisha said as she crossed the room. "Now, hold still."

"Why?"

"Because your ponytail is still smoking." She turned Harri around and patted the ends of her tresses, nipping out the glowing embers.

A crackle and hum preceded a different kind of boom. Sparx must have taken out the fake transformer the guys had rigged.

"She is going to pay Jeremy's fee for fixing this," Harri grumbled.

"He'd do it for free," Aisha shot back. "He's been wanting to fix your my-ex-left-me-and-I-don't-give-a-fuck hair for two years."

"It was a mutual split," Harri growled. Then in a less aggressive voice, she whispered, "Here comes Miguel."

Anxiety roared back in full force and threatened to upheave Aisha's stomach. The problem was she hadn't eaten the toast and coffee Tim had offered this morning after she spent the night on his floor.

Miguel pushed through the front door. Sweat shone on his forehead. He took in the minor damage Sparx had to inflict before he launched into his speech. "Ms. Winters, come quick! The supers. They fight. They hurt *mi hijo*! He was playing in the Canyon Building. He's hurt bad!"

His barely-there accent had turned thick and juicy. At belt level, he made a thumbs-up gesture.

Aisha wanted to sag in relief. Tim had signaled Miguel he had rescued Francisco, and the child was safe. But a cold shiver rippled along her spine when Miguel followed with three fingers spread wide. Shift had a wire on him and was listening to everything they said. That was why Miguel had laid on the thick accent. She didn't blame him one bit for using Shift's bigotry against him.

She shared a quick look with Harri, who straightened though fear shone in her eyes. Fear Aisha was sure was mirrored on her own face. If their plan didn't go perfectly, Seismic Shift could bring all thirty-four stories of the Canyon Building on top of Harri and Miguel even without his augmented powers.

Harri nodded. "Give me the emergency flashlight."

"I have one, Ms. Winters," Miguel said for Shift's benefit.

Patty reached somewhere behind her desk and produced a bright red one.

"We'll need both." Harri took the flashlight Patty held out. "Arthur, tell the paramedics where we are when they arrive," Harri added before she turned back to Miguel. "Show me."

Aisha watched the two race out the front doors and across the street. The icy feeling spread along the rest of Aisha's nerves when they entered the Canyon Building's main entrance.

She pivoted to face Patty and Arthur. "Okay, you two are done."

"But Harri—" Patty started to protest.

"No 'but's." Aisha jabbed a finger in Arthur's direction. "Get her out of here." Eddie had given him directions where to meet a couple of agents, who would then whisk the pair to an FBI safehouse.

Arthur wrapped an arm around their assistant. "I want to stay, too, but we can't endanger the baby, Patty," he murmured.

Wetness filled her eyes. "I know. It's just—" She swiped at her face before she glared at Aisha. "Call us as soon as you know everyone's safe."

"I will." Aisha laid a hand on the other woman's shoulder. "I promise."

Once the pair had disappeared down the back alley in Patty's little car,

Aisha nibbled on her thumbnail while she watched the building across from her. Her role as the clean-up wouldn't come until the end. This waiting thing sucked.

Silence had fallen over the neighborhood, which meant Rey and Sparx had moved to their part of phase two. No sirens yet, but then CPPD was notoriously slow responding to this side of the city. Dammit, all she wanted was a sign. Any sign.

Please, God, let everyone be okay and I'll give up cigarettes for the rest of my life.

———·●·———

Harri watched Miguel's flashlight bob ahead of her own as he led her down the stairwell into the basement. If only she could talk to him . . .

But who would be reassuring who?

Stick to the plan, Harri, she could hear Aisha saying. *Don't bulldoze your way through this. Everything has to be timed perfectly.*

Except Aisha wasn't carrying a smart phone turned into a detonator.

Harri resisted the urge to reach into the pocket of her slacks. As much as she was sweating, she might accidentally short out the phone. Or worse, drop it.

Her stream of thoughts turned to a new worry. What if she was sweating too much? What if Seismic Shift could see the wire Eddie had taped to her torso through the forest green silk shell she wore?

A bead of moisture trickled between her breasts toward the microphone nestled in her bra. If she electrocuted herself, it would save Shift the effort of killing her.

"Watch the last step, Ms. Winters." Miguel grasped her hand with his free one. It was a relief to find he was sweating as much as she was despite the chill, damp air that permeated the underground section of the central tower.

Once she found her footing, she trudged behind him, deeper into the basement. She tried to memorize the route, then realized it didn't matter when she spotted the first red "X". Her escape route was marked as Tim had promised.

A faint scraping sound came from behind her. It could be Seismic Shift following them instead of waiting at the exchange point. It could be Tim in full Ghost Owl regalia, watching out for them as promised.

Or it could simply be humongous sewer rats searching for their next meal.

Harri shivered and tried to ignore that image.

"That's far enough."

She recognized the voice that echoed off the concrete. A figure stepped out of the shadows of a side corridor. The flashlight beams bounced off Seismic Shift's red and gold superhero togs. He held a small black device in one hand.

The demolition team's remote detonator.

Harri crossed the fingers of her free hand. If Arthur missed changing the frequency of one of the charges, she and Miguel were screwed.

"She's here. Now where's my son?" Miguel demanded.

"Tie her up first." Shift pointed to some rope coiled on the floor.

Bloch, Harri reminded herself. *He's Darryl Bloch. Not a superhero, just a run-of-the-mill bully.* And she hated bullies.

Miguel looked at her, at Bloch, then back to her. "Run, Harri!" He clothes-lined Bloch and took off down the corridor.

Harri whirled and ran. Shouting came from behind her. *Don't be stupid now, Bloch. I'm the one who knows your secret. Follow me.*

Footsteps pounded behind her. Coming closer, not in the direction Miguel had raced. Red 'X's whizzed by on the walls, the floor, the pipes. She didn't dare look behind her. If she saw how close Bloch was, she really would panic.

Her lungs burned. Muscles ached. A sharp stitch dug into her side. She couldn't run much further.

She raced around a ninety-degree turn and nearly cried in joy. The huge circled "X" on the floor gleamed under the dim sunlight filtering through the grimy windows high on the walls of the delivery dock. More fear ate the bit of relief at finding the right spot. The next part would be trickier.

She jogged past the temporary retaining wall and stopped well on the opposite side of the painted circle. Her fingers trembled as she pulled her phone from her pocket. Bloch charged around the corner and skidded to a halt. His expression turned wary as he saw her standing there, panting.

"You know . . . I could have . . . made this . . . quick and . . . painless," he said. Good to know he was as out of breath as she was. But he wasn't close enough to the retaining wall.

"Why? Is this all because of the lawsuit over the Lake County Retirement Home?"

"You know why," he snarled.

"You mean the assassinations you committed?"

Bloch sneered. "I'm not an assassin. I'm a hero."

"Not anymore. Maybe you never were." Harri shook her head. "I didn't know about your extra-curricular activities, Bloch. Not until you came after me. Not until you tried to kill me and my friends. If you hadn't done those things, I wouldn't have gone looking for the evidence that will put you away."

He spread his arms wide. A sick, twisted smile spread across his face. "What evidence?" Of course, he believed everything was destroyed in the City Hall fire.

She ignored him. "Then there's the fact you blackmailed a superheroine into killing me by threatening her son. That evidence I do have with me." She thumbed the icon for the audio playback. Bloch and Qiang's voices filled the cavernous area from the tiny speaker.

"Give that to me," he snarled and took a step closer. But not close enough and she still needed his confession on the FBI wire.

"Touch me or use your powers, and this will go out to every law enforcement organization in the country."

A demented chuckle erupted from him. "Go ahead. It won't do you any good. The signal can't get out of this basement. And even if it could, we control everything. And everyone."

"Who? The supers? Or Corvus?"

Bloch hesitated, but he quickly hid his surprise. "I have no idea what you're talking about."

Harri projected nonchalance she didn't feel. "You know, my partner and I have a bet. Aisha says you're behind everything. Tim Canyon's frame-up, the plot to kill me, the land deal for this neighborhood. On the other hand, I don't think you're that smart."

A low sound, the same tone as a dog growl, rumbled from Bloch's throat.

"But then, you wouldn't be anything without Tim Canyon's invention, would you, Bloch? Another two-bit player with token powers."

He lurched a few steps closer. His thumb twitched on the remote trigger.

Harri skipped back a foot. Time to try a different tactic. "Tell me the truth and I can help you cut a deal."

"Stupid bitch." But as he muttered the insult, his gaze roamed around the room. "There's nothing you can offer."

He's thinking too much. Can't let him catch his balance. His confession was the one thing that would end this. "The only thing I can't figure out is why you killed Canyon's family. If you wanted to keep him quiet about the power enhancer in your belt, why not kill him instead?"

"Canyon shoulda played ball when the boss wanted the sonic tech. His family would still be alive. The kid was an accident."

A sick feeling spread through her gut before she said, "The wife wasn't."

His leer made her want to vomit. "Well, I was supposed to entertain her a little. But the bitch fought back. Pulled off my mask. When she saw me, I had to slit her throat."

"So you got your rocks off a second time by stabbing a child?" Bile burned at the back of Harri's throat.

Bloch shrugged. "He saw what I did to his mommy. I had to take care of him."

"You mean kill him?"

"Of course. Just like I'm going to kill you." He shuffled closer to the retaining wall and eyed her warily before he stepped within the circle Tim had drawn on the floor.

Bingo.

"Think twice before you kill me while I'm wired, Bloch." Harri yanked up her shirt. "The FBI's listening to everything you say."

The bare part of his face beneath his mask paled. Then he snarled again. "Like I said, a signal can't get out of this basement."

She released the hem, and the silk fluttered down her abdomen. "Listen to me, Bloch. I can help you cut a deal. Put down the detonator."

His attention flicked between her and the little black device in his hand. Maybe Aisha and Tim were wrong, and Bloch would actually listen to her.

But his fingers tightened around the plastic. Cold, hard eyes stared at her. "If you're really recording me, then we're both dead."

"Neither of us has to die today. But before you blow up the building, I'd like to point out one thing."

"Oh, yeah? And what's that?"

She smiled, the one Aisha and Jeremy called her "evil bitch" smile, and held up her phone. "Ladies first." She pressed the button Tim had preprogrammed.

The world detonated in blast of thunder.

CHAPTER 34

Dust clogged Harri's nose and throat. Her ears rang. Every muscle and bone in her body vibrated with echoes of the blast. Her hips, back and shoulders ached.

Tim and Arthur had assured her that standing behind the huge, red 'X' on the floor would keep her out of harm's way, but she'd landed a few yards from where she'd been standing. Somehow, her head hadn't smashed into the concrete, too. She needed to have a very serious talk with those two geeks about what constituted harm.

She rolled over and spat out the dust turning to mud in her mouth. Sitting up, she lifted the neckline of her shell to cover her nose and mouth. It helped a little.

The emergency lights the guys rigged had kicked on, and the bloody-colored fog started to settle. Thank god, Tim and Miguel had restored some of the power to the basement, or she'd be blind down here.

A few yards away, a still figure lay partially under the collapsed non-load-bearing wall her guys had rigged. Bloch was no longer recognizable as himself, much less as Seismic Shift. His rug was gone, and powder-fine concrete particles collected on his bald head. A soft moan indicated he was still alive.

A shadow drifted through the clouds, coming closer until it resolved into Tim dressed as the Ghost Owl. He carried the oxygen tank she was supposed to grab on her way out.

Tim slipped the mask over her face. At the first sip of clean air, a coughing fit rattled her.

His chuckle was muffled under his visor, which meant he had his own breathing supply. "I thought you might forget this in all the excitement." His gloved hands skimmed over her body as he checked for injuries.

"I'm fine," Harri said. "Just bruised." There was so much more she wanted to add, but she didn't dare. Not with an audience.

"Can you stand?"

"I think so."

He wrapped an arm around her and lifted. She wasn't sure how given the state of his knees. Her own felt like Jell-o, and her head pounded, but she remained upright.

While she was grateful for his assistance, she prayed his voice was unrecognizable through the wire Eddie made her wear. Assuming the dang thing still worked after that explosion.

Shouts echoed through the basement of the Canyon Building. In the distance, the yellowish beams of the FBI-issued flashlights bobbed.

"I've got to go," Tim murmured. "And I've got to take your tank."

"Harri!" Definitely Eddie's voice, and it was getting closer. He wouldn't be alone either.

"Go." Harri slipped off the oxygen mask before she pressed it into his hand with a squeeze. Without another word, the Ghost Owl disappeared into the swirling dust a few seconds before Eddie emerged from the opposite direction.

"Harri, why didn't you answer me?" He grabbed both her shoulders, but it was the really sore one that elicited her squeal of pain. Which in turn prompted another coughing fit.

"Medic!" Eddie yelled over his shoulder before he turned back to her. "Are you okay?"

"Yeah," she rasped. "Please tell me you got everything."

He grinned. "Every damn word. Seismic Shift will be enjoying a long stay in maximum security." He glanced around. "What I don't get is why his remote didn't set off the rest of the charges?"

Harri almost smiled at his ass covering. Almost.

Instead, she coughed some more before she said, "I wouldn't be a bit surprised if the Ghost Owl knew about Bloch's plan. If he stays true to form, you might have an early Christmas present waiting for you at your office."

— • ◆ • —

Aisha breathed a small prayer of relief when Harri, with Eddie's help, emerged from the Canyon Building. Across the ruined entryway, their gazes met. Her right eyebrow rose a fraction. Harri nodded in return. They could fill each other in on the details later. It was enough to know everything had gone as planned, and that Harri, Miguel and Francisco were alive.

She turned back to the statements Rey and Qiang were giving to the two FBI agents. They kept it simple. Miguel had come to Captain Justice for help after Miguel's son was kidnapped as insurance he would lure his boss into the Canyon Building. Captain Justice enlisted Sparx's assistance to clear the homeless from the area, but before they could attempt to rescue either Francisco or Harri, the explosion occurred.

As long as the adults kept to the script, everyone would be fine. On the other hand, little Francisco would be the only one to tell the absolute truth— the Ghost Owl rescued him from the bad man and returned him to his daddy. Aisha resisted the urge to smile at the irony of the situation.

A round of shouting rose from the reporters as the FBI completed her clients' interviews. The police had cordoned the area, but that didn't stop the pack of screaming journalists and flashing lights. Every news station in the city had a van parked out front.

And in front of them all stood Ted Meadowfield. Beside him, Bob had his camera on his shoulder. He grinned broadly and flashed Aisha a thumbs-up gesture.

Nothing wrong with spreading the love, and money, around. A little extra moola from the exclusive footage they allowed Bob to shoot would go a long way towards positive coverage anytime Rey was in public as Captain Justice.

Unfortunately, Harri had to go past the gauntlet of news crews to reach the ambulance Eddie guided her toward. No doubt her best friend was grumbling all the way.

"Harri! Harriet Winters! Ms. Winters!" The pack had spotted her, and they smelled blood. Meadowfield howled the loudest.

Aisha turned back to her clients. "Okay, folks. Time to flash those super smiles to the nice reporters." Louder she said, "Captain Justice and Sparx can answer your questions now."

All it took was two very attractive supers, and the news crews ignored the battered victim. Harri's grateful smile was the last thing Aisha saw before waving arms and station cameras obscured her vision.

She raised her hands. "Ladies and gentlemen, can we have a little order? My clients are happy to give you all equal time."

Rey answered a couple of questions, but deferred most of them to Sparx.

Any worries Aisha had about Sparx disappeared as the woman deftly handled the reporters.

Or she did until Meadowfield asked, "There's a rumor the Ghost Owl was involved in the attempted murder of former city attorney Harriet Winters. Can either of you confirm this?"

By the time Aisha took a deep breath to prepare herself to step in, Rey and Qiang shared a quick look before she loudly proclaimed, "We can. He rescued the son of Ms. Winter's employee, Miguel Esperanza."

"Jatz'om Kuh, the one you know as the Ghost Owl, has been the only superhero who cared about this area of Canyon Pointe." A hint of righteous anger flavored Rey's voice. "Without his help, without the intel he provided, Sparx and I wouldn't have saved as many lives as we did. If anyone deserves the credit for today, it's Jatz'om Kuh!"

When they heard the name of their hero, a roar went up from the civilian bystanders. Their chant of the Ghost Owl's Mayan name rang off the bricks.

Rang with pride in their heritage.

Maybe she'd been wrong about insisting Rey change his superhero moniker. And maybe this 'hood was where they belonged after all.

— • ● • —

Late that night, Harri listened from her hospital bed as Aisha related everything that happened at the Canyon Building after Eddie hauled her away in the ambulance. As much as Harri hated the place where her beloved grandmother had died, everything ached too much to escape.

"... then the weirdest thing happened. Total silence. Then they erupted in applause and cheering. Not for him, but for what he said." Aisha shook her head. "No question about it. He's definitely got a career in politics."

"Don't do that to him." Harri glared. "Don't even suggest it. I want him to stay as innocent as he can." She let her glare turn into a smirk. "At least, not any more jaded with you already corrupting him."

"You know." Aisha nibbled on her bottom lip a bit before she added, "I fucked up."

Harri snickered. "Well, yeah, if you two were flying while doing it."

"We are not discussing this right now. Shut up and let me finish."

Aisha was right. It wasn't the time or place to have this particular conversation. For one thing, she didn't want to be high on painkillers when she bitched out Aisha for breaching her ethical duties to a client. She waved her unencumbered hand for Aisha to continue.

"Nella Lopez from Channel 12 stopped by the office after all the hoopla."

Harri groaned and pulled the pillow over her head. "Just shoot me now."

"Don't get pissy. She asked for exclusives with any of our clients who are supers."

Harri lifted the corner of the pillow and peeked at Aisha. "Not for free."

"Give me a little credit." Aisha named the figure. It was well beyond what Harri expected.

"For all of them?"

"No. Per super per interview." Aisha grinned. "I told her I had to run it by you and our clients."

"What did they say?"

"Sparx started crying."

Harri couldn't imagine the badass super shedding a tear over anything, but the money would definitely help with her autistic son's care. Everything came down to her family with Qiang, so maybe she wasn't as badass as she acted. Maybe Sparx was more like her than Harri felt comfortable admitting out loud.

She shoved the pillow back behind her head, and an ugly thought occurred. "Do we really want to subject our clients to Ted?"

"I made that part of the deal. Only Essie Morales is allowed to interview them, both in the studio and at any press conferences." Aisha grinned even wider.

"Their new investigative reporter?"

"Yep. Nella totally agreed after she saw Bob's footage of Ted ambushing you and Patty, plus Essie's handling of the first Captain Justice story." Aisha finally relaxed in her chair. "Anyway, Essie has Nella and Bob's seal of approval. Apparently, she was already on Samuels' trail over a couple of bribes when she got a mysterious package from a concerned citizen. The paperwork in the package showed the extent of our mayor's dealings. And she was smart enough to record Samuels threatening her if she interviewed Captain Justice again."

Harri started to laugh at Tim's "help" to the young reporter, but her throat reminded her of its irritation. Aisha rose and patted her back until the coughing subsided. Then she handed Harri the hospital-issued sippy cup.

A sippy cup. God, she hated being helpless. The lung specialist said she'd have issues for a while between the exposure to the acidic fumes and the possible asbestos dust from the explosion. She really needed to convince Aisha to give up smoking before they both ended up with lung cancer like Grandma Harri, but that was a battle for another day.

Harri handed back the cup. "I think Eddie got a similar package."

"So did Cal." Aisha grinned and slid into her seat again.

Harri stared at the ceiling. "Is it just me, or is it weird working on a case with our exes?"

"Beyond weird."

The odd catch in Aisha's voice made Harri look at her. "What's wrong?"

"As the only senior attorney in the department who hasn't been indicted in this mess, Cal's the acting DA with Michaels' arrest." She sighed. "But word's already out that he was the whistle-blower."

"You think he's in danger?"

"Not from Corvus or the supers." Aisha shrugged. "It's crap from others in the department for being a tattletale. His tires were slashed tonight in his driveway."

"Shit," Harri muttered. "Is there anything—"

"Tim and Arthur are at Cal's house setting up a new security system."

"And it's done," said a familiar voice. A bouquet of daisies preceded Tim around the edge of the door. "How are you doing?"

The beep of Harri's heart monitor sped up. Cal wasn't the only tattletale around.

"Better now that you're here," Aisha said. She stood and slung her third new purse in the last two weeks over her shoulder. "Don't keep our girl up too late." She pointed a finger at Harri. "Call me for pick up when they let you go."

"You don't have a car, remember?"

"Miguel's letting me borrow his minivan."

"What minivan?"

Aisha grinned. "A certain national car manufacturer gave Rey his choice of vehicles as the signing bonus for his endorsement. He blew their minds when he asked for a minivan." She waved a hand. "Until Captain Justice donated it to the poor working family whose youngest child he helped rescue. I arranged the transfer from Rey to Miguel so it's in Miguel and all the kids' names so they don't have to pay gift taxes."

"You've been busy today."

"One of us has to work while the other lays around." Aisha winked and strode out of the room.

Tim set his vase next to the obnoxiously huge arrangement Jeremy had delivered earlier in the evening. He turned to Harri with a curious expression. "Should I ask?"

"Our flamboyant mutual friend. At least, he didn't sprinkle glitter over the lilies to make a point."

Her answer seemed to relieve Tim, so she added, "No roses this time?"

"If you're going to smash the flowers I give you over people's heads, I decided cheaper was better." He lowered himself gingerly into the chair Aisha had vacated and propped his cane against the wall. "So how are you feeling?"

"Like I was too close to a stick of dynamite." She held up the button to the Demerol dispenser. "But this stuff is wonderful."

"I've had my share." He smiled, but it faded as the silence stretched between them.

"Thank you for the flowers," Harri said. Anything to break the tension.

"You're welcome."

More silence. And in that quiet, a little voice reminded her she couldn't give Aisha a lecture about her relationship with Rey when she had come so close to doing things with the man in front of her.

Tim clearing his throat jarred her back to reality. "We need to talk about the book."

"All right."

"I don't want to publish it after all."

"Okay." She wasn't sure if it was drug haze or Tim's habit of playing close to the vest, but she couldn't figure out where he was going with this. "Does this mean you're staying in Canyon Pointe?"

"Yes."

"So you don't want me to represent you anymore?" Her heart thumped, and the stupid monitor blabbed her hope.

"Yes. I do want you and Aisha to be my lawyers."

Harri's heart started to ache as much as the rest of her body.

"I'll need assistance patenting my inventions." In a softer voice, Tim added, "Rey and Qiang aren't the only ones who need my help. Powers are one thing; survival is another. There're others who haven't been totally corrupted by Corvus. And Trubble is still in charge. I was hoping Bloch would roll over on him, but Eddie says he's tighter than a clam."

"I see." If she had the energy, she would have kicked herself for foolishly wanting him to give up the superhero game or revenge for his family's murders. It was as stupid as expecting Eddie to give up his desire for kids.

"You're angry."

"No." *I want you to tell me you're staying in Canyon Pointe because of me.* "Rey needs a mentor in the same profession. There's only so much Aisha and I can do for him."

"You're angry," Tim repeated.

The dam holding back her emotions crumbled. "Yes," she hissed. "I want you to give this up before there's no knees left to replace. I want—" The harsh breath she sucked in stung her damaged throat, but dammit, she wasn't going to beg, and she sure as hell wasn't going to cry.

"Has it occurred to you I want that, too?" Glacial fury shone out of his dark blue eyes.

"Then give it up."

"Why can't we have both? You and I—"

"Because I can't handle you dying, too!"

There. The truth was out. The giant whale of her issues. Everyone she loved left her. Mom. Dad. Grandma Harri. Everyone.

Tim stared at her for a long moment before he breathed, "Wow. I thought my head was screwed up. I also believed you had Rey's best interests at heart."

"What's that supposed to mean?"

"You're not worried about Aisha violating attorney ethics. You're jealous she and Rey are paying more attention to each other than you."

Harri sat up abruptly.

And immediately regretted it. But the pain in her muscles and head was nothing compared to the rage pumping through her blood. "How dare you."

Tim reached for his cane and climbed to his feet. His expression when he met her gaze was no longer angry. Just weary and sad. "I care about you, Harri

Winters, but this almost thing between us—" He waved his hand between them. "—won't work until you let go of your past. It's hard. It's painful. But it's doable. I know. I've been there. Call me when you're ready."

When the nurse came to check on Harri, she blamed the tears on the pain, pressed the button on the medication pump, and let the drugs take her away from reality.

CHAPTER 35

Four nights later, Aisha stared around the loft apartment in amazement while Miguel and his sons beamed proudly. Hardwood floors gleamed golden under the setting sun. The smell of fresh paint filled the space. Brand-new black and silver fixtures and appliances shone from the corner kitchen. And the boxes of things she'd managed to salvage from her condo sat against the far wall. "I can't believe you did this all in four days."

"Pfft." Miguel flicked the fingers of his right hand. "It was nothing."

"Rey did the heavy lifting," Javier said. "Literally. The dude carried the refrigerator up the stairs by himself!"

Rey remained silent. He leaned against the counter dividing the cooking and living spaces and smiled that secret smile of his that made her toes curl.

"We helped," Francisco chimed in. "I painted your bathroom."

"You did an incredible job, Francisco." The boy beamed as she shook her head. "You all did. Miguel, you and the boys should be moving in here, not me."

"You did not have a place to live until we get the rest of the apartments finished. We do." He jabbed a thumb at the old hotel. "The other rooms in this building won't be ready as fast as this one because you'll be keeping our Rey busy."

It was an innocent statement, but her cheeks heated nonetheless. "This place is gorgeous. Thank you."

"Okay, boys!" Miguel clapped his hands. "Let's head over to Marta's for dinner, and let Ms. Franklin get settled."

The entire Esperanza clan demanded hugs before they left. She was still laughing by the time Francisco darted out the doorway after his second one.

"Don't I get a hug for my contribution?" Whatever shyness Rey exhibited their first night together was gone. His steamy expression was pure male lust.

"I get the feeling you want more than a hug."

"Well, duh." He held out his arms.

This is so, so stupid. But the internal admonishment didn't stop her from drifting into his embrace. His kiss was tender at first, but he coaxed her mouth open and explored her thoroughly. He tasted of fresh papaya and spice.

Rey didn't even break their contact when he lifted her onto the granite countertop and inserted his body between her thighs. She half-expected him to take her then and there when an odd rumble interrupted them.

They parted, and his bronze cheeks flushed crimson. He muttered an obscenity in Spanish, turned his head and stared at the door.

"Was that . . . your stomach?"

"Yes."

"Are you okay?"

"Just hungry." He wouldn't meet her gaze.

She pursed her lips for a moment to keep from laughing. "It's okay, honey. It's a normal body function."

"Not when you're trying to impress your girlfriend," he grumbled.

"Girlfriend?" What had she done?

He finally looked at her. "Well, yeah. I thought . . ."

She could hear Harri now. *I told you not to mess with him.*

Aisha stared anywhere but at his earnest expression. "Well, it's that most guys—" *Your age are only looking to screw around, and I thought that's all this was.* Somehow, she managed to keep from saying the words out loud. Not to mention it wasn't exactly fair. The last time she'd been with anyone Rey's age, she'd been twenty-one as well. She glanced up at him.

Mortification flared in his golden eyes. "I really screwed this up." He pushed away from the counter and stalked over to the windows, his arms crossed.

Girlfriend. Harri was right. He really was too good to be true.

Aisha jump down from the counter and crossed over to him. "Rey . . ." She touched his upper shoulder. "I'm sorry. You took me by surprise. Most guys . . . only a couple of nights . . ." The right words usually tripped from her tongue. Why couldn't she find them when she needed them?

He looked down at her. "I'm not the other men in your life, Aisha. I'm not Cal."

"I know. Intellectually, I know that." But dammit, Rey was so young. He had so much ahead of him. And he made her feel young, too.

The hard muscle under her fingers relaxed a fraction. "What does your heart know?" he murmured.

"That I could love you. That I am falling in love with you." She dropped her hand to her side. "But I'm scared of getting hurt again. Stupid, huh?"

He turned to face her and gently cupped her cheeks. "No, it's not. I never thought I would meet someone that I would—" He grimaced as he searched for the right words.

"Give it up for?" she volunteered.

A wry smile crossed his face. "Well, yeah. For some reason, I'm not worried about hurting you. I don't think I ever could."

Aisha smiled back. Yep, he was too good. Too good for her. And that little voice sounded like her mother. Maybe that was the problem. Despite what Dad said, maybe she was more like Mom. So afraid of time that she was letting all the good things slip past her.

"I know you wouldn't." Aisha wrapped her arms around Rey's waist. "But I don't want to hurt you either. Maybe that scares me even more."

— • —

Two hours later, they lay entwined on her new mattress. Between Rey and Cobblestone, it didn't make sense to buy anything larger or more expensive than a Japanese-style platform bed. Ambient light from the streetlights filtered past the vertical blinds in the master bedroom. Aisha traced the spots and streaks of light across Rey's chest. "I suppose I need to look for some new furniture. I can't entertain on just a bed."

"Why not?" Rey grinned at her. "You could go for the minimalist look. The Japanese have more than their beds on the floor."

She rose on her elbow and propped her head on her palm. "Why? So you and Cobblestone can wrestle some more. You may have cracked my headboard, but Cobblestone helped crush the rest of the frame."

Rey rolled his eyes. "The way you say that sounds so . . . wrong."

"I can think of more wrong things." Her fingers walked their way down his torso. His stomach rumbled as she reached his belly button, and she laughed. "Still hungry?"

"I worked up an appetite." He grinned again.

"Then I better feed you." She stretched, rolled to her feet and headed for the main room.

"You can't go out there naked," he protested. "I haven't put up the blinds in there yet."

She turned back to find him standing with the sheet wound around his waist. He was so cute in his modesty, considering his assets and enthusiasm.

"It's dark. No one can see in, assuming they are high enough." She waved in the direction of the buildings across the street. "The stairs between the second and fourth floor are gone in the hotel. And the police officers watching the Canyon Building aren't crazy enough to go inside until the demolition specialists remove the remaining charges."

"But—"

"If it makes you feel better, I'll leave the lights off." She pivoted and stalked out of the bedroom. Her own stomach was demanding food.

From the slap of feet on the hardwood, he followed. "If I could convince the rest of the folks in the hotel to move out permanently . . ." Rey wasn't grumbling this time. He was genuinely concerned about them.

So was she. "Your micro-loan idea is great, honey, but you've got to give them a chance to come to terms with the offer."

She yanked open the fridge and pulled out—well, she wasn't sure. Meat, peppers and rice baked in a bed of tortillas, but it looked wonderful and smelled even better though it was cold. Miguel swore it was Marta's house-warming gift.

"So far they're only contracted to work here." Aisha handed the casserole-looking dish to Rey and reached what she really wanted, the chocolate-cinnamon mousse that was a Marta original. "Once they see this isn't a flash in the pan, they'll lighten up." She reached into another cupboard for the plastic spoons and forks.

Her great-grandmother's silver hadn't survived Cobblestone landing on her antique buffet either. On one hand, she mourned the loss of the family heirlooms. On the other, she was secretly glad to never have to polish the collection again.

"You think I'm loco for wanting to buy the Canyon Block," Rey said as he followed her back to her bedroom.

Cal would have screamed bloody murder if she'd brought a snack to bed, post-sex or not. Rey was simply happy to have sex and food, as shown by the way he plowed into Marta's dish once they were seated.

Aisha really needed to stop comparing the men. It wasn't good manners, which brought her back to his statement.

"Normally, I'd tell a client there are better investments, then line up a few financial planners for him to interview. In your case, you're trying to give back to your community. I think that's admirable." She forked a bite of casserole. Paradise hit her taste buds.

"But . . ." he prompted around his own mouthful.

"No 'buts' here. Investing in the families here will make you a more attractive prospect to other parents, which means there will be more demand for products with your logo and likeness on them."

"And more demand means more money, yada, yada, yada." Rey waved his own fork. "You're answering as my attorney. I want to hear my girlfriend's opinion. What do you really think?"

Aisha sighed. This wasn't the time to hash out their relationship status. Nor was his request about the money so much as Rey worrying about other people's approval. "Honey, our pasts color our opinions too much. You have to remember Harri and Tim grew up with silver spoons in their mouths. Their grandparents doled out charity to make themselves feel better about being rich. My grandparents were activists. They had nothing, therefore nothing to lose when they fought for the basic right to exist. It's your income. Do what you think is best."

Rey poked at the casserole. "The money doesn't seem real to me."

She took the dish from his lap and set it aside before she grasped both of his hands in hers. "That may be a good thing. I'm not going to pretend to know what it was like for you growing up. Despite my parents' issues now, they loved me and my sibs. They made sure we were taken care of. We always had a roof over our heads, food on the table, and clothes on our backs. We had hugs and kisses every morning and every night. I'm lucky. I know that.

"You got to understand despite all the money, Harri's mom died when she was very little, and her dad considered her an inconvenience. Grandma Harri and my mom and dad tried to give her that love, but it's not the same. All the money in the world can't change that."

Aisha released Rey's hand, reached over and tilted his chin to face her. "Your mom loved you and cared for you as long as she could. I don't want you to think you need to buy love. It doesn't work that way."

"So Harri and Tim's advice about investing my money is wrong?" And just like Harri, whenever the topic turned to her mother, Rey changed the subject.

Fine. She wouldn't push it. Not tonight.

"As your attorney, I would agree with them." She shrugged. "But as your girlfriend, I have totally different perspective than they do. If you're expecting me to agree with them, I don't. It's your money. It's your decision. All we can do is show you the various options."

He nodded. "Do you think their family problems are why Harri and Tim can't admit they love each other?"

Oh, boy. This wasn't a subject Aisha wanted to touch. Harri and Tim had been fine when she left the hospital Wednesday night. But Thursday morning when she went to pick up Harri . . .

The last time Aisha had seen Harri look this bad was the night she showed up at Aisha's condo, red-eyed and pale. The night Harri and Eddie decided to split.

"Yeah. That's part of it. The other part is her ex."

"Why did they break up?"

Aisha got the sense that Rey wasn't asking out of morbid curiosity. "Honey, you can't fix her problems."

"I know. It's just—" He took a deep breath and released it. "I get the feeling it's similar to why you're scared of being with me."

She jerked away from him, jumped to her feet, and strode into the living room. It was rude. She knew it was rude. And she was running away, just like Harri would do. But she couldn't think past the surge of adrenaline. Or the shame.

"Aisha?"

She couldn't turn away from the city glowing through the huge plate glass windows. Couldn't speak.

He enveloped her in the sheet and pulled her tight against his hard muscles. "Talk to me. Why are you so scared of us?"

"Besides the age difference? Besides the fact that I'm breaking an entire section of the attorney ethics code?" Her bitterness wouldn't allow her to sink into his heat like she craved. It wasn't fair. None of this was fair.

"Give me a little credit. There's more to it." His lips brushed her shoulder. "It's the reason Cal abandoned you."

She blinked, tried to keep the old tears from falling. Rey had his whole life ahead of him. He would leave if she told him to. She didn't deserve him. She'd seen the way he'd watched Miguel's kids. He deserved the truth.

"I can't have children," she whispered.

Rey's hug tightened. "That's the reason?" Anger rumbled beneath his soft voice. "That asshole left you because he couldn't prove his manhood? Are you sure he's not shooting blanks?"

"Yeah, I'm sure." Wetness trickled down her cheek. "I lost the one baby we conceived, and th-there was a lot of damage to my body. The fertility treatments didn't work. Adoption was out because h-he wanted one of his own. And now—" Her throat hurt too damn bad to continue.

"You wanted one of your own as well, and now you can't," Rey finished.

"Yes," she whispered. A bitter sound stung the back of her throat. A sound that wanted to laugh and scream at the same time at the absurdity of her life. "I got the test results that I'd started menopause early the same day Harri called me about you."

He held her while she silently wept.

Aisha wasn't sure how long they stood there when she finally scrubbed her face with a corner of the sheet. Turning to face him, she said, "This is why it isn't fair to you. You need to find someone young. Pretty. Like Anna."

A low note sound deep in his chest, almost a growl. "I don't want Anna. I don't want babies. I want you."

Aisha sighed. "Maybe you don't now, but someday, you will want children."

He shook his head. "Aren't you the one just telling me I need to make my own decisions? Here's one for you. I'm sorry Cal was an asshole. I wish I could give you all the babies you want. And I'm never going to leave."

Rey's kiss was as fierce as his voice. It wasn't until he laid her on the mattress she realized he had flown her through the loft. He unwound the sheet from them and did his best with his body to convince her he was right.

CHAPTER 36

The next morning, Aisha could hear activity in the office as she climbed down the stairs. It was five after eight. If Harri said a damn word about punctuality before she had her coffee, she'd punch the bitch, best friend or not.

"Good morning!" Patty beamed from her desk. If she hadn't found them such a great deal at a used office furniture warehouse, Aisha would have kickboxed the perky assistant, pregnant or not.

"Good morning. Do we have coffee yet?"

"Of course." Patty stretched as far she could in her condition without somersaulting off her chair to make sure Harri's office was closed before she motioned Aisha closer to her desk. "I spoke with Becky over at Dewey & Cheatham."

"Becky?" Who the hell was Becky?

"The receptionist. She told me how you like your coffee." Patty reached into her drawer and pulled out a cup with a familiar green logo. "A large no-fat, no-whip mocha with sugar-free peppermint, right?"

Aisha grasped the hot cup like it was a lost treasure. The rich steam blessed her nose. She took a sip and her taste buds erupted into hallelujahs. "How did you keep this warm?"

"One of Tim's inventions." Patty grinned. "Of course, if we had a real espresso machine, I could make them fresh for you."

"Make them?"

Patty shrugged. "I worked my way through paralegal school as a barista."

Aisha leaned closer and whispered, "Start researching machines, and I'll make sure you get a raise."

"Deal." Patty's smile faded. "Also, I added Becky to your appointment calendar. She's coming in at noon. Something about one of the partners sexually harassing her."

A sliver of satisfaction inserted itself into Aisha's heart. "Stuart Cheatham?"

Patty snapped her fingers. "That's the name."

"He's not a partner. You did tell her that employment cases aren't our specialty?"

The assistant's blond curls bobbed. "Yep, but she still wanted to talk to you."

As much as she wanted to put the screws to her old firm, she needed to discuss this with Harri before taking the case. And there were a few personal issues they needed to talk about as well.

———— •◆• ————

Harri glanced up at the knock on her door. She frowned at the cup in Aisha's hand. There wasn't a storefront for the popular chain for blocks. Definitely too expensive for the clientele on this side of Canyon Pointe.

"Rey fly out and get that for you this morning?"

Aisha scowled. "If you're going to get snotty before I finish my coffee, then let's throw down, bitch." She closed the door and attempted to stomp across their brand-new carpet before she dropped into the visitor's chair. "Wanna tell me what happen between you and Tim?"

Heat flooded Harri's face. "We're not discussing—"

"It has everything to do with you copping an attitude about my personal life, and we both know it." Aisha took a sip and licked her upper lip before she continued. "What happened? Everything was fine between you two when I left the hospital."

For an instant, Harri wished she had superstrength, just to throw Aisha out of her office. She didn't want to talk about this. "Maybe I came to my senses and realized screwing a client was a bad idea."

"Ah." Aisha nodded. "The old 'piss 'em off to drive them away' trick. Here's your options, Harri. Either you talk to me now." She took another drink of her coffee for effect. "Or I call Jeremy."

Harri's fingers dug in the slightly used leather of her office chair. "You wouldn't."

"I would and you know it, bitch." Aisha pulled her phone out of her hip pocket. She held it up to show her thumb hovering over the "2" button. Her speed dial for Jeremy. "You got three seconds."

"This isn't anyone's business."

"One."

"You're really threatening our partnership over this?"

"Two."

"Fine! We had a fight."

Aisha lowered her phone. "About?"

"I want him to stop superheroing," Harri mumbled, staring at the top of her desk.

"What was that?"

Harri raised her head and glared. "You heard me."

Aisha leaned forward and set her cup on the desk. "What I heard was you planning to make the same damn fool mistake you made with Eddie."

"It's not the same," Harri snapped.

"When you're trying to mold everyone in your life into what you want them to be, then yeah. It is." Aisha flicked her immaculate fingernails. "I'm not saying Eddie was blameless. You both thought you could change the other one's mind about kids through sheer inertia. But you knew what Tim was upfront. What he's been doing for the last twenty years. You're not going to bulldoze him the way you did the city council to get your way."

She leaned back in the visitor's chair. "So the question is, can you accept him, tights and all."

It was the same question Harri had run through her mind over and over again for the past five days. And it always came back to the same answer.

"I can't handle it if he dies," she whispered.

She could feel Aisha watching her. When she finally looked up, Aisha's expression held a mixture of sadness and understanding, but not pity. Never pity. She'd kick Harri's ass first before she'd pity the rich little orphan girl like so many others had.

"I have just one question for you, then I'll let this drop." Aisha's gaze bore into her. "Why are you so worried about Tim when I never saw you this worried when Eddie was on patrol while you were married?"

Harri rolled the new idea around in her mind. And it exploded and smeared logic over every brain cell. Had she truly been that callous when it came to her ex?

"I guess I owe both guys an apology."

"Yeah, I think you—"

The sharp rap on Harri's door was followed by Patty's head poking around the corner of it. "Sorry, but—" She sucked in a harsh breath. "General Byron Trubble of Corvus is here to see you. And yes, that is exactly how he introduced himself."

Harri shared a look with Aisha. "Tell him we'll be right there."

Once Patty closed the door, Aisha muttered, "I don't like this."

"He's come during office hours in broad daylight. Too many witnesses."

"That's why I don't like it," Aisha shot back.

Neither did Harri. Trubble knew too much about all of them, so why the hell make a show now that Bloch was in jail? She pushed back from her desk and rose. "We won't find out what game he's playing by hiding in my office." Aisha followed her into the reception area.

Retired Army General Byron S. Trubble stood ramrod straight next to Patty's desk. He was older than the picture Tim had shown her. The gray hair had gone white. He wore a tweed jacket over a black turtleneck with matching black slacks. The body underneath his clothes showed a broad-shouldered man who still tried to stay fit, but time was winning the race.

When he spotted Harri, his smile didn't meet his hard blue eyes. "Ms. Winters? A pleasure to meet you at last." He held out a beefy hand that Harri ignored.

"What do you want, Trubble?"

Her slight didn't faze him, and he lowered his arm. "I wanted to say thank you for exposing a bad apple in the superhero community."

Harri smiled, the one she knew wasn't very nice. "I'm sure you did. And?"

The door to the basement opened and Tim appeared, his expression schooled to one of serenity. The movement caught Trubble's peripheral vision. His head turned slowly, and Harri followed his gaze.

In addition to Tim, Arthur stood in the archway to the building's main staircase. Rey and Qiang strode into the office through the street entrance in casual clothes. For an instant, a flicker of worry darted across Trubble's face.

The head of Corvus faced Harri again, the genial smile restored. "A little bit of overkill for a social visit, don't you think, Ms. Winters?"

She shrugged. "Given the number of attempts on the lives of me and my associates over the last twenty years, no."

The smile didn't twitch, but emotions behind his eyes did. Rage. Harri would bet every penny she had left Trubble was furious over losing control of the situation.

"It'll be interesting to watch your careers." His attention swung around the room again before it settled on Rey. "All of them."

The supers tensed, but Trubble merely nodded at Harri. "Until the next time, Ms. Winters."

He swaggered to the main entrance. Rey and Qiang parted to let him by.

Once Trubble was through the door and out of earshot, Aisha blew out a harsh breath. "Well, that was educational."

"Definitely," Harri said.

Qiang's head swiveled as she looked at Harri and Aisha as if they'd lost their minds. "You're not going to do anything about him?"

"No." Harri grimaced. "The longer we keep the status quo, the longer we, and especially innocent civilians, will be out of the line of fire." What she dreaded was the proverbial straw that would break their little cold war between Corvus and the rebellious superheroes.

"And what happens if more supers than Cobblestone and Sparx leave Corvus's embrace," Aisha murmured.

"We take it one superhero at a time," Harri whispered back.

"All right then." Aisha pointed toward her office. "Ms. Reilly, we need to review interview questions."

"Wait a minute." Harri raised her hands. "How'd you all know Trubble was here?"

Arthur stepped forward, a certain authority in his movement. "Tim and I installed a panic button on Patty's desk."

"And I panicked," Patty added.

"You have nothing to be embarrassed about." Arthur crossed to Patty. "You did the right thing. Are you okay? Do you want some water or juice?"

Harri suppressed the urge to gag at his lovey-dovey act, but Patty lapped it up. The other thing she couldn't ignore was Tim's attention focused on her. Yeah, she needed to apologize, but she wasn't about to do it with an audience.

She wasn't sure how long the moment lasted when Tim growled, "If the excitement's over, I'll be in the basement." He slammed the door behind him.

Aisha caught Harri's eye, scowled some more, then mouthed, "Talk to him," before she guided Qiang into her new office.

"I'll go help Miguel," Rey volunteered. He pivoted and head for the main door.

"Hold it right there, mister!" When he looked back at Harri, she pointed toward the stairwell. "Absolutely no flying right outside of my law office while you're in civilian clothes."

"Yes, ma'am," he muttered sheepishly and trotted out of the reception area.

Harri glared at Patty and Arthur, but her assistant pretended to type, and her computer geek practically ran to the break room. She stomped back to her office and slammed the door. For a moment, she understood Trubble's rage at rebellious underlings.

⸺ ·•· ⸺

Well after sunset the following evening, Harri swiped at the sweat beaded across her forehead. Even with the A/C cranked in her townhouse, she'd worked up a healthy odor while packing up her home office. The meeting with the realtor had gone well. If she got close to the asking price, she would have a decent chunk of change after paying off both mortgages.

She walked into the kitchen and opened the fridge. As much as she wanted a glass of wine, she reached for a diet soda. The last thing she needed was a headache when Jeremy arrived in the morning to help her pack the rest of the house.

Harri dropped into a kitchen chair, popped the top of the can, and took a healthy swig. Both of her phones remained silent, like they had all evening. She was the one who let her fear overwhelm her. She was the one who had thrown the ultimatum in Tim's face. She needed to make the first move.

She snatched the receiver for the landline. There'd be no excuse for a dropped call this way. She punched in the number she shouldn't have memorized. The other end rang.

Hang up now. There's no reason to make a further fool of yourself.

And rang.

What makes you think he'll forgive you? You drew the line in the sand.

And rang.

This was a stupid idea. You're too old for this bullshit.

"Hello?" Tim sounded breathless.

Words stuck in her throat, backed up in her esophagus. Nausea came in waves. She was going to screw this up again.

"Harri? Is everything okay?"

"Y-Yes." The logjam ached, but she pushed past it. "I-I'm fine. I just called—"

She couldn't remember the last time she had actually apologized to someone. Maybe that was part of the reason her marriage fell apart. She never apologized when she had done something wrong. It had never been big things. Always little ones. Maybe the little ones mattered the most.

Static crackled in her ear. Static and the faint whisper of breathing. He hadn't hung up. He waited for her.

"I-I called to say I'm sorry for what I said to you at the hospital. I have no right to tell you what you can do with your life."

"No, you don't," he agreed. At least he didn't sound angry.

"I can't stop the worry."

"About me?"

"Yes."

"That the closest I'm going to get to a declaration of affection?"

"Probably." A little smile tugged at the corners of her mouth at his teasing. "You could have told me you were staying in Canyon Pointe because of how you felt about me, you know."

"You're right. I should have." Air whistled across the receiver. "Guess we both suck at communication."

"When it comes to emotions, yeah." She rubbed her thumb along the condensation collecting on the side of her soda can. "We also both suck at letting people into our lives."

He chuckled. "I don't know about that. I rather like the new tenants at my building."

"Enough not to kick one of them out when she says stupid things."

"Enough to say can we please start over."

"I'd like that." Harri swallowed hard to rid herself of the lump in her throat. "I'd like that very much."

CHAPTER 37

◆─────◆ ◍ ◆─────◆

Two weeks later, Harri jogged down the stairs from her brand new apartment in the Lechuza Building. Happiness gave her a spring in her step. She couldn't complain about the commute anymore. With Aisha, Jeremy, and Rey's help, Harri had packed and moved her belongings in record time. Her old townhouse already had a bidding war so hopefully that would be off her plate soon.

And Tim wasn't pushing her. They were living in the same building. A building she and Aisha now co-owned with him since Tim had nothing to pay them with yet. When Harri protested, he called it the retainer for all the patents Aisha would be filing for him.

Still, he called Harri from his quarters in the basement every night before bedtime. Just talking with him was nice. The thought of more sent a delightful shiver across her skin as she unlocked the door to the law office.

Change was in the air this morning. No doubt about it.

She headed for the breakroom for coffee. The very expensive espresso machine Aisha had demanded, and her father had paid for, sat quietly in its corner. The smile Harri didn't realize she had faded. This was damn weird. Patty usually beat her here, even with Patty's drive across the city.

Even stranger, the door to Aisha's office was shut.

Before Harri could do more than register the oddity of her best friend awake before seven in the morning, her phone vibrated in her pocket. The caller ID added to her unease. If it was important, Arthur would have simply come downstairs from his apartment to tell her.

She pressed the answer button. "What's up, Arthur?"

"Please don't be angry I didn't call sooner."

"Where are you?"

"At the maternity ward. Patty swore it was Braxton-Hicks contractions when they started around midnight." So, Arthur was spending nights at her assistant's apartment, another new development. "But I insisted we go to the hospital."

The wonderful feeling Harri woke up with evaporated. "You didn't kidnap her, did you?"

"No!" His tone carried a ton of offended feeling. "The fact her water broke on the way proved I was right." His voice softened. "She's asking for you, Harri."

"I'm sorry for jumping down your throat. Let me tell Aisha, and I'm on my way." She punched the appropriate button. Good thing she'd pulled on her good jeans and flats this morning.

Harri crossed the reception area and knocked on Aisha's door.

"Go away!"

Harri could count the number of times she'd seen Aisha cry on one hand with fingers to spare. And right now, her best friend sounded pretty damn weepy.

"Aisha? Is everything okay?"

"Leave me alone!"

Concern for Aisha warred with fury. Harri clenched her fists. Everyone decided to ignore the budding romance between Aisha and Rey, including her. If they were already on the outs, Harri wasn't sure which of the two she would kill first.

But right now, Patty needed her.

Which meant telling her law partner she'd be out of the office for the day.

Relaxing her fingers, Harri grabbed the handle and shoved the door open, half-expecting a cloud of cigarette smoke.

Aisha halted in mid-step, obviously pacing from the stiletto marks on the brand-new carpet. No smoke. No makeup. Hair barely tamed. Harri examined Aisha's hands. Her nails looked like a dog had used them for chew toys. She hadn't bitten her nails since high school.

Oh, this was not good at all.

"Shut it," Aisha hissed.

Harri complied and decided to force the issue. Better to face the music now. "Did you and Rey have a fight?"

"No. It's nothing like that. It's just—" Aisha wrung her hands like the heroine of a really bad romantic comedy. "I never expected—they said I couldn't ever—"

Harri grabbed Aisha's wrists. Their motion was starting to make her dizzy. "Take a deep breath, sweetie."

"I-I don't know what to do—" Aisha's words broke off into a half-sob, half-laugh sound. "I never dreamed this would happen. Of course, I dreamt it but . . ." She looked like she was going into shock.

Harri sagged in relief. Reality was finally settling into her best friend. This was fixable. "Sweetie, there's nothing wrong with falling for a younger man—"

Her words roused Aisha, and she yanked out of Harri's hold. "That's just it! He's too young for this! He's got his whole life ahead of him! And if I take care of it, you'll yell at him for not standing up to his responsibilities! Just like you're trying not to do with Patty! Besides, Arthur—"

"Wait. Slow down." Harri waved both hands. She had the sinking feeling they were having two different conversations. And what the hell did Arthur have to do with this? "I'm not mad about Patty and Arthur's relationship. And why would I yell at Rey about his superhero responsibilities?"

"What? No." Aisha gulped in air. "It's—it's—" She was going to hyperventilate at this rate.

"We can fix this," Harri said. "Calm down, and tell me what's wrong."

"How can I calm down! I'm pregnant!"

Harri felt her jaw drop. After the last month, she didn't think anything could surprise her anymore. When she gained control of her mouth, she said, "Are you sure?"

Aisha whirled away, hands in the air. "Yes, I am sure! I took six fucking tests! I'm forty! The father is twenty-one! And we're guessing about that fact! But I'm not even supposed to be able to get pregnant!"

Harri winced at her own initial reaction to Aisha's freak-out. That wasn't what her friend needed right now. And from what she was seeing, Aisha may need more help than Harri could give. "Sweetie, I really need you to calm down."

"Why!"

"You're floating."

Aisha looked down. Her heels were a good two feet above the floor as she drifted in the middle of her office. "Oh, shit."

The lights had been out for a couple of hours in the high security section of the Canyon Pointe jail when Darryl Bloch heard the faintest scuff of shoe leather on painted concrete. His sixth sense said it was another super. He rolled into a sitting position.

About fucking time. Sure, the boss had to be pissed about his freelancing, but Seismic Shift was the best when it came to coups and wetworks. The boss wouldn't let such a valuable asset rot in prison. Not to mention, he had more than enough stashed in his offshore accounts to smooth over the general's ruffled feathers.

But it wasn't Trubble or any of the other escape specialists outside the bars of his cell.

"You?!"

"The general's not happy with you, Darryl."

Bloch's heart pounded as he watched the man dressed in black. He hadn't bothered with a mask. "I can pay you. Anything you want. You know I can deliver."

"What about my family, Darryl? Are you going to give them back to me?"

"That wasn't my choice!"

"You're right." Icy rage tainted his voice. "It was mine. Just like tonight when I volunteered to deal with you."

"You can't get into my cell," Bloch sneered. "Not without setting off the alarms. And I'm not about to get close enough for you to touch me."

"Who says I need to touch you?"

"Y-you have to—" His words choked off as the sharp tang of copper filled his mouth.

"What? You're surprised I lied about my powers?" the visitor mocked. "When you've been lying about yours for years?"

Bloch made one last wet sound in his throat before he fell back on his pillow.

The man in black grunted in satisfaction before he pivoted and headed for the elevator shaft. Bloch's death wouldn't win Patty back. Wouldn't make up for missing the birth of his daughter.

But it was a damn good start.

So who is Patty's mysterious baby daddy, and is he a threat to the team? Even worse, why is Aisha floating around her office? Find out in *Hero Ad Hoc*!

For a sneak peek, turn the page!

HERO AD HOC

Aisha Franklin stared at her brand-new office carpet nearly a yard beneath her favorite Christian Louboutin stilettos. And the carpet was drifting farther away by the second.

"How the hell do I get down!"

Her best friend and legal partner Harri Winters stared up at her. "Honey, I don't even know how you're flying to begin with."

"I'm not flying!" Aisha yelled. In her panic, she bounced up another foot. "I'm floating, and I can't get down!"

Harri waved her hands. "Keep your voice down. We don't need to freak out the neighborhood."

Aisha glared at Harri. "I'm pregnant, I'm floating in mid-air, and we exclusively represent superheroes. Not to mention, our IT guy is a former supervillain. I doubt if this is the weirdest thing they've ever seen or heard."

But Harri was right. Aisha glanced at her windows. She'd opened her office blinds when she came downstairs. Thankfully, their building was on the downtrodden Canyon Block, and no one was on the sidewalk this early in the morning.

"It is when you're not a super." Harri crossed her arms. "I can't leave you like this, but I can't reach you. Do you want me to call Rey?"

"No!" Aisha winced as her head bumped against the plaster medallion on her office ceiling, but it gave her an idea. She reached up and pushed hard against the ornamentation.

The floor rushed toward her, and she stumbled slightly on her leopard print stilettos when she landed. She straightened. So far, her feet remained in contact with the carpet.

Harri sagged. "Do I need to get a rope and tie you to your desk? Because I can't stay here and babysit."

When the weird light-headed feeling rushed through her again, Aisha grabbed the edge of her desk. Just in case. "What are you talking about? We've got a meeting with a new client this morning."

"You can handle Screaming Orgasm. Rebranding her will be totally in your court anyway." Harri dropped her arms to her sides. "I came in to let you know Patty's in labor. I need to get to the hospital."

"Why are you in here yakking with me?" Aisha made shooing motions. "You need to get her there before her water breaks. You're her birthing coach."

"It already broke, and Arthur already took her."

At Harri's grimace, Aisha realized the real problem. "He spent the night with her, and she didn't tell you before they left for the hospital."

"Keep your phone in your pocket." Harri looked around the office, ignoring her own feelings as usual. "If you get into trouble again, call Tim. He's downstairs tinkering." She finally met Aisha's gaze again. "We'll talk about your situation as soon as I get back. I promise."

"I know." She gave Harri a wry smile. "Sorry, I freaked out on you."

Harri chuckled. "It can't be any worse than what Rey did."

Aisha nibbled her lower lip.

Harri's face fell. "You did tell him, didn't you? Oh, God, please tell me he's the father."

"Of course, he's the father," Aisha snapped. "Why do think I was freaking out? He's doesn't need this shit when he's just getting his career off the ground!"

"Given the circumstances, I totally get why you're upset, but I really need to go. I'll call you once Patty has delivered." Harri waggled the fingers of her right hand before she marched out of the office.

Aisha held her breath until she heard the side door slam shut, followed by the distinctive thud of the deadbolt and the beep of the security system. Was Harri that irritated about Aisha's pregnancy she was abusing the building?

Aisha released her breath and her hold on the edge of her desk. No, Harri was probably freaking out being Patty's birthing coach, and half-afraid she would ask the same. Which she wouldn't do because Rey would be there.

Wouldn't he?

The panic from the six pregnancy tests reared its ugly head again.

And she immediately started floating upward again.

She dug her fingertips around the wooden lip of the desk and pulled herself down. She couldn't lose it. Not today. Not with a new client coming in this morning.

Aww, who the hell was she kidding? She'd already lost it.

How the hell was she going to explain this to Rey? She'd told him she couldn't get pregnant. That's what all those damned expensive fertility experts had said after she'd already lost one ovary to an ectopic pregnancy. Calvin had left her because of what those doctors had said. The kicker had been last month when her doctor said she'd started perimenopause.

Her fingers twitched. God, she needed a cigarette. But she didn't dare. Not now.

She rubbed her still flat belly. There was someone else she needed to worry about for the next eight months. And she knew exactly what she was going to tell Rey.

Because Captain Justice sure as hell couldn't be seen with a family, no matter how she felt about the man behind the mask.

***

Acknowledgements

I've been a comic book fan for decades. The twenty-plus boxes as well as the numerous t-shirts in my closet are only a slight indication of my obsession. The credit goes equally to DC and Marvel for inspiring me to want to read. The list of writers and artists who influenced me could fill a book by itself, but special mention must go Chris Claremont and George Perez. Their stints on The Uncanny X-men and The Teen Titans respectively during my teen years affected my own style of action-adventure stories in all my series, not just 888-555-HERO.

Additional thanks must go to . . .

Elaina Lee of For the Muse Design, who took my vague ideas for the series' covers and ran with them.

Jaye Manus of QA Productions, who does the interior formatting with style.

And Darling Husband and Genius Kid for taking care of everything at home.

The initial chapter that would become *Hero De Facto* was written in January of 2015. After several false starts, I finally finished the first draft on April 17, 2018. Two days later, I was diagnosed with breast cancer.

So a special thanks goes numerous medical personnel in Findlay, Ohio, and Detroit, Michigan, for the story you have in your hands. This novel would never have seen the light of day without them.

About the Author

Suzan Harden is a recovering attorney who writes fiction to regain her sanity. She currently lives in the Great Lakes region with a husband who believes writing is a practical career option and a kid who thinks she's too enamored with superheroes.